Too Many Princes

Deby Fredericks

www.dragonmoonpress.com
www.debyfredericks.com

ISBN 1-896944-85-X Printed Version
ISBN 13 978-1-896944-85-2

ISBN 1-896944-87-6 Electronic Version

CIP Data on file with the National Library of Canada

Dragon Moon Press is an Imprint of Hades Publications Inc.
P.O. Box 1714, Calgary, Alberta, T2P 2L7, Canada

www.dragonmoonpress.com

Printed and bound in Canada

Dragon Moon Press and Hades Publications, Inc. acknowledges the ongoing support of the Canada Council for the Arts and the Alberta Foundation for the Arts for our publishing programme.

The Alberta Foundation for the Arts
COMMITTED TO THE DEVELOPMENT OF CULTURE AND THE ARTS

Alberta
COMMUNITY DEVELOPMENT

Canada Council for the Arts   Conseil des Arts du Canada

TOO MANY PRINCES

Deby Fredericks

www.dragonmoonpress.com
www.debyfredericks.com

CHAPTER ONE
THE DEAD DONKEY

WHERE is he?" Therula fumed as she stalked from the stable of Crutham Keep. "Where is my worthless half-brother?"

Brastigan was supposed to be helping her with Fire Rose, the chestnut colt their father had given her. The young horse was so beautiful; she had been longing to ride him, but he was still too skittish. No one was better with horses than Brastigan, and he'd promised to help train Fire Rose. Instead, he went off to the low-town getting drunk again, no doubt. He did that far too often.

Therula stormed angrily across the packed earth of the castle courtyard. She realized what she was doing when a pair of serving maids bobbed in nervous curtseys. Therula drew a deep breath and slowed her pace, consciously assuming a calm expression. She could practically hear her mother telling her that a royal princess must not stomp and scowl, however frustrated she might be. She would simply have to find Brastigan later and express her disappointment directly.

As Therula continued toward the inner keep, a falcon winged between her and the granite towers. A shrill cry came, thin with distance. Therula paused, looking up and down the broad courtyard. No one was near the mewes, nor did she remember anyone planning to hunt with falcons today. If they had, Therula would have been invited.

The bird of prey banked and soared over Therula's head. It was a prairie falcon by its brown and buff coloring, but much larger than any she had seen before. She saw its wings with feathers spread wide, like hands with too many fingers. Something white was clutched in its talons perhaps a scroll of parchment?

What she didn't see was the dangling strap of a falconer's jesses. Intrigued, Therula turned to follow the falcon with her eyes. If this were a wild bird, what was it doing here, above the king's fortress?

The falcon banked again, still descending, and gave another shrill cry. A word came to her clearly over the air: "Unferth!"

Therula took half a step backward. Unferth was her father, the king of Crutham. Then she shook her head. Birds couldn't speak. She must not have heard correctly.

The falcon glided down toward the great hall, where King Unferth and Queen Alustra should be holding court at this time of day. It stretched out its talons and beat its wings to alight on the peaked roof. The falcon settled its wings and stood in proud silhouette. Therula could have sworn its fierce, pale eyes were fixed on her.

"Unferth!" the falcon shrieked.

There was no mistaking that time. Therula stared back at it, fear fluttering in her chest. Birds did not speak unless magic made it so.

"Unferth!" it cried again.

This creature was no mere falcon. Whatever it was, it wanted her father. Therula *forced herself to move, lifted the folds of her riding skirt with a pretense of regal dignity, and hurried toward the great hall. All thoughts of Fire Rose and Brastigan had vanished from her mind.*

* * *

"Hey!" Brastigan yelled. No one looked around. It took more than that to get yourself noticed in the Dead Donkey.

The Dead Donkey was a low-town alehouse, one of a dozen crabbed together and fighting for life along one narrow, cobbled way. The city guard's barracks were just down the street, and despite its name, the Dead Donkey was a favorite of the garrison. Not because it was a safe place, nor for the sake of good ale, clean women or honest games. The Dead Donkey boasted none of those things. What it did have was an evil reputation. Men liked to brag that they had been there and lived.

The gaming tables were crowded with folk of every size and description. It was hot as a smithy. The air was thick with pipe smoke and a reek of sour beer. Conversation was a deafening, constant roar, punctuated by shouts from the gaming tables. Fortunately, the senses numbed quickly.

A mixed lot of soldiers and tradesmen wenched and swilled. Others elbowed up to the bar, which defended itself with an array of splinters and nails. Many wore the black tower badge of the king's livery. Others wore a commoner's woolen trews, with shirts of coarse linen and heavy leather boots.

An even less promising assortment of women wove their way among the men, giving voice to easy laughter. A few carried pitchers to excuse their presence. It was these Brastigan called out to.

Brastigan sat alone against the back wall. His chair was tipped back to lean against the rough planks. One booted foot hooked under the near edge of his table. He seemed no more than a common sword for hire, clothing threadbare and none too fresh. A sword belt hung from the back of his chair. It and the blade were plain and serviceable. They were well worn, but cared for in a manner that belied their owner's unsavory appearance.

"Hey, sweetheart!" Brastigan called again. He grinned ruefully. Usually he didn't have this much trouble catching a woman's eye.

Brastigan had the fair skin and bright, dark eyes of an Urulai warrior. Glossy black hair fell well past his waist, beaded and braided in the fashion of that barbaric race. His features were narrow, almost angular, and he looked no older than five-and-twenty. Even seated he was a tall fellow, wide shouldered, narrow waisted, well muscled.

One of the alewives passed nearby. She was a cozy blonde with a peasant blouse and bodice barely laced. Her full skirt was stained with ale, and perhaps other things. Brastigan spied his chance.

"Hey, are you busy right now?" He pitched his voice low, but she heard the familiar invitation.

The alewife smiled and sauntered over. "I'm never too busy," she crooned. "What can I give you?"

Brastigan turned his tankard over, sprinkling the last few drops of ale on the tabletop. The alewife leaned forward to refill it. As she did, her sleeve slipped off her shoulder.

"Anything else?" she asked hopefully.

"Well..." Brastigan drawled. He flipped her a copper bit. "You can stand there for a while, if you want to."

The alewife straightened. She plucked the coin from the air with an offended snap and strutted away. Brastigan grinned over the rim of his dented tankard and took another pull at his ale. It was his third or fourth. He hadn't bothered to keep track, and he was feeling fine. The alewife glanced back at him. Brastigan grinned at her, a laughing wolfish grin. It was probably her first blush in years.

Mirrors were no stranger to Brastigan. He was better than good looking. He knew it, and he reveled in it. What he didn't know was that while he was staring at the alewife, someone else was staring at him. And not happily.

What little light filtered through from the door was abruptly blotted out. On the opposite side of the table was a man as big as a house, with straw-colored thatch of hair cropped at ear length. His face was brutally flattened, as if his horse had run him into a wall or two. It seemed luck had deserted him at the gaming tables, for he wore no shirt, but there was no hint of softness in the massive exposed chest.

The table creaked warningly as the fellow set both fists on it and leaned over. He squinted mean, pale eyes. "That's my girl."

Typical Cruthan. No beating around the bush, just an open challenge.

Brastigan came easily to his feet, with a greasy clap of chair legs hitting the floor. Around them, others turned sharply, alerted by the sound. Alewives squeaked and scurried for cover.

"No problem, friend." His voice was lazy, mid-ranged, but his grin was a little dangerous now. He extended his right hand, as if in greeting. "Brastigan."

The house looked from him to his hand and back. He straightened slightly, suspicion evident in the set of his shoulders. Then an answering smile whitewashed his blunt features.

"Herut." He smirked confidently.

Herut's huge fist closed over Brastigan's long one. Closed and clinched hard. Brastigan responded with equal pressure. The two men stood there, eye to eye, smiling and trying to break each other's hands.

This went on for several minutes, as those around them tensely looked on. Gamblers whispered, calculating the odds. A fine sheen of sweat appeared on Brastigan's face. Herut more grimaced than grinned. Neither would yield.

Who can say what would have happened? Before the contest could be won or lost, violent shouts erupted from one of the gaming tables. Everyone turned to look. As they did, Herut suddenly yanked on Brastigan's arm, trying to pull him into a bear-hug. The swordsman tensed, pushing back against the edge of the table. With a shriek of wood over flagstones the table lurched forward, catching Herut in the groin. He doubled over and Brastigan pulled free. He danced backward, grabbing for his weapon. Not that he needed her yet, but Victory had been with him for a long time. He didn't want her damaged.

Within moments, the whole place was a-brawl. Ale splattered everywhere. Cheap furniture shattered, or was ripped up for cudgels. Fists and bodies flew. Brastigan crouched low against the wall, working his fingers to restore circulation. He grinned unconsciously at the familiar, primal roar. In all the world, there was nothing better than a good brawl.

Then he recalled the alewife, and his grin widened. Maybe there was one thing better.

Herut had recovered from his momentary distraction. With all the subtlety of a bear, the man bellowed and charged. Brastigan tucked Victory under his left arm and waited. At the last moment, he leapt aside. Herut caught himself just short of the wall. As he spun, Brastigan reached down. Magically, as if from nowhere, he produced a brawling pin. Crusher was another of his most trusted old weapons, a foot-long hardwood club, well seasoned and lovingly tended in the hope of just such need. He tossed the club, caught it lightly. Herut charged again. This time when Brastigan leapt away he delivered a smart rap to the chin. It couldn't have hurt the fellow, but it added insult to injury.

Whatever control he'd had was gone in an instant. Herut charged, flailing his brawny arms. Again he missed Brastigan. This time, he blundered into a pair of off duty soldiers who were almost as big as he was. Brastigan leaned against the wall, laughing silently as they instantly turned on Herut. He almost felt sorry for the fellow. Almost.

Brastigan had survived enough brawls to know that danger could come from any direction. He kept an eye out as the two soldiers demolished Herut. That habit saved his life. He caught a flicker of motion in the corner of one eye. Instinct took over before his brain understood what it saw. Long legs collapsed, sending him to his knees in a controlled fall. There was a sharp, splintering smack. Brastigan hugged Victory as he rolled and came to a limber crouch. He wasn't laughing any more. A long dagger quivered in the wall where his chest had been only a moment ago.

He spared it but a glance. Dark eyes searched for signs of the assassin, without success. It could have been anyone in the struggling mob, maybe even one of the alewives.

The melee was over as quickly as it began. Howling riot gave way to shouts of alarm as a column of big, black-clad men forced their way in from the door. Suddenly no one wanted to be seen fighting. Weapons dropped to the floor, or vanished up sleeves. Men stood apart, allowing the soldiers passage. Some showed innocent, empty hands. Even Herut, breaking free of his assailants, thought better of coming after Brastigan again.

A heavy silence fell, broken by much shuffling of feet and a single semi-conscious moan. The soldiers parted, roughly clearing an isle. Between them strode one who was even more imposing.

Prince Habrok, Champion of Crutham, stopped in the center of the room. The cloth of his surcoat would have been enough to make shrouds for a trio of lesser men. A hauberk gleamed beneath it, though the prince didn't seem to feel the weight. Silently, great arms akimbo, he surveyed the wreckage of the Dead Donkey's common room. The injured man groaned again. The prince's helmeted head turned in that direction.

"Somebody help that man," Prince Habrok ordered. His voice was deep as a bull's. Four of the soldiers leapt to obey.

Habrok beckoned to his sergeant. "I want the names of every man involved in this."

The off duty soldiers in the crowd suddenly looked apprehensive.

"At once, my lord." Though Stam was by no means a small man, he sounded like a boy compared to his commander.

Then Habrok turned in Brastigan's direction. Cold eyes, surprisingly blue, glinted in the shadow of his helmet's heavy nasal bar. A blunt, gloved finger thrust out. "You. Come with me."

The tension was thick enough to cut with a sword as Brastigan unbent his lanky knees. For a moment, the onlookers thought – feared? hoped? – he would defy Prince Habrok. Then long fingers touched his forehead in a sketchy salute. With a sweep of black hair, he turned to seize the dagger that still stood in the wall. The blade grated as it came free. He paused a moment more to lock eyes with Herut.

This time it was Brastigan who smirked. "Good fight, friend. Have to do it again sometime."

Herut ground his teeth, but the presence of so many soldiers restrained him.

"Prince Brastigan!" Habrok's voice rang impatiently from within his helm.

Brastigan had the pleasure of seeing Herut's fury turn to alarm. It was never wise to provoke a royal prince, even if there were dozens of them in Harburg. He flashed another mocking grin.

Jauntily, then, Brastigan strode out past the watching soldiers. Shards of crockery and splintered wood ground under foot as his half-brother followed him through the door. The porch shuddered with each step.

Brastigan paused to restore Crusher to his boot-sheath and belt Victory on. Then he took a good, long look at the dagger that someone had tried to sheath in his heart. It was, unfortunately, a completely ordinary blade. Well worn, cross-wrapped leather on the haft. Dung. There could be hundreds like it in Harburg alone.

"So, brother," he inquired casually, as Habrok loomed over him. "How did you find me?"

Prince Habrok pulled off his round helm and the attached mail coif, revealing square, solid features. Blond hair was neatly tucked under a quilted arming cap. He eyed Brastigan with a mixture of envy and disgust.

"Easily," he rumbled with what might have been humor. "I just looked for the fight, and there you were. As for why..." he shrugged with a muted whisper of mail links. "Father sent me to find you."

"And you never asked why?" Brastigan snapped. Habrok was by no means his least favorite half-brother. Still, there were times when the great hulk seemed to be deliberately dense.

"I ask when it's my business," Habrok retorted. He proved it by jabbing a finger at the unsheathed dagger. "Where did that come from?" he demanded.

Brastigan glanced up. He hadn't been mistaken. There was a current of suppressed alarm in his half-brother's voice.

"I don't know," he replied softly, for Habrok alone to hear. "But if I were just a bit slower, you'd be carrying me home on a table. You might ask Stam to keep an eye out for a man with an empty sheath. I'm taking this up to show Eben. If anyone can find out where it came from, he can."

Habrok might be slow, but he wasn't stupid. No less than four of King Unferth's illegitimate sons had died within the past year. Aric had been killed by bandits, Mathas choked on a bone, Rickard in a hunting accident, and young Luvan drowned while fishing on the Great Bay. Brastigan would have been the fifth. Given his well-known liking for such places as the Dead Donkey, who would have questioned it? Nevertheless, the surviving Princes of Crutham were watching each other's backsides these days.

"I'll stay myself and see what I can find out," Habrok decided. He gave Brastigan a clout on the shoulder that fairly knocked him over. "You get up to the keep. It took me almost an hour to find you."

Brastigan grimaced, but stepped off the porch.

"And make yourself presentable," Habrok called after him. "It's for official business."

Brastigan glared over his shoulder. "The only time I ever see our father is for official business," he growled, not really meaning Habrok to hear.

It didn't matter. His half-brother was already plowing a path back into the inn. A pair of soldiers passed him on the way out, unceremoniously dumping an unconscious man into the horse trough just outside the alehouse. The resulting fountain of water restored Brastigan's humor somewhat.

* * *

The most important thing in Harburg was the great, gray keep. There lived King Unferth of Crutham with his wife, several consorts and numerous offspring. Theirs was a sizable court, bustling with soldiers, officials, servants and assorted other hangers-on. Not surprisingly, since it housed all these people—and their chickens, pigs, cows, horses, goats, dogs and falcons—the keep was easily the largest thing in Harburg. That wasn't saying a lot. Crutham wasn't much as kingdoms went. Queen Alustra had pointed this out to her husband on more than one occasion.

The keep was built from the gray stones of the craggy mountains that loomed behind it. It stood on a promontory overlooking the rolling plains of Daraine. From the uppermost tower, one could see well in every direction. Alas, there was little more to see than mountains. Mountains to the north, in Verelay. Mountains to the south, in Gerfalkan. Mountains in Firice and Begatt. Crutham would have been twice the size if so much of it weren't vertical. They weren't even wild or dangerous mountains, but sad old peaks, worn down like the teeth of an aged dragon. To the west, the sea ran out and away. Far, far across the Great Bay was the desolate coast of Urland. That was where the *real* mountains lived.

The city swirled, like a raggedy skirt, out from the knees of the keep. Neither looked as though it had been washed in quite a few years. Thus, Harburg was known to be very strong, and in more than one sense of the word. Especially so on an afternoon in spring, with the day almost visibly lengthening toward summer.

Long legs carried Brastigan rapidly down the street. He skirted vendors and heaps of refuse. The common folk gave way before him, and not just because of the knife he bore. His lips twitched in what could have been a grin but wasn't. Brastigan swished his dark mane and stalked on.

All his life, Brastigan had been a misfit. He wasn't one of them; he didn't belong. Oh, he hadn't been told in so many words. No one dared insult a prince that way. But any reasonably intelligent boy would have taken their meaning. His mother had been a foreigner, Leithan by name. A wellborn lady, or what passed for it among the Urulai. Accepting concubinage to King Unferth had been the price of safety for the tattered remnant of her people who'd fought their way free when Sillets conquered Urland.

Leithan had died when he was young. Some said she had been poisoned by Queen Alustra. Personally, Brastigan didn't believe it. He couldn't imagine stuffy Alustra being so overcome by jealousy that she plotted against another woman's life. That would have required emotion, of which he doubted the bitch was capable. Except where matters touched Oskar, her only son—but he was a different problem.

All of this was meaningless, of course. Brastigan's mother was so long dead he had never known her. His father was, to put it kindly, a loving man who had sired so many offspring he probably couldn't remember all their names. And Brastigan was a half-breed misfit who didn't have the sense to be ashamed of his differences.

His upbringing had been left to Joal, an old Urulai who'd been Leithan's servant during her life. In that respect, Brastigan had to admit he'd been luckier than he deserved. Joal had been both father and mother, had wiped his nose and his behind, washed his cuts, and paddled him when he needed it. It couldn't have been easy. Brastigan had been a wild brat, more beast than boy, but Joal had been like the mountains, everywhere and immovable. He was the one obstacle Brastigan could never get around.

Always, he'd been teaching. Oh, not reading, or any of that nonsense. On important subjects, Joal had taught Brastigan everything. Not just how to ride, but how to gentle a horse so that it served him out of love. Not just how to shoot from horseback, but how to make the bow he shot with. How to move silently, leaving no trace, and how to track one who didn't wish to be followed. How to hold his own against boys—and later men—twice his size. Brastigan was arguably the best swordsman in Crutham: maybe the best in the world. That was only part of the debt he owed to Joal.

Oh, there had been complaints. Queen Alustra, for one, hadn't approved of a savage Urulai being brought up in her court. Unferth hadn't seemed to care what Joal did, except when Brastigan was in trouble for one thing or another. Fortunately, he'd been all but eighteen when Joal stopped breathing one night. Brastigan scowled, remembering. Those had been bitter days. Then, despite himself, Brastigan's lips twitched into a smirk. It was lucky he'd been too old for any more fostering by then. He could have been stuck with some stodgy old lump of a nursemaid, like the one who'd badgered Lottres half to death, poor pup. Neither of them would have survived his adolescence!

A clatter of hooves on cobblestone jarred his thoughts. Brastigan looked around quickly, then relaxed as he remembered he hadn't done anything blameworthy. At least, not today. He was at the base of the ramp that led up to the keep, and a mounted patrol was coming down. Around him, commoners hurried out of the way. Brastigan toyed with the idea of standing where he was, forcing the riders to break around him. But no, he recognized the troop leader. The man had no sense of humor. Grudgingly, Brastigan stepped to the side of the road, concealing the dagger he still carried behind his arm. He shook his head at the ugliness of the passing chargers. Those weren't horses. They were barrels with legs! Finally they were gone, leaving only a few heaps of steaming dung to mark their passing. The waiting populace surged out into the street, and Brastigan with them.

The ramp wove twice across the face of the bluff below the keep. The rock walls were sheer, to prevent any attackers climbing up from below. At the first bend was a guardhouse, where Brastigan passed unchallenged. They knew him—there weren't many Urulai left in Harburg.

From that point, the ramp was walled. Anyone foolish enough to try fighting his way through would face a host of defenders and a dozen dirty tricks: concealed archers, boiling oil, caltrops, or worse. Siege warfare wasn't a pretty business. Brastigan hoped to avoid it for many years to come.

The ramp was steep. Brastigan kept an even pace, but he was sweating by the time he reached the top. Guards at the gatehouse questioned him about the dagger, although, being a prince, he could fairly well do what he wanted. Then it was into the gatehouse, under the barbed portcullis and the murder holes, and out into the yard.

Within the keep was a wide rectangle of packed earth, oriented west to east. The low dwellings of the servants were tucked under the northern wall. A planted garden occupied most of the western end, along with penned animals. Those provided the fresh morsels Queen Alustra demanded. Along the southern wall were interior barracks for the soldiers on duty. All roofs were of slate, a ward against fire.

On the eastern side was the high walled inner ward, where the king and queen dwelt with their personal attendants. Their quarters were finer than the rest, but not much larger. There wasn't enough room inside for all of the king's offspring, so additional housing had been constructed inside the southern wall. Brastigan made his way toward this.

At Queen Alustra's insistence, one wing of the two-storied dwelling was occupied only by men, including the princes and gentlemen of the court. The other wing was reserved for the king's daughters, who, since Luvan's untimely passing, outnumbered his sons.

Along the northern wall, the new Great Hall thrust out into the courtyard. Brastigan avoided that, since the royal court conducted most of its business there and it was always crowded. He toyed with the idea of cutting through the women's wing and seeing how much fuss he could stir up. Grinning, he reluctantly decided not. He angled his long strides toward the men's wing.

There always seemed to be someone loitering beneath the high, arched entry. Courtiers and toadies, Brastigan thought with an unconscious sneer. Today one of them hurried out to meet him. To his surprise and pleasure, he recognized a friend.

Lottres was another of Unferth's bastards, but he too was an odd one among them. Perhaps that was why he and Brastigan had become such friends. Brastigan's lanky height often outstripped that of the burly Cruthans, and he had his striking good looks to add insult to injury. No such good fortune had visited Lottres.

Folks said he had the look of Merowen, his dam. She had been a foreigner, too, the daughter of a diplomatic envoy from Forix. Lottres was shorter than almost everyone at court, including the ladies, and frankly scrawny. He had reddish brown hair that curled far too much. Muddy brown eyes were set in a face too finely drawn to be a man's. Even a thick fleece of beard couldn't hide that. At twenty, Lottres still had the gawky, unfinished look of a half-grown pup. He'd followed Brastigan around like one, too, starting when he was three and Brastigan five. Brastigan hadn't been too happy about it, but Joal had taken a liking to the younger lad. Under his patient tutelage, Lottres had slowly learned to manage his unruly limbs. He would never be a great swordsman, but he could defend himself. And in other ways, he was as gifted as Brastigan. If not for Lottres, Brastigan wouldn't have been able to do more than scrawl his own name.

So he genuinely smiled as Lottres scurried up to him. "Hello, Pup."

He hadn't slackened his pace, so Lottres was forced to whip around and follow. "Bras, we've been looking high and low. Where were you?"

Brastigan shrugged. "Well, first I was at arms practice this morning." He smirked. "Whipped the snot out of Tarther again, too. Then I had to try gentling that colt of Therula's." He grimaced, and shook his head to toss black hair over his shoulders. "That nag isn't worth a heap of dung, but it's pretty, so she won't let go of it. After that, I needed some relaxation, so I went down to the low-town. Ran into a little trouble."

Brastigan flipped the dagger into the air, spun on his heel and caught it. Lottres ducked nervously. The courtiers by the door applauded politely. Brastigan managed not to sneer at them.

"Worthless toadies," he told Lottres in an undertone. "Come on. Let's go somewhere we can talk."

"But Brastigan, Father wants us. Now!"

"He'll like me better when I've bathed," Brastigan promised.

"True," Lottres retorted. Brastigan grinned and punched his shoulder lightly.

The courtiers bowed as they passed, a habit which never failed to grate on Brastigan's nerves. He swept through without acknowledging them as Lottres jogged to keep up. Just inside was a steep stairwell. One flight led downward, to the subterranean bath-house and stores. They took the other, upward, to the quarters of the junior princes and gentlemen of the king's household.

"Brastigan, would you please slow down?" Lottres sounded slightly winded. "You know I can't keep up."

"The exercise will make you strong," Brastigan teased, but he did wait.

The long corridor was hushed, since most of the suites were empty at this time of day. At the far end, a lone servant went scurrying about some errand. The two men had adjoining chambers near the center of the wing. Brastigan unlocked the wooden door to his own suite and pushed through.

Since he wasn't one of the legitimate or important princes, he had only a pair of middle sized rooms, linked by an arched portal. One was a sitting room, the other his bed chamber. They were furnished not richly but comfortably and, he noted with irritation, had been tidied during his absence.

"Now tell me what really happened," Lottres said, following Brastigan through to the bedchamber.

"I don't know," Brastigan replied, voice muffled as he rummaged through a chest of clothing. "I was at the Dead Donkey having a drink, and I was looking at one of the alewives. Some big fellow saw me and didn't like it. Seems she was his girl." He emerged long enough to toss a garment onto the bed.

"What happened?" Lottres picked up the dagger, which Brastigan had left atop another chest.

Brastigan shrugged. "Nothing much. We were clinching hands, and a fight broke out at one of the gaming tables. Nothing I couldn't deal with," he insisted, seeing Lottres's worried expression. "Then, in the middle of the fight, someone threw that at me. I couldn't see who it was. Let me tell you, it's a good thing Joal trained me. One of Tarther's whelps would've been dead for sure."

"You never saw who threw it?"

"Habrok and his bully-boys showed up before I had a chance to ask any questions. As if I could have, with a brawl going on." He dug deeper in the chest, this time bringing out a pair of dress boots. "I kept the knife, though. Eben might be able to learn something from it."

Lottres frowned slightly, leaning in the door. "Eben can't work miracles."

"Well, we have to start somewhere. Be assured, I have no intention of ending up like Aric." By this time Brastigan had found what he needed. He gathered the armload of clothing. "Come on. I just need a quick rub down, and then we'll go see what Father wants. Bring that, would you?" he added, meaning the dagger.

Lottres stuck it through his belt and stood aside to let Brastigan pass. Together they moved down the corridor and descended the stairs. The lower level was dimly lit by smoky candles set on wall brackets. Widely spaced doorways hinted at storage rooms beyond. The lower hall took a sharp turn and gave out into the main bath. Again, the room was nearly empty except for a single manservant who bowed at their approach. Arrel was a wizened little scrap of an old man: toothless, bald, and deaf as a post. He had worked in the baths as long as either of them could recall. Brastigan waved him away.

There was a main pool, rimmed with tile, and beyond it a row of partly enclosed stone basins. The pool was drawn directly from subterranean springs. Its water was cold at best. In the basins, one could draw hot water from a tank heated behind the main ovens in the kitchen. Queen Alustra had insisted on many innovations, when she was newly come from Tanix. Hot water for bathing was probably the only one that had been accepted gladly.

Brastigan set his clean clothes on a low bench, and quickly stripped to the waist. Arrel shuffled after them with towels and a bucket of cold water from the pool. This Brastigan accepted, motioning the man to leave. The servant bobbed his hairless skull several times before obeying. A smaller basin was cut into a rock ledge at the back of the cubicle. Brastigan drew hot water until it was half full, and added a dollop of cold. Lottres settled on the bench.

"Your turn," Brastigan told him. "Any idea what Father wants? I assume he sent for both of us, since you're all dressed up, too."

"No and yes," Lottres replied, examining his good clothing carefully. He wore traditional Crutham garb, that being a simple, long sleeved tunic over close fitting trews. The tunic was of finely made cloth, embroidered about the cuffs and t-slot collar. Polished boots gleamed softly. This particular shade of blue was one of the few that went well with his rusty hair. Lottres carefully straightened his belt. "Yes, he sent for both of us. No, I don't know why. I think there was an emissary of some kind. The men were telling me about it when you arrived."

Brastigan snorted as he washed. "I don't know why you waste your time with those fellows."

Lottres shrugged. "They like to gossip, and sometimes they know things. Rodrec said a falcon landed in the courtyard, calling Father's name. 'Uh-herh!'" he said in a shrill, high voice, trying to imitate the bird's speaking. "It sounded like that, Rodrec said. There was a message of some kind in its talons, but it wouldn't let anyone touch it. They took it in to Father and he read it. That's when he sent for us."

Brastigan stopped and twisted around to stare at Lottres. "That sounds like a winter tale," he remarked, but he didn't feel sure. Magic was a force in the world, as real as the tides on the Great Bay — and potentially as dangerous.

"I don't think they were joking." Lottres shook his head soberly.

"I don't like the sound of it." Brastigan scrubbed his back with a long-handled brush, holding his hair aside to keep it dry. "Sounds like witch work."

"It could be." Lottres sounded interested. "I've never met a witch. I wonder what they're like."

"Dangerous, if you listen to the tales." Brastigan reached for a towel. "At least for normal folk like us. People who get involved with them come to bad ends."

"Or become heroes," Lottres argued.

"Heroes!" Brastigan gave a bark of laughter. "I've been on raids, Pup, and let me tell you, it isn't as much fun as you think. Trust me — you don't want to be a hero."

"That's easy for you to say," Lottres murmured resentfully.

Startled, Brastigan twisted around to look at him. They traded stares for just a moment, Lottres's brown eyes betraying old hurt and resentment. Then the younger man looked away, shrugging uncomfortably. Brastigan shifted restlessly as the silence stretched between them. Despite their friendship, he knew Lottres must sometimes envy him, wishing he could be as handsome, as quick with a sword. Well, there was no way for either of them to change what they had been born with.

Brastigan reached to clap him on the shoulder. "Pup," he said gruffly, "for every live hero, there's a dozen dead fools. I'd rather have you alive."

Lottres managed a smile in response.

CHAPTER TWO
THE VOICE OF THE FALCON

LOTTRES said nothing more as his brother changed into court clothes. When Brastigan was in this mood, you couldn't say anything that didn't set him off. Lottres was feeling nervous enough without being sniped at.

Instead, he watched as Brastigan dressed. First were the trews, replacing dusty leather ones. He stamped his good boots on over them. Then a shirt of fine, soft cloth, tied at the wrists and throat. Lottres would have offered to help with that, but he knew Brastigan wouldn't accept it. Next, the tunic. It had long sleeves and came to mid-thigh. The fabric was dark green, embroidered in a pattern of yellow and red. Over this, Brastigan belted on Victory. The ends of his long hair were caught behind the sword belt. He pulled them free.

"Too bad I didn't know I would be in court today," Brastigan said, mostly to himself. "I would have put on something more colorful."

Lottres glanced at the beads in Brastigan's hair. They were simple, of dark wood.

"There's more to life than annoying the queen," Lottres pointed out. Brastigan snorted at that, neither agreeing nor disagreeing.

Brastigan was always saying how he detested the bright colors some of the courtiers wore. For all that, Lottres thought, he always made sure he looked good. He went out of his way to be noticed, too, whether that meant showing off in the practice arena or pulling some juvenile prank on their sisters. It was a kind of revenge, Lottres guessed. Brastigan had to be better than everyone else, because it was so painful to be different.

Truthfully, it wasn't all bad for Lottres. Brastigan had always been quick to jump in when one of the bigger brothers, like Albrett or Rickard, sat on Lottres and wouldn't get off. Sometimes, when you were the smallest, it was good to have a shadow to hide in. Lottres knew Brastigan didn't mean to overshadow him so completely.

Still they weren't boys any more. No one sat on Lottres, not literally, and Rickard wouldn't be bothering anyone, ever again. Lottres was fully grown. He didn't need a champion to defend him, and he couldn't help resenting that it was all so easy for Brastigan. So easy, he never considered it might be hard for others.

"Well, how do I look?" Brastigan asked. He straightened the hem of his tunic and struck a pose.

Lottres stood, eyeing his brother critically. "They'll never know it's you," he joked.

* * *

If the jest was a peace offering, Brastigan was willing to accept it. He grinned and punched Lottres's shoulder lightly, extending a hand to take back the mysterious dagger. He tucked it into his belt again.

"Come on. Let's get this over with."

"It doesn't have to be something bad, you know," Lottres remarked, following Brastigan out of the bath. Just beyond the arched portal was a broad stairway, curving upward. They began to ascend.

Brastigan snorted. "When has our father ever called us to court for something good?" he shot back.

"We've grown up," Lottres argued. "We aren't a couple of trouble making brats any more."

"Yes, and have you noticed how boring it is around here?" Brastigan retorted. He had always hated court, and he made no secret of it. It didn't help that court was the only time he ever saw the king. Bad enough to be a bastard, ignored by his father. The pompous formality of such occasions only grated on his nerves.

They emerged at the top of the stairs. The great hall, where the king and queen held court, was directly ahead. The crowd made it impossible to see into the chamber.

"I hope there's someplace to sit down," Brastigan grumbled. Lottres merely sighed in response.

After much nagging on the part of Queen Alustra, the great hall had recently been enlarged and rebuilt. The rest of the keep was constructed in true Cruthan style: simple, massive and defensible. This hall, by contrast, looked as though it had been built for pixies. Its ceiling arched high, with long, thin, elegant pillars and fancy windows. The stonework was elaborately dressed in the style of Tanix, Alustra's homeland. Even the entrance was carved to look like a bower. There was a gallery from which the court could be viewed, too. Brilliantly colored banners hung along the length of the great central chamber. It was ridiculous, if you asked Brastigan. Totally indefensible.

From the angle of the sunlight pouring in those egotistical windows, it was late afternoon. Even so, the hall was crowded. Brastigan used his height shamelessly to seek a path. Most of the people, he noted, were dressed like himself, in sober and practical colors. Only a minority had given in to pressure, adopting the bright hues and elaborate costumes Queen Alustra encouraged. Brastigan tried not to sneer as he shouldered a way through for Lottres and himself. Such fancies might be bearable in Tanix and Forix, rival kingdoms in the warmer lands across the sea. Crutham was cold a good part of the year, and her people ought to dress for the climate.

King Unferth and Queen Alustra sat on a dais, raised several steps and canopied in the Tanixan style. The canopy was of pale gold satin, brocaded with a pattern of black towers. Beneath it were the thrones, of dark wood carved and inlaid with gold. Brastigan glanced at his father, and then quickly looked away. It wouldn't do for him to be seen wearing such an unfilial expression of contempt.

King Unferth lived well, as everyone knew. It showed. His beard was still golden, but it flowed down over a belly that strained against the fabric of his purple tunic. His face was red, and he sipped frequently from a golden cup. Still, the old man's eyes were keen as he watched the guildman making his presentation before the thrones. They were bright blue, like Habrok's. His crown was a band of beaten gold, etched with the symbols of his various provinces. As Brastigan looked again, Unferth shifted the coronet. He rubbed his temples briefly, as if the weight troubled him.

Beside him was Queen Alustra, his first lady in name only. She was a plump woman, dressed in a brilliant blue gown with the huge sleeves and upstanding collar of the Tanixan style. It was an unfortunate choice. Instead of making her look young, as she doubtless intended, the over-done garb only emphasized that she was aging. Alustra's crown wasn't permitted to outshine the king's, but she made up the lack with a jeweled net covering her pale hair. Queen Alustra sat very straight. She, too, paid close attention to the prating merchant. Unlike King Unferth, she seemed to actively enjoy sitting on a throne, in the eyes of all the watchers. She often, and ostentatiously, advised her husband on matters of state.

Near Alustra, Brastigan glimpsed two of her children. Therula loitered near Unferth's chair, eyeing Brastigan and Lottres with curiosity and a trace of concern. Closer to Alustra as another of Brastigan's unloved ones. Oskar, her only son, strolled through the first rank of courtiers with a self-satisfied air. As Unferth's legitimate heir, Crown Prince Oskar had a clear advantage over his baggle of brothers. He was fair enough in his dealings with them, but with a condescending kindliness that made Brastigan grit his teeth and gag. He knew he wasn't the only one who felt that way. Brastigan might not have much in common with most of his siblings, but they could at lease trade jibes or ride together. Oskar, he just stayed away from.

Today, it was hard to miss him. For one thing, Oskar's pacing created a constant swirl of movement that drew the eye. For another, he was garbed in a doublet of dark red velvet that made him seem to smolder in the sunlight from the windows. The big shoulders looked swollen, Brastigan thought sourly, and the doublet was short enough to show a bit too much leg clad in black hose. His red velvet shoes had toes that curled absurdly upward.

Oskar was handsome enough, so the ladies said, with the sleek look of a well-fed feline. He accepted the flattery of the court with smug aplomb, but his eyes were like his mother's: heartless and cold. Like a cat, he felt no true affection for anyone but himself. Brastigan had good reason to know that.

How much longer would the idiot tradesman drone on? Brastigan held his place with difficulty. Why had they been summoned, if they weren't wanted?

Lottres sensed his agitation, for he murmured, "It won't be long now."

"Will that be before I've died of old age?" Brastigan hissed back.

He tried to keep his voice down, but the queen turned her head. Their eyes met, and her expression hardened into a familiar, prudish sniff. Moving her lips as little as possible, she mouthed a few words to her husband. As Therula watched, Unferth briefly glanced toward them and then returned his gaze to the petitioner before him.

The dark prince stiffened, stung by the slighting appraisal. It was all he could do not to turn and stalk out. Why, if the old man weren't king... But he was, and even Brastigan knew better to ignore his summons, however much the old man ignored him. So he waited, and fumed, and it seemed an eternity before the guildman finished his over worded and pompous request for an exemption from some tax or other. Which the king, in a mere handful of syllables, denied. Then the queen, showing off her influence, laid her hand on his arm and craved him to reconsider. And so the matter was set aside until a week hence.

By this time Brastigan was grinding his teeth to keep back a shriek at the tediousness of it all. As the merchant withdrew, trying to look properly meek, a scream did ring in the palatial hall—but no human voiced it.

Brastigan wasn't the only one who started at the shrill echoes among the banner hung arches. A snap of movement made him look up, where the largest falcon he had ever seen unfurled its wings atop the royal canopy. The strong sunlight turned its tawny breast to gold. Its wings, barred with rusty brown, made a striking pattern, blood and gold, against the shadowed gallery.

The bird kicked away from the canopy and dove into flight with a motion so graceful and economical that Brastigan thought of a dancer—a dancer of the air. Yet it was swift. In but a moment, it stooped upon them. He instinctively stepped back and raised his arm, but the great bird flared its wings wide and dropped, lightly as a bit of thistledown, onto Lottres's shoulder. The crowd shank back, murmuring what this must portend. They were left, at last, with room enough to breathe. The falcon closed its wings with a matter-of-fact rustle. Its claws curved cruelly, but did not so much as pin the cloth of Lottres's tunic together. The eyes it turned upon the bystanders were pale as gold coins.

If the bird hadn't been so intimidating, Brastigan would have laughed at his brother's stunned expression. Or, he might have cried warning. For Oskar, across the court, was smiling in a way Brastigan didn't like at all.

Then, in a quiet thick with whispers, came the rustle of movement. King Unferth arose and handed his cup to a page, who sprang forth to receive it, then descended the low stairs to the floor of the chamber. He crossed the broad floor with a dignity at odds with his girth, until he drew near his two sons.

It was the closest Unferth had been to Brastigan in years. He had gained weight, and his face had a pouchiness about the nose and eyes. However, his gaze wasn't on Lottres or Brastigan. Instead, he bowed to the falcon, showing his sons a wide pink spot of bare skin parting his hair. Many strands of silver glinted among the gold.

A fresh wave of whispers washed over the hall as the great bird inclined its head in return. Then it spoke, in a shrill, strange voice like the squeak of a whistle you could make by splitting a blade of grass. The sound of it made the hairs rise on the back of Brastigan's neck.

"Unferth of Crutham," it said. The words were clear despite their weird pitch. "In accordance with the ancient pact, my mistress Yriatt now calls upon you for aid."

Though Lottress appeared entranced, Brastigan felt his stomach sink. Aid? What pact?

"Crutham shall not forget our debt of honor," the king replied. His voice wasn't quite as deep as Habrok's, but a lifetime of political practice made it sonorous, cultivated. "Thus I shall send to the Lady of Hawkwing House these two of my sons."

For Brastigan the room seemed to fall silent, save for the echo of those callous words: "I shall send... shall send these two... send these two of my sons."

Rage scalded in his veins. Sent away, banished maybe, on the whim of a *bird?*

The tramp of booted feet drew him back to himself. A column of ten liveried and armored men marched to a halt before the king and princes.

Their leader dropped to one knee with a rattle of chain mail on plate legs. "My lord king."

"Pikarus," Unferth intoned. "You will accompany my sons to Hawkwing House. Guard them and serve them well."

"Aye, your majesty."

"And you, my sons..." Now, at last, the king looked at Lottres and Brastigan. His face was calm and without expression. The pause lengthened. It seemed he awaited something. Over his shoulder Oskar smiled, showing many teeth, while the queen looked as though she smelled something sour. For her part, Therula watched with barely concealed anxiety.

Lottres shook himself. He also dropped to one knee, and Brastigan followed with a rebellions jerk. The anonymous knife poked him in the ribs as he did so.

Unferth told them, "You shall accompany this messenger to Hawkwing House, and do whatever Lady Yriatt requires of you. Do not return until you have her leave." As if he didn't even wish to look at them, his gaze shifted to the falcon. "Is that acceptable to the noble lady?"

The great bird nodded. "It is."

"Then so be it."

Brastigan swallowed, keeping back angry words. The old man didn't even ask for their agreement, just packed them off like unwanted luggage!

Unferth was saying, "Go forth, my sons, for the honor of Crutham."

If the king thought Brastigan was going to mouth some prettiness in agreement, he was mistaken. Lottres did find his tongue. "It shall be as you say, Father."

He rose, and Brastigan, stiffly, as well. What he really wanted was to spit in the old man's face, but that would give Oskar and his toadies too much satisfaction.

"We shall depart at once." Brastigan couldn't quite keep the snarl from his tone, so he contented himself with that and a curt bow. Then he stalked from the room as quickly as his long legs could carry him. After him came Lottres, with the men at arms behind.

They were a good ways out in the courtyard before Brastigan's fury cooled enough that his pace began to lag. Even Lottres didn't try to calm him. They simply concentrated on keeping up.

Brastigan stopped as quickly as he had started. Lottres regarded him anxiously, with the falcon, like some unnatural growth, on his shoulder. The men fell into military lines. There was an awkward pause as everyone waited to see who would take charge of the situation.

"All right, you heard him," Brastigan snapped. "Get your stuff together, if you haven't already."

He knew the squad leader well, for they often trained together. Pikarus was too good a soldier to reveal his thoughts, but some of his squad were less experienced. Their expressions confirmed his suspicion, that King Unferth had planned this eviction well in advance.

Before he could question them, Pikarus ventured, "Your highness, I must point out that you are not permitted to carry an unsheathed weapon in the castle."

He was looking at the unidentified dagger, still braced in Brastigan's belt. The dark prince had forgotten about it, but he wasn't about to admit that.

"Too late now," he sneered.

Ordinarily he liked Pikarus, but at the moment he didn't like anything at all. What he really wanted was to punch someone, but he knew better. Bare knuckles against armored men would only hurt him, and the king would feel no pain at all. Anyway, the brawl earlier nearly came to a bad end for him. He was in no mood to press his luck. Brastigan swallowed the fire in his chest and consciously diverted himself back to the matter he had been pursuing before King Unferth pronounced his sentence of exile.

"I'll get rid of the knife," Brastigan told Pikarus. "We meet at the stables at dawn." He spun and stalked off, hoping the crowd would stay behind for once.

In his wake, Lottres was smoothing ruffled feathers. "Let me talk to him."

"Very good, your highness," Pikarus said, his bland voice fainter with distance.

"Brastigan..." The younger man puffed, hurrying after him.

A weird, thin voice advised, "Let him sulk. It's best he get it out of his system early."

Brastigan whirled with a hot cry: "Iamnotsulking!"

He knew he shouldn't let the king's "deed of honor" bother him so much. After all, he should be used to Unferth's rejection by now. It shouldn't have mattered. Yet still, his pride smarted. After all the years of boredom, something interesting was finally happening in Harburg—an attempt on his life, no less—and the old fool had to send him off on some idiot quest. Instead of defending himself, he'd be at the beck and call of... What? The Lady of Hawkwing House? He'd never heard of her, but the talking falcon alone made him wary. There was witchcraft at work, and that was bad news for sure.

But he wasn't going to argue with some stupid bird. "Come on, Pup."

Brastigan turned to walk on, but at a reasonable pace, and he did his best not to shuffle like a sulky boy.

"Where are we going?" Lottres asked patiently.

"To see Eben, remember? Before I lose the chance. Or," he mocked, "get arrested for bearing naked steel in the castle." Tarther, the captain of the keep's guard, would love to have the chance, too.

"A wise choice," observed the falcon.

He didn't want its advice. "Why don't you go catch a mouse or something?"

The bird blinked at that. Had he annoyed it? Good.

"All right, Bras," Lottres agreed. No doubt he thought he should go with his brother and keep him out of trouble. "But why are you so angry?"

"Father always makes me mad," Brastigan growled with a renewed surge of irritation. How dare he, the old man... Just because he was king... Why did he have so many kids, if he didn't want them around?

"I know," Lottres answered. He sighed. "Maybe I'm so used to being a disappointment to him, it just doesn't surprise me any more."

"That is untrue," the falcon told them.

"What do you know about it?" Brastigan snarled.

Archly, the great bird answered, "I think I will go catch a mouse."

"Wait!" cried Lottres, but it was already flapping away from his shoulder. It passed over the wall, from the shadows of the courtyard into the evening sunlight, and glided out of sight.

Lottres turned to Brastigan, sighing again. Brastigan wished he would stop doing that.

"What did you do that for?" The creature must have caught Lottres with its claws, for he rubbed his neck and winced.

"Because it isn't natural," Brastigan snapped. "How can I talk to you with that thing listening to us?"

"I wanted to hear what it was saying," his brother complained. "The information could be useful."

"Or it could be feeding you a cock and bull story. Don't get sucked into this romantic garbage, Pup. Ancient pact, my eye! Sorcery is nothing but bad news to plain folks like us."

"Bras," Lottres began to argue, then stopped. "It's only for a little while. We'll see what Lady Yriatt wants and be back before you know it."

But Brastigan wasn't sure he wanted to return. Not after this.

* * *

Eben lived in the northernmost tower on the inner ward. It was the also highest, built more for spying out invaders than defense. Still, its slender column contained more private space than even the king and queen had. That in itself was odd, since Eben wasn't an official of the court. He was the king's close friend, however, and he had been there for so long that nobody questioned it any more.

Like a good brother, Lottres trailed after Brastigan. He was left behind, as usual, but his mind was as much in a hurry as his legs, thinking about Eben and the falcon, and their quest.

Brastigan might be too caught up in his temper to see the advantages, but Lottres wasn't. A talking falcon! It was the most exciting thing to happen in years—and they got to be part of it. Lottres looked forward to the brotherhood of the road, new places, thrilling exploits. He could have danced for joy, if his brother would just slow down a moment.

Because he was good with numbers, Lottres spent his days in a fusty port office, calculating tariffs and the like. He never saw anything interesting, aside from the occasional transposed number. Lottres felt so bored and cooped-up, he was ready for any adventure. Even Brastigan felt the same way. He'd said it himself, "Have you noticed how boring it is around here?" Brastigan didn't like being surprised, that was all. Surely he'd come around once he got over the shock.

Meanwhile, Lottres could never pass up a chance to see Eben. He felt a shiver of anticipation. Eben was a wizard. He seldom showed it off, but everyone knew. If you wanted to know somebody's secrets, Eben was the one to ask.

Ah, how Lottres would love to do that! It would set him apart from all his burly brothers, and no mistake. Of course, he was already set apart just by being so short. What Lottres wanted was to choose the difference for himself.

To reach Eben, they had to pass through the massive gate to the inner ward and cross the narrow courtyard beyond. As a child, Lottres remembered hearing the stone walls echo with voices of the king's offspring, for the children and their mothers had lived directly across from the royal chambers. Sometimes they could see their father watching them, smiling when they waved to him. Alustra hadn't liked it, not the noise or the proximity of the other women, with the result that the current living quarters had been constructed away from her sight. Since then, none of them saw Unferth often enough. Lottres suspected that weighed on Brastigan, as it did on him.

The vacant rooms had since been converted into royal archives and the offices of various functionaries. It was a strange feeling to pass through his old quarters, which had seemed so large, and find them stuffy and cramped.

The two princes began to climb upward, into territory that had been forbidden them as youngsters. The castle watchmen still used the two lower stories. Eben had the upper three and the roof. That was where they found him, leaning between two crenels to watch the sunset. Amber light ran like syrup over the slate roofs of Harburg. Far below, a mote of bright gold glided against the weathered gray of the mountains. The falcon?

"Welcome," said Eben in his dry, smooth voice. He smiled and nodded to Lottres, who felt a flutter of pleasure. He could see why Brastigan, too, trusted Eben. He was a lot like Joal.

The king's unofficial advisor was not elderly. Still, he had a timeless, leathery look. Hair and eyes were dark brown, the hue of well-worn hide. His garb was simple, a woolen robe of deep blue with a hood to raise against foul weather.

It didn't take long for Brastigan to explain what had happened. The wizard's eyes lit with delight when Brastigan showed him the dagger. Lottres felt a squirming jealousy, deep inside.

Eben took the weapon, supporting the pommel and point with his fingertips, and held it up in the light. "Ah," he breathed, as if it were beautiful. "At last, something I can work with. You have no idea how long I've been waiting. Excellent work, Prince Brastigan."

"Actually, since my brothers keep dying, I think I do know," Brastigan retorted.

"Of course," Eben said, ignoring the sarcasm. "Thank you for sharing this with me, your highness."

Brastigan shrugged, and Eben went back to gazing at the dagger, turning it thoughtfully from side to side. The two princes waited and exchanged glances. Lottres wasn't sure what was supposed to happen next, but he felt disappointed somehow.

"Master Eben," he suddenly said, "may I ask a question?"

Eben blinked. He seemed surprised they were still there, but he nodded. "Of course, your highness."

"Who is the Lady of Hawkwing House?"

Eben's face, his whole body, went still. Only his eyes, hooded suddenly, flicked to Brastigan for a moment and then returned to Lottres.

"So the message has come," he mused.

"Message?" Lottres pressed. A surge of excitement returned to his belly.

"You knew about this?" Brastigan interrupted.

"I was aware of the possibility," Eben admitted, "but there are many possibilities. Not all become realities. I truly hoped this one wouldn't."

Despite the suggestion of an apology, Brastigan wasn't mollified.

"I'm sure," he snapped. "Well, let me know what you find out. If it's *possible*."

"Bras!" Lottres gasped. Even as well as he knew his brother, Brastigan's rudeness still shocked him sometimes.

"You must learn to trust your father's counsel," Eben answered, unruffled. Meaning that they should trust him. Lottres did trust Eben, but Brastigan seemed determined to view this as a personal betrayal.

"Leave me alone!" He stalked across the flat roof and stared at the darkening mountains.

Lottres tried to swallow his own irritation and concentrate on his question.

"Master Eben," Lottres persisted, "who *is* the Lady of Hawkwing House?"

"Mistress Yriatt is an ally to Crutham," Eben replied, "just as I am. The rest is for the king to explain."

Brastigan gave a sharp bark of laughter. Lottres winced.

"Your highness?" Eben asked politely.

Brastigan tossed his raven hair over his shoulder. "That would mean he'd have to talk to us," he explained caustically.

Eben gave Brastigan a probing stare. "Shall I suggest it?"

"Don't bother," he answered bitterly. To Lottres, he snapped, "You might as well give up, Pup. He isn't going to tell you anything. He's part of the whole scheme."

"You assume I mean you ill," Eben countered, though he didn't deny Brastigan's accusation.

"What else can I believe?" was Brastigan's scathing reply. With a snort, he told Lottres, "I'll be downstairs packing."

"Bras, wait!" Lottres cried as Brastigan started down the stairs. He wasn't sure what he was going to say, but Eben interceded.

"Prince Lottres, if I may have your attention for a moment longer."

"Yes, Eben. I'm sorry, he's..." Lottres began, then stopped. He shouldn't have to apologize for Brastigan. Let him do it himself, or not.

"This isn't your fault," Eben said quietly. "Nevertheless, your queries speak well of you. I can tell you that I know Mistress Yriatt well. She has my deepest trust. You need fear no evil of her."

"I never said I feared it," Lottres reassured him. Then, hopefully, "Do you at least have a map to Hawkwing House? I'd never heard of it before today."

"Not many have," Eben said, "and that is as she desires." She being the mysterious Yriatt, Lottres assumed. He was already anxious to meet her. The king's wizard continued, "I fear I do not have a map, for I do not need one. A copy may exist in the royal archive. You should seek there."

"Very well, I will." Lottres nodded. He had used the archive before, and thought he might even have an idea where to look first. Lottres glanced at the lowering sun, trying to gauge his time for a search before supper. Then he realized Eben was still watching him with a strange, penetrating gaze.

Belatedly, Lottres asked, "Is there something else?"

"Perhaps," Eben said. "It has seemed, of late, that you grow restless, Prince Lottres. That you wish for more in your life. Am I correct?"

Lottres stared for a moment. He had no idea how Eben knew this when he hadn't even told Brastigan about it. Yet Eben spoke Lottres's heart exactly. Wishing for more was undeniably how he felt.

"Yes," Lottres answered, fumbling for words. "I realize that, as a royal prince, service is expected of me. Yet... just because I can add, doesn't mean I want to spend all my days in a counting house."

Eben's leathery face creased with gentle humor. "Or a scribe's copy house," he said, nodding. "I, too, once felt the same. Only it was no falcon that landed on my shoulder." Lottres listened with intense interest, but Eben retreated from whatever tale he had to tell. He went on, "I have sensed your interest in my arts, your highness. What is more, I believe you do have an aptitude."

"I do?" Once again Lottres felt a thrill go through him. He could hardly believe what he was hearing. "You mean, be a wizard, like you?"

"I am not wise enough, myself, to be your teacher," Eben said firmly. "It would be foolish of me to try, and dangerous for you. Yet there is one who could."

Lottres became aware that his mouth was open. He closed it, and swallowed. "You mean, Lady Yriatt?"

Eben nodded. "I have already spoken of this to Unferth, but in truth the choice is yours. Do not decide too soon," he cautioned. "Do not choose what is new, only because of the novelty. It is lonely, also, to be set apart from other men."

Lottres scarcely heard Eben speaking. He was so excited, he found it hard to breathe. Lottres almost expected to wake up and find he had dreamt it all, down to the stinging cut on his neck.

"If you wish," Eben was saying, "I can demonstrate the first exercise, which will begin to train your mind for the rigors ahead. You may practice on your journey, as time allows. Mistress Yriatt would then have a basis for judgment when you arrive."

"That sounds logical," Lottres agreed. In his heart he was begging, "*Oh, show me. Yes, please, show me.*"

CHAPTER THREE
THE KING'S CONSPIRACY

BRASTIGAN lay on his bed, hands clasped behind his head, and stared at the ceiling while daylight faded from the window. Out in the hallway, muffled footsteps approached his door. Lottres? After a lengthy pause, they moved on.

Fine, thought Brastigan. He wanted to be alone anyway. He liked it here, in his familiar room, where he could brood—not sulk!—without anyone commenting. It seemed to him he had reason enough. The whole situation was ridiculous, unfair. Anyone would brood. Anyone.

When the chamber was almost completely dark, Brastigan took a candle out into the corridor and lit it from a wall lamp. By that light he shoved some clothes into a canvas bag and gave his armor a careful inspection. The hauberk was of stout chain mail, worn over a gambeson of thick, padded cloth. Unlike Habrok, Brastigan didn't rate a pair of steel plates to cover his chest and back. He did have vambraces for his arms, and demi-greaves for his legs. Brastigan flexed the joints dispiritedly, making sure they didn'tt stick or squeak.

It was all in good order, not that he got to use it much. Crutham was at peace, and there were at least ten princes champing at the bit whenever a bandit got too bold for his own good. Brastigan laid the whole harness out on his bed. It was one of the few real expenditures Unferth had devoted to him, but it was no more than any of his brothers had, and far less than some, like Habrok and Oskar. Even Victory had come to Brastigan by other hands. He had chosen it from the armory because it had once belonged to Unferth. Such things had mattered when he was a young lad.

Finally he'd have the chance to ride out again. That should have pleased him, bored as he was with court life, but the circumstances chafed worse than leather straps on bare skin. For the honor of Crutham? They were being kicked out, that was all. Everyone, from Eben to Pikarus, was in on it. That was hard to stomach.

Brastigan straightened, frowning to himself. What if..? No. Eben couldn't be involved in the murder attempt. He had been too happy to receive the dagger. That was a separate problem, and the king's wizard was still the best one to find out who was behind it. At least, he'd better hope so. Brastigan had left the weapon with Eben, and there was little chance he'd get it back soon.

A rap came at the outside door, which opened before Brastigan even had a chance to respond. "Your highness?" called a familiar soft voice.

Appetizing odors of roast meat and vegetables reached him even as he strode, scowling, into the main chamber. There was Margura with a tray of food. The shapely blonde dipped a curtsey at his approach.

She adopted a soothing tone on seeing his frown. "I heard what happened. When I saw you weren't at dinner, I thought I'd bring you something privately." She smiled coyly.

Privately. Right. Margura was one of the queen's wellborn attendants, though she clearly hoped to find a more permanent position in Harburg. Since four or five of the various princes' wives had once been royal attendants, there was some reason for optimism. Brastigan knew she spent time, beyond her official duties, with more than one of the bachelor princes and noblemen. Margura was a slut and a leech, but that could be said of most court women. He didn't hold it against her.

Indeed, he appreciated her charms as much as any man would, and the low curve of her bodice certainly showed them. Besides, the food did smell good.

"I won't be much company," he warned as he sat at the table.

Margura set down the tray with a shrug. "You'll always be good enough for me."

He had to smile, obvious though the flattery was. Brastigan began to eat with real appetite. Kitchen-cooked meals would be few after tomorrow morning.

Margura sat across from him, leaning forward slightly to pour ale. It was a favorite ploy to secure his attention.

"I'm sorry you're going," she said softly.

"So am I. But when the old man says go..."

"Did the falcon really talk?" Margura asked eagerly.

Brastigan grunted at that.

"Do you know where you'll be?"

His shoulders jerked in a shrug. He should have asked Eben, but other things had distracted him. Lottres probably knew. Pikarus must have been told, anyway.

Margura rose and came to stand behind Brastigan, rubbing his neck and shoulders with skillful hands.

"I'll miss you," she purred.

"You'll be the only one." Brastigan was feeling sorry for himself now, and his ale wasn't nearly strong enough.

She leaned to whisper in his ear, "As long as I am the only one."

"Since when do you pick favorites?" Brastigan asked mockingly. He turned, and found his eyes on a level with Margura's bodice.

"Just don't forget me," she said, and slipped into his lap. The scent of rose water clung to her skin. Of their own accord, his arms circled her waist. Her teasing kiss quickly turned passionate.

Before things could get really interesting, there was another knock at the door. Brastigan held Margura a moment longer, hoping whoever it was would go away. The sound came again, and it annoyed him enough to break the mood. Margura murmured a protest, but rose from his lap when she had to.

With an irritable sigh, Brastigan strode to the door. Somebody short squeaked in dismay as he yanked it open. Brastigan looked down into a pair of wide blue eyes and forced himself to relax.

"Hello, Princess," he said.

Cliodora was the youngest Cruthan princess and the very last of Unferth's offspring. She had two long pale braids, a cute freckled face, and the coltish form of a girl about to emerge into womanhood. Despite being ten years younger, Cliodora had a special place in his heart.

She seemed to realize she was interrupting, for she hesitantly glanced behind him. "Did I come at a bad time?"

"Nah," he answered genially.

"Well," she said in her sweet little voice, "Therula and Agiatta asked if you could come see us tonight. Before you go away, I mean."

Brastigan felt a touch of guilt. He had forgotten about saying good-bye to his sisters, and he would have felt badly about that. That they hadn't forgotten made him happier than all of Margura's ministrations.

Still, there are things you can let your sisters see, and some you can't. One of those was waiting for him. Glancing over his shoulder, Brastigan could see Margura busying herself with the supper dishes. Her pouting face was slightly turned away.

Leech, he reminded himself. *She just wants you for what she can get.*

On the other hand, home cooking wasn't the only thing that would be in short supply while he was on the road.

"How about if I stop by a little later?" he suggested.

Clio smiled shyly, a bit of pink misting her cheeks beneath the tawny freckles. "I'll tell them," she giggled, and started back down the hallway.

Brastigan closed the door and locked it. He quickly got back to what he had been doing.

* * *

After a good meal and some delightful private entertainment, Brastigan left his chambers in a much better frame of mind and began to make his way toward the women's wing. He proceeded slowly because, it seemed, he was destined to meet each one of his sisters and brothers, and also most of their hangers-on and toadies, and they all wanted to say something to him on the eve of his glorious quest. Especially Agiatta and Orlyse, who were full of advice even though they knew nothing of wilderness travel.

Still, Brastigan managed to keep his sense of humor. When at last he reached Therula's apartment he greeted her with a brisk kiss on the cheek. She regarded him suspiciously.

"What are you so happy about?" When Therula saw his grin, she corrected herself. "No, never mind. I don't want to know."

Therula was Unferth's youngest daughter by Alustra. She was near to Brastigan's own age and probably should have been married away, but the king seemed to be in no hurry for that. For all that she resembled her mother, she was a comely enough maid. Alone among Alustra's children, Therula made the effort to be friendly with her many half-siblings and treat them like true family. Unfortunately, she did follow the queen's gaudy taste in clothing, and her golden hair was done in a fanciful coil on the top of her head. A cap of silver filigree covered this, almost like a crown.

Therula's chambers were similar to his own, except that her suite was on the inside of the building and had a fireplace rather than a window. A merry blaze crackled behind the iron grate, though it wasn't really necessary to warm the room. Like her clothing, Therula's apartment had always struck Brastigan as being overly adorned. Elaborate tapestries, most woven with her own hands, covered every patch of wall. Silver sconces held wall lamps that amply lit the room. The cushions on the furniture were so fine and fancy, they looked like they weren't actually meant to be sat on.

"Fire Rose and I missed you this afternoon," Therula went on with barbed sweetness.

Brastigan shrugged, keeping his opinion of the horse to himself. "I guess I won't be able to help train him after all," he said, trying to sound as if he felt badly about it.

"Apparently not." Therula smiled tightly around her annoyance.

Brastigan strolled on into the room. He was met by Cliodora, who stood up to her tallest to kiss his cheek. He picked her up and swung her around, which evoked fresh giggles.

"You're so tall! What have they been feeding you?"

"Bread and water," said Therula teasingly.

"Liver," Cliodora retorted, wrinkling her nose in mock disgust.

"Well, no more liver for you," he scolded, "or you'll be married and gone before I get back."

Therula snorted at that, but Cliodora looked stricken. "You won't be gone that long, will you?"

"I don't know, Princess," he answered, recalling their open-ended instructions. "I guess it depends on how hard this hawk lady is to please."

Brastigan now saw that Lottres was sitting in a wooden chair near the fireplace, staring at the flames. He was slouched over in a way that must have been uncomfortable and seemed completely unaware of it.

"Where are we going, anyway?" Brastigan asked. He seated himself on a cushioned settee opposite Lottres and stretched out his long legs. Cliodora curled up against his side like a kitten. "Hey, Pup!"

Lottres started out of his thoughts. "What?"

"This Hawkwing place," Brastigan repeated. "Eben told you where it is, right?"

"Oh. No," Lottres said, "I found it in the archive, on a battle map from the last Silletsian invasion. I sketched us a copy."

"Good." Brastigan grew thoughtful himself. It wasn't on the current maps, not heard of since the last big war. Which was, what, 70 years ago? "You're sure it's still there?"

"Eben says it is," Lottres said.

"Someone must live there, since you've been summoned," Therula pointed out. She sat, making a great production of smoothing her skirts, and reached into a bag beside her chair for an embroidery hoop. One fair brow arched when she saw him make a wry face. "You'd better mind your manners there. That would be my advice."

Though irritated, he forced a smile. "More advice, dear sister, is not what I want. A little more concrete information would be nice."

Cliodora stirred restlessly. "Well, it doesn't have to be all that bad, does it?"

Brastigan laughed. When she winced, he added gently, "I suppose not." He was old enough to know that any court scheme boded ill. He was also old enough to envy his little sister her innocence.

The girl murmured restlessly, "At least you get to go somewhere. I never get to do anything except sewing." She made a face.

"It's a useful skill for a lady," put in Therula as she sat, serenely sewing.

"You, too, eh?" Brastigan smiled ruefully. First Lottres, now Cliodora. Everyone wanted an adventure. He hugged her lightly. "Well, I'd love to have you with us."

She brightened. "You would?"

"Sure! You'd—"

"The queen would never hear of it," Therula interrupted severely.

"I know," Cliodora sighed.

"Oh, come on. A princess needs to know practical things. Right?" Brastigan turned to Lottres for support, and found him again deep in thought. It didn't look like he was mooning over the forthcoming noble mission, but still...

"Hey, Pup." Brastigan reached out to kick the leg of his brother's chair.

Lottres again started. "Hmm? Oh, I'm sorry, Clio. What were you saying?"

"Nothing," she answered softly, pouting.

Therula relented. "It is a bit dull here in the castle. Perhaps Lionor and I can come up with something suitable for an all girls excursion. For now, I want you to run along, Cliodora. Your mother will be worried about you."

"She's just down the hall," the girl protested.

"Cliodora." Her older sister fixed her with a stern gaze.

Reluctantly, Cliodora turned to hug Brastigan, burying her face in his chest. "Be careful," she said to his tunic. "And come back soon."

"Of course I'll be careful!" He laughed to reassure her. "Why are you going on about this? Sure, the talking bird is weird, but I'll be in no danger."

"I hope not." She didn't sound convinced.

"Besides, I'm the greatest swordsman in Crutham," he boasted cheerfully. "Come on, now. Nothing is going to happen."

Both Lottres and Therula rolled their eyes at his bravado.

Perhaps it was paranoia, but Clio's distress seemed off to him. So did Therula's bossiness and Lottres's distraction. What else was going on that he didn't know about?

Another prim glance from Therula herded the younger girl from the room.

"You wouldn't really bring her along, would you?" Lottres asked doubtfully as the door swung shut.

"No," Brastigan drawled scornfully. Then he darted a glance at Therula. "But don't you tell her that. Just because she's youngest, she gets left out of everything."

"As if I would," Therula sniffed, but then she smiled. "And since when are you the concerned older brother?"

"Maybe you don't know me as well as you think," he retorted.

"Well, don't tease her," his sister advised.

"How could I take her with us when I don't even know where we're going?" Brastigan added, shooting another glance at his brother. Lottres was staring at the fire and didn't answer.

Brastigan didn't care much for book learning, but he knew vaguely that Sillets was an empire across the high mountains of Verelay, to the north. Crutham and Sillets warred periodically. In fact, Joal had once told Brastigan that Sillets had invaded Urland because its attempts to conquer Crutham kept failing. The invasion of Urland had had a much more satisfactory result for Sillets, though it took ten years to finish. Since then the northern border had been quiet. Perhaps a bit too quiet, one might think.

Logically, Hawkwing House must be somewhere along the Silletsian border. Wonderful. The talking falcon would fit right in with the dragons, griffins, and other fell beasts he heard rumor of. And he was supposed to lead a band of men into that? With a sketched map and a bird for a guide?

True, no one had said he was in charge, but Pikarus would follow military order, and that meant he wouldn't issue commands to a royal prince. Brastigan was the elder of the two princes, not to mention Lottres's lack of field experience. That left it to him. He was beginning to think ten men might not be enough. The lofty peaks, and the dragons, formed a protective barrier, it was true, but who knew what might be lurking in those mountains — and beyond, in Sillets, where black magic was said to reign?

In the quiet room, the rattle of the door knob sounded abnormally loud. Brastigan heard Lottres's sudden catch of breath. His heart was already thumping at the sound of a tread he hadn't heard for years and yet recognized instantly. By force of will, he kept his eyes focused on the flames crackling behind the fireplace grate.

"Father," Lottres said, surprised.

"Good evening, Father," Therula said tranquilly. "I was wondering where you were."

Brastigan bit his tongue to keep back harsh words. What did the old man want here? Wasn't it enough he was sending them off to nowhere?

Unferth was saying, "I meant to be here sooner." It wasn't his usual tone of voice, the public proclamation that commanded immediate obedience. Despite himself, Brastigan looked around to see Unferth bend and kiss the top of Therula's head. His stomach clenched at the sight. "I was wondering where you were?" So this was another plot, and Therula had contrived to bring them here. Was Cliodora part of it, too?

Therula must have guessed his thought. "Don't look at me like that," she said coolly. Her needle flashed as she sewed.

"Fine," Brastigan said between his teeth.

The old man was gazing at them with an expression Brastigan didn't recognize. Lottres stood up. Brastigan looked back at the fire, unable to believe the gall of the man. First banishing them, and now sneaking in to see them. He heard the rustle of fabric and slap of hands as Unferth embraced Lottres.

It seemed the old man regarded Brastigan for a while before sighing. Then, to his infinite annoyance, the king came and sat down beside him.

"Well, lad." Unferth laid a broad hand on Brastigan's knee. "You're taking this personally, aren't you?"

"Shouldn't I?" Brastigan wanted to knock the offending hand away, but he couldn't seem to move.

"No, of course not," Lottres answered. Brastigan glared at him. "Affairs of state aren't personal. If Father believes we're the best suited for whatever the noble lady wants, then I will do my best."

Unferth and Therula seemed to exchange a glance, and the king said, "Well, son, it isn't quite like that, either."

"See?" Brastigan growled with bitter triumph. "It's all a scheme. I knew it. You just want to get rid of us." Unable to sit still any longer, he jumped up and began to prowl the room with fierce energy.

"Bras," Lottres protested. "Stop it!"

And Therula chided, "Brastigan, that tongue of yours will get you in real trouble one day."

Unferth hadn't yet answered, and Brastigan saw that he was sitting still, eyes closed. Then his shoulders gave a jerk, and he made a noise that Brastigan had never heard before. It took a moment to recognize that the old man was laughing. Hearty guffaws shook his fat belly, his whiskers swayed, and he leaned back on the settee to make more room for it. His three children looked on silently. Brastigan, in particular, stood with hands on hips, wondering what he had said that was so very amusing.

"Father?" Lottres finally ventured.

"Ah," sighed the king. His eyes twinkled merrily at Brastigan. "Now I remember why I kept you around for so long. You make me laugh. You have no idea how your escapades have kept me entertained over the years."

"How nice," his son snapped. "I wasn't aware I was providing such a valuable service."

"Of course not." Unferth still smiled, but with a trace of melancholy. "Alustra wanted me to be stern and discipline your misconduct. I have tried not to disappoint her." Then he chuckled again, shaking his head. "You made it hard, you rascal. I'll never forget the time you snuck that frog into Bettonie's bed." He leaned back to laugh again.

"Rascal?" The childish word was almost an insult. Brastigan felt an unaccustomed tightness in his chest. He drew deep breaths to keep his composure.

"That was you?" Therula demanded indignantly.

"Maybe." Brastigan was too upset to take pleasure in such an ancient exploit.

"Now, look. Sit down." The king patted the cushion beside his. "I need to talk to you both before you go."

Lottres obediently seated himself, but Brastigan tossed his dark hair restlessly. "I feel better standing up."

And he did. There was too much anger inside him, years' worth. The king's uncharacteristic warmth only churned up more.

"As you wish," Unferth answered mildly. "I know it hasn't been easy, but I couldn't favor you, either one of you, in front of Alustra. It's been hard enough for her."

"Her," Brastigan snorted. "You had half a dozen kids before she married you. Didn't she know what she was getting into?"

Therula frowned sharply, but the king answered with guarded equanimity. "It was discussed at length in the prenuptial negotiations, yes. However, you will learn, if you should survive long enough, that living in a situation is different than talking about it. There were other factors involved, such as the political need of Tanix for alliances to balance Forix."

"It wouldn't hurt you to think of others' feelings from time to time, Brastigan," Therula put in. Normally she favored the king's temperament, but she could convey all her mother's cold hauteur when she wished—as she was now demonstrating.

"I've already told you," Brastigan snapped back. "I don't need any more advice."

The king chuckled wryly at that, but said with a trace of sternness, "It hasn't been easy for any of us, you know. It hurt Alustra to see me with other women, and more, to see my crowd of youngsters running through the castle when she had so few of her own. It was easier for her to permit me affection toward my daughters, but it galled her to see me with you boys. So I restrained myself, and gave you to the care of strangers."

Brastigan stood still, not even realizing he had stopped pacing. All his life he'd thought he was Unferth's least favored son, the misfit, the disgrace, the wastrel to be ignored whenever possible. Now the old man said they were actually the favorites, he and Lottres. Everything he had believed was wrong. Brastigan was used to being angry all the time. Now he didn't know how he felt. Numb, maybe.

Then Lottres asked, greatly daring, "Father, why do you have so many of us? I mean, it's got to be a burden on the treasury..."

"The people you love," Unferth interrupted, "are never a burden. Make no mistake, I do love you. *All* of you."

Brastigan's habitual sarcasm took over. Here was another amazing statement, considering they hardly ever saw him. He began to pace again.

"I'm glad you asked, for this touches on the matter I wished to discuss." Unferth's voice now took on the courtly ring they were accustomed to. "Long ago, before I was even your age, I was privileged to receive information from a very wise man which I have kept to myself all these years."

"You mean Eben?" Therula asked, so confidently that Brastigan wondered how much she already knew. He had thought from time to time that she might not be quite as vain and self-involved as she made herself out to be. It seemed his suspicions were well founded.

Yet Therula was disappointed, for the king answered, "No, although Eben was present at that time. I speak of Ymell, he who was Eben's master."

"Never heard of him," Brastigan muttered.

"Bras..." Lottres hissed reprovingly.

"Would you please shut up?" Therula added in a way that made Brastigan think she might not be quite as much in the king's confidence as she had supposed.

"You wouldn't know Master Ymell. He has his own domain and seldom visits us," Unferth said. Now his voice was strange, strained. "On this occasion, he came to Harburg to tell me that if I did not have at least twenty sons, there would be no heir to survive me."

Therula gasped, and Lottres sat up straighter. Brastigan stared, intrigued.

"And so, I began to beget. Despite what you may think, Brastigan, fatherhood has never been a game. Habrok taught me that. As you noted, he and Haraldine had already been born at the time of my marriage. Meranca arrived soon after."

"But that prophecy..." Therula breathed.

"For a long time, I thought our family was safe. Now I fear his prediction is proving true," the king said grimly. "When Rickard and Aric died, it seemed mere chance. Such things happen." Despite his effort to sound calm, there was a tremor in Unferth's voice. "Now that Luvan is gone, I know Ymell's words were correct. With Eben's assistance, I have begun making other arrangements to protect my remaining family. We are too vulnerable, living so close together in Harburg. I plan to settle as many as I can elsewhere."

This wasn't welcome news, though Brastigan had to admit it was in line with his own suspicions. If some unknown enemy had a grudge against the royal family, they were all in danger.

"Did you know someone tried to kill Brastigan today?" Lottres asked, tautly.

Unferth and Therula stared at Brastigan in shock. He shrugged uncomfortably. "I ducked."

"No," Unferth breathed, suddenly shaken. He seemed to gather himself. "This tells me my instincts were correct. I will miss the others, but you, my clever boy," he smiled wanly at Lottres, "and you, you rascal," he looked to Brastigan, "you two, I want safe.

"So, Brastigan, you are quite correct in thinking I arranged for your departure. Eben was very helpful in passing a message to his good friend, Mistress Yriatt. Coincidentally, she requires the assistance of the crown in a matter of legitimate concern to Crutham. Nevertheless, I am sending you to her in hopes you will be safe. I would appreciate it if you'd waste a bit of time there, until Eben can figure out who's behind these murders."

It seemed too good to be true. Brastigan regarded his father warily.

"Do you think we'll be safe out in the wilderness?" he sneered. "Oh, good idea."

"The Lady of Hawkwing House is puissant and wise," was the king's patient reply.

"You mean she's a witch."

"Brastigan," Therula warned. He made a face at her.

"That is such a coarse and vulgar term," the king smiled. It took Brastigan a moment to realize he was mimicking Alustra.

Lottres said, "Do you trust her, father?"

Unferth nodded. "I do. It isn't widely spoken of, but Mistress Yriatt and her household play an integral part in Crutham's defense, as do Eben and Master Ymell. That could not be so if I didn't trust in their loyalty and judgment."

The room was silent for a time, save for the crackle of the fire. The flames had begun to sink low. For lack of anything better to do, Brastigan stabbed at the fire with the poker.

"I guess we'll have to watch each other, then," Lottres said. "We'll do our duty by the noble lady. Have no fear of that, Father."

He sounded very certain. Oddly, Brastigan felt just the opposite. The sound of steel biting into a wooden wall sounded loud in his memory.

"I know you will." At the tenderness and pride of Unferth's tone, Brastigan's vision suddenly blurred. He blinked fiercely, hating himself for his wayward emotions. "I have faith in both of you, but I do hope you'll be careful and avoid any unnecessary risks."

He looked straight at Brastigan, who retorted, "How much fun would that be?"

"You," the king growled. "I mean it. Be careful."

"I'll tell you what I told Clio," Brastigan snapped, annoyed by the fussing. "I'm the greatest swordsman in Crutham, and nothing is going to happen to me."

"Braggart." Therula smiled fondly.

"It's true," he smirked. The familiar banter was far preferable to dwelling on his unaccustomed emotions.

"So I hear," Unferth chuckled, "and that's another reason to get you out of here. Not everyone enjoys how you hone your skills."

"Ha!" Brastigan gave a bark of laughter. "So Tarther's been whining, has he?"

"Actually, yes, and I have to agree with him. How can his men respect him when they see him get thrashed?" the king asked reasonably. "It would be one thing if you were interested in leading the guard yourself. We all know that isn't the place for you."

"What do you mean?" Brastigan demanded. "I have the skill — ."

Then he closed his mouth. An endless round of patrols, watch posts, honorary guards, always ready for action but never seeing any? The old man was right. He would hate it.

"What do you mean? You'd die of boredom," Therula laughed mockingly.

"And you'd have to work with Captain Tarther," Lottres added slyly.

"Take orders from that dull blade?" Brastigan gagged dramatically, and set them all laughing, but he didn't smile for long.

"Really," he said to no one in particular, "these quests are all well and good, but I'm still twelfth or thirteenth in line for the throne, and Lottres is behind me. Oskar's got the position secured anyway. What are we supposed to do with the rest of our lives?" It wasn't a question that had occurred to him before, and it sat on his stomach like a stone.

"Maybe," Lottres suggested quietly, "we'll find something else to do on this trip."

"Perhaps," Unferth agreed. He gazed at Lottres fondly.

Therula glanced sharply between them, and Brastigan was left wondering what he had missed. Then the king leaned to one side, drawing something from his belt. He extended it toward Brastigan. "Here."

"What is it?" Brastigan asked suspiciously.

"I'm not sure," the old man confessed. "It belonged to Leithan. I want you to have it before you go."

This was low. First Unferth got all fatherly, then he brought up Brastigan's mother. Still, how could he refuse? Brastigan took the small, dangling object and turned it over in his palm.

It was a flat disc of dark stone, perhaps black, perhaps blue, with a dull sheen on its surface. It was about half the length of his thumb and fastened to a leather thong with a simple knot. Roughness caught at his fingertips, and he angled it against the light. On one side a dogwood flower was carved, and on the other side, a snowflake.

Slowly, drawing on memories from twenty years ago or more, Brastigan recognized it. Leithan had worn this token about her neck. She was never without it. It seemed distinctly strange to see it, now, without her. Joal had worn one, too, but his had been a rusty color, perhaps red jasper. Brastigan couldn't remember exactly, but he was sure the carving had been different. A pine cone, maybe.

Unferth spoke with old sadness. "I always wondered who she really was. She said she wasn't wellborn, that they had no such rank as king among their folk. And yet, as long as she was here, the Urulai stayed. There were quite a lot of them, you know, down in the town. They kept to themselves, kept together."

"I remember them," Therula put in thoughtfully. "And their horses."

Brastigan remembered, too. The lanky steeds, always gray or white, with a shy dignity and lively spirit. Their milky manes were braided and beaded like those of their riders. He remembered looking up at the proud strangers, so dark and tall among the heavier, blond Cruthans. All of them had worn these necklaces. What could they mean?

"Once Leithan died, they all just left," Unferth was saying, "We thought nothing of it then, though I recall Eben made mention of it. It's been fifteen years. I don't know where they would be. But as to your question, son, I believe the answer must lie with the Urulai. You should find them if you can."

Brastigan stared at the incised flower in his hand and said nothing. He couldn't remember much of his mother. She had had fair skin and dark eyes, with fine black hair trimmed to shoulder length. Each morning, Joal had bound it for her in a brief stub of white cloth. No other Urulai he had ever seen wore her hair that way. Leithan had been tender with him, but she seldom smiled. In a soft voice, she sang words he didn't understand. Urulai, it must be. He regretted, now, that he didn't know their tongue. Joal had never offered to teach him.

Who was she? A leader of some sort, it seemed, among the ragtag exiles. What must she have thought of the tame farmland, the thick city walls? She had not been old when she died. How did she feel about exchanging her body for the safety of her landless people?

"Didn't Joal know who she was?" Lottres asked.

"Of course. I asked him once, but he didn't answer." Unferth shrugged. "I think he felt that it wasn't my business."

"You are the king," Therula objected, frowning.

"Not their king," Unferth answered.

"I doesn't matter," Brastigan said. He tied on the necklace and stood, feeling stiff all over. "Thank you, Father."

It felt strange to say those words. He was so accustomed to bitterness instead of gratitude, and he had never called the man father before. Yet it had to be said. Too much was going on, and he didn't know when they would speak again.

"Of course, son."

Brastigan merely nodded. There was so much more to say, and yet, suddenly, he couldn't bear any more talking. More than anything, he wanted to get out of Therula's chambers. There was too much new insight, too many unfamiliar words. He had to get away, to walk and walk and walk and think.

"Pup, we'd best get going. We ride out early." Brastigan kissed Therula again, quickly, and strode from the room without waiting for an answer.

Truly, he should try to get some rest. The road before them was long, his destination uncertain, but somehow he didn't think he would sleep much that night.

CHAPTER FOUR
FORWARD AND FAREWELL

SHOULDN'T they be here?" Therula wondered aloud.

"They will come," Pikarus replied.

Therula looked up at her companion. Their eyes met, and his smile filled her with warmth. She didn't speak for a moment, just drank in the sight of him against the long drought ahead.

There was so much she was going to miss when Pikarus was gone. His quiet strength, as he stood watch at mother's door. His courage, for he didn't quail in the practice ring, not even when facing Brastigan. Nor did he later complain of the results. Most of all, that he kept his own dignity while surrounded by men of higher rank. No groveling from Pikarus, no jealous posturing, and never a sly remark. Oh, how she was going to miss him!

Therula couldn't remember, any more, when or how she had recognized his virtues. It seemed she had always known him. Their love had grown as naturally as green grass under the sun. Now duty was taking Pikarus away from her. Perhaps, in truth, Therula didn't mind so much if her brothers were late.

A light mist from the bay mingled with fumes from the castle ovens to form a tinny haze. The cool air was ripe with scents of the sea and oiled metal. All around them came the muted rustle of men in armor, the thump of horses' hooves, and the creak of leather. Pikarus's squad had gathered just outside the stables. A small group of women mingled with the men, wives and lovers who gave hugs and small parcels of food. A few sleepy-eyed children, too, took kisses from fathers who were leaving. Therula saw one woman, heavy with child, clinging to the arm of a doting soldier. Soft voices, here and there, urged the men to do their best, to be careful. One or two couples embraced passionately, speaking no words at all.

Therula was dressed simply, as one of them, in a long-sleeved gown fitted close through the body and flowing down to a full skirt. Her golden hair was braided and pinned in a circle around her head. Over her shoulders, a hooded cloak kept the damp air out of her hair. Only the elaborate stitchery set her apart. That was as she wished. This was no time for her to flaunt her rank. For the moment, she was merely a woman like the rest of them, sending her loved one off to places unknown.

Some shadow must have shown on Therula's face, for Pikarus said, "Try not to worry."

"I'm not worried," Therula said, though it was only partly true.

She envied the soldiers' wives their simple farewells, for she was too much a princess to give any public displays. Yet neither would she send her beloved off with nothing. Therula reached under her cloak and drew out a pair of fine leather gloves. Embroidered lilies and roses surrounded her own initial, T, on the cuffs.

"This is for you," she said. "You shall keep one, and I shall have the other. I won't wear them until you have come back to me."

Pikarus made a solemn bow. "I will keep it near me always." He stood quite still as she tucked the glove into his sword belt, making sure the initial hung on the outside, for all to see.

Softly, Therula said, "When you meet those other girls on your journey, I want them to know..." She couldn't finish. It was hard to even think that her beloved might betray her, but considering her father's example, she had to be realistic.

"There are no other women for me," Pikarus answered quietly. "This I swear."

Therula wanted desperately to believe him. She leaned against his shoulder, searching for warmth through the stiff mail hauberk.

"I will miss you," Pikarus said. From his voice, she could tell he understood how small a comfort he offered.

"It is what we must do," Therula answered. She didn't look at him, now. "It will be worthwhile, when it is over."

"For you, I would do a thousand times more," Pikarus said.

Before Therula could answer, a new voice among the many caught at her ear. It was Lottres, out of breath.

"Hurry up!" he panted.

"Why?" came Brastigan's lazy retort. "They won't leave without us."

Reluctantly, Therula stepped a little away from Pikarus. Her two brothers emerged from the mist, wearing full harnesses and swords. Like all the soldiers, they wore black surcoats with yellow badges bearing the black tower of Crutham. Lottres stopped near the horses, turning in a circle as he searched for someone. Despite his frequent protests at being called bookish, Therula noted Lottres clutched a roll of parchment in his hand.

Brastigan was fussing with his hair under the heavy leather aventail behind his helm. On top of his surcoat, Therula saw the dark disc of Leithan's pendant. Despite his many annoying habits, Therula had always felt sympathy for Brastigan, separated from his mother so young. She wondered, sometimes, what kind of man he would have been if Leithan had lived longer. Would he still show off and take foolish chances? Would someone still want him dead?

Unaware of Therula's scrutiny, Brastigan brushed past Lottres and approached the line of horses. Most of them were bay with white faces or stockings. The pair of white chargers near the head of the line stood out with their shining liveries. As Therula watched, Brastigan's lips twitched in self-mockery. Therula couldn't help smiling, too.

"What is it?" Pikarus asked.

"Why did you choose a white horse for Brastigan?" Therula asked. The virtuous color certainly did contrast with her half-brother's rough ways.

"They were the only two that matched," Pikarus replied with a trace of humor. "Prince Lottres deserves it, at least."

"I suppose you're right," she said.

Lottres had spotted who he was looking for. He trotted over, calling, "Pikarus!"

"Good morning, your highness," Pikarus answered.

"Good morning, brother," Therula echoed.

"Oh, good morning." Lottres kissed Therula's cheek, then unconsciously shouldered her aside so he could unroll his map in front of Pikarus. "Sergeant, do we have enough pack beasts? We're going all the way to Glawern, aren't we?"

"There's no need for concern, your highness," Pikarus patiently reassured him. "We won't be away from shelter for more than one night at a time until we reach Carthell. We will acquire additional pack mules there."

There was something symbolic, Therula thought, in the way Lottres came between her and Pikarus. She tried not to hold it against him. Over Lottres's shoulder, she caught sight of Brastigan. He looked at Pikarus and then at her. One eyebrow twitched, and he smiled knowingly. Therula returned his gaze coolly. Still grinning, Brastigan sauntered toward them.

"You've studied the map?" Lottres fretted.

"Yes, your highness," If Pikarus was annoyed, he didn't show it. "Princes Eskalon and Sebbelon added their observations, as well. They recommend we ride over Daraine, and thence into Carthell. From Carthell Keep, we will turn north into the mountains. Would that be acceptable?"

"Yes," Lottres said, but he continued to scan his map as if it were telling him something else.

Brastigan gave his brother a casual clout on the shoulder as he joined them. "We'll be fine. I'm sure it's all been planned out for us." He turned to Therula with a ribald smirk. "Come to see us off, dear sister?"

"Of course, dear brother. We don't often have such valiant deeds to tell of." Therula spoke smoothly, sweetly. She offered her hand, and when he took it, she pinched him. Brastigan's grin broadened.

"Indeed!" trumpeted another voice.

A hush fell over the crowded staging area. There was a flurry of salutes from the armsmen, and the women sank in deep curtseys. Therula did, too, hoping it would hide her surprise.

She couldn't think why Oskar had come here. He never did anything without some gain to himself. Perhaps he wanted to show everyone he was still the most royal of the princes. Oskar was sensitive about that, Therula knew. He certainly spoke loudly enough to draw all eyes.

While Therula and Lottres made their obeisances, Brastigan stood tall and nodded pleasantly to Oskar.

"You go with the gratitude of our nation!" Oskar proclaimed. He stopped and made a broad gesture which took in the soldiers and horses. "My heart is full of pride at this gallant sight, and that you, my good brothers, have sworn your service to our kingdom."

Therula tried not to wince as Brastigan proclaimed right back at Oskar: "If only you knew what that means to me, my brother!"

Oskar's eyes narrowed, but he held his smile. He had definitely come dressed to be looked at, Therula thought, in a short tunic quartered with Crutham's black and bright yellow. The two legs of his hose were of opposite colors to the tunic, and the shoes were of opposite colors to the hose. Even his hat and its feathers were parti-colored.

Behind Oskar stood Captain Tarther, the commander of the palace guard and Pikarus's immediate superior. He was the only soldier present who didn't wear armor. Instead, he wore a full length robe, dark gray, with Tanixan styled shoulders. A highly ornamented sword was belted over it. Tarther had come to Crutham as Queen Alustra's liegeman, and made no secret that his loyalty was to her and her son, rather than to Crutham. Ignoring Brastigan and Lottres, Tarther nodded to Pikarus with a military jerk.

"You have your orders," he grated out. "Fulfill them well, and your service will be rewarded."

Pikarus saluted. "Aye, Captain."

"Take good care of my brothers, Sergeant," Therula added.

"I will, your highness." Pikarus's voice gave no hint of his feelings now.

"And you," Therula's eyes strayed to Lottres, and then Brastigan. "Guard each other well."

Brastigan rolled his eyes and opened his mouth for some scornful reply, but Oskar must have realized people weren't looking at him, for he began to expound again.

"Great is the glory of Crutham!" he declared. "Great is the honor of her sons. Go forth, my good brothers, to seek your destiny. We shall remember you daily, and our every wish shall be for your speedy and safe return."

Not to be outdone, Brastigan then cried, "Come, my comrades! Mount your steeds!"

With a sweep, Brastigan turned his back on Oskar and Therula. He strode toward the two white chargers. Lottres hurried after. With a leap, Brastigan was in the saddle. He whipped out his sword and flourished its bright length over his head.

Brastigan cried, "The hour is at hand! Farewell, my noble brother! My sister, farewell!"

Therula did her best not to laugh at his outrageous showing off. Oskar wouldn't like it, she knew. Then, suddenly, it was very easy not to laugh. Pikarus delivered a smart salute, taking in Oskar, Tarther and Therula at once. Then he, too, went to take his place in line.

All about Therula, there was a flurry of last kisses and murmured farewells. Some of the women were weeping now, the pregnant one especially. Therula concentrated on maintaining a facade of royal grace, even as she felt her heart tear in two.

Therula and Pikarus had kept their feelings quiet, not out of shame but to protect him from the envy of others. However, they hadn't made the mistake of trying to hide it from her parents. Unferth made no secret, either, that he didn't want to see Therula leave, and Alustra, for all her pride, was still a woman. Therula knew she grieved that her older daughters had married so far away. This gave Therula and Pikarus a chance, however slight.

Alustra herself had pointed out that a political alliance could be internal as well as external, and Pikarus's family, in Gerfalkan, had proven their loyalty to Crutham many times over. If Pikarus did well on this mission, Therula was sure her father would sanction their marriage.

Even that left too many questions. Therula didn't believe the quest would be as simple as it sounded, and Pikarus was going to be right in the middle of it. Therula could only hope the fates would be kind and bring her beloved back soon.

* * *

Brastigan held Victory aloft until his shoulder started to throb, waiting for Lottres and the others to mount up. A casual glance through the thinning mist showed no one outside the immediate circle of onlookers. Brastigan hadn't expected Unferth to attend, but it would have been good to see Habrok or some of their other brothers.

There was someone else he hadn't seen yet today—or something. Brastigan stood in the stirrups, frowning over Oskar's head. Where was the falcon? His restless gaze searched the castle roofs, but there wasn't a feather to be seen.

Once Lottres and most of the soldiers were up, Brastigan flourished Victory once again. "Now we shall ride, my valiant men! We shall never return until our deed is accomplished. Forward!"

Therula waved to them, smiling and yet serious. Tarther glowered his disapproval. And Oskar must have known he was being mocked, for his expression was more snarl than smile. Brastigan felt his own resentment burning like hot coals in his chest. Pale eyes and dark eyes met, across the noise and hurry, in a moment of understanding. He raised his free hand in salute, acknowledging their mutual hatred.

Then he tapped his horse with a booted heel. The white charger lumbered forward, and the rest fell in behind it. The racket of so many hooves absorbed all other sound as they trotted toward the castle gate. The portcullis rose as they drew near. With a final shake of his sword, Brastigan passed beneath the bars and left his childhood home. He was not, after all, sorry to be going.

A short way down the sloping ramp, Lottres drew up beside Brastigan. "My valiant band? What's all that about?" he called above the clatter of hooves over cobbles.

"He started it." Brastigan sheathed his sword and grinned at his brother.

Lottres seemed to slump in the saddle. "Does everything have to be a fight with you?"

He sat up straighter. "It wasn't my idea, good brother."

But Pikarus was of like mind, for he brought his bay up on Brastigan's other side. Over the bobbing ears he asked, "Is it wise to antagonize Prince Oskar?"

"Hah!" Brastigan gave a bark of laughter. "What a pair of old women! He'll have plenty of time to forget about it before we see each other again. Anyway, Pup..." Brastigan reached over to give Lottres a playful shove. "Relax! We haven't even left the shadow of the castle walls."

Lottres winced from his roughness, and restlessly picked at his helmet's chin strap.

"You got your wish," Brastigan reminded him jauntily. "We're off on an adventure. What's the point, if you don't enjoy it?"

Instead of cheering Lottres, the suggestion seemed to make him thoughtful again. Pikarus dropped back, and the two of them rounded the first switchback in silence. Slowly, one jolting step at a time, Harburg rose from the morning mist to greet them.

"Maybe you're right," Lottres murmured, long after Brastigan had forgotten what he said to be right about. "Maybe I will."

"Will what?"

Lottres shrugged. Brastigan stared at him sidewise until his shoulders hunched defensively. "Cut it out, Bras. I won't know until we get there."

"Won't know what?"

"Nothing."

By the time they rode through the Butcher's Gate on Harburg's heavily fortified eastern wall, the sun had turned the mist into butter and was melting it from the morning air. The rolling hills of Daraine were laid bare as an endless tapestry of farm fields stitched together with seams of stone fencing. Here and there were clusters of buildings: farm houses, barns and sheds. Groves of trees grew on any hillside too steep to plow. The patches of darker emerald suggested what wild land this must once have been.

Southward, toward the mountains of Gerfalkan, a taller hill was adorned with a single great stone. At its base, unseen from the lands below, was a pool of clear water. No other structures marred the smooth sides of the mound. Whatever the season, that spring was ever flowing. Brastigan knew, because he often rode up to see it. The view from the height was so expansive, he could almost conceive of a future outside Harburg.

The local people spoke of the place with vague suspicion and avoided visiting. The Dragon's Candle, they called it, though none knew why. Brastigan, who was neither sentimental nor superstitious, felt a little sorry there was no time, this trip, to ride up and see it again.

The falcon unexpectedly swept from the sky and plucked some small, wriggling thing from beneath a dense carpet of turnip leaves. It glided to a roadside fence and stared at them with eyes like tarnished coins. Lottres raised his hand tentatively in greeting, but the falcon didn't speak. It bent its beak to peel off strips of gore and fur, and snapped them down. That was its good morning to them.

The days quickly settled into a rhythm: riding, resting the horses, riding, stopping for luncheon, riding, resting the horses, riding, stopping for the night, rubbing down the horses. The king's highway was well made and cared for, with a surface of clay that had gravel beaten into it. It was broad enough for two carts to pass abreast, as they frequently did. Since it was a main thoroughfare, the horsemen frequently passed rows of neatly kept houses, shops and inns. The abundance of taverns made stops far more refreshing.

For the most part, the falcon circled high above them. Sometimes it vanished for hours at a time, but it always returned. Brastigan thought it must find the horses' land bound pace unbearably slow, but it didn't descend to say so. Where it roosted at night, he had no idea and little desire to know. All in all, he was content to know the falcon hadn't drawn them out of Harburg and left them.

The weather held fair as a handful of days went by. Brastigan passed some of the time on the road with idle speculations. Such as Therula and Pikarus, for one thing. He couldn't help wondering if that situation was as it seemed Pikarus was wearing a fancy glove, all of a sudden—one with Therula's initial on it. Brastigan hadn't seen it before, but he would have bet it was Therula's own handiwork. Pikarus wasn't talking about the relationship, and no wonder. It would be a real coup if a lowly man-at-arms could win the hand of a royal princess. That wasn't likely to happen, in Brastigan's opinion. If it did... Queen Alustra as a mother-in-law? What a nightmare!

As a military convoy, they took lodging at whatever fortress they came across. That occurred every two or three days. There was always room, for Crutham was at peace. Other nights, they chose among whatever inns presented themselves. Brastigan let Pikarus choose, so they had modest accommodations and simple meals.

That was as well. The kind of inn Brastigan favored wasn't to be found along the king's highway. Nor would he bring Lottres into the back alleys. Moreover, Brastigan wasn't interested in carousing. He only sought rough company when he was bored. In Harburg, that had been a daily occurrence. Now it wasn't.

Even on the royal road, the innkeepers seldom saw real royalty. Brastigan and Lottres had seldom been the center of so much attention. They had too many older brothers. The fawning had its charm, but Brastigan found it soon began to pall on him. As did the flirtation of the alewives. These women were of a better class than his accustomed lot but Brastigan enjoyed them only with his eyes. He wanted no brats brought to his door, as had befallen his father and a number of his brothers. Most nights, he retreated to the sanctuary of a room he shared with Lottres.

Curiously, it was the younger prince of Crutham who stayed up late drinking as they traveled on. Perhaps Lottres took advantage of the maidservants, though his stammering when Brastigan ribbed him suggested otherwise. Most days he seemed to ride in a stupor, contemplating his horse's pale mane. The reversal was amusing, when Brastigan thought about it.

It wasn't so funny when he woke by himself one night. Through the floor he could hear muffled sounds as the last patrons were ushered from the common room below. The alewives bade the innkeeper good-evening and the bar fell to shut out the night. After a few brief words to someone else, the proprietor shuffled upstairs. Brastigan heard the door across from his own open, then close softly.

He rolled over but couldn't get comfortable, so he got up to use the chamber pot. As he turned back, the wan moonlight showed him Lottres's empty bed. The sheets lay smooth, the blanket still folded at the foot of the bed. Brastigan frowned, scratched his head, tried to marshal a sleep-heavy brain. The last he saw, Lottres had been in a deep consultation with some scruffy minstrel. Hearing more tall tales, no doubt. He sure was fond of them.

Brastigan sighed as he turned from the warm, waiting blankets on his own bed. It took a bit of shuffling in the dark to locate Crusher. He stubbed his toe in the process and, thus painfully awakened, padded down the stairs.

The common room was dark and silent, of course. The scent of the fireplace hung in the air faintly, bitterly. A single tallow candle had been left burning. This revealed the welcome sight of Lottres sitting near the fire. The slim young man had pulled a bench practically onto the hearth, where embers glowed dully under the blackened log rack. He was leaning forward so far he seemed about to fall into it.

Fire-gazing again. This was becoming an unsettling habit.

Brastigan hadn't realized how worried he was until he saw his brother safe. Then he released an exasperated breath and stepped forward purposefully. As he walked, he kicked a spoon under a bench and sent it singing into the darkness.

Lottres straightened at the sound. At least he had some awareness of what was going on around him, Brastigan thought. Hands on hips, he stood over his brother.

Lottres blinked up at him. "What are you doing down here?"

"Getting you up to bed," Brastigan answered gruffly. "You're going to fall from the saddle one day if you don't start getting more sleep."

His brother smiled wryly. "Yes, Nursie."

"I'll nurse you!" Brastigan knocked his curly head lightly with Crusher. "Come on."

Lottres rose stiffly, as if he had been sitting in that strange position for some time. As his brother followed him toward the stairway, Brastigan muttered, "What are *you* doing in here? That's what I'd like to know."

"I was listening to the fire," came the desultory explanation. Lottres sounded as if he was already half asleep.

Brastigan's snort echoed up the stairs. "The bards, you mean. Why do you waste your time with them and their wild stories?"

"I'm looking for news." Around a yawn, Lottres repeated his familiar argument. "I'd like to know what lies ahead of us. Wouldn't you?"

"You're going to start rumors about yourself."

"Instead of rumors about you? That would be a change," Lottres teased. "What, are you jealous?"

"Ha!" Brastigan swung open the door to their chamber. As he did so, he saw Pikarus opening the door to his own room, just down the hall. Speaking of nursemaids... Brastigan nodded to the squad leader before following his brother into their room.

"Get to bed, Pup," Brastigan yawned, "so I can get to bed."

More shuffling in the dark commenced, as Brastigan returned to bed and Lottres got ready for his. Finally, the room was quiet. But only for a short time.

"Bras?" Lottres's voice came from the darkness. "I meant to tell you, I think we're being followed."

"What?" Rushes crackled as Brastigan rolled over.

"There's a tinker. Maybe you've seen him." Lottres paused to yawn again, while Brastigan waited impatiently. "He's been at every inn where we've stayed for the past five days."

"I couldn't see past the boot-lickers and flunkies," Brastigan answered. "Anyway, we were at Rockaine Keep last night."

"I know. The only nights I haven't seen him were then and when we stayed at Belegoth Keep the third night out. You'd think, if he were a wanderer looking for work, that he'd be stopping along the way."

Brastigan said nothing, so Lottres continued, "I walked by his table two days ago, and again tonight during supper. His tool pack doesn't even look like it's been opened."

Brastigan rolled onto his back, hands clasped behind his head, and stared into the darkness where the ceiling was supposed to be. He searched his memory for any suspicious travelers.

"You're right," he said after a moment. "I think I've seen him a couple of times."

Brastigan poked at the image in his mind: a shabby fellow with a long nose, drooping moustache, matt of brownish blond hair beneath a battered felt hat. Always hunched over his food as if someone might steal the plate from him. Or as if he wished to hide his face? To all appearances, he was the vagabond blacksmith, but Brastigan was sure he'd seen that hat before.

Lottres said, "Tinkers never have any money, either, and there are less expensive places he could be sleeping tonight. He always sits near us at meals. I can't say what it means, but I thought I'd better tell you."

"Does Pikarus know?"

"Not yet."

"Hmm," Brastigan said slowly. "I think I might know him."

"The tinker?" Lottres demanded. "From where?"

"The Dead Donkey." Brastigan grinned to himself as his brother groaned ominously.

Yes, he was sure of it. Wolf...no, Wulfram. They had a passing acquaintance, played dice upon occasion. Once, they had clenched hands.

Brastigan lost the match.

When he had been quiet for too long, Lottres asked, "What should we do?"

Brastigan shrugged, causing the mattress beneath him to crackle again. "Will he be in the common room for breakfast?"

"He should be."

"Then I'll look for him in the morning." He was getting too tired to think any more.

"All right." Lottres sounded faintly disappointed.

"What do you want me to do, start knocking on every door in the inn?" Brastigan demanded irritably.

"No, no. But..."

"If he is following us, we won't have to look hard to find him," Brastigan yawned. "He won't go away, and if he wants trouble we'll deal with him in daylight. Get some sleep, Pup."

Lottres said nothing more, and his breathing soon deepened into sleep. Yet if Brastigan's body was weary, his mind was wide awake and running in fevered circles. The stranger looked a little like Wulfram, but he couldn't be sure. He remembered the man having a beard. It might be someone else.

In a way, Brastigan hoped it was. He'd seen Wulfram in a brawl. He was fairly sure he could beat the man, but he would rather not try.

LOTTRES woke with a flutter of excitement and vindication in his chest. He was right about the tinker! He had sensed something amiss the moment he laid eyes on the fellow. Now, even Brastigan agreed the tinker was suspicious. Maybe what Eben had said was true, after all. Maybe Lottres could be a wizard.

His self-satisfaction was shattered by a brisk tap on the door. Lottres sat up, rubbing his eyes. Daylight brightened the room's curtains and showed him Brastigan stretched out face down on the bed. Black hair obscured his features. As Lottres's muddled brain fumbled to think what was wrong with that, the door opened. Pikarus leaned in and murmured, "Your highness, you have overslept. If you would come downstairs, the men are ready to ride."

"What?" Lottres gasped. Before Pikarus had to repeat himself, Lottres said, "No, I heard you. I'm sorry. Of course, we'll be right down."

Pikarus nodded, a sympathetic gleam in his eye for Lottres's confusion. He closed the door.

"Wake up, Bras," Lottres called.

"I am awake," Brastigan replied, though he didn't much sound like it.

"Hurry, get dressed," Lottres urged. He frantically grabbed for his own clothing. Slept late? How could they, when they were supposed to confront the tinker at breakfast? "We'll miss him. Brastigan, get up!"

His brother responded by indulging in a long stretch. "That's what you get for staying up so late," Brastigan said, but he did roll out of bed.

A few minutes later, Lottres rushed down the stairs to the common room. Brastigan followed at a deliberately slower pace. The soldiers made no comment on their tardiness, but Lottres could feel their eyes pricking at him. The two princes tied down their baggage while Pikarus settled their account with the innkeeper.

They had missed breakfast, but that wasn't the worst of it. All the other guests had already departed. There was no sign of the tinker on the road outside, either. They went on their way with slices of bread and cheese for the morning meal. Lottres chewed listlessly. His eyelids felt sticky and stiff. Brastigan's words of the night before, "if he is following us, we won't have to look for him," gave scant comfort. They couldn't even try to hurry, or the tinker might realize they were aware of him.

Well, Lottres wasn't ready to give up. Not yet. As they rode, he tried to follow Eben's instructions. Lottres let his eyes slip shut and relaxed so that his body would adjust itself to his horse's strides.

"Listen," Eben had told him. "Be as one with the air. Listen, and breathe."

Eben called this the first form. Lottres had practiced it every day of the journey. So far, he had learned that a man could hear and smell many more things with his eyes shut than open. He knew the scent of a muddy road, the sharpness of green fields, even the slight difference in pungency between horse and chicken manure. Lottres knew all the men in Pikarus's squad by their voices alone. He had learned how frightening it could be when your horse suddenly jumped underneath you. He was also learning, slowly, to sense the horse's tension just before it jumped.

Perhaps Lottres was trying too hard, for he had never felt anything out of the ordinary. Most days, he heard only the singing of blood in his ears. He definitely couldn't hear past the drumming of horses' s hooves to the slither of wind in the turnip leaves—not the way Eben said he should.

Of course, Brastigan's teasing didn't help. Last night, when Brastigan came to fetch him, Lottres had been trying to use the second form, using fire to focus his senses. He had even been tired enough to let slip that he was listening for sounds in the fire. Fortunately, Brastigan had mistaken his meaning.

Lottres sighed and opened his eyes. Any idea that he and Brastigan would renew their boyhood closeness on this journey was turning out to be hollow. Brastigan never missed a chance to mock the falcon and their quest. Of course, Brastigan didn't know he was also mocking Lottres's fondest dreams. Even if he had known, Lottres couldn't guess whether Brastigan would have stopped baiting him or done it even more.

Lottres wasn't sure what his brother would say when he learned that Eben thought Lottres could be a wizard. Brastigan had made his feelings about magic quite clear. Even less did he like events that weren't his own idea. The sullen way he had been acting ever since Unferth announced the expedition gave witness to that. Look how he had corrected Lottres last night, speaking so scornfully, as if Lottres didn't know what he himself was doing.

It wasn't just that, however. Lottres had to admit that he liked having a secret. He wanted to keep this to himself for a while longer. After all, he might not be able to master even the first form. No one could ridicule his failure if they didn't know what he was trying to achieve.

Even with this doubtful safeguard for his pride, Lottres's confidence was flagging. Five days of effort, and nothing to show for it. Nothing but the jingle of harness and mumbling of the men. Except...

Except, Lottres reminded himself, he had been right about the tinker. It was little enough, but this minor achievement was sufficient to make him keep trying.

* * *

Lottres nudged Brastigan and whispered, "There he is!"

"I told you," Brastigan muttered back.

With evening the tinker appeared again, though they hadn't seen him all day. As a test of Lottres's theory, Brastigan had told Pikarus to choose the most expensive inn. Though puzzled, the squad leader had complied. Now they sat with a much finer meal before them, pretending they weren't staring at the stranger two tables off and one down. Brastigan had no doubt that it was Wulfram. He could only speculate whether the man had shaved his beard as a disguise or for some other reason.

"He's right over there," Lottres said as he passed a plate of steaming roast mutton across the table. "What should we do?"

Brastigan took it and speared a couple of tender slices. "I see him. Don't look around! He'll know we're watching."

"Sorry," Lottres muttered as he reached for the bowl of mashed parsnips.

"Now, listen," Brastigan began, but Pikarus interrupted.

"Is it the tinker you're not looking at?"

The squad leader was seated next to Lottres. He helped himself to the platter of meat, although Brastigan wasn't offering it.

Brastigan merely nodded, but Lottres leapt on the words. "You've seen him, too?" he triumphantly demanded.

"Shhh," Brastigan warned.

Pikarus nodded and ladled gravy over his platter before passing the gravy boat on to Brastigan. He kept his voice low. "I didn't want to alarm you, your highness, but Javes and I have been keeping an eye on him for a few days now."

"You should've mentioned it sooner," Brastigan answered, annoyed.

"I could have said something the day after Rockaine." Lottres seemed far too happy about the confirmation of his suspicions.

"Never mind," Brastigan snapped. "I think I know who he is, and I have a plan to deal with him."

"What plan is that?" Pikarus asked.

Brastigan had filled his mouth with food and had to chew before he spoke. He used this time to glance along the table, where he saw every man of Pikarus's squad who was in hearing distance was listening quietly. Good—there would be less explaining later.

"Finish your supper," he told them, "and don't get excited. Just do what you'd normally do. I'll pick the moment to have a friendly talk with him." He smiled ironically at this description.

"By yourself?" Lottres asked anxiously.

Pikarus asked, "Will you at least tell me his name?"

Brastigan nearly refused, but then thought better of it. "Wulfram. From Carthell, or so he says. Ever heard of him?"

"No," the man-at-arms replied after a moment's thought.

That was a good sign. If Wulfram had been arrested for a violent crime, Pikarus should know his name.

"Are you sure it's safe?" Lottres pressed.

His worrying was an unpleasant reminder of the assassination attempt, which Brastigan had nearly managed to forget. He grunted, "Pup, I'm not sure of anything, but I'll hear what he has to say before I jump to conclusions."

Lottres looked unhappy, and Pikarus carefully asked, "Your highness, can we talk about this?"

"What's to talk about?" Brastigan retorted, irritated by their caution. "Do you think he'd start trouble in a place like this? There are too many witnesses." He gestured to their busy surroundings and speared a piece of onion with his fork.

"Agreed. However," Pikarus said, "it might not be wise to let him know we've seen him. It could push him into something. Can we discuss our strategy beforehand?"

"Yes," Lottres said. "I have some ideas, too. You can always talk to him later, if we all agree."

Brastigan looked his brother over while he chewed his food. It wasn't like Lottres to be so assertive. He wasn't sure he liked it. Still, he could see the conversation was about to get heated. That alone might draw Wulfram's attention. He shrugged, taking another bite of mutton to conceal his annoyance.

"If it makes you old women feel better," Brastigan said, "when you see me go upstairs, wait a few minutes and then join me. You two only." He turned his dark eyes to Lottres and Pikarus. "The rest of you, keep your distance and act natural."

There were nods of assent along the table, though Lottres frowned at being called an old woman.

With a hint of relief, Pikarus said, "Very good, your highness."

Brastigan turned back to his meal. The mutton was rare and juicy, the vegetables tender, and he didn't let them get cold on his plate. Afterward, the ale warmed him nicely. Pikarus and his squad separated, some joining a dice game at a neighboring table and others strolling toward the fire, where a fiddle was starting to whine. Brastigan had to practically shove Lottres after them.

"You've listened to the minstrels every night so far," he growled. "If you don't do it this time—"

"I know, I know." Lottres sulked off.

The common room was much like those of the other places where they stayed: noisy, crowded, and dark. Even a blazing fire couldn't completely light the cavernous spaces. This inn was newer than some, with fewer drafts and more comfortable chairs. As a result, the room grew warm rather quickly. Brastigan sipped his ale and waited for the atmosphere to get good and hazy before he moved.

While he waited, he considered the few details he had. Wulfram was what they called a "man of work," which could mean anything, except that the work wasn't likely to be legal. There were less savory characters at the Dead Donkey, to be sure. Brastigan was reasonably certain Wulfram didn't cheat when he gambled. On the other hand, Brastigan had been trying to think if Wulfram had been at the Dead Donkey the day the knife was thrown. He couldn't remember.

Brastigan watched the tinker a while longer. Nothing raised his suspicions. Still, he didn't like the feeling it gave him. Hadn't he been thinking, earlier, that he didn't want to cross swords with Wulfram?

The dark prince drained his tankard and sauntered toward the stairs. The room he and Lottres shared was large and comfortable. There were two beds, a pair of dressers nearly buried in baggage, and a small table with chairs. A fireplace provided both light and heat. Brastigan added more wood to the fire and dragged three of the chairs over to the hearth. Then he checked his luggage to assure nothing had been pilfered in their absence.

The room was quiet, save for an occasional sputter behind the fireplace grate. Brastigan dug out oil and a honing stone. He sat down to give Victory a good cleaning while he waited for his comrades.

It wasn't long before Lottres arrived, scuttling in as if he were the one who had something to hide. His face was full of anxiety as he took the chair nearest his brother. The dark prince merely nodded and returned to his work. The honing stone hissed softly along the length of the blade.

"I'm glad you didn't talk to him," Lottres began.

"I'm not," was Brastigan's curt reply. "A man should have the chance to speak for himself."

An exasperated breath wafted the whiskers on his brother's chin as he slumped back in his seat. Brastigan almost expected Lottres to start staring at the fire again, but he folded his arms and fixed a determined gaze on Brastigan. Who, in turn, determinedly continued cleaning his weapon.

Some minutes passed in this stubbornness before a gentle knock sounded at the door. Pikarus entered swiftly, closed it behind him, and took the remaining chair.

"I don't like the look of that tinker," Lottres burst out, as if Pikarus's presence gave him courage to speak his mind. "He's dangerous. I can tell."

"It could have nothing to do with us," Brastigan reasoned. He gave Victory a final swipe and returned her to her sheath.

"You don't believe that," Lottres accused. "You just don't want to admit it."

"Don't put words in my mouth," Brastigan warned.

Pikarus cleared his throat. "There was no secret to our going," he said. "Anyone could know where we are bound."

"No, not with the falcon shouting it out," Brastigan snorted. He raised a hand to still Lottres's angry protest. Then he tightened the cap on the oil jar and turned to toss it and the stone lightly toward his bed. "I'm not saying I don't agree with you, Pup. I like Wulf, but I don't trust him. I could never be sure of him unless I paid him myself."

"Is there anything about him that you can be sure of?" Pikarus asked.

"He's mostly a messenger, so I've heard." Brastigan wiped his hands thoroughly on the rag. "It could be he's carrying a message now. It could be the message has to do with us, or it could be it doesn't. Carrying a message isn't the same thing as intending to harm us."

"I suppose such men make a great deal of those fine distinctions." Pikarus's mouth twisted with disgust. Brastigan shrugged.

"What does this have to do with our situation?" Lottres asked irritably.

"It's like you've been saying all along, Pup," Brastigan answered. "There's no reason for him to be here, instead of at the brothel down the street. He should be keeping clear of you, too." Brastigan glanced at Pikarus. "You could have him clapped in irons."

"We're a little outside my authority," Pikarus answered moderately. "I'm just a palace watchman."

"Ha!" Brastigan retorted. "If you were just a palace watchman, you wouldn't be on this trip with us. You and all your men who know to keep mum at the right times."

"Our squad was chosen because my men are so reliable," Pikarus said blandly.

Lottres interrupted, "The local commanders would listen to you, wouldn't they?"

"Is that what you want me to do?" Pikarus asked. "Arrest him?"

Brastigan stretched out his long legs to prop his boot heels on the hearth. He linked his fingers behind his head.

"Not yet," Brastigan decided. "There's no real reason to think he's dangerous. At least, not to us."

"What's that supposed to mean?" Lottres asked.

"This road doesn't go anywhere but Carthell," Brastigan explained. "He might be part of something going on there."

"What business could he have in Carthell?" Pikarus asked.

"Maybe he's going home to visit his poor old mother," Brastigan suggested wryly. "He says he's from Carthell."

Lottres frowned. In an odd voice, he asked, "Bras, doesn't our brother Albrett live in Carthell?"

"Albrett?" Brastigan asked, confused by the non sequitur.

As in any large family, the full- and half-kindred of Crutham's royal family included an array of factions and cliques based on age and other variables. The sheer number of Unferth's brood made this inevitable, and perhaps even necessary. It helped to organize the unruly company. Brastigan and Lottres had formed such an alliance years ago. Likewise, Albrett had united with Rickard. The two, full siblings, had shared a nasty sense of humor. Albrett, in particular, had always seemed to be involved in some cruel practical joke. Lottres, being small and gawky, had been a favorite target until Brastigan's stout fists convinced the two older boys to leave off.

The matter had been so long settled, Brastigan hadn't bothered to think of them in years—except recently, when Rickard had been killed. Quite naturally, Albrett had been the one to escort his body back to Carthell, where their mother lived. Her brother, Johanz, was the Duke of Carthell.

Yet Albrett hadn't come back to Harburg. Until this moment, Brastigan hadn't questioned it. Now, he felt a niggling itch in his brain. Rickard and Albrett were among the more mature of Unferth's sons. They both had families, held positions at court. Why hadn't Albrett returned? For that matter, he didn't remember seeing their wives around the keep, either. Where were they? In Carthell?

"Do you think Prince Albrett is in danger?" Pikarus's concerned question jarred Brastigan from his thoughts.

Brastigan shook his head. All this guesswork confounded him, and that made him peevish. "This might not have anything to do with Albrett. Wulf could be following us out of curiosity."

"Curiosity?" Pikarus asked.

"Sure, just in case he saw something he could tell someone about later. For a price, of course." Brastigan leaned forward, pushing back the sleek, dark strands that slipped over his shoulders. He sighed. "We don't really know that, either."

"That's not it," Lottres answered, a flat statement. "I don't like this, Bras."

"You think I do?" he snapped back. "Look, we'll be staying over at... Where was it? Cobble..."

"Caulteit Keep," Lottres answered. "That's where we'll be tomorrow night."

"Do you know the garrison commander?" Brastigan turned to Pikarus. "Can we trust him?"

The soldier rubbed his temples thoughtfully. "That would be Captain Morbern. I don't know much of him personally, but there's no reason to suspect his allegiance."

"What are you planning?" Lottres demanded.

"I'm planning to send a message to Albrett when we get to Caulteit," Brastigan said. "This Morbern can send a dispatch ahead and let Duke Johanz prepare his household for whatever might happen."

"May I suggest we also alert the constable in Carthell?" Pikarus put in. "I'm sure he has informants to keep track of such men."

"Then they would know Wulfram is coming." Lottres sounded relieved.

Brastigan nodded firmly. "Good idea. Yes, do it."

"Very well," Pikarus agreed.

He should have felt badly about warning the constables of Wulfram's presence. Should have, but didn't. Whatever their past association, it hadn't kept Wulfram from spying on him. Blood was blood, even if it was the blood of a worthless bully like Albrett.

The fire had burned down, leaving the chamber nearly dark. Lottres crouched on the hearth to add more wood, which the fire accepted with a greedy crackling. Over his brother's head, Brastigan studied Pikarus in the ruddy shadows. A round face with pug nose, short hair a shade darker than the usual bright blond, no beard. Pikarus wasn't that much older than Brastigan and Lottres. What was he, really? Bodyguard, nursemaid—or a spy himself?

Pikarus looked up. Their eyes met momentarily. Then he blandly looked away. Brastigan opened his mouth to speak, but Lottres abruptly straightened between them.

"Sending a message isn't enough," he fretfully announced. "I don't think we should stay on this road. Not if this wolf fellow is sniffing after us. We should take precautions."

Brastigan didn't mind being diverted. Pikarus was a friend, too. He didn't like doubting his loyalty.

"What's your alternative?" he countered. "We can't go back home. We haven't even left the king's highway yet. What kind of adventure is that?"

Lottres returned a sour smile for the baiting, and Pikarus said stolidly, "No, we must go to Hawkwing House."

"Ah, but we don't have to go through Carthell," the younger prince declared. He rose and went to the beds, where Brastigan heard him rummaging through his bags. Returning with a stout tube, Lottres explained, "I've been thinking about it all day. If we ride north from Caulteit, instead of east, we could follow the River Ogillant up to Glawern, and from there go straight to Hawkwing House. Look..."

He drew a scroll of parchment from the tube and spread it over the hearth. A hastily drawn map of Daraine and Verelay lay revealed in the renewed firelight. As Brastigan and Pikarus each held down some of the curling edges, Lottres's index finger followed the wavering line of a watercourse between two mountain ranges.

Pikarus was frowning, and Brastigan thought he knew why. The River Ogillant flowed straight out of Sillets. A tower-shaped scribble, presumably their goal, was marked just at the edge of the blankness designating unknown Silletsian territory.

"It could be dangerous," the man-at-arms observed. He ran a blunt finger over the mountains around the village of Glawern. "Some of this is wild country. We'd be far from any help if danger came upon us, or if we ran short of supplies."

"It's flat land most of the way," Lottres said. His brown eyes roved over the surface, planning. "We can resupply at Rowbeck or Glawern."

"Not so many comfortable inns on that road," Brastigan teased.

In truth, his gut reaction was to stay on the highway, where they could draw upon their prestige as royalty. Also, Pikarus was correct that help might be hard to find if they got too far from settled land.

"It would save us time," Lottres argued with some enthusiasm. "If we went all the way to Carthell, we'd have to back-track through the mountains, here, at Carthell Cleft."

"I don't know," Brastigan said, seriously now. "I thought maybe we should talk to Albrett while we're there. You know, find out how he's doing." Or, perhaps more importantly, *what* he was doing.

Lottres regarded him suspiciously. "You don't really want to see Albrett again, do you?"

"You were the one who was so worried about him," Brastigan retorted.

"Prince Lottres," Pikarus inserted, "you have been asking the minstrels for news of the road. Have you heard any reports of this region?"

"Nothing out of the ordinary," Lottres said. He tugged on his map until the other men released it, and began to roll it back up. "The crops are growing well and people I never heard of are getting married. Oh, and there was a huge migration of crows, all heading north. The farmers are a little worried they'll eat the whole crop if they're still there at harvest time."

"Crows?" Pikarus repeated, puzzled.

"I didn't think crows migrated," Brastigan remarked.

"I have no idea. Maybe that's why they're all talking about it. Still, if crows are the worst of our problems..." Lottres shrugged as he sealed the map into its oiled tube.

Brastigan leaned back in his chair again. "Falcons and crows," he snorted. "What's next? Storks?"

Pikarus murmured something under his breath that sounded suspiciously like griffins, and he wasn't laughing.

Lottres smiled, but pressed his point. "I really think we should do this, Bras. We know this fellow is following us. What if there's someone else we haven't noticed yet?"

"You're just not having enough fun, are you?" Brastigan scoffed. "You're determined to make it more of an adventure."

"No!" his brother protested. "I just..." He shut his mouth angrily.

Brastigan poked his shoulder. "Don't get mad. I don't care which way we go. I just don't like the idea of all this magic in the first place. You know that."

"All right, then," Lottres mumbled.

"What I really wonder," Brastigan said slowly, picking out his own thoughts with the words, "is what Father would say. He wants us to go to a place of safety. If we take a dangerous route to get there, doesn't that defeat the purpose?"

"What, you—frightened?" Lottres mocked.

It was Brastigan's turn to glare at him. "Iamnotscared!"

Pikarus considered the two of them. "I, too, dislike being followed," he offered tactfully, "and it's been my experience that a man should trust his instincts at times like these. If Prince Brastigan doesn't object to turning north..."

"I've slept outdoors before," Brastigan assured him.

Pikarus nodded and continued. "Also, I hesitated to suggest it, knowing how you feel—" he glanced apologetically at Brastigan, "but perhaps we should consult the falcon."

Lottres's face lit up. "I forgot about that! It must have flown to Harburg from Hawkwing House. Maybe it saw things on the ground."

Brastigan grimaced sourly, but then shrugged in deference to his brother. "I don't have to be there, do I?" he asked hopefully.

* * *

They were up at cock-crow the next day. Lottres made good and sure of that. He sprang out of bed and had the drapes open at first light, then bustled around the room packing. Brastigan couldn't have slept long if he wanted to.

The morning meal passed in silence, but that was busy with glances darting across the boards. From Lottres to Pikarus they flashed, and from Pikarus to Javes, a kind of wordless swordplay. Brastigan, watching sardonically, had to wonder how much the men had been told. Yet that was a petty concern when the real problem, Wulfram, sat just a few seats down, chewing his eggs and bread. They had all gone back to pretending they didn't see him. Wulfram drained his morning ale and shouldered his pack. Many watchful eyes followed as he tramped out the door.

The words they had been holding in broke loose the moment their backsides touched the saddle. Brastigan heard low rumbles of talk along the line as the horses clattered down a cobbled lane between shops and houses. He and Lottres took the head of the column, with Pikarus and Javes close behind. The squad followed in what seemed a much tighter line than the day before. Since they all rode so near, it was easy to talk. That they did.

The plan that emerged was simple: they would change mounts at Caulteit and head north before sunrise. Later in the morning, a party of soldiers from the fort would ride out with their steeds. If luck held, these would lure Wulfram on after them.

Lottres was much pleased by the acceptance of his ploy, and eager to consult the falcon at their first rest. As if he needed some excuse for that, Brastigan thought sourly. He strolled around, stretching saddle-stiff legs, and left his brother to it.

Brastigan hadn't bothered to keep track of the falcon's whereabouts. It hunted for itself and that contented him. Now he watched with veiled amusement as Lottres waved and shouted up to the sky. After much exercise, he succeeded in catching the falcon's attention. It streaked downward on folded wings. Brastigan could faintly hear his brother explaining their intent, and see the tawny head jerk in what served as its nod. No other approached that council. From their expressions, Javes and the other men shared Brastigan's misgivings.

Yet there was a thought he had, one that wouldn't leave his mind. He didn't like it, but this was his command. Even Brastigan knew better than to put selfish feelings before safety. He kicked his way through the grass toward Lottres.

The falcon's beaky face snapped around as Brastigan approached, but he didn't speak to it. Instead, he told Lottres, "Ask it if it can follow Wulf tomorrow."

"Why?" came his brother's wary demand. Lottres turned away, as if shielding something precious.

The falcon regarded Brastigan over Lottres's head. Dark lids ran down and up over its pale eyes, but it said nothing.

"Wulf's not stupid," he snapped, unnerved by that feral regard. "The bird's been with us all the way so far. If it doesn't follow the decoys, he'll know it's a trick."

The falcon cocked its head, blinked again. Then came the strange voice: "That is well thought of."

"I didn't ask you," Brastigan snarled.

"But we'll need him!" Lottres protested as if they were boys again, and some bigger child was about to pry a wonderful new toy from his hands.

"It can fly," Brastigan reminded his brother with patient sarcasm, "and it can see long distances. Let it keep high enough to be out of bowshot, and stay long enough to see if Wulf follows them."

"We shouldn't get separated," Lottres insisted.

"I agree with Brastigan," the falcon said. Brastigan clenched his teeth at the sound of his name coming from such a source. "It is the wiser course."

"But..."

"Pup, the bird flies faster than we can ride." Brastigan linked his thumbs and made flapping motions on the air. "As long as we stay on the road, it will find us."

"It is even so." The falcon dipped its curved beak toward Brastigan. "Tomorrow, then."

It launched from Lottres's shoulder, barred wings beating swiftly upward. Brastigan watched it away and Lottres watched him, and both of them were scowling. The younger prince rubbed his shoulder and muttered rebelliously.

Brastigan was in no mood for dissent now. "What was that?"

"I said," Lottres answered, speaking as slowly as Brastigan had a moment ago, "why am I always the one who gets scratched? You're the one who can't be polite."

"Sorry," Brastigan shrugged. Manners were irrelevant as far as that witch-thing was concerned. "If you don't like it, don't let it sit on you. You're not a tree, you know."

"You..."

Brastigan looked around sharply. He scarcely recognized his brother's voice, but his hackles were still up from the parley with that cursed bird. Their glances caught like crossed swords.

"You just want to get rid of it!" Lottres burst out, eyes blazing and fists clenched white at his sides.

"Oh, do you think so?" Brastigan widened his eyes with feigned astonishment. Then, "Of course I do! It's unnatural!"

His brother stepped back from him, as if the words were blows, and his face above the curly beard was ashen.

"You don't even know —." Lottres began hotly.

Then Javes's loud whistle cut between them, summoning the riders back to the saddle. Brastigan didn't move, didn't blink, but Lottres let an angry breath hiss between his teeth and stalked off to join the others.

There was little talk thereafter. Lottres rode fuming, and Brastigan rode aloof, determined to ignore his brother's temper. He had nothing to apologize for. A commander had to make decisions sometimes, that was all.

Still, he found himself chewing on the problem as the column trotted between pastures and fields. It irked him that Lottres set such a great store by the falcon. As if it were an honor to be perched on by a creature that might bloody him at any moment. Brastigan glanced aside, taking in his brother's frowning profile. Lottres was such a sensible lad, normally. How could he be so smitten with the romance of wizardry? Worse, how could Brastigan save him if he willingly ran after danger?

For the moment, Brastigan let Lottres keep his silence. At last the waning day showed them the blunt gray towers of Caulteit Keep. A goodly town clustered near the fortress. Behind them all the mountains of Carthell loomed closer now than not. As the convoy approached the castle walls, Brastigan hoped tomorrow's exploits would cure whatever ailed his brother.

CHAPTER SIX
DIVIDED ROADS

ALL the way to the north tower Therula told herself she was being an idiot, but she couldn't shake the feeling that something was wrong. She nodded, acknowledging the guardsman who swung the heavy oaken door open before her. As soon as her feet touched the ancient stone steps, she lifted her skirts and ran upward.

Part of the problem was her father. The king seemed distracted in court. Granted, he had once told Therula it was only the pleasant haze of wine that made the long-winded presentations bearable. Yet he didn't seem sleepy to her. Instead, he was edgy and alert. He had been for several days. When Therula attempted to raise the subject, Unferth merely shook his head, silencing her.

There wasn't much in the realm of public policy that Unferth didn't share with Therula. Nor of private matters, either. His silence now suggested this might have something to do with Oskar. Since Unferth had declared an end to his pursuit of younger women years ago, Therula couldn't think what else it might be.

In an interesting coincidence, Oskar was also behaving oddly. Ordinarily, he liked to make himself visible at court, but Therula hadn't seen him for several days. Not since the morning of Brastigan and Lottres's departure, in fact. When he did appear, his merriment seemed slightly forced.

Just because the king wasn't talking didn't mean Therula couldn't ask Oskar about it. They had never been close—Oskar was nearly twice her age—but Therula didn't think he would lie to her. Still, it seemed more suitable to consult her mother. Alustra would know what was happening, especially if Oskar was involved. It wouldn't have been the first time Therula acted as peace-bearer between her two parents.

Even so, Therula knew, it wasn't her family's maneuvering that troubled her. It just seemed that something was wrong, somehow. As if the sea air suddenly smelled of dust. With the utter paranoia of true love, Therula was sure it all had something to do with Pikarus.

Pikarus. He had only been gone a few days, but Therula missed him so much she sometimes felt she could hardly breathe. That was what finally drove her to Eben's door. She could wait for whatever news her father might have, if she only knew her beloved was safe.

The lowest level of the tower, where she had entered, held Eben's sitting room, where he gave formal consultations. With supper just over, Therula didn't expect to find him there. She climbed to the second level and Eben's personal chambers. By the time she reached the door, her legs ached and she really was fighting for breath.

Therula stopped on the landing to compose herself. When her heart had stopped hammering against her lungs, she adopted an expression of regal calm and raised her hand. The plain wooden door swung open before she even touched it.

"Oskar," she said, surprised. "I didn't expect to see you here."

Her older brother wore a tense expression, which he quickly turned into a genial smile.

"I was just leaving," Oskar said. "You are free to drink from the fountain of wisdom." He took Therula's shoulders, kissed her cheek lightly, and then swung her around as if they were dancing on a feast night.

"Warn me, brother," Therula protested. Dizzy, she leaned on the inner wall. Oskar merely chuckled and was off down the stairs. Therula watched him for a moment, wondering at his sarcastic tone.

When she turned to enter Eben's chamber, her dizziness suddenly returned. Therula's knees wobbled, and she clutched at the door handle to keep from falling into Eben's chamber. As she caught her balance, she had the confused impression of a stranger inside. His features were distorted, and he was crowned with something like tree branches. Candles, burning behind him, made Therula blink and shield her eyes.

Then it was only Eben, in his plain blue robe, hurrying forward to steady her.

"Your highness, are you well?" Eben asked.

"Oh, that Oskar," Therula managed to laugh although her heart was beating hard. "He put me off balance."

"Then do come in, your highness," Eben said. "Tell me what I can do for you."

"I..." Therula found herself tongue-tied. For a moment, she couldn't remember why she had come here. Oskar's prank must have startled her more than she knew.

Eben guided Therula forward with a gentle hand on her elbow. He showed her to a seat and offered a cup, which steamed invitingly. Then he waited, all patience and consideration.

Therula sipped at the cup, and tasted spearmint tea. "My favorite," she murmured. Somehow it seemed she had forgotten that, too.

Eben's smile slowly widened, and he said, "You are always welcome to drink my tea."

Therula drank again, savoring the warmth of the tea and Eben's presence. She remembered now why she had come to see him. He was so wise, so kind. She felt she could tell him anything.

"I came to ask about Pikarus," Therula said.

"Pikarus?" Eben repeated.

"Yes." She hesitated, then asked, "Were you aware of our feelings for each other?"

"No," Eben admitted. "Your father hadn't mentioned it."

"Well, it's true," Therula said. "Since Pikarus left, I've felt... I don't know, that something is wrong. I can't help worrying. Can you tell me if he is all right?"

"I can try, certainly," Eben said. Then he cautioned, "It may take me some time. Perhaps a few hours, or even a day or two. Shall I send a message when I have the information?"

"Of course." Therula sipped her tea again, trying to hide her disappointment. Days? She had never asked Eben for anything before, but she had been hoping for more immediate results.

"Tell me, before you go," Eben went on. "What do you mean that something is wrong?"

"Oh, it may be nothing," Therula said. "I feel something is out of place. You know how it is, when the staff cleans your room and they don't put things back right where they were?"

Eben nodded, cupping his chin in his hand thoughtfully. "When did you first notice this?"

"After they left," Therula said. "Pikarus went with Brastigan and Lottres to Hawkwing house. You knew that?"

Eben's eyes narrowed, glinted thoughtfully. Then he said, "Perhaps that is what is out of place, as you put it. Simply that you are accustomed to seeing Pikarus and now he is absent."

"No," Therula said. She shook her head impatiently. "I know something is happening. Father seems distracted to me. So is Oskar." Therula looked toward the doorway for a moment, remembering how Oskar had swung her around. She asked, "Have either of them mentioned anything to you?"

"If they had, I couldn't break confidence," Eben said gravely. "You understand."

"Yes, of course," Therula murmured, feeling rebellious in her heart.

"I think," Eben went on gently, "the heart of the matter is that you miss your dear friend. There is no shame in this. At such times, it is easy for imagination to run wild." Eben pressed Therula's hands gently. He took the empty cup and drew her toward the door. "Let me see what I can learn, princess. I will send word as soon as I know anything of his whereabouts."

"Very well," Therula sighed, wishing for more but knowing she couldn't demand it. "Thank you, Eben."

"It is no trouble, your highness," Eben assured her.

He closed his door, and Therula was left alone in the stairwell. It seemed very dark after Eben's lighted room. She descended slowly, measuring her steps with care, but felt no more dizziness on the way down.

What she did feel was a sharper confusion than she had before. Could she be imagining it all—Unferth's distraction, Oskar's forced good humor? Therula didn't think of herself as being prone to flights of fancy. Yet Eben thought she did. He was so wise. Tomorrow, perhaps, or the next day, Eben would let her know Pikarus was all right. When he did, Therula would laugh at herself and her silly fears.

She would.

* * *

It didn't seem to matter that Lottres wasn't speaking to Brastigan. Captain Morbern, the commander of Caulteit Keep, was willing to talk enough for all of them together. Before the end of supper, everyone knew more than they wished of Morbern's life. He was a local man, proud indeed of how well he'd done in the king's service. A wife and children dwelt in the town and, by his wide grin, he adored them all.

Morbern's broad good humor made Lottre's own anger into an anti-climax. No one even noticed that he wasn't talking, because no one could get a word in.

"I wonder if he's even seen combat," Brastigan muttered, while Morbern had the whole table roaring with laughter at his older son's escapades.

Lottres shrugged. Who was he to judge? He hadn't seen combat himself. He couldn't help wondering if Brastigan had forgotten that, or if he was reminding Lottres of it. Trying to prove how much more he knew. When Lottres didn't answer, Brastigan shrugged himself, irritably.

At least Morbern did give a satisfactory response when Brastigan finally got him to focus on their situation. He dispatched a message to Carthell at once, then applied himself to the business of detaching the unwanted camp follower. Morbern also offered the squad mules in exchange for their horses, a suggestion Brastigan was quick to approve.

Pikarus looked askance at the loss of the valuable horses, but Brastigan insisted. He said the mules would be sure-footed and hardy, an asset in rough country. Despite their greater size, the chargers were delicate by comparison. They needed more water and special care, and they were no faster once you left the high road. Morbern assured them the mules were war-trained, not as skittish as horses, and they were easily strong enough to bear the weight of armored men.

"Besides," Brastigan said, "I don't fancy us being set apart by the color of our steeds. You might as well shout, "Look! I'm important! Shoot me first!""

At this, Pikarus reluctantly agreed. Not that it really mattered, Lottres thought bitterly. Brastigan thought he knew so much about horses, and he wouldn't listen to anyone else, anyhow. He had to have everything his own way.

Lottres slept poorly that night, despite Brastigan badgering him to an early bedtime. He hadn't been able to practice the second form, and it made him irritable. Lottres was sure that tonight he would have heard something in the fire. Instead, he turned over and over, shifting between sleep and wakefulness.

Once Lottres woke suddenly, with his skin prickling. He was certain he had heard Eben's voice calling out to him from far away, but now there was only darkness and snoring.

* * *

They emerged from the fortress in a pre-dawn gloaming. The chilly air held wisps of steam from the breath of men and beasts and the drumming of hooves along muddy streets was the only sound. Soon they crossed an ancient, moss grown bridge over the River Ogillant and left stone walls behind. The dark waters rushed between narrow banks, as if they would flee their origins in the north.

Daybreak found the riders on a river plain striped with low hills. At first, clusters of flickering light showed where farms and houses bestrode the hills, but these showed fewer with the rising sun. The hills started out bald — the woods, no doubt, cut down for firewood — but soon grew shaggy with trees. Plowed fields yielded to pastures, and then to marshy grassland. As they crossed the first rise, the plains below were dappled green and gold. The river lay in braided channels, now dark, now silver bright. It looked like a tapestry of Therula's weaving, save that now and again the whole scene shimmered with sheets of tall grass bowing to the wind. The desolate loveliness helped, in a small way, soothe Brastigan's concern at Lottres's stubborn silence.

No longer held down by the weight of wagons, the road wandered freely across the plain. It skirted the deepest pools, but Brastigan often smelled stagnant water and heard the sodden thump of hooves on spongy wooden spans. They saw myriad birds — ducks, cranes, yellow-headed blackbirds — and met swarms of bloodthirsty bugs, but no other travelers shared the road. Brastigan was sure of that, for the sun-gilt plain gave no cover at all. Still, whenever he looked behind, his brother's face was turned back and up, and he knew it wasn't Wulfram that Lottres watched for.

Well, Brastigan had endured enough snubs from that quarter. He reined in his gray mule to ride beside his brother's dun.

"Looking for those migrating crows?" he teased.

Lottres gave back a narrow glance. "Storks," he replied with a sour humor.

Brastigan laughed, perhaps as much to reassure himself as to placate his brother. "Don't worry. The falcon will find us. It said so itself."

He couldn't believe he was quoting that creature, and Lottres didn't seem impressed, either. He barely nodded.

"Anyway," Brastigan went on, determined to pierce his bad humor, "it looks like you chose the better path for us. There's no way anyone could follow us out here." He gestured to take in the open terrain. "We'd see him too fast."

Finally, Lottres relaxed. "I hope so."

Brastigan, in his turn, rode with a better heart. As if their talk had summoned it, the falcon drifted down to them shortly afterward. Defiantly, Lottres raised his fist to receive it.

Brastigan swallowed his ill feelings and turned in the saddle to signal a halt. He loitered only long enough to hear confirmation that Wulfram had gone after the decoys before leading his mule to drink. Lottres and the bird continued talking, but he didn't stay to hear what they spoke of. The whistling voice made his teeth clench. While his mount stood in the shallows, sucking in the brackish water, Brastigan kicked at the wildflowers along the stream bank.

The slither of approaching feet provided a welcome distraction. Brastigan nodded at Pikarus's approach.

"News?" the soldier asked.

"It worked." Brastigan snapped off a long grass stem. He stuck the frayed end in his mouth and sucked in the taste of green. The seed head bobbed before him like an old man's pipe.

Pikarus eyed him. "But..?"

"It won't fool him for long, I don't think," was Brastigan's reply. "He knows me, remember? Morbern's men may be loyal, but they can't fake my height—nor my hair. If he follows them to the inn again tonight, he'll have no doubt."

"And then he has a choice," Pikarus said softly, with all his contempt of the night before. "He can keep his paid appointment, or turn and follow us."

Brastigan spat out the grass stem and yanked another from its roots. "If he does that, we'll know where the money is."

"If he does that," asked Pikarus gravely, "should he be allowed to live?"

In his heart, Brastigan knew the answer to that, but he merely shrugged. "I'll want to talk to him. Find out whose man he is."

Pikarus nodded. "I understand. We do have a watchdog of sorts." A glance over his shoulder suggested the falcon, but offered no opinion on its provenance.

"Wulf might not be our only problem," Brastigan said around the stem in his teeth. Thinking again of the fight that nearly took his life, he added, "It's the one we don't see who'll get us, so just you keep a good watch."

"Aye."

Pikarus said no more than that, merely looked across the river with narrowed eyes. The water, running past them, seemed to murmur in its bed of secrets from the north. Brastigan studied his comrade in the silence. For all that he spat on Wulfram, Pikarus was just as much a cipher. At least the man of work said plainly what he was. Not so for the man at arms. Was it the memory of Therula's blue eyes that drove him, or some other duty? Brastigan didn't ask, and the soldier kept his thoughts to himself, and then it was time to ride on.

The party hadn't made any great haste in the days before this, but now they pressed their speed. Nothing like an enemy to spur you on, thought Brastigan sardonically. Though they made good time, the land about them seemed oddly lonely under the noonday sun. By the time of afternoon shadows, he found himself seeking some sign of man—a stone fence, a cow shed, a dock on the river bank. He saw none, and that was eerie. He hadn't known such a stretch of land lay empty in Crutham.

Dusk met them at the base of a wooded knoll. A wide, flat spot had been leveled from the slope and extended out above the standing water. Fire pits, lined with stones from the hillside, held cold ashes of other fires. There was even a series of rusted metal posts at just the right distance to tie up the mules.

As Brastigan sat his long-eared steed, taking in these details, Javes drew up beside him. "Set camp here, your highness?"

Brastigan shrugged. "No place better."

"Very good." Turning in the saddle, Javes bellowed to the others, "All right, you men, let's get to it!"

The quiet order of the riding line gave way to a bustle of activity as the soldiers set about pitching tents, gathering wood, carrying water. It was obvious they had set camps before from the way each took up his task without assignment. Only the two princes were left without duties.

"This looks like a regular way station," Lottres observed. The falcon had left his shoulder bare, a great improvement in Brastigan's eyes.

"Probably is," he agreed. "The road looks well traveled. I'm surprised we didn't meet anyone today."

"Not the season for it?" Even Lottres sounded doubtful of that.

"Well, this is no good," Brastigan decided. He swung down from the saddle.

"What?" Lottres asked.

"Sitting here, watching. I'd rather make myself useful, wouldn't you?" Brastigan wanted to be accepted among the soldiers, not regarded as a royal snob who had to be coddled while others worked. "Come on, Pup. I'll teach you something useful."

Lottres hesitated, and Brastigan thought he might make some retort. Then he climbed down from his mule. "Of course. You teach, I'll learn."

Brastigan frowned, but decided not to ask what his brother meant. They were just in time to take the reins while the last of the pack mules had their burdens pulled off. Together with two other soldiers, they led the animals off for a drink and a rub-down. Brastigan savored the familiar work. He also thought his brother had been riding too much apart. Lottres needed normal activities to take his mind off other things. Winged things.

By the time the beasts were staked out securely, fires were blazing in the pits and cider was being passed in steaming cups. Javes got out his bow and brought back a brace of hares from the marsh, and so they ate hot meat. The stars above shimmered through the rising heat of the fires.

Lottres left off his fire-gazing at last. Brastigan was glad to see that. Instead, the younger prince sat in the rank grass on the bank above the water. The soldiers turned questioning glances in that direction, but Brastigan thought it too soon to renew their quarrel. As long as Lottres stayed in sight of the camp, he wouldn't press the issue

Later, he lay in his tent, listening to frogs belch and mosquitoes whine and thought with satisfaction that he didn't miss the soft bed of an inn at all.

* * *

Thus passed a handful of days, in hot sun and the smell of swamp mud. Camp was set each night in much the same way. Soon Brastigan no longer needed to take duties for himself. Their participation was expected. In daylight, the two brothers rode in a comfortable silence, for the falcon once again kept its distance from their kind. They scarcely saw it, save on the evening of the third day, when it descended to report there were no tinkers on the road behind them.

By then, Brastigan had something else to distract him. A grassy hill rose tall from the plain before them, its conical sides too perfect for any work of nature. Frowning against the sunset, he could barely pick out the vertical stroke of a single stone at the summit. When a rise in the trail permitted, Brastigan turned in the saddle to stare westward, behind them. Sure enough, there lay the distant wart of the Dragon's Candle. Lottres, reined in beside him. "What's wrong?"

"That." Brastigan jerked his thumb at the nearer mound. "I didn't think there was more than one of those."

"Yes, I'd seen it." Lottres regarded the monument with interest.

Riders were backing up on the trail behind them. Brastigan was about to move on when a new voice interrupted.

"There are at least two others," said Egger, one of the soldiers who rode nearest. "I've seen them. One in Carthell and another in Firice."

"What are they?" Lottres wanted to know.

"Ah, well, that's beyond me, your highness," Egger demurred. "I just know I've seen them."

"He's no help," Brastigan grumbled, urging his mule forward.

"You could ask around in Rowbeck," Lottres suggested. "We'll be there tomorrow."

Without a ready answer, Brastigan could only watch the hill grow larger as they drew near. The valley pinched in around it, and the river flowed more swiftly. River plains gave way to fields and farms. The road once again ran straight and flat, deeply rutted with wagon tracks. At last, they rounded a wooded thumb of hills to see Rowbeck lying before them in twilight.

The hill, standing above the town, was still bathed in fiery sunset rays, but the buildings lay in shadow. Plumes of chimney smoke drifted in feathered layers above slate roofs and the river ran in a rocky bed close beside buildings of rough timbers. The water's chatter was nearly loud enough to cover the sound of hooves as they entered the square.

The town had but a single inn, which was so small the royal party filled the handful of guest rooms to overflowing. The common room featured rafters too low for Brastigan's comfort and a haze of smoke in the air. The locals who came in for a flagon of ale had trouble squeezing in. The overcrowded chamber stank of tallow and sweat and burnt meat. After the silence and clear air of the marsh, the voices of men seem coarse and irritating, like a stifling wool blanket over the room.

Worse, from Brastigan's viewpoint, there were no women that he could see, not even a cook in the back. You could tell from the stew, which tasted strongly of cabbage. Brastigan knew he wasn't the only one to grumble at the flavor. Without other options, he could only eat more quickly to end the torment of the ill-cooked meal.

Still, the hard bed waiting in the chamber upstairs offered little enough comfort that Brastigan chose to linger over a draft of the local barley brew. It, at least, was properly stout.

As he drank, Lottres nudged him and murmured, "There's your source."

"My what?" Brastigan followed his brother's gaze to behold a wizened old man seated at the fireside.

"The hill," Lottres prompted, pushing his bowl of stew away half eaten. "It's the old ones you want to ask about such things. They know all the best tales. Look, he's practically by himself."

Indeed, there was a strapping young man beside the oldster, but he sat turned toward a group of men his own age, shutting the old man out of their conversation.

"By all means, let's pay our respects." Brastigan followed as Lottres made for the hearth, and he didn't leave his ale behind.

The young men (farmers, by the mud stuck to their cleated boots) didn't so much as look around as Brastigan and Lottres pushed through to the old man. His face, they now saw, was so wrinkled it seemed about to fold in half. One eye was vague and milky beneath jutting brows, but the other one was clear and sharp as a nail. A long pipe lay cradled in his lap.

"May we join you?" Lottres began politely.

"If ye can find a space," came the laconic retort. "Busy tonight, it is."

"That's our fault, I'm afraid." Lottres maintained his humor as they crowded onto a bench facing him. "We're just passing through, and we couldn't help noticing that mountain outside the town."

The old man made a noise between his nose and chin that might have been a chuckle. "The Dragon's Tooth, is it? I knew it. You strangers always ask." His good eye, beneath the brim of his cap, fastened on Brastigan's hair with friendly contempt.

"Well, what is it?" snapped Brastigan, who didn't like feeling that he was being laughed at.

"Wait," his brother interrupted. "Strangers? When?"

The old man's gaze was keen on Lottres's face. "Oh, now and again."

"Where from?" Lottres frowned.

"They didn't say." He cocked his eye at them in a way that reminded them they hadn't given their names, either.

Brastigan nudged his brother. "No one we need to worry about." It hardly seemed worthwhile to pull rank in a tiny place like this. He pretended not to see Pikarus and Javes, seated nearby and clearly more interested in keeping sight of the two princes than in their dice.

Lottres looked abashed. "Well, I'm Lottres, and this is Brastigan, my brother."

The one bright eye roved between them. "Spitting image of each other, you are." Brastigan had to laugh at that, a sharp bark. The old man waved in dismissal as Lottres began to stammer an explanation. "It doesn't matter, boy. I'll tell you what I told the others. And that is... I can tell you nothing."

There was silence as he took a pull from his long pipe.

"But surely—" Lottres started to argue.

"Wise men don't go there," the oldster growled. In the noisy room, if they wanted to hear, they had to lean closer and smell his sour breath. "It's a haunted place. You come back strange, so they say."

Now Brastigan snorted. "There's nothing haunted about it."

The old man squinted at him. "Oho. Been up to the Dragon's Tooth, have you?"

"And you haven't?" Brastigan retorted. In a rural area, with not much for entertainment, he couldn't see a young man refusing a challenge like that.

A glint in the old man's eye told him he was right.

As usual, Lottres tried to smooth things over. "We live in Harburg, in sight of another mountain just like yours called the Dragon's Candle. That's the one we've climbed. We were just surprised to see another one so like it."

The fire at their backs was growing overly warm, and Brastigan was glad his brother sat nearer than he. The old man didn't seem to feel the heat, for he leaned closer and spat into the flames.

"Pah. Been up there, so you say. Then you've seen the fairies a-dancing?"

That was a test, Brastigan guessed, a falsehood to see if they really knew what stood on the hilltop.

"Fairies, my eye," he scoffed right back. "We saw a standing stone and a pool of clear water."

Lottres tensed, no doubt preparing another reprimand for Brastigan's ill manners, but he didn't get the chance.

"Oho." The old man leaned forward, keenly interested. "Did you see the lights in the water? Hear the stone sing?"

"Lights?" Lottres repeated, baffled.

"Singing stone," Brastigan retorted, but with keen interest.

"Aye, lights in the water, always moving, like the sun shining through a tree's branches. They come and go, but it's easier to see them at night." He squinted past the two princes as if visualizing something seen long ago. "The stone sings, it does. Whistles like the wind on a still day, or crackles like a fire, or roars like the salt sea waves—but we're inland, you see. A fey thing, it is. A man could think he heard voices."

At those words, Lottres shifted suddenly in his seat, drawing the old man's gaze to him. The pale eye held something like sympathy. "You've not heard it, then."

Lottres shook his head silently, and Brastigan put in, "We were only up there in daylight." If they hadn't returned to Crutham Keep, the guard would have been sent to collect them. "What makes it sing?"

"Well, lad, nobody knows that." The old man smirked, enjoying their intense interest.

There was another brief silence. Brastigan, studying his brother's profile, thought he could guess Lottres's thoughts. Truth to tell, he wanted to see this singing stone for himself. But not today, nor tomorrow.

His heel thumped against the bench his brother sat on. "We don't have time for it."

Clearly Lottres wanted to argue that point, but he reluctantly nodded.

Seeing the oldster's curious look, Lottres explained, "We're summoned."

"To Hawkwing House," Brastigan added, thinking the old man might have information on their mysterious destination. He was disappointed.

"Where's that?" The oldster's voice was hazy now, as if the change of subject made his mind wander.

"North of here," Lottres prompted, "up above Glawern."

"Ah? It's a bad road you're on, then." Their companion shook his head grimly. "Too close to Sillets. Better to go home, say I."

"I wish we could," Brastigan muttered to himself.

A looming form interrupted them. The two princes looked up to see a weather-worn, younger version of the old man standing over them.

"Come on, Gramps," he ordered curtly. "Time to go. You know how Ma worries."

"Aye, she does, aye." Reluctantly, the old man let his hulking grandson stand him up and guide him from the room. Brastigan watched them hobble out, shaking off the sense he had been dozing in his seat.

The old man and his grandson weren't the first to leave. The room was emptying quickly as the locals sought their own homes. There wasn't much life in Rowbeck after dark, it seemed. Without women, why would there be? Pikarus, still seated nearby, seemed fully involved with his dice, but Brastigan saw his wary gaze following the farmers from the room.

Lottres, however, sat quiet and thoughtful beside him. The crackling of the fire, unnoticed moments ago, now sounded unusually loud. Brastigan remembered the old man saying the stone made a sound like voices in fire, and he felt the fine hairs rise at the back of his neck.

Brastigan clapped his brother on the shoulder, declaring cheerfully, "No mountain climbing in the dark, Pup. We've a long road ahead of us yet."

Lottres screwed up his face and stuck out his tongue. "Bleah for you."

CHAPTER SEVEN
A PASSING OF POWER

WHERE are you going?" came Cliodora's indignant demand.

Therula smiled at her younger sister. "I just need to see Father for a moment."

"But we were supposed to go riding!" Clodora followed Therula, dancing with agitation. "You said we can gather shells at the seaside, and see the galleys go by."

"We will," Therula answered.

The two princesses crossed the great court and passed bowing guardsmen at the gate to the inner keep. They were both dressed for riding, in simple gowns with divided skirts and warm cloaks against the sea wind. The excursion included some half dozen of Unferth's youngest daughters — Cliodora, Frella, Leoda, Alista, Agiatta and Orlyse — plus guards and grooms to help Therula keep a rein on the younger ones.

"You promised," Cliodora grumbled.

"I did promise, and I meant it." Therula did her best not to be annoyed by her little sister's fixation.

Cliodora had been reminding her about the promised outing all week. In truth, Therula looked forward to it. She liked spending time with her sisters, and it would take her mind off her worries. She couldn't have known Eben's message would reach her just before their departure.

The two princesses were inside the keep now. Soft steps echoed off stone walls as they approached Unferth's door.

"Is my father in?" Therula asked as the guard bowed to them.

"I believe so, Princess," the guard replied. "He may still be sleeping. He hasn't called for his manservant yet."

"Then you can come back later," Cliodora said eagerly. "Come, sister, let's go."

Therula hesitated. She couldn't remember any court feasts or carousing that would have kept Unferth up late last night — but she did remember the bright sunshine in the courtyard outside. Even kings couldn't lie abed all day long. It set a bad example.

She set her hand on the latch. "I'll just look in," Therula said. "If Father is asleep, I'll be right back out."

The guard didn't try to stop her, though Cliodora gave a dramatic, impatient moan before dragging her feet in after Therula.

"Father?" Therula called softly. She let Cliodora enter, then closed the door behind them. "It's Therula. Are you awake?"

The room was very dark. Cautiously, Therula made her way to the narrow window, where heavy drapes were tightly drawn to shut out the day. She stubbed her toe only once in progress.

"He's not awake," Cliodora complained from the shadows near the door. "Can we go now?"

"I have news, Father," Therula went on, ignoring her. "Eben found Pikarus. He's with Brastigan and Lottres in a town called Rowbeck. They're doing just fine. I know it's silly, but I can't help worrying about them. I'm so glad to know they're all right, aren't you?"

As she spoke, Therula pulled on the edge of the drapes. The rich fabric slid aside, admitting a shaft of light that cut through the gloom like a sword blade. It fell across the bed, where Unferth lay on his side. A green bottle glinted on the bedside table, liquid like a shadow within it. The king's face was pale against the darkness, his expression serene.

"You're being rude, Therula," Cliodora scolded, "talking to Father when he just wants to sleep."

Therula stared at Unferth, wondering why he didn't blink against the bright light. She felt a sudden chill of fear.

"Father?" Therula called more loudly. He didn't respond.

Therula's knees didn't want to move, but she forced herself to walk the few steps to the bedside. She could see, as she drew closer, that her father's eyes were partly open. They glinted dully, and he wasn't breathing.

"Fa... Father?" she stammered.

Therula reached out, hesitated, and drew back. Then she forced herself to touch him. Unferth's cheek was dry and cool. Even his hair felt stiff under her fingers. Therula jerked her hand away. She took a step backward, rubbing her two hands together in a vain effort to warm them.

Unferth was dead. She didn't understand how this could have happened. His calm expression gave no hint of pain or fear. He must have died in his sleep. Therula turned away with a choked cry, trying to shut out the sight. How could he look so peaceful when something terrible had happened!

"Sister, what's wrong?" Cliodora's voice at Therula's side startled her. Then the younger one was staring, too, transfixed by the sight of their father's calm, dead face. Cliodora's blue eyes were pale as glass in the dim light.

"Go get my mother," Therula said quietly. Panic churned in her stomach, until she felt she would vomit it out. She had no idea what to do. Alustra would know. Therula felt sure of that.

"I..." Cliodora backed away, still staring at Unferth with her hands pressed to her mouth.

Therula grabbed Cliodora's shoulders. It wasn't fair, she knew, but she was glad to have someone to yell at.

"The queen," Therula insisted fiercely. "Go quickly, go quietly. Tell no one else, but bring my mother here. She deserves to know first."

Cliodora nodded and stood up straight. A measure of clarity returned to her eyes as the effect of this simple, important duty took hold. She whispered, "You can count on me."

The younger princess left, walking with her arms held stiffly to her sides and her hands clenched into little white fists.

Therula returned to the window. Defiantly, she flung the curtains wide. It seemed wrong to admit the pitiless light, and yet she couldn't bear to be alone in the silence and gloom.

The waiting seemed endless, an agony of her own fears magnified by the terrible stillness. Finally, the door flung open from the outside. Therula turned, longing to rush into her mother's arms. She stopped before she had even lifted a foot.

"Oskar?" she choked.

Her brother ignored her. He strode into the chamber, leaving the door open. Therula could see the guard looking in, his mouth agape. Oskar went to the bedside and bent over the dead man, his expression as stunned as Therula's must have been.

"So it's true." Oskar spoke softly, almost to himself. "I didn't want to believe it."

Therula watched, too numb to move. How could Cliodora have told Oskar, after Therula ordered her not to tell anyone except Alustra? But she was too stunned to feel the rage she should have.

Oskar looked up, then. He seemed surprised, as if he hadn't known Therula was there. Then he said, "Sister, dear, you're shaking."

He was right. Therula was trembling, and she couldn't seem to stop. Oskar crossed the room and reached to embrace her, but she jerked away. She wanted her mother, and she didn't want anyone else to touch her.

"I was... I was waiting for Mother," Therula mumbled.

Oskar frowned, but he let his hands fall to his sides. "You found him? Oh, dear."

"I'm fine," Therula lied. With a conscious effort she straightened, folding her hands before her to keep them still.

"You are a strong woman," Oskar said. Carefully, moving slowly, he reached out to squeeze her two hands. "I will need your support, my sister. You and Mother are all I have now. I know I can depend on you."

Therula nodded with a jerk, though she was feeling the opposite of strong. She watched as Oskar returned to the bedside. He knelt there, head bowed, in a classic pose of grief, yet he shed no tears. Instead, he posed for the audience, making sure everyone saw him as a loyal, grieving son.

And his words, "I can depend on you." As king to subject, he meant. Therula looked out the window again. She was ashamed of her disloyal thoughts. Oskar was her brother. Even so, she had the feeling his grief was just that, a pose. She wondered who he posed for.

Therula blinked away the tears that had gathered in her eyes. She forced herself to view her brother dispassionately, as an outsider would. Oskar wasn't a living image of Unferth. He favored their mother too much. Yet he did look like a king, she thought with a start. In fact, he was a king. Oskar was the heir. With Unferth dead, he was king already.

She couldn't believe it, couldn't imagine anyone but her father sitting on

Crutham's throne. Oskar would, of course. It was what he had been waiting for. All his life, waiting for the chance to rule Crutham and justify their mother's many humiliations.

Therula looked out the window again, trying to hold back the tears that blurred her vision. She turned with a start at the sound of rapid footsteps. This time Alustra did enter the room. It was the first time Therula had ever seen her regal mother run. Alustra's cheeks were flushed, her dark eyes wide with shock. Two attendants came behind her, and Cliodora last of all.

Alustra rushed to the bedside, where Oskar rose to greet her.

"Mother," he said mournfully.

Therula's knees wobbled with relief as she went to join them. Alustra was here now. She was in charge, and everything would be all right. But she was not to experience the comfort of her mother's embrace. Alustra kissed Oskar's cheek briefly, but her eyes never left the bed. She moved past him, ignoring Therula, and sank down on the soft coverlet. Alustra reached out slowly, just as Therula had done, and brushed Unferth's forehead. Therula heard her mother sigh, saw her shoulders bowed as she bent forward to kiss her husband's cold forehead.

Margura, one of Alustra's attendants, now stepped forward. She sank in a low curtsey. "Your majesty, is there anything I can do?"

Her voice was husky, kind and thoughtful, yet Therula realized Margura wasn't speaking to Alustra. She was looking at Oskar. And he was smiling back at her.

"Leave me for a time," Alustra answered, for she didn't see them behind her. "Return to my chambers, and see that suitable raiment is prepared."

"Yes, my lady." Margura curtseyed again, and followed the other young woman out. Cliodora, left alone, drifted uncertainly toward Therula. Abandoning pretense, Therula embraced her little sister tightly, let her sob on her shoulder.

"We were to have gone riding with our sisters, Mother." Therula managed to speak, though her throat felt tight and hard. "They are waiting at the stables. I'll go tell them what's happened."

"That is well thought of," Oskar added smoothly. "I will summon our brothers and do the same. If that is what you want, Mother?"

"Yes," Alustra said. Her voice was as calm as Unferth's dead face. "Now, leave me."

Oskar went first. Therula made sure to close the door behind them, though the guard was no longer staring. She patted Cliodora's shoulders soothingly, but her eyes followed her brother as he strode away from them.

Oskar wasn't married, though he had been once. His wife, the delicate Cyrille of Erlixen, had died in childbed, taking their son with her. Oskar hadn't remarried, despite Alustra's best efforts. Therula had the impression that Oskar hadn't liked being married, having to share his quarters and answer to another. Cyrille had been one of the most docile creatures Therula had ever known, and she couldn't imagine what restrictions the girl might have placed on Oskar.

Whatever the reason, Oskar was an eligible king who lacked an heir. Besides their brothers, of course, but Therula knew very well he wouldn't settle for that. No, Oskar would be looking for a wife, and there were plenty of women willing to take that part. Margura was only the first. Crutham Keep was going to be a circus until Oskar chose a wife. Just thinking of it gave Therula a headache.

The two princesses left the inner keep and made for the stables. Therula walked slowly and let Cliodora cry. As they went, wellborn and servants alike passed them, running the other way. All the court was learning that Unferth had died. They were all in a hurry to speak to Oskar, Therula thought bitterly, wanting to keep their positions or even improve on them.

Meanwhile, she couldn't think what she could say to their sisters. "Father is dead" was truthful, yet it seemed so harsh. Perhaps she could start with something like "I have some bad news," or "I'm sorry to tell you..."

Cliodora stopped crying long enough to sniffle out, "We aren't going to go riding today, are we?"

Therula laughed sadly at the lesser loss among greater tragedies. "I'm afraid not, little sister. Oh, but I do wish I had listened to you."

"Me, too," Cliodora whimpered.

* * *

The beds of the Rowbeck inn were as hard as Brastigan feared, and lumpy as well. Even so, he and Lottres were lucky. Others slept on a floor not swept for months. With such comforts to goad them, the whole squad was up and ready to be away in the chilly dawn. None cared to try the kitchen's mercy in breaking his fast.

In leaving Rowbeck behind, they also left the open spaces and easy trails. The road abandoned the river, which now lay in a chasm roaring with foam and spray. Wooded heights beckoned from above, and the road answered with sharp turns that challenged even the sure-footed mules. The beasts earned their fodder as they moved into true mountains, which must be crossed to reach their next goal of Glawern. Rests for them were fewer, for there were few level places for resting.

If the beasts labored harder, Brastigan relaxed as he breathed the earthy scents of trail dust and cedar. He had always felt at home in the woods. The trees covered him like a blanket, warm against the piercing chill of the mountain air. After the noise of the town, the sense of peace was welcome. There was little talk among the men, just the thump of hooves and creak of harness, the jingle of armor and the deep breath of the mules. The forest about them was dense and shadowed. It was all conifers now—pine, spruce and fir—dripping with dew like murmurs of strange voices. The mist lingered beneath those boughs well into midday.

The land between Rowbeck and Glawern was mining country, mating iron ore from the mountains and charcoal from the woods to make steel. Ever, as they passed, were small signs of human industry: tailings banked on either side, or wood and stone waterworks, or the black slots of mine openings. Rusty streaks leaked down the mountainsides, as if the earth bled. Nor was all the mist in the woods mere water vapor. Some carried the bitter tang of smoke from charcoal kilns. Often, too, they crossed foul smelling rivulets which Javes said flowed from mines unseen in the peaks above.

The trail could no longer be glorified as a road. Still, there were places to camp along the way. Most of these were too small for tents. The men slept beneath the trees, with stars winking at them through the boughs. With plentiful small game, they continued to eat well. There was deer sign, too, and sometimes, in deepest night, the distant scream of a panther.

Though they saw the works of men, the makers were visible only at a distance, and that began to weigh on Brastigan. Lottres had reported no rumors of trouble in the town, but Pikarus and Javes often spoke between them in low tones, falling silent when others walked near. Even the falcon stayed close. Brastigan often glimpsed it gliding above the treetops or perched on some snag as it waited on their coming.

Only the mules seemed unconcerned, laboring on with stolid patience. Brastigan wanted to take reassurance from their indifference, but that failed him as the days went on. He couldn't help sneering at his own fears. Was he such a soft city boy, dependent on walls to feel safe? No, he loved the wilderness too much for this whining. What lay before them, the unknown of Hawkwing House, was what unnerved him. That, and what might come behind—Wulfram, or another of his ilk. Time and again Brastigan thought to ask the bird if any strangers rode the trail behind them. Pride stopped him. Anyone would be a stranger, here. He wouldn't show such a dependence on their guide, not in front of Lottres.

So passed a string of days. By the end of the ninth, Brastigan felt as grubby as he was nervous. He longed for hot water, a shave, and the shelter of stone walls against the night's biting cold. Late that afternoon, they crested a ridge and gained sight of their goal. A narrow valley lay below, shockingly bare among the forested peaks. In the center was a walled town, and beside it the gaping sore of an open pit mine. Dust belched into the air, laying a pall over the landscape.

A mining town might be dirty, but it promised many comforts for bachelor men. Brastigan looked upon it with longing. They soon dropped from their vantage, and the paradise was lost to sight. It still gave him heart. One more safe place awaited before they must leap into the unknown.

* * *

The passing days only added to Therula's depression. Kinfolk came to Harburg for Unferth's funeral and Oskar's coronation. Therula knew every one of her full- and half-siblings, but she had forgotten, somehow, just how many of them there were. It was hopeless to find room for everyone in Crutham Keep, even with the recent deaths and the fosterings Unferth had arranged. Alustra struggled to find suitable accommodations in the town below. Therula worked alongside her, fulfilling the duty of hostess when the press of events was too much for her mother.

In a way, Therula was glad of the distraction. It kept her from dwelling on her own grief and fears. Yet she felt isolated among the influx of visitors. Therula hadn't been included in organizing either the funeral or the coronation. She was accustomed to being a part of such plans, and she didn't appreciate being left out. Especially in the funeral. Eben's eulogy had been lovely, but Unferth was her father. She would have liked to help say good-bye.

By custom, they did not eat before a funeral, and the feast for Oskar's coronation was some while away. Therula's empty stomach gnawed at her ribs, even as her fears did on her heart. Perhaps it was merely this that made her so irritable. Therula reminded herself to keep a cool head as she entered the great hall. Later, she would be able to compare observations with her mother.

It was, of course, crowded and noisy beyond the elaborately carved lintel. The wellborn folk of Crutham were crammed together. Weaving through their voices, a somber melody wafted down from the balconies. The ladies wore mourning black with shoulder-length veils, while the men wore heraldic colors to signify their loyalties.

Above them all, a single throne stood on the dais, draped with a gold-and-black state cloak. It was empty, waiting to be filled. Therula felt her throat tighten with emotion. She had always seen two thrones for Unferth and Alustra. Now there was just Oskar, until he chose his own queen.

Nor was that the only change she noted. Right away, Therula could see how the courtiers's garb reflected the change in power. There were fewer of the plain Cruthan robes and tunics now, more puffed shoulders and full skirts. Knowing of Oskar's honor for his mother, everyone wished to emulate her Tanixan influences.

It didn't take long to pick out Oskar. Therula's brother stood at the foot of the dais, receiving a throng of well-wishers. He looked magnificent in a knee-length tunic and hose, both black and stitched with golden towers in a deliberate reprise of the state cloak. He was bare-headed, a practical choice since he would soon enough wear the crown.

Although he looked solemn, as befitted the occasion, it struck Therula that Oskar was happier than she had seen him for some while. He always did enjoy being the center of attention, and this was unmistakably *his* day.

Then again, it might have to do with the number of young women in the press around Oskar. Each noble man or woman who came to give condolences had a comely daughter to be presented, it seemed. Even though they wore the proper black, some of the gowns were quite daring, especially in the bodices.

Perhaps that was why Therula's older sister, Bettonie, was standing so close at Oskar's shoulder. The eldest daughter of Unferth and Alustra had always taken her position seriously. Her cold stare made more than one of the approaching maidens flinch, however much their fathers might flatter the new king.

Therula nodded in response to a curtsey, but didn't stop to talk. She wanted to look around more, assessing the situation as her mother had taught her to do. The fine nuances of who spoke to whom, and how, gave her something to think about besides her fears. She soon found that she had a good deal to think about.

Eben stood near Oskar, a rare venture into public life for him. The wizard wore a full-length robe of midnight blue, and a striking dragon horn headdress that Therula had never seen before. Eben was speaking with some of the ambassadors who had been invited to attend the coronation, including a representative from Tanix, whose extravagant attire made some of Alustra's most elaborate gowns seem plain in comparison. Near them, keeping a little apart, was a more surprising arrival: an emissary from Sillets.

Therula knew she wasn't the only one who eyed the man with curiosity and distrust. He wore a very tall hat with a flat crown, a close-fitted jacket and trousers in a handsome, dark brown. The arms of Sillets were sewn over the breast, a red dragon on a white field. By contrast, his hair was bright red and very curly. Therula longed to know if this was natural, or if he somehow had it styled that way. The whole outfit gave the Silletsian a straight standing look, broken only by the line of a thin moustache over his thin mouth.

Alustra had told Therula that Oskar had expected his invitation to be rebuffed. It was true, the Silletsian was not wellborn, but a mere merchant. Still, it would be a hopeful sign if Sillets sought increased trade, rather than the warfare that had held sway for generations.

And yet, there was something unsettling in his presence here. And in Eben's demeanor, chatting so casually. Eben looked rather pleased with himself, Therula thought. He should have been mourning his close friend, Unferth. Shouldn't he?

A harsh echo of voices distracted Therula. She glanced over in time to see Bettonie imperiously dismiss their younger sister, Frella. Therula winced. She had noticed this during the funeral: that Bettonie was trying to push aside those she deemed unsuitable—in particular, the illegitimate siblings.

Perhaps it was inevitable that Oskar would treat the others as rivals rather than allies. Particularly their brothers. It seemed unnecessary, a waste of true loyalty to Crutham. Bettonie preened smugly, as if she had done a brave and noble deed. Therula felt uneasy watching her. This wasn't what Unferth would have wanted, especially on this day, when they all had one thing in common: the loss of a father.

Nor had she any intention of giving up life long friendships just because of her sister's pride. Therula made her way through the press, trying to find Frella. The girl had looked crushed, and Therula wanted to reassure her. After a few minutes, she began to wonder if Frella had fled the Great Hall.

It took effort and persistence, but she did find Frella, sobbing in her mother's arms. Nearby, Cliodora looked stricken and helpless. Therula hesitated, hoping her presence wouldn't add to Frella's distress. Then she raised her chin and strode forward.

Frella's mother, Diona, turned slightly away, shielding her daughter, as Therula approached. Softly, Therula said, "I'm sorry about Bettonie. I didn't hear what she said to you, but she doesn't speak for all of us."

"You have always been kind to us, your highness," Diona answered, though her voice was strained. Frella sniffled, peering over the velvet of her mother's sleeve. "I know you mean well, but Princess Bettonie may have the right of it. Mayhap our time here is at an end."

"Bettonie is a guest in this house," Therula said, more sharply than she intended. "She no longer lives here, and she has no right to speak for Crutham. I assure you, I will speak to my mother after the coronation and do my best to ensure you're not displaced." More gently, Therula squeezed Frella's shoulder. Glancing at Cliodora, too, she said, "You will always be my sisters."

Cliodora smiled, but she too was red-eyed beneath her veil. Therula felt a surge of pity for all her younger sisters. Most of them, like Cliodora, were daughters of the common houses, merchants and sea traders. If Oskar chose to vent his ill will on these young women, their families could do little to protect them.

Timidly, Cliodora asked, "Are you still angry, sister?"

"Oh, no," Therula said. Even she knew she spoke too quickly. Cliodora sighed, and hugged her tightly.

The youngest princess insisted she hadn't told Oskar that Unferth was dead. She said she hadn't even seen him that morning. Which raised the question, how had Oskar known? That question haunted her. So did the memory of Oskar smiling at Margura. Unferth had died of old age, nothing more—that had been Eben's announcement. Yet he didn't seem to miss Unferth. He was so friendly with Oskar now. Therula tried not to dwell on these things, since they changed nothing.

Therula gazed at Oskar over the top of Cliodora's head. During the long, sleepless night after their father's death, she had realized her future with Pikarus was now in question. Their unspoken agreement had been with Unferth, a king secure in his realm and his alliances. A new ruler changed everything. Oskar would want to make his own alliances. Therula had already seen that her desires mattered little.

She hadn't yet dared to mention this to Oskar. Dread of the future soured every bite she ate, squeezed her lungs with every breath. Therula had been right all along, she thought bitterly. Something was wrong. She just hadn't imagined that disaster might fall upon her, safe at home, instead of on Pikarus, far away on his mysterious quest.

Cliodora tugged at her elbow. "I think Calitar wants you."

"Oh? Where?" Obediently, Therula looked around. The noise of the gathering suddenly swelled around her. She hadn't even realized she wasn't hearing it.

"I'll take you." Cliodora dragged on Therula's arm. She barely had time to nod in farewell to Frella and Diona before the crowd swallowed them.

Calitar stood talking with Axenar, his full brother, and Habrok and his wife, Gunnheld. Calitar and Habrok were the true leaders among Unferth's sons. Therula knew they had prevented many quarrels when the boys were all younger. Both Calitar and Axenar had married into the household of the Duke of Daraine, and Therula seldom saw them now.

All four were somberly dressed, and wore serious expressions, but they greeted Therula courteously with bows and kisses to her hand. Habrok embraced Cliodora with great care, as if he might bruise her.

"Clio said you wanted me?" Therula asked.

Calitar nodded. "We were wondering if Albrett will be here. Has there been any word from Duke Johanz?"

"Mother made the invitation," Therula said. "Johanz sent his best wishes, but he said his wife is ill. He won't leave her side."

"Such devotion," Axenar said, but he glanced slyly at his brother.

As he spoke, Therula frowned slightly. She thought she understood why the men wore such sober expressions. Carthell was the highest ranking of all Crutham's duchies. It had a rich history of its own, and had been independent until Unferth's grandfather married the duke's daughter and joined their domains to form present day Crutham. Johanz' nephew, Rickard, had been one of the princes who died recently. Could he possibly be using the loss as a pretext to assert his independence?

"Don't tell me you wanted to see Albrett," Habrok rumbled, glancing sidelong at Calitar and Axenar. Those two had had their share of quarrels with Albrett and Rickard, in times gone by.

"Of course we do," Calitar answered. His face was perfectly composed, but there was a twinkle in his eye.

"We like him much better now that we only see him once a year," Axenar added.

"You know," Therula said quietly, "the dukes of Verelay, Begatt, Daraine, Gerfalkan and Firice are all here, but Johanz isn't. I wonder who will represent Carthell."

"So do we," Habrok said.

"Have you had a chance to talk to Oskar about it?" Therula asked.

"No," the big man said plainly. Gunnheld laid a hand on his arm. Without asking, Therula knew Habrok must also feel excluded from the centers of power. Before she had a chance to respond, trumpets rang out. Heads turned expectantly, and the babble of voices died away.

"Here they come," Cliodora exclaimed, nervously excited.

"I know. Hush," Therula murmured.

The procession appeared at the far end of the hall. Above the crowd, Therula could see the banner of Crutham, glittering cloth-of-gold stitched with a black tower. Behind it came banners of the provinces. Therula counted quickly. Carthell's banner was there, the silver wolf on a purple field, but it was hard to feel reassured by that alone.

Glorious music floating down from the gallery as the rest of the procession came into view. Tarther led off, in his full array as Captain of the Royal Guard. He carried the Cruthan sword of state before him, sheathed, point down. Tarther's face was solemn, but his cheeks seemed to sag with the weight of age.

Therula wished Oskar had listened to her and let Habrok carry the sword. After all, Habrok was the Champion of Crutham, leader of all its armies. What better chance for him to show solidarity with his brother, the new king? Tarther was a timid choice. He represented continuity and took no risks. It was a missed opportunity, and an unnecessary snub to Habrok, who had always been loyal, even submissive, toward Oskar.

Next came Alustra, bearing Unferth's crown on a cushion of black velvet. The symbolism was obvious, a passing of power from one generation to the next—and Alustra's support for her son.

She moved with measured steps, resplendent in a black brocade gown with Tanixan styled shoulders and collar. Her veil was sewn with bits of polished onyx which flashed in the candlelight as she moved. Therula felt deep sadness as her mother passed. This would be one of Alustra's last official duties as Queen of Crutham. Her face, beneath the veil, was perfectly composed. It was impossible to see the emotions Therula knew must be raging within her. Certainly Alustra must feel proud of her son, but she loved being a queen. It had to hurt that she had been supplanted, even by her own child.

Behind Alustra came more banners. Begatt's blue stag head on silver, Daraine's green with golden sun, Firice's red with silver sword, Verelay's gold griffin on a field of blue, and the wolf of Carthell. Behind each banner came a delegation of noblemen to witness the ceremony. Most of them were led by their own dukes. Carthell was an exception. Therula glanced aside as the purple banner passed and saw her brothers' intensity as they watched.

"They're mostly soldiers," Calitar murmured.

"Even if Kathlen is ill," Axenar added softly, "Johanz should have sent his son as a representative."

"Or our dear Albrett," Calitar said.

"I'm sure Oskar is aware of this." Habrok spoke just a bit too calmly.

"If he isn't, Mother is," Therula told them reassuringly. "She will know how to handle this."

"I'm sure you're right," Gunnheld whispered back.

The courtiers stepped back, clearing an opening at the foot of the dais. Alustra mounted the steps, while the procession divided and formed a half-circle at the perimeter. The queen stopped at the edge of the platform and turned to face the assembly, and the music echoed away.

"Here I have the crown of Crutham." Alustra spoke slowly, pitching her voice to be heard clear and far. "As the king has died, it is my duty to summon our heir, who will take his father's place as king. Come forth, Oskar of Crutham."

Oskar stepped forward and bowed low. "I am here, Mother."

"My son." Alustra allowed a hint of warmth to color her official voice. "Are you prepared to carry out all the duties of your royal office?"

"Yes," Oskar answered firmly, "I am."

"Then kneel," Alustra instructed. Oskar obeyed, bowing his head with exaggerated humility. A page stepped forward to take the velvet cushion from Alustra, while she held the golden crown glittering before her.

In a ringing voice she cried, "I, Alustra, Queen of Crutham, declare before all noble witnesses and our honored guests that this man, my son Oskar, is the true and legitimate heir to the throne of Crutham. I entrust my authority to him and pledge my loyalty until the day I die."

Therula swallowed a lump in her throat as Alustra raised the crown high and then bent forward, placing it carefully on Oskar's head. A sigh went through the watchers, whispering like the wind. Therula glanced at Habrok. He, who could have worn the crown himself, showed no emotion at all.

Movement on the dais drew her eye back with a jerk. Oskar mounted the steps slowly, dramatically. As he climbed Alustra stepped back, bowing before him with sweeps of her veil. Tarther approached from the other side. He knelt, offering the Sword of Crutham with both hands, haft outward.

"Into your hands I place this weapon," Tarther intoned, "as the emblem of your power and rightful authority. May your justice be feared."

Oskar laid his hand briefly on the hilt. "I accept this sword, and I shall use it to defend my people and to carry out justice."

He turned to face the audience and stood still, allowing Tarther to belt the sword on. While Tarther did that, Alustra lifted the royal cloak from the throne. As soon as Oskar's sword was buckled on, she laid the cloak over his shoulders. Alustra let her hand linger on his shoulder for a moment in a loving gesture. Oskar turned and took his mother's hand. They both bowed, as if in a dance, and Tarther offered his arm to guide Alustra down the stairs.

Slowly Oskar sat on the throne, shifting the Sword of Crutham so that his right hand could rest lightly on the pommel. He sat for a moment, alone and splendid, looking over the silent court.

"I accept these honors with grief in my heart," Oskar declared. "In my father's name, I swear I will do all to uphold the honor of Crutham."

Therula tensed. Was that a jab at Unferth?

Oskar went on, "Although my sword is ready for the defense of my kingdom, I would have it known to all that Crutham would rather offer the hand of friendship than the fist of war. Let this be so."

Tarther, at the base of the platform, bellowed out, "All hail King Oskar!"

The Great Hall erupted into cheers as the courtiers released their restrained emotions. Therula joined in, wishing she felt true joy in her heart. She should have been happy, yet tears pricked at her eyes. There was something hateful in Oskar's aplomb, the way he accepted the applause as his just due. As if their father's death meant nothing. Near the dais, Eben leaned toward the Silletsian representative, perhaps explaining some detail of the ceremony. Therula's sister, Bettonie, stood embracing their mother at the base of the steps. Therula wondered what was wrong with herself, that she didn't feel the same joy in Oskar's triumph.

As the cheers began to fade, Duke Edwarin of Daraine stepped forward.

"All hail King Oskar!" he cried. "Before these witnesses, we of Daraine declare our duty and faith to King Oskar and his realm of Crutham. May your reign be rich in years and goods."

More cheers rang out as Edwarin bowed before Oskar. Even as he stepped back, the Duke of Verelay strode to take his place.

"All hail King Oskar!" Duke Robbart began.

As Verelay began to pledge his fealty, Calitar murmured, "I guess we'd better get in line."

"Aye," Habrok said firmly. "We want no question of our loyalties now."

"Too true," Axenar agreed.

Technically, Edwarin's oath should be binding upon Calitar and Axenar, since they were part of his household, but Therula understood why they needed to make their own oaths.

While the men began to work their way forward, Therula eased herself backward. This part of the ceremony would last for some time, until every vassal had renewed his vow of loyalty. By tradition, all who spoke could also offer the new king their advice, or bring forth grievances. Some of them would go on for quite a time, as Robbart of Verelay was demonstrating. Oskar's siblings would also need to pledge to him, including even Therula and Cliodora. Therula was in no hurry to speak her oath. In truth, she had no idea what she would say.

CHAPTER EIGHT
VOICES ON THE WIND

IT had been twenty-two days since they left Harburg, and Lottres found himself wondering desperately when the journey would be over. A bitter wind came gusting from the heights as they made camp. It suited his mood perfectly.

Twenty-two days of Brastigan's selfish strutting and cutting remarks. Twenty-two days of Pikarus pretending he didn't hear it all. Lottres couldn't believe he had once admired Brastigan, wanted to be more like him. How had he thought this journey would make them closer? The two princes might work side by side, picketing the mules as they did every day, but together? Never.

The men had started campfires, but even in fire pits they could scarcely stay lit. Supper was eaten half raw, a taste that soon lost its novelty.

Twenty-two days of trying to see visions in the fire. Twenty-two days of relaxation techniques that left him feeling tense and frustrated. Just before Rowbeck, Lottres had thought he finally heard something. He had been so sure he had reached a turning point! Since that tantalizing moment, Lottres had felt nothing. Nothing but his own fears.

The wind made the whole forest shout with unrest. Loose needles and twigs drizzled down on the men. Through he rolled himself into thick woolen blankets, Lottres could feel the wind pricking at him, like cold cat claws in the darkness. The bare earth had never seemed harder for resting on.

Lottres was exhausted, but sleep came and went. The falcon hunched in a tree near them, gripping tightly for balance. Lottres was afraid to ask its advice. In the noisy darkness, he couldn't help wondering if Brastigan was right. Maybe he had just been dreaming. Maybe he should just stop trying. Go back to being the man his brother approved of—a boring nobody.

The very thought made Lottres grit his teeth until his jaw ached. Admit that Eben had made a mistake? Let Brastigan be right? No, he couldn't stand it. Not after twenty-two days.

The man on watch, Aglend, turned with a snap when Lottres sat up and groped for his cloak. It flapped hard as the wind tried to jerk it from his hand. Somehow Lottres managed to wrestle the cloak around his shoulders. He tottered toward Aglend, who self-consciously took his hand from his sword hilt.

"I can't sleep," Lottres told him. "Go lie down. I'll take over for you."

Aglend hesitated, then said, "That's good of you, your highness, but I can't leave my position. I'll watch with you, and be glad of the company."

"Very well," Lottres agreed.

If he were to use the second form, he would need a fire. Lottres chose a fire pit and sat, putting his back to the wind. He stared at the coals struggling for life in its depths and thought about what he was trying to do. After twenty-two days, he had it by heart. "Relax your body," Eben had said. "Breathe deeply, and hear what the fire has to tell you."

Lottres tried to relax the way he was supposed to. He was aware of Aglend's curious gaze. Unspoken questions stung like the grit the wind blew into his eyes. All he felt was the hard ground and cold gale. Trees moaned in the wind, as if they couldn't sleep, either.

A wave of exhaustion swept over Lottres. His head and eyelids grew heavy. He forced his trembling eyelids up, trying to focus on the fire. The glowing coals flickered as the wind blew. It was so cold, he felt numb all over.

Or was he? Lottres suddenly felt he was floating, at peace. The wind's noise was all around him, an indistinct roar, yet the roaring had the cadence of a distant voice. Lottres listened, trying not to strain. If he tried too hard, his excitement might shatter the fragile moment. Perhaps he slept, and this was but a dream. Still, he focused on the voice, and the words came more clearly.

"Hear me, Eben. Hear and answer."

It was a woman's voice, Lottres was sure. Something was moving in the fire, too, shifting forms of amber and rust. Then the blurs cleared and he saw her. It was a woman of strange, angular beauty. On her head was a shadowy headdress, like the twisting horns of a dragon.

"Eben, you are needed. Please answer me."

Lottres sat still, quivering with excitement. It was really happening! He was seeing something, just as Eben said he should.

Then the coals popped, and the image burst apart in a spray of sparks. Lottres choked back a cry. He leaned forward, trying to reclaim the experience.

"Your highness?" Aglend called anxiously.

"It's nothing," Lottres said.

"You can go lie down, if you're sleepy now," the guard said.

"In a moment," Lottres murmured. He tried again to relax and listen to the wind.

It came more quickly this time, the narrow face with stern dark eyes. It seemed she saw Lottres, too.

"Eben?" Lottres sensed the presence clearly, as if she sat just across the fire from him.

"No," Lottres answered. He wasn't sure if he spoke aloud, but she seemed to hear. The woman frowned, and he felt a gathering menace. "But I know Eben," he quickly explained.

"Who are you?" she demanded.

"Lottres, son of Unferth," he began. Lottres stumbled awkwardly as he tried to understand just how he was doing this.

"Of Crutham?" The woman finished for him. For a moment, Lottres wondered if Eben had mentioned him to her. Before he could ask, she demanded, "Where is Eben?"

"I last saw him in Harburg," Lottres said. He had the vivid impression of her eyes narrowing in thought.

"You are in a dangerous place, son of Unferth," the woman said abruptly. "For your sake, and for Crutham, come to me quickly."

"Mistress Yriatt?" Lottres dared to ask. "Eben said..."

"Do not speak my name!" she answered so fiercely that her image rippled again. It steadied quickly, though Lottres had the impression that was her doing, not his. "Only hear this. You stand in the path of an avalanche. Crutham is in dire peril. An army has massed to invade. I seek to warn Eben, but he does not hear me. This I do not understand. Yet I must stand against them."

"Who is it?" Lottres dared to interrupt.

"Sillets," Yriatt replied, as if he should have known without asking. "It is always Sillets."

Lottres felt his stomach drop. "We have only ten men," he protested.

"No matter," she answered briskly, "if they are the right ten. Make haste, son of Unferth. Follow my companion," he sensed she meant the falcon "and be at my side within two days."

Her face vanished. Lottres was left blinking. The fire was no more than a sullen glow in the darkness. As if, he thought, their brief conversation had consumed it. He closed his eyes for a moment, clinging to the incredible memories and sensation. His breath came faster; elation made his heart beat harder. Eben had been right all along. He had done it! He wanted to do it again as soon as possible.

Fast after that came a sickening dread. Crutham stood on the threshold of destruction! It couldn't be, and yet he didn't doubt it. Lottres stretched his legs, and found himself stiff and sore. The stars had moved, and a mere glint between the branches showed where the moon had sunk behind the trees.

There was no time to congratulate himself. Lottres had to get his party to Hawkwing House within two days, and he didn't know how he would ever convince Brastigan to go along. Still, even with the bad news, the twenty-two days of struggle were worth it.

***

Brastigan slept only restlessly, waking with a start when the wind dropped a pine cone on his head. As his blurred vision came into focus, he saw Lottres at the fireside. And that was odd. He didn't think Pikarus had assigned Lottres a watch. The slight frame was unmistakable, outlined against the faint orange glow of dying coals. His shoulders, beneath a hooded cloak, were shrugged against the punishing wind but his head was erect. There seemed something purposeful in his stillness, but Brastigan couldn't bring himself to care.

It wasn't easy to settle back down with the wind still blustering in the treetops. When Brastigan did sleep, it was with Victory clasped in his arms. This time he dreamt of Margura. The minx sat in his lap, raising a tankard of beer from which he drank thirstily. With her other hand, she teased the soft hairs at the back of his neck.

Even in his sleep Brastigan knew he had been away from civilization too long if he was dreaming of that wench. Then her breath came suddenly cold on his cheek, and he was blinking into wakefulness again. Brastigan tried to curl away from the chill into his warm bedroll, but a hand caught at his shoulder.

"Brastigan," a voice said with low urgency. "Bras, wake up."

"I'd rather not," he mumbled, but he rolled back over and squinted up at a sky just turning creamy with dawn. Black branches bristled against the lightening sky. From somewhere nearby, the harsh croak of a raven rang in the still air. A far-off echo answered it.

The lingering stars were blocked by his brother's anxious face. Beside it was the falcon's fierce profile—an unwelcome sight, indeed.

"Come on, get up." Lottres pulled at his shoulder.

Brastigan ignored his brother and stared at the bird. "Don't do this to me," he groaned.

The falcon didn't deign to reply, but Lottres insisted, "You have to get up, Brastigan. We're not safe here."

"Why?"

Lottres ducked closer to him. "Something is coming. I heard a voice. We have to get out of here."

"You heard what?" Brastigan's voice came overly loud in the pre-dawn stillness, but he didn't care. Even half asleep, he knew Lottres didn't just mean he heard someone talking in the woods.

"A voice," his brother repeated.

Brastigan sighed loudly, irritably. "If you don't stop staring at that fire, you're going to burn your wits, Pup."

Lottres ducked his head for a moment, his features reflecting controlled annoyance. Chin set, he answered, "It wasn't the fire. It was the wind."

The wind? Brastigan rolled clear of his blankets at last. "Wait a minute," he groaned. "Wait."

The morning air was brisk indeed, so much that it didn't matter if the wind had finally stopped. A few paces from the fire pits, a little stream ran gurgling down the mountainside. Kneeling beside this, Brastigan splashed his face with water cold enough to burn his skin. Thus washed, he tottered back to slump on his bedroll, shaking the last icy droplets from his hands, his hair.

Shivering slightly, he wrapped his blankets around his shoulders, craving their scratchy woolen warmth. "Okay. Tell me again."

Lottres winced from his scathing tone, but though his face was pale, the gaze of his red-rimmed eyes held steady. "I heard a voice in the wind."

"Oogh." Brastigan flopped down on his back and his head struck a partially buried rock.

Lottres hurried on, "I know you don't like it, but we have to move. There's an army. We're not safe here." While he spoke, Lottres looked over his shoulder as if expecting an attacker in the dim light.

Brastigan sat up again, scowling as he rubbed the back of his head. "We're supposed to run with our tails between our legs because of the wind?"

"Yes," his brother answered defiantly. "I'm not mad, Bras. We're in danger, real danger."

"You're a danger to your own mind," Brastigan retorted.

The falcon on Lottres's shoulder rustled its wings impatiently.

"Sillets is on the move," the creature announced in its strange, small voice.

Nearby there came a rustling, and Pikarus sat up from his bedroll. He must have slept in his harness, for he was fully armed except for his helmet. A sword rested in the crook of his arms. While Brastigan was taking this in, Javes rolled over, too.

"Help me out, here," he said to them. "My brother has lost his wits."

"I have not," Lottres protested. "It's the truth!"

To Brastigan's chagrin, the soldiers seemed to take the falcon as seriously as Lottres did.

"I'm not sure of that, your highness," Pikarus answered. "We have feared such an event."

"Who's we?" Brastigan asked through gritted teeth. He hugged his blankets around himself and found they did nothing to warm the chill in his heart.

Pikarus didn't answer directly. "Our commands have come from the falcon, since it is our link to the Lady of Hawkwing House. Since Prince Lottres also agrees, I believe we should give heed to its counsel."

Javes put in, "A force this size can't hold off an army. If your brother is right, shouldn't we move?"

Lottres said nothing to that, but looked smug. All this while, the falcon looked upon Brastigan with inscrutable amber eyes.

The dark prince lay back again—carefully, this time—and ground the heels of his hands into his eyes. Green and yellow lights played against the darkness behind his eyelids. He didn't want to consider too deeply what it meant that Lottres was hearing things. He'd said he was listening to the fire, but Brastigan had hoped it was just some fireside fancy. If it wasn't... If some spell had snared his brother...

Aloud, he mumbled, "How long will it take us to reach Glawern?" Once there, perhaps the men could be persuaded to delay departing.

"We can't go to Glawern!" Lottres sounded shocked at the idea. "We'd be trapped there."

Brastigan propped himself up with elbows behind him and glared at his brother. "Do you hate me now? All I want is a hot bath!"

Lottres's face flushed a red that didn't blend well with the ruddy brown of his beard. "Just because you don't understand something, do you have to..."

"You don't know what you're playing at..."

"I know what I'm doing..."

Words tumbled over each other, as fighting dogs roll in the dirt.

"You're going to get yourself killed!"

"I'm trying to live!" Lottres exploded, momentarily silencing his brother. "And you keep standing in my way. Everything always has to be your idea, your way. You can't keep holding me back!"

As Brastigan sat blinking at him, stunned by the ferocious accusation, Javes cleared his throat. "If there is an enemy nearby, they're sure to hear the two of you."

It was almost a relief to turn from Lottres's angry eyes to sneer at the soldier. "And you two are no help, playing along with his fancies like this."

"Your highness," Pikarus began in a distant, formal tone Brastigan had never heard him use before.

"It isn't a *fancy!*" Lottres hissed. "Don't mock me. I know what I heard."

Ignoring them, Brastigan appealed again to the falcon. "Can't you talk some sense into him?" he asked with dramatic despair.

"Sillets is on the move," it answered solemnly.

"How do you know that?" Brastigan demanded.

The creature regarded him with no pity. "My mistress has seen such creatures as will only heed that command. It can be no other."

Brastigan's back was aching from how he sat. He straightened, rubbing his neck with one hand. Lottres's face, seen in profile, was stormy and unforgiving. Brastigan had the feeling he was supposed to apologize, but the words stuck in his throat.

Meanwhile, eyes were open all over camp. The men, awakened by the shouting, lay staring uncertainly. Javes and Pikarus waited, too, for some clear command. Brastigan felt suddenly helpless with his brother and both officers arrayed against him. As the silence lengthened, he realized he did have power, of a sort. Pikarus wouldn't leave a man alone in these mountains, even if he did believe Lottres. They would follow, if Brastigan insisted, to Glawern or anywhere else.

Of course, Lottres would never forgive him. Brastigan found that his nerve quailed from outright refusing what his brother was so set on. Lottres was caught, even as a fish on a line, and reason alone would not sway him. All Brastigan could do was stay close and try to save him. Or bury him, maybe.

Brastigan forced a laugh. "Well, we're commanded to Hawkwing House. As long as we end up there, one road is as good as another, I guess."

The words sounded strained, but Lottres let go a harsh breath. "All right, then." The younger prince rose swiftly enough to make the falcon beat its wings for balance.

Pikarus stood, too. "Let's go."

Though he spoke softly, his voice carried over the camp. Lottres's agitation was catching. Within moments, the area was full of movement and noise. By the dull dawn light, men got into armor, rolled up their gear, loaded the mules in anxious haste. Lottres was in the thick of it, lending a hand wherever needed. The men, oddly enough, seemed to regard him with a new respect. Brastigan, watching, thought he no longer seemed such a gawky pup. And when, he wondered, had this transformation taken place?

For the first time in weeks, Brastigan was left to get into his gear without assistance. He took his time in combing out his hair, doing up the braids with bits of black leather, dragging on his hauberk over the leather gambeson. By this time the men were mostly in the saddle and Brastigan was aware of irritated glances from his brother. He deliberately worked more slowly as he rolled up his bedding, laid it over his shoulder, and sauntered toward the waiting riders.

The mule Brastigan rode was tethered at the head of the line, as usual. He tied his baggage on and casually led the beast back down the line. Just in front of Javes, he swung his long legs over the saddle. Lottres was left conspicuously alone at the head of the column.

There was a resounding silence before Pikarus said, "Your highness?"

"Don't look at me," Brastigan drawled scornfully. "This was his idea. He can lead off."

Lottres turned sharply to glare at him. As their eyes met, Brastigan awarded his brother a mocking salute. No one could accuse him, now, of standing in Lottres's way. The younger man regarded him warily, as if reluctant to let go of his anger. Then he looked pleased.

"There is one thing," Brastigan went on, keeping his face and voice bland. "If you're all so convinced that Sillets is invading, I want a rider sent to Glawern with warning, and then on to Carthell. I want another sent back to Harburg. My father will need time to gather his forces."

It wouldn't be an easy trip in such rough country, nor was it safe for a man to ride alone. Worse, it would reduce the strength of the main party. The faces turned toward him reflected all these doubts.

Brastigan pushed on, "Are there any volunteers, or should I just choose?"

Pikarus looked as if he had something to say, but a new voice cut him off. "I know the road from Glawern to Carthell. I'd take that trip."

That was the fellow who had spoken of the other mysterious mounds. Egger, his name was. Another hand went up at the rear of the file.

"I'll ride for Harburg," Duale said. His wife, at their parting, had been great with child. By now he must be a father, so it was no surprise he offered for the homeward duty.

Brastigan looked again to Pikarus, waiting for some argument. Whatever the soldier had to say, he kept his peace. Brastigan nodded to the departing armsmen.

"Good speed, then."

"Aye, your highness."

There was little more in farewell, just salutes along the line and the thump of hooves on the trail. Then Lottres started off. He didn't choose a gentle path. They went first by miner's tracks, and then on game trails angling ever farther up the mountains. On some stretches they had to ride bent forward, with their faces in their mounts' manes, to avoid low-hanging branches.

Brastigan gave little heed to that. He watched his brother riding ahead of him, and couldn't decide just what he felt. Frustration, certainly. Annoyance, too. He had never held Lottres back, and didn't like the accusation. If he often led, it was because Lottres was the laggard, so awkward and unsure. Why should Brastigan wait while another man wavered? Now Lottres made a grudge of that.

But beyond those things... What?

For certain, the two of them hadn't argued as much in ten years as they did on this trip. Lottres's sudden anger left Brastigan bewildered. He didn't like this feeling he had, that even while they rode on the same trail, they no longer rode together. That, in fact, his closest friend was disappearing on some other road where he couldn't go.

The cold thought touched him: what would he do without his brother?

Brastigan rode without seeing, let his mule shuffle after the beast before it. The reins were knotted in his fist hard enough to make his shoulders ache. A nudge from behind made him turn from his thoughts, and glad he was to do it. Over his shoulder, Javes offered a short hank of summer sausage. The soldier wore an expression as if to say he would listen to whatever the prince might tell him. Brastigan turned from that, but took the food. With sausage, cold water, and trail bread, they broke their fast in the saddle.

While he chewed, Brastigan looked around him. It was an erratic trail they rode, the country too broken for a straighter course. As for the falcon, the bird flitted forward and back above them. Brastigan soon saw that the bird was indicating, by its perch, where a branching path lay. From time to time, two sharp calls would drift down from above. At that, Lottres would find them some shelter—a stand of dense trees or a rocky overhang—where they halted for what seemed a long time. Not until the falcon gave a single long cry would he let them move again. There seemed no purpose to this, and the delays made Brastigan's stomach grow tight with frustration.

At the third halt they dismounted, crowding men and mules into the shadows of an abandoned mine shaft. With his height, Brastigan had a good view out the cavern mouth. He saw the falcon making itself small against the trunk of a tree nearby, and a narrow valley spread out below them with a glittering thread of water in the bottom. Something was moving in the air. Large, dark shapes gliding on powerful wings, hunched-backs and bald heads with a ruff of black feathers behind them. They were condors from the highest mountain peaks, but these didn't spin above some dying thing. No, they flew in a straight line, three of them in a file just like the soldiers if they could ride on air. After the condors came perhaps a dozen crows, laboring to keep pace with their larger companions.

From the quality of the silence in the mine, it was obvious everyone saw the passing formation. Brastigan couldn't help wondering if this had to do with Lottres's rumored crow migration. He leaned over his mule's saddle and muttered to Pikarus, "What do you make of that?"

He was instantly aware of a sharp glance from Lottres. Pikarus seemed to consider before replying, as softly, "Sillets has black magic. If there is an army, I'd call those the advance scouts."

"I was afraid you'd say that."

The squad waited out a long, tense time before the falcon spread its wings. Its piercing cry said they could move again.

There followed more hours of punishing travel. Progress seemed slow, since they must go and stop, skulk and hide. The sun, as it arced across the sky, told Brastigan they were heading as much straight north as they could. Sightings of the aerial patrols continued, though not as frequently and more often composed of crows than condors. Brastigan marked the time in his mind, and wondered where Egger and Duale might be. They were both hardy fellows, and he was sorry to lose them from his company. Watching a flight of ravens pass, he hoped he hadn't sent them into the jaws of some evil thing.

Not that they would complain of it, being soldiers, but a commander might have such regrets.

Night found them sleeping behind a tangle of deadfall. Camp was cold, without fire that might betray them. Brastigan felt chilled to his core, but the colder heart was in Lottres. His brother seemed intent on whatever goal he had, and thus immune to temperature. They seldom spoke.

Staying to cover became more difficult the next day, as the mountains jutted ever taller. Trees could grow only so high and they fell ever lower on their flanks. The upper reaches were left bare, spires of dark gray rock patched here and there with snow.

That evening found them riding a mere goat track, which showed signs of travel despite its difficulty. They topped a sheer ridge and saw below them a hanging valley where some glacier used to live. Far below lay yet another spectacular vista of deep green forest and barren peaks.

Drawing the eye was a fortress wall and a pair of watchtowers cupped between two rocky horns of the mountains. The snow had melted or blown away, exposing a field of gravel mottled with stunted vegetation. This was divided by a running stream that fell from the lip of the hanging valley in a gossamer cascade. The dwelling seemed small with distance, a desolate aerie indeed. The falcon, their guide, descended before them in slow spirals.

This, it seemed, was Hawkwing House.

The bitter air was making Brastigan's nose run, and he drew a gloved hand across his face to blot wind-stung tears. More bothersome was their exposed position on the crown of the ridge. Anyone in the world could see them up there.

"Let's get going," he called, his voice a cross bark.

Lottres, forgetting his anger at last, flashed a smile of triumph. With the sun already dropping, Brastigan was even willing to enter this inhospitable place if it meant avoiding another night outdoors.

Eagerly, then, they began to inch their way down toward their goal.

* * *

"Good day, Oskar." Therula curtseyed as she entered her brother's chambers.

Oskar inclined his head, indicating a small table near the window. "Sit down, dear sister."

There hadn't been time to refurbish the royal apartments yet. Oskar was still using his private chambers. One couldn't call this a private meeting, with black-clad servants flitting around them. One laid out plates and knives, another cups and saucers, while still others poured tea or offered trays of pastries. Yet it was the first time Therula had seen the new king since the coronation. She found herself scrutinizing him, seeking any small sign of change.

Sunlight from the nearby window gilded Oskar's sleek face, turned details of stitchery to fire. He wore a red-brown tunic with the usual Tanixan shoulders, but he had also adopted the Silletsian's tall, straight hat. Its crown puffed out, echoing the tunic's rounded shoulders. At the base, circling his head, was a thinner band of gold: a modified crown. Given the height of his headgear, Therula thought, he might need the weight to secure it.

She had noticed in the past two days that Oskar never seemed to take the crown off. Perhaps he could be forgiven if he enjoyed wearing it. It might be that the novelty hadn't worn off yet. Still, she didn't remember Unferth and Alustra wearing theirs so much. In fact, Unferth had taken his off at every chance he got.

Oskar returned her gaze now with a hint of a smirk. Therula had the feeling he knew something she didn't. She didn't like that feeling. Therula tried to push her speculations to the back of her mind and waited while the servants poured tea.

Only when they had withdrawn did she ask, "You sent for me, brother?"

"You seem troubled," Oskar replied. He gestured genially, offering a sweet, flaky pastry. "Since my position has changed somewhat, is there any way I can help you?"

"I..." Therula hesitated a moment, surprised by his preening. "I miss Father," she managed to say.

"Yes, this is a big change," Oskar said smoothly. Therula noticed he didn't say he regretted it, or that he missed Unferth. "It will take time for all of us to adjust."

Therula nibbled at her pastry, barely tasting the strawberries inside it.

"Have you learned any more from Eben?" she asked.

A trace of some expression passed over Oskar's face, too quickly for Therula to really see. Eben had been the last person to see Unferth alive. They had supped together, as they often did. There was no reason to suspect Eben of anything, though Oskar and Tarther had spent several hours the day before in Eben's tower.

"Eben has requested time away for contemplation," Oskar said with the appearance of regret. "To tell the truth, I don't think he wishes to remain in Harburg."

That was odd; Therula had thought Eben and Oskar were getting on very well. Then she felt a pang. Eben was her only connection to Pikarus.

"He must do as he thinks best," she murmured. "Father always relied upon him. You should, too."

"I can't constrain him," Oskar said with a trace of impatience.

"I suppose not," Therula sighed.

"There is one thing Eben mentioned," Oskar said, "and Mother, as well."

He spoke carefully, calmly, but he was watching her closely. Therula felt her throat go dry as he left her to ask the dangling question.

"What is it?"

"There is a young man you fancy, I hear." Oskar smirked over the rim of his teacup. His mockery wasn't reassuring.

"It isn't a fancy," Therula answered in what she hoped was a composed tone. "I've known Pikarus for years. We care for each other..."

"Yes, I'm sure," Oskar interrupted. "His love is as pure as wine and as deep as your purse."

Therula felt her mouth drop open. She closed it, and swallowed hard. Her mind whirled with hot words—"He isn't like that," or "Pikarus would never betray me"—and she cast around for ones that couldn't be twisted.

"That is cruel!" she finally blurted. "It isn't true!"

"I know men, dear sister," Oskar answered with steely amusement. "Who wouldn't desire a maid like yourself—one whose wealth and position are as lovely as she is?"

Therula twisted her hands in her lap to hide their trembling. A calfskin glove was tucked under her belt, mate of the one she had given Pikarus. She felt its soft edge and summoned a cold smile.

"Pikarus knows well how crowded Harburg is, and how little of Crutham's wealth belongs to me," Therula said. She thought she might have an argument that would sway Oskar. "Think of this, brother. In Harburg are five princes, and twice that in the provinces. Pikarus would be the least among them. In Harburg also are twenty princesses, and a queen besides.

"Now consider Gerfalkan, where there is a mere hand-count of wellborn men. Pikarus stands high there. In Gerfalkan also there are a duchess and just four of her daughters. Where, my brother, would I shine more brightly? Where could my husband best advance our fortunes—here, or in Gerfalkan?"

Oskar leaned back in his chair, brows raised in amusement. Therula went on.

"Gerfalkan is loyal to Crutham, a suitable match to stabilize internal allegiances. Mother thinks so, and no one knew when we spoke of it that Carthell might rebel. You are preparing for that, I assume?"

Oskar nodded, his eyes narrowed.

"It is wise to court new friends," Therula said, "in Sillets or elsewhere, but you must not forget to reward your old and faithful supporters, as well. You may need such alliances as Gerfalkan in times to come. Now, since we are speaking of this, what of your own plans?"

Oskar put his fork down abruptly and reached for his tea to clear his mouth.

Therula pressed, "You will marry, brother. You must, for I know you won't be content when your heir is..."

She broke off when Oskar burst out laughing.

"Enough, my sister!" he chuckled. "You and Mother are of one mind, but I must beg more time. I am still grieving." Oskar leaned back in his chair, striking a pose like a widow in a drama.

"I, too, am in mourning," Therula said softly, "but I know my own heart."

If she hoped to seize on Oskar's sympathy in this playful mood, it didn't work.

"I merely wish to spare you pain," he said, so sincerely that she knew he was lying. "As I have told you, a handsome man is least to be trusted."

"I believe in Pikarus," Therula said without hesitation. "I fear no pain from him." From Oskar—oh, yes, she did fear him.

"Ah, my poor sister," Oskar murmured. Therula frowned at his feigned sorrow. "Perhaps we can agree to a test, of sorts."

"What kind of test?" Therula asked. She sipped at her tea, though her heart was jumping like a young hare. Brastigan's quest was a test, but if Oskar didn't know that, Therula wouldn't tell him.

"Let us wager," Oskar said. "You believe your sweetheart is faithful. I say he may not be. When he returns—or should I say, if that fool Brastigan brings him back alive..."

"Don't mock him," Therula interrupted, for Oskar touched on a matter she had been longing to speak of. "Brastigan is no fool. Nor is Habrok, or the others. Even when you snubbed them, they still swore their faith with you."

"Not all of them," Oskar answered in a clipped voice. "But I was saying, when Pikarus returns I will investigate his conduct during the journey. If you are right, dear sister, then I won't oppose Pikarus's suit if he brings this to our mother. But if I'm right..." He trailed off with a shrug.

"If you are right," Therula snapped, "then I won't marry him, regardless of any wager."

Even as she spoke, she caught the gleam in Oskar's eye. Immediately Therula paused. Did she really want to commit to this... this wager of Oskar's?

"There can be no tricks," she said. "No hiring a whore to tempt him, or any such a thing."

Oskar didn't even pretend to be hurt by her accusation. "Of course not, sister," he purred. "If I'm right, you will permit me to choose the husband I think best."

"You can do that anyway," Therula was forced to admit.

"I would prefer your cooperation," Oskar said. "Once you see that I am right about him, I'm sure you will."

For a moment, Therula didn't listen to Oskar. Her mind was crowded with questions. She didn't trust her brother's smile. She did trust Pikarus. Therula didn't need proof of his love. This gamble seemed unnecessary, when all she had to do was wait. Worse, it was insulting to treat her lover as a plaything.

But, another voice whispered to her, what would it all mean if Oskar forbade them to marry? Here was a chance to assure that he wouldn't interfere. Shouldn't she seize the opportunity, if Pikarus was the man she really wanted?

"Sister?" Oskar's voice called her back to herself.

"I want to witness the questioning," Therula said. Her voice was tight. "So that we both will have no doubts."

"Very well," Oskar nodded. "Is it agreed?"

Oskar extended his hand across the table. His mocking gaze challenged her. Therula longed with all her heart to slap that smile from his face. She felt a moment's vertigo, and then her own hand was reaching back. Oskar's fingers were hard and cold. Her own felt hot and limp, like cooked sausages. Unexpectedly, Oskar patted Therula's hand gently.

"If you are right," he said, "there is nothing to fear."

Therula fought the reflex to tear her hand away. Oskar murmured something she didn't hear, stood up, and left her sitting alone.

Therula leaned her elbows on the table. She still felt dizzy, and the smell of strawberries was nauseating. In her heart, she knew she had done the wrong thing. She had betrayed her lover by playing Oskar's game. How could she explain this to Pikarus, even if she won?

CHAPTER NINE
HAWKWING HOUSE

THE way down was long, and it was not friendly. The mules moved slowly on a track that descended so sharply it seemed they might topple right off. Brastigan thought he wasn't the only one who leaned inward, away from the dizzying height. He resisted his vertigo by focusing on the signs of other riders who had passed before them. Hooves left no mark on the bare stone, but pale fibers clung to the rocks on the sharper corners. It wasn't cloth. Horse hairs, maybe.

While the animals inched downward, the day was quickly waning. Shadows lengthened as they reached the gravel field below. Larger spruce trees grew on the sheltered flanks of the mountain, with patches of snow stark white in shady places. The riders hurried deeper into the shadow of the peak, crossing the brook despite the protests of their thirsty mules.

"We're nearly there. Come on!" Lottres sounded eager as a child at midwinter, Brastigan thought sourly.

Himself, the dark prince watched the approaching keep with wary eyes. It stood squat and solid, similar to Cruthan construction, but rather than being level, the towers were crowned with conical slate roofs.

The fortress walls were built nearly flat against the steep mountainside and of the same rocks. They seemed to grow from the slope. Narrow slits served as windows, behind which were barely discernible flickers of movement. Strangely, Brastigan saw no movement at all along the battlements.

Nor was there any hail from the walls, though the riders must have been well in sight. Every step of a mule's hoof on the cobbles grated loud in the chilly silence. Those small sounds echoed from the ramparts as they approached the gate. The stones were roughly finished, with patches of mortar sticking out in many places. A part of Brastigan scorned the poor workmanship. Attackers could climb right up that wall. The gate was secured by a door of thick planks stained dark with oil or tar for weatherproofing.

The column of mounted men halted when they drew near enough to smell the tar. The mountain stillness quickly became oppressive.

The hawk had been sitting on the peak of one tower, watching their progress. Now, it swooped down to resume its perch on Lottres's shoulder. As if that gave him courage, Lottres hailed the walls. His voice sounded thin and small in the open air.

"If there's nobody here, I guess we can all go home," Brastigan quipped.

Javes chuckled nervously behind him. Lottres hailed again. The falcon added an imperious shriek of its own.

No human voice came in reply, but a low steely groan. Stout chains became visible as the gate lowered away from them. There were murmurs of relief along the line and the men kicked their mules forward. As the riders passed beneath the portal and through the thick wall, a second gate sank before them. The two gates joined to make a bridge over a startling gulf. A deep trench lay between the wall and mountainside, half filled with musty dark water. Hooves thumping on the planks drew faint echoes from the depths.

"No wonder they call it Hawkwing House," Brastigan muttered. "You'd need wings to get in."

Javes chuckled again. "Not quite what it seems from the outside, is it?"

Brastigan grunted dourly. As they crossed the drawbridge, he could see wooden platforms braced against the inner wall. The walkways extended from the two towers to barred doors in the cliff. The center lay bare, and this explained the lack of movement there. Any invader who succeeded in scaling the barrier would find no footing, but a long drop into the moat. Even the walkways had drawbridges operated from within, meaning the towers' defenders could be cut off if an enemy overwhelmed them. It was a ruthless strategy, and it made him wonder.

"Yes, but what are they so worried about?" Brastigan muttered back at Javes. "This place is pretty remote. Who is there to be afraid of?"

"Sillets?" Javes replied cautiously. "Look—the walls are old, but the platforms are new."

Indeed, the stones were weathered and crusted with lichen, but the wood was fresh and bright. On the tower platforms, men worked in pairs to turn the cranks that lowered the gate. Or, were they men? Brastigan turned sharply in the saddle, drawing a snort of protest from his wooly steed. He focused his gaze on one figure in a stiff leather jerkin with a full skirt below it. A round leather cap crowned a head of long, black hair. The bulky garments hid everything, yet concealed nothing.

"Your highness?" Javes inquired.

Brastigan answered, "Those aren't men."

Now Javes turned, too. Brastigan kept his eyes fixed, just to be sure. That was no man—it was a woman dressed for war. She held a short bow, loosely drawn in case of trouble, and over her shoulder a bristling bundle of arrows in a quiver. Her feet were set as if she knew exactly how to use these weapons.

"They aren't Cruthan, either," Javes said.

Brastigan had just realized the same thing. The sheet of hair wasn't blonde, but dark as night. These were Urulai women. Brastigan rode with his head turned, staring, until a pain in his neck forced him to sit straight and face the gloomy entrance.

Passing that portal, the riders were forced to halt, for darkness fell on them like a black cloak. Daylight, fading as the door rose behind them, showed the outlines of a spacious chamber. Shadows suggested a ledge above them where more archers might perch. Arched portals led onward from three sides, but there wasn't enough light to see the way ahead.

A bleak welcome, indeed. Mutters around Brastigan told him the other men liked this no more than he did. Their distress, after they had blindly followed Lottres here, annoyed him.

"Quiet," Brastigan snapped. His voice rang more loudly than he intended. Startled, his mule shuffled beneath him.

Brastigan shut his eyes and breathed in. The air had a heavy texture, an herbal scent he didn't recognize spiced with body odors and wood smoke.

Before he became completely disoriented, there was a rustle of clothing and the soft patter of footfalls. Then came a flickering light. Slender shapes in dark clothing filed into the chamber from the arched portal in front of the riders. Some bore tall poles mounted with carved deer antlers. Upon these, pale candles shed the mellow scent of beeswax. Faces sprang out, ghostly in the dim light: fair skinned women, dark eyed and unsmiling. Yet they didn't wear the dull gaze of servitors. Rather, they were wary and alert.

These ones didn't carry weapons, but the wavering lights picked out gleams from beads of jade or bone woven into their sable hair. Their dresses were plain and loose, a uniform brown in color. They weren't linen or wool, but a supple leather. Tanned elk hide, Brastigan guessed. Four of the women had tied on aprons of a crude weaving, like cheesecloth. These had about them the stench of manure, as Brastigan could smell when one came to take his mule's reins.

There was no word of welcome, but Lottres's confidence seemed buoyed by the falcon on his shoulder. Still astride his mule, he declared, "We are the sons of King Unferth, summoned from Crutham by the Lady of Hawkwing House."

One of the candle-bearers replied, "She tell us you come at this house. You follow now."

It was hard to understand such broken grammar, yet the sound of her voice stirred Brastigan's memory. Come at instead of come to—Joal had always said it the same way. They *were* Urulai.

Lottres seized on the scanty invitation and swung out of the saddle. The others did likewise, Brastigan last of all. The rustle of armor made the women step back, as if they had never heard such a sound. Noting their reaction, Lottres removed his helmet, showing a human face beneath helm-matted curls.

Now that they were all afoot, the eyes of the silent women were even with most of the men's. Though not quite to Brastigan's height, they shared his lanky frame. Unaccountably, he felt a tightness in his chest.

The mules were led off, and the men followed their guides through a warren of chambers where echoes of creaking harness sounded like whispering voices. The walls were plastered, concealing the stone beneath. Some of these were covered in mosaics of colored pebbles. It was hard to make out the subjects, since the women walked quickly, but once Brastigan glimpsed something much like the snowflake on his mother's pendant.

The transit offered a few glimpses of people in the chambers as they passed. There were women, and occasionally children, but nowhere did

Brastigan see a boy over the age of twelve.

He considered that as they walked. Where were the men? Why were the Urulai in this place of witchery, rather than in Crutham? And why did women hold the walls? It seemed a bizarre thing. Joal had never told him of any such custom among their people.

They followed their guides to a ramp sloping upward in a tight spiral, and emerged into a rounded chamber with a high center. There was more light here, enough to make the men blink and rub their eyes. No plaster or pebbles adorned these walls. Rather, veins of some mineral glinted from the domed ceiling above, as if they stood beneath unearthly skies. The unknown, herbal scent was now very strong.

Candles glimmered where carved antlers stood in brackets shaped to hold them, but most of the light came from a raised hearth at the far end of the room. Brastigan had seen such hearths before, in peasant huts on the plains. This one was narrower and taller than he recalled, and set within an oval niche. Squinting past the fire's glare, Brastigan could see yet another female seated within the alcove, her waist at a level with the flames.

The candle-bearers stopped a few feet away, and the men halted behind them. The woman who had first spoken murmured something softly, in Urulai, but the seated woman was already rising.

She seemed to be another Urulai, clad in a brown leather dress, but her garment was stitched with some shiny stuff, and she wore a fabulous headdress of two great, twisted dragon horns. Sheer veils fell behind it and passed beneath her chin. Those horns and her night-dark hair were draped with beads and fine chains that winked as she moved. She had an angular face, not beautiful but arresting. Her eyes were the deep gray of wet slate.

"Welcome." Her voice was deep for a woman's, and her Cruthan was perfect. Like her attendants she gave no smile of greeting, but remained stern and calm. "I am Yriatt, mistress of Hawkwing House."

Eagerly, Lottres began, "I am Lottres of Crutham, and..."

The woman interrupted his fawning. "I know."

She raised her hand, and the falcon flew to her. It was a regal gesture, yet unaffected. Brastigan thought Alustra would have been jealous. Yriatt stroked the falcon briefly, and it bent its fierce head to her caress.

She murmured something to her attendants in Urulai. The women withdrew, making no obeisance and yet showing the deepest reverence. It was just as they had done with Leithan, Brastigan remembered. As feet whispered out of the room, the sorceress brushed past the Cruthans, striding to an antler perch where the falcon debarked.

The armed men shifted, looking to Lottres, but he stood mute, silenced. The younger prince regarded the witch with the stunned gaze of a man who has just had his first sight of the most beautiful lady in the land. A hot surge of irritation roiled in Brastigan's stomach. He had been careful, these past days, not to say what he was thinking or do anything that might be taken as hindering his brother's mad pursuit, but this cowed silence was more than enough.

Yriatt turned back toward them, and Brastigan stepped out to meet her. His helmet was braced on his hip, and his demi-greaves made a sound like the snap of a whip.

"Well, what do you want?"

Brastigan couldn't see Lottres's face, but he heard a choking noise from that direction. He stood straight and stiff, making a conscious effort to keep his sword hand away from Victory. The witch ran her dark eyes appraisingly up his long form. Then she had the nerve to laugh at him.

"You're her son, I see," the witch replied wryly.

She must mean Leithan, so many years dead. Through gritted teeth, Brastigan demanded, "How would you know?"

Yriatt was no longer smiling. Almost tenderly, she said, "I ought to know. She was my sister."

Now it was Brastigan's turn to stand dumb, horrified to think he had any blood tie with this witch-woman. Over her shoulder, the falcon on its perch seemed to be sneering, and there was a hissing gasp from Lottres. The fury in Brastigan's stomach turned to nausea. He felt he must force himself to breathe.

Yriatt moved past him, her veils wafting behind. Brastigan turned to watch, for he wouldn't take his eyes off the witch. When she drew even with Lottres, she paused.

"You must be my eavesdropper," she remarked.

"I didn't mean to..." Lottres began. Then he drew himself up. "But yes, I did."

Yriatt tilted her head, and beads tapped against the horns of her headdress. Sharply, she asked, "Eben sent you to me?"

"Yes." Lottres's voice was oddly steady, now.

The witch permitted herself a meager smile. "He chose wisely."

Brastigan had a sick suspicion what she meant by that, for Lottres looked happy enough to swoon. Then Yriatt turned again, with an abruptness Brastigan suspected was calculated to unnerve them.

"As to your question," she said to the whole of them, "you will accompany me on a further journey."

"I thought we were to do your will here." Brastigan scarcely recognized his own choked voice.

Lottres sharply countered, "We will do whatever she asks of us!"

Their gazes caught again in a ferocious exchange. Lottres glared, as if to reclaim dominance from his brother. Or as if, maybe, he was jealous of Brastigan's kinship with Yriatt. Well, Brastigan was done with giving way before his foolish brother. He held his dark eyes steady.

Yriatt ignored their sparring. "All changes, does it not?" Her dry words didn't truly make a question. "The task I had for you is pointless. I believed Sillets was preparing to invade. You were to spy out the country and confirm it." She shrugged with a tinkling of baubles. "But we know that, now."

Finally, Lottres broke his angry stare to look at Yriatt. "Then you don't need us?" His expression was strained.

In the next moment Brastigan demanded, "If you knew Sillets was getting ready for war, why didn't you tell our father?" The task she mentioned didn't seem to match with the safe haven the king had intended.

"I told Eben," she answered, "which amounts to the same thing. If Unferth didn't share the knowledge, that's between him and you."

Brastigan felt his hackles rise, to hear his father's name spoken in such a casual way. Yriatt turned back to Lottres. "Fear not, young man. We shall be in company for some while. Now that Sillets has moved, another task has become far more urgent. But you and your men have traveled far already. You must be tired and hungry. Rest now, and refresh yourselves. We will speak again at supper."

* * *

An hour later, Brastigan was still fuming at the abrupt dismissal. They were men of Crutham and owed no allegiance to Hawkwing House, yet Yriatt spoke to them like lackeys. Now she had some other errand for them, but could she say plainly what it was? Oh, no. She had to surprise them at dinner.

And she claimed to be his mother's sister. Brastigan blew out a harsh breath. No, he refused to believe it. No kin of his would ever wear such a ridiculous hat.

The bath was a long, narrow chamber, half of it occupied by a shallow pool. Brastigan was seated on a cut-rock bench, water lapping at his ribs as he picked the largest twigs out of his hair. The water was tepid, thanks to baskets of heated rocks the silent women had dumped into the pool. Steam lingered from the simple technique.

The women had also provided modesty towels of their loosely woven cloth. These fit properly, so there must have been men in the settlement at one time. Brastigan still wanted to know where they were. Behind him, he could hear clanks and thumps as the soldiers helped each other out of harness. Chairs made of what looked like bent branches groaned beneath the weight of chainmail hauberks. Sweat-soaked gambesons added a tang to the air.

Brastigan glanced aside, where his brother was just entering the pool. He caught the end of a resentful glance, but no word of greeting. Well, Brastigan wouldn't beg for company. His brother, grandly ignoring him, ducked completely under the water.

The dark prince picked up a rag and a bit of soap that looked like it had been hacked off a larger block. The lather carried a now familiar herbal scent. Maybe it was a flea repellent, like the herbs they burned in Crutham. Maybe it was the only herb that grew in these high peaks. Whatever, the soap cleaned his hair well enough.

He had scrubbed his body and was trying to reach his back when someone sat down beside him. Pikarus. Saying nothing, the soldier took the soapy cloth from Brastigan's hand and began to wash his back. Brastigan sat silently, enduring the vigorous rubbing only because it felt so good.

"Are you all right?" the soldier asked in a low voice.

Maybe he thought to make amends for supporting Lottres against Brastigan's wishes. Well, Brastigan was in no mood to be appeased. Pikarus was no better than Yriatt, keeping secrets as he did.

"Of course," Brastigan lied airily. "I got my bath. I'm perfectly happy."

He spoke loudly, goading his brother, but Lottres didn't respond. Pretending nothing was amiss, Pikarus said, "How about that mural?"

Brastigan frowned through gauzy wisps of steam at a mosaic on the opposite wall. On the left hand side, three strangely elongated human figures stood with arms raised. On their heads were twisting horns, like those Yriatt decked herself with. No features or expression were discernible. Facing them on the right hand side was a huge, dark form. A dragon, legendary scourge of these mountains. Flames wreathed its head, outlining dagger-like teeth, spines, claws. On its head, too, were the great, twisted horns.

"I wonder what it means," Pikarus mused.

"They dance with dragons?" was Brastigan's scathing suggestion.

Looking at the mosaic, he considered the horns Yriatt sported on her headdress. Wearing them might be a kind of boast. No housebound mumbler would obtain such ornaments. Winning those would take guts, and real power.

Ironically, there was nothing especially magical about Hawkwing House so far. It was foreign, yes, but ordinary candles lit the halls and the folk within seemed to be flesh and blood. The prosaic setting must be a disappointment to Lottres.

More men were in the water now, voices running together as they rid themselves of the accumulated grime from the journey. Even through the echoes, Brastigan heard a sloosh of falling water. He turned in time to see Lottres rise from the pool and drip his way over to a chair stacked high with towels. Lottres wrapped one of these around his narrow chest as he left the chamber.

Frowning, Brastigan gathered himself, but Pikarus laid a hand on his shoulder. "He has to walk his own road," the soldier said.

Brastigan turned, fast enough to break Pikarus's grip. His hands tightened into fists. "Not around here, he won't," he answered, hotly enough to warm the bath water. "I don't want anyone wandering off by themselves. We stay together, and that goes for every one of us."

There was an awkward silence. While the men were trying to pretend they hadn't heard his angry words, Brastigan felt how cold the water was getting. He stood up and yanked a towel from the stack. Lottres might be a prince, but he didn't need a bunch of lackeys to coddle him and agree with all he said. He needed someone to talk sense, and that was what Brastigan planned to do.

He followed his brother to their assigned quarters, a square hall with a raised hearth at its center. A series of chiseled alcoves held leather pads stuffed with rushes, where the soldiers could lay out their bedrolls. At present, baggage was piled outside the bunks, making it hard to move through the room without tripping. There was no fire on the hearth, and the few candles gave little heat.

Lottres crouched, partly dressed, beside his bags. The damp towel lay discarded on his bunk. He looked up when Brastigan entered and quickly turned away, shoulders hunched.

Brastigan's mind whirled with things he wanted to say, but his tongue seemed numb. Kneeling beside his own baggage, he ordered gruffly, "I don't want you going off by yourself, Pup."

"I'm not a pup!" Lottres barked back. "Don't try to put me on a leash."

Brastigan felt his veins tingle with fury. He yanked clothing out of his duffel without really looking at it. "It's not like that."

"Yes, it is." Lottres's voice came muffled as he pulled on a dress tunic. "You came here to put me back in my place. I know it."

"I never put you any place," Brastigan snapped. He dried his body with angry strokes of his towel. "I never stood in your way, so quit making this stuff up."

"Then why are you here?" Lottres demanded, as if his presence somehow proved a point.

Trying to control his fury, Brastigan slouched on his bunk and yanked at his trousers. They stuck against his damp legs. He pulled harder. "Because you're my brother. I'm worried about you."

Lottres gave a brittle laugh. "You don't have to treat me like a baby. I know what I'm doing."

"Oh, yes. You and Pikarus. He must follow his own road," Brastigan intoned, imitating the soldier's unwanted advice. He stood, pulling his pants up the rest of the way.

"Well, I'm going to." Lottres fastened his belt with a defiant snap.

Brastigan stared at him, wishing it could be some other way. He knew what he must do, but it scared him. That made him mad again. He all but snarled, "Fine, but who says you have to do it alone?" Lottres regarded him suspiciously, and Brastigan went on, "You know I don't like this. I think it's dangerous, but you aren't going to listen."

"Guilt won't change my mind," his brother interrupted.

"Would you listen?" Brastigan stopped just short of saying "Pup." It felt strange to censor the habitual nickname, and he resented it, but he had to make Lottres accept his presence. Otherwise, he would never know what he was up to. "Maybe I can't stop you, but I will back you up. Just quit trying to make me out as your enemy."

Clearly Lottres didn't believe it, but he said, "Then hurry up. I'm going to see Yriatt."

There was a gleam in the younger man's eyes, as if he dared Brastigan to make his word good.

Brastigan rolled his eyes. "Dinner wouldn't be soon enough?" His brother's scowl warned he wasn't forgiven yet. "How do you know she's got time to see you? If she's in charge here, there might be other things —."

"She'll talk to me," Lottres answered confidently.

Why, Brastigan wondered. Because Eben had chosen him? For what? He shut his mouth on the question. Brastigan's hair fell into his face, tangled and wet, as he bent to close his duffel. He pulled a comb out and tucked Victory under his arm.

"Coming," he muttered, and added, "I wanted to ask her a question, anyway."

"What question?" Lottres frowned, jealous again.

"Oh, get off yourself." Brastigan pulled his mother's pendant out from under his tunic, dangling it by its cord. "She might know what this is for."

"We're wasting time," Lottres snapped, not giving in on the point. He yanked a candle from the nearest antler. "Let's go."

So saying, he stalked from the room—and now it was Brastigan who hurried to keep up.

CHAPTER TEN
A TESTING

THE inner ways were as black as Brastigan's hair, lit only by the feeble flame of the candle Lottres carried. Despite this, he strode along without hesitation. The cool air held many scents built up in the closed caverns, but Lottres smelled more than cooking smoke and stabled beasts. He smelled possibilities, thick and ripe.

Yriatt's presence was everywhere in the tunnels. Lottres followed as it drew him onward. Partly, he wanted to test himself and see if he could find his way to Yriatt without help. Partly, he admitted to himself, he did it to tweak Brastigan's nose.

For his part, Brastigan followed so closely that Lottres caught an anxious grumble: *"...Hope he knows where we're going..."*

Lottres turned to snap at Brastigan, only to see his brother's eyes veer away. It was then he realized Brastigan hadn't said anything. At least, not out loud. He was hearing Brastigan's thoughts. Lottres held back an excited smile. For a moment he concentrated on Brastigan rather than Yriatt.

"...Can't stand this, trusting his gut instead of my own," Brastigan's inner voice complained. *"I like this place less the longer I'm in it."*

Scowling, Lottres broke contact. That was Brastigan all over, so surly when things didn't go his way.

They passed many side tunnels and work rooms while Lottres struggled to find his way to Yriatt again. The corridors were all alike, save for the occasional pebble pattern to relieve the monotony.

Just as Lottres was starting to worry, he found the spiral ramp. As they climbed, Lottres felt a sudden pressure at his temples. She was aware of them! He hesitated, started to form words in his mind, but the presence withdrew. It seemed Yriatt had only wanted to know who was approaching.

"What?" Brastigan demanded in a low voice, and his thoughts whispered, *"I knew it. There's something wrong..."*

"Nothing," Lottres said. He climbed on, heart fluttering with nerves and exertion.

Yriatt was at the hearth. The falcon still rested on its antler perch, eyes closed and feathers fluffed, but Lottres hadn't expected to see someone else with them under the glittering rock dome.

It was another woman. Lottres had heard Javes and Brastigan muttering to each other about all women and no men at Hawkwing House. As if Brastigan wouldn't enjoy the situation, given a chance! This was a Cruthan girl, slim and pale as an icicle in the shadows of the chamber. She sat quietly near the hearth while Yriatt, standing behind her, combed out her fair hair.

Lottres paused in the doorway, drinking in the power of Yriatt's presence. From the moment of their first meeting, he knew he wanted to be just like her. The sorceress scarcely looked up as they entered, and the nameless girl didn't so much as blink. She was pretty, in a bland way, but even with eyes open her expression was of deep slumber. She sat tamely, oblivious to the twists and tugs that made her head rock.

"Feeling more yourself?" Yriatt looked past Lottres to address Brastigan with a hint of mockery.

Lottres drew a tense breath. This interview was supposed to be about him, not bratty Brastigan.

"I was always feeling like myself, noble lady," he replied. Lottres marched to the hearth and turned his candle over, snuffing it on the stones.

For his part, Brastigan dragged a bentwood chair a little away from the fire and slid into it with Victory propped at his right hand. Ignoring Yriatt's question, he began to work his comb through the tangles of his wet hair.

"Were you?" Yriatt mused. Her hands drew a comb through the girl's tresses, but her gray eyes were now fixed on Lottres. That was what he wanted — except that his confidence suddenly wavered.

"I had been content as I was, but..." he faltered.

She angled her head in cool curiosity, and gems winked in the flickering firelight. Lottres knew she would interrupt a moment before she spoke.

"Ordinarily, you see," Yriatt said, "Eben would send someone to me who is... unwell. They come to me for curing."

"No, I'm not unwell." Lottres hastened to correct her. "My life has never lacked in comfort, but I've felt lately that I could be more, *do* more."

"More what? More powerful?" Yriatt's eyes were sharp beneath the spiral horns, though her hands wove golden locks into neat plaits. "Would you command the clouds to rain, and lightning to smite your foes? Would you send plagues upon your enemies, or summon wealth for yourself alone?"

Lottres felt the pressure again, her latent disapproval making the very air weigh down on him. With difficulty, he drew breath to protest, "Lady, I am a king's son! I could have wealth if I wanted it. I could manipulate affairs of state." He had certainly seen enough of his brothers pushing themselves to the fore. "I don't need your teachings to get what I already have."

"Her what?" Brastigan's horrified thought came clearly to Lottres. The younger prince shrugged irritably, trying to shut out the distracting protest.

"Do you assume my teachings are for all?" came Yriatt's whip-crack reply. "You would demand this of me?"

Lottres floundered momentarily. He was only doing what Eben had told him, and she had said earlier that Eben chose well. But Lottres knew he must win this argument on his own merits. Whining and crying Eben's name wouldn't be enough.

"I do not demand, no. Of course not." Lottres tried to keep his voice calm, while fear felt near to choking him. "Yet, noble lady, I will beg if I must. I have never been quick or strong. I'm not suited to war, but neither do I wish to spend my days in a stronghouse, counting out coins to serve the realm. I had felt I was wasting my talents, but I didn't know what else to do. The moment Eben said the words, I knew." Lottres clenched his fists in the air before him. "I want to be greater than a king's son. I want to feel that power within myself. Power like his— like yours. He said he wasn't wise enough to teach me, and sent me to you."

Brastigan had stopped pretending to comb his hair. He gave Lottres a black stare, and Lottres heard the whisper, *"...a score I'll settle with Eben one day..."*

Lottres gave Brastigan a scornful glance, but his words were for the sorceress. "Perhaps I am unwell, noble lady. Will you cure me?"

Yriatt gave a low laugh. Lottres sensed her approval, that he turned her own words back on her.

"We shall see," she said. "Did Eben teach you the first form, then?"

"Yes, and the second, as well." Lottres's words came in a fretful rush. "I tried it with fire, at first, and also with water. Nothing worked, until two days ago. I did what he told me, the breathing and all, but I don't understand it."

"Of course you don't," the witch answered with equanimity. "Do you need to understand it, to pick it apart and measure each portion? Can you not take it on faith, and simply believe?"

"I already believe," Lottres answered, confused by her challenge. Or, maybe just afraid to say the wrong thing and face rejection. "I thought... That is, the forces you summon, there must be consequences. Hadn't you better understand what you're doing?"

It seemed he had passed some sort of test, for Yriatt smiled. Lottres felt a rush of relief at her approval.

"The mind is stubborn," Yriatt said. "It knows only the physical. It is filled with reasons why magic cannot be real, and what you *know* cannot be true. Remember this, young man: what seems solid is an illusion, just as distance and silence. Spirit and body are both the same."

Her words were baffling, yet Lottres felt that he understood them. They resonated in his heart. Lottres groped for a chair to sit down in, never taking his eyes from Yriatt.

"To become what you desire, you must put aside the mind's insistence on the barriers of the physical," Yriatt said. "Fire, wind or water are merely tools to do that. Working late at night also helps to break the grip of rationality. All of these provide a means to release your inborn power. Soon you will not need them."

Yriatt had finished with the girl's hair, and now fastened it into a crown with a brisk pat. She sat down at the hearth, assessing Lottres across the fire.

"I haven't heard anyone else but you, that one time," Lottres confessed. "Since then, I..." He hesitated. Brastigan wouldn't like it if he found out Lottres knew what he was thinking. Awkwardly, he concluded, "Sometimes, it seems I can almost hear people around me."

She didn't seem impressed. "When one is beginning, those nearby are easier to find than those distant. This simply shows that your gift has begun to blossom. Did you say you had tried both fire and water?"

"Mostly fire," Lottres said. "We weren't near water most nights, but there was always a fire."

"Interesting," Yriatt said. "Wind is often the more difficult tool. Still, it has succeeded for you. It's best to continue with that."

Lottres leaned forward, afraid to ask what he most wanted to know. He blurted, "Then, I am your student?"

Brastigan snorted to himself. Lottres turned to glare at him, felt his fists tighten with rage. This was his moment, a precious validation. Leave it to Brastigan to spoil it.

* * *

He didn't mean to do it. He just couldn't help himself. After all, he had been sitting quietly through all Yriatt's drivel. Barriers of the physical, indeed. She sounded like a marketplace fortune-teller. Next the witch would be telling Lottres the lines on his palm betokened a long journey—as if they weren't already in the middle of one.

But there was no taking back that one ill timed sound.

Brastigan drawled, "Why would she be telling you all this blabber, if you weren't her student?"

"It isn't blabber!" Lottres protested.

Yriatt merely appeared amused. "What is your interest in this?"

"I'm not interested," Brastigan retorted. His comb jabbed in the air, pointing at Lottres. "I'm here because he's here."

"Your mother would be disappointed," Yriatt said.

Brastigan felt his brows tighten in a scowl. Still, she had given him an excuse to avoid hearing any more of her gibberish.

"Speaking of her," Brastigan lifted the pendant he wore about his neck, "Father gave me this just before we left Harburg. He said it was hers. Any idea what it is?"

Yriatt didn't even look closely before answering, "It's called a *jeup*."

"Joop?" he repeated.

"*Jeup*," she corrected, stressing a slide on the J that gave it almost a Z sound. "They cast the stones at birth, so I'm told. One side represents the spirit and the other is destiny."

Still frowning, Brastigan turned the smooth sphere, looking at the snowflake, the flower. "How do you know which one is which?"

Yriatt shrugged. "I do not know. I did not think she wore one, though I suppose it should not surprise me. They were very precious to her, the Urulai. She sacrificed much for them." The witch gave Brastigan an inscrutable, dark look.

Brastigan stared for a moment, trying to take in what she had said. Yriatt spoke of his people as strangers. That didn't make sense.

Lottres heard that, too, for he asked, "Aren't you also..?"

She cut him off with a sharp laugh. "No! Remember, *Thaeme,* the things of the physical world are illusion. I wear this seeming because it comforts those who share my dwelling. It reminds them of *her,* and I would not deprive them of any solace, but I have never been one of them."

Brastigan felt his stomach grow tight and sour again. Roughly, he demanded, "Are you saying my mother wasn't Urulai?"

"She became one," Yriatt corrected soberly, "and that was a very sad day. Even the name, Leithan, was given to her afterward. Her name at birth was Yrien, if you wish to know."

Brastigan stared at his mother's *jeup,* trying to absorb this new knowledge. If Leithan wasn't Urulai, then he wasn't really half Cruthan and half Urulai—he wasn't any part Urulai. Joal must have known this. No wonder he had never taught Brastigan their tongue.

That left the question, if Yriatt and Leithan weren't Urulai, what were they? Did his mother once wear dragon horns on her hat? He stuffed the pendant under his tunic, not wanting to look at it any more.

For the first time in days, Lottres regarded Brastigan with sympathy, but this latest news had thrown any thought of his brother or his foolish ambitions right out of Brastigan's mind. He gazed into the empty eyes of Yriatt's pet girl and felt exactly that hollow and numb.

* * *

One never shouted in Urulai, it seemed, but murmured and whispered. So it seemed to Brastigan as he sat at Yriatt's table.

The entire community gathered for the evening meal, in a long hall with a raised hearth running down the center. Spits and kettles hung at regular intervals, but no smoke stung the eyes. The smoke-blackened ceiling must hide air vents. The tables were set near enough to feel the fire's warmth, but far enough to give the cooks working room.

The Cruthan men were seated at a head table, along with Yriatt. Small roast fowl had been set before them, one for each man. There was also a strange vegetable rather like thick blades of grass but with a sharp flavor. The plates and utensils were of polished wood. The goblets had the curl of carved sheep horns. Brastigan ate slowly, out of habit rather than hunger. He scarcely tasted what had been set before him. Lottres sat on Brastigan's right, but he didn't speak. Lottres's training had continued after Brastigan left, and his mind was probably busy picking out meanings from some vague word of Yriatt's.

Pikarus sat on Brastigan's other side, with Javes next over. Their bracketing him might have been a gesture of support, but Brastigan didn't take it so. More likely, they were positioned to jump on him if he spoke out of turn again. It didn't seem to matter. Brastigan wondered if even Lottres could understand the black gloom he felt. His outland heritage was the core of his pride, of everything he believed about himself. How could he *not* be Urulai?

The breathy cadence of Urulai speech came from tables around them, where the women and children were seated. Brastigan felt more conspicuous than he had in all his years at Harburg. With his braided hair, he looked like an Urulai man, the only one here. He should have felt at home. He didn't.

Seek the Urulai, Unferth had said. Brastigan looked down the ranks of tables, counting heads. Had the old man known how little there was to seek?

Two distinct generations sat there. The majority were elders, with silver streaked hair and faces lined by their suffering and exile. A sizable minority were girls Brastigan's age or younger, whose giggles and bright eyes somewhat relieved the glum atmosphere. Many of these had babes or young children, squirming in their seats and kicking each other under the benches.

There must have been young men here to sire these whelps, but even accounting for their absence the Urulai numbered well under three hundred. That was shockingly scant. Urland was a large country. Could this be all that was left?

From his youth, Brastigan remembered the exiles being mostly women and children. The warriors, as he understood it, had remained behind to fight the invaders. And what of those who didn't escape? The red dogs of Sillets must be lording it over the lofty peaks these days. What Brastigan didn't know was if they had exterminated their captives, or kept them as chattel. Sillets kept a ruthless hold on its provinces, and it was sure death to try the borders. Rumors of Urland were more rare now than snow in summer.

There was movement to Brastigan's right as Lottres stirred from his thoughts. The younger prince turned to his right, where Yriatt was seated. That was a deal too close for Brastigan's liking. On the other side of her was the strange, silent girl. At intervals, the witch gave her plain bread, without butter or jam, and helped her sip from a bowl that might contain water or broth.

Brastigan braced himself for more drivel as Lottres opened his mouth. For once, he was pleasantly surprised.

"Noble lady," Lottres frowned, as in puzzlement, "when I heard you calling for Eben that night, it sounded like he wasn't answering. Was I mistaken?"

There was a flicker of emotion in Yriatt's slate colored eyes. "You were not mistaken. I have been unable to reach Eben for some days." Coolly, she drank from her cup. "For some while before that, I could not reach my father, Ymell, who holds the vale of Altannath. That was how I guessed Sillets might be preparing to move. To enter Crutham they must pass Altannath, and to pass Altannath they must first overcome Ymell."

She spoke so blandly, it was hard to credit the disaster she spoke of. Brastigan remembered how he had thought, during their journey, that Crutham was ill prepared for war. The country had been at peace for many years. The garrisons were poorly staffed and their commanders, like Morbern of Caulteit, inexperienced. All along the tables, Cruthan men who were close enough to hear were muttering this news to those who couldn't.

Lottres frowned more deeply. "If he doesn't answer you..."

"It is more than that," Yriatt interrupted. She glanced along the table, at the eyes on her, and beyond, where even the Urulai grew still. The dark eyed women might not understand the language of their visitors, but their expressions made it clear they knew what was being spoken of.

The witch seemed to reach a decision. "If this is a council, so be it. Then I will tell you plainly, I can sense nothing from Altannath. Spying into Sillets has always been difficult, but it was sometimes possible. Now, I am as one blind."

"Then your father..." Lottres blanched and chewed his beard, unable to bring forth the words.

Brastigan was not so hobbled. Baldly, he asked, "Do you think he's dead?"

Lottres let go an exasperated breath, and dug an elbow into Brastigan's side. Yriatt's brows bent just enough to let him know he had annoyed her. Well, good.

"If I knew that, I would not have sent for you," came the crisp reply. "There is reason to believe my father yet lives. Our enemy will not kill one who may be useful, not even his sworn foe."

Quietly, Pikarus asked, "We'll be going to Altannath, then?"

"We will begin there," Yriatt said.

"Wait a minute!" Brastigan cut in. Her words implied a journey even beyond Altannath, and he didn't like the sound of that. "You just said Eben doesn't know the invasion has started."

"Eben has his own resources," she answered. "Still, it is troubling, I agree."

"Troubling?" Brastigan all but shouted. Obviously, Lottres would go along with whatever the witch suggested, so it was up to him to demand some sanity. "They'll be caught flat-footed. We must return to Harburg. Father needs us!"

Some of the men murmured agreement, but Lottres argued, "No, if Mistress Yriatt is correct and Master Ymell has been captured, we should free him first."

The witch nodded, swinging her horns for emphasis. "Ysislaw is the ruler of Sillets. He has trained some of his vassals in our arts—his *eppagadrocca*— but no more than he can keep under a watch for signs of rebellion. With Ymell's power removed from opposition —."

"Wait a minute," Brastigan interrupted. He knew little enough of geography, but he did remember the emperors of Sillets always had the same name. "I thought his name was Silester. Silester the Tenth."

"Twelfth," Lottres corrected, though reluctant to concede the point.

Yriatt said, "What is a name but another illusion?" Brastigan groaned out loud. This wasn't the time for more of her nonsense. "Call him what you will. It is the same individual. He takes whatever seeming serves his purpose."

Just as Yriatt did, Brastigan thought. Before he could say so, Lottres asked, "The same man has ruled Sillets for all this time?"

"Since the very beginning," she answered.

A man who lived forever? Now that was something to think about. And Yriatt had said "our arts." Did that include Leithan, as well?

In the silence that filled the hall, Yriatt said, "Ysislaw can be defeated, but only if—"

"Meanwhile, Crutham lies open to destruction. By the time we find this Ymell, it may be too late," Brastigan argued. He didn't need any magical powers to know how bad this news was.

"Do not think me cold," she answered softly, coldly. "Eben is near to my heart. Yet we must determine what's happened to my father. I have already taken the steps I could to aid Crutham."

Lottres let his shoulders sag with relief, and Pikarus asked, "What steps, noble lady?"

"Ysislaw's *eppagadrocca* are not strong enough to conceal the invaders movements from me," Yriatt explained. "A small force has besieged Glawern, while the main army passes by. Presumably, they will be going on to Harburg."

This sounded logical, so Brastigan didn't question it. Her next words surprised him.

"I asked the Urulai for their aid. Because they are grateful to Crutham, and because they hate Sillets, they have agreed. The Urulai warriors have gone past Glawern and will hold Carthell Cleft against an incursion toward that province. If no attack occurs, they will attempt to raise the siege on Glawern."

At least that explained where the men were. They had the satisfaction of honest bloodshed, it seemed. Brastigan heartily longed for the same.

"This ensures that Sillets won't come up behind us," Pikarus remarked, pleased.

"Correct. There is also another who depends on me. We will join her at Altannath."

"Who?" Brastigan demanded suspiciously. The witch seemed to have planned well, and that annoyed him. He wanted something to find fault with.

"My *thaeme*, Shaelen," Yriatt said. Lottres twitched beside Brastigan, perhaps reacting to the knowledge there was another student—a potential rival. The witch continued, "She is wise in the ways of the forest. When I could not see into Altannath, Shaelen offered to go there and find Ymell. When we meet again, I will know what must be done to save my father." She gestured to the pale girl on her right. "This one will come with us as well."

"Oh, a girl!" Brastigan sneered. "Well, a pretty girl makes all the difference." Some along the table chuckled, but Lottres was intent on persuading him.

"There are too few of us to make any difference in Harburg, if we can even get there," he said. "We must heed the noble lady's counsel."

Yriatt said, "I have not survived so long with Ysislaw as my enemy by making foolish errors. I need Ymell, and Shaelen needs me."

Brastigan slouched, bracing his elbows on the table. "I guess you're not so powerful, then."

The witch regarded him with impatience, and Lottres hissed into Brastigan's ear, "Is this your idea of support? You said you would back me up, but all you've done is—"

"I'm trying to point out the problems with what she's suggesting," Brastigan answered loudly, mocking his brother's whisper.

"Your highness," Pikarus put in, and both princes turned. "I've been considering the options ever since we learned of the invasion. Every man here has." He glanced down the line, drawing murmurs of support. "Glawern may be taken by now, and possibly even Carthell. There is no easy, safe way. I don't see how a group so small can defeat an army, but the noble lady says she does. We must listen to her."

"Must?" Brastigan retorted. Even with Urulai opposition, Glawern and Carthell would make a third of the nation in enemy hands. There was no time for mistakes.

"Yes, we must." Lottres spoke more calmly, but forcefully. "Father trusted her, and I trust her."

Just because he wanted her precious training, Brastigan thought bitterly. Yriatt could turn into a snake and bite him, and still the fool wouldn't hear a word against her. Glancing at the tables where the soldiers sat, he saw many doubts, but no one seemed to agree with him.

Yriatt's broke the impasse. She dabbed at her mouth with a cloth and rose purposefully from the table. "I will depart in the morning. It is your choice to accompany me, or not."

She took her strange ward by the elbow. At her touch, the girl meekly followed.

Lottres stood, too. Looking down on his brother, he said, "Remember what you told me." Then, looking over Brastigan's head, he said to Pikarus, "I will ride with Yriatt."

Pikarus paused, waiting for Brastigan's response. When none came, he answered, "Yes, your highness."

Once again, Brastigan felt like the stranger among them. He had the right of primacy, and he knew the men would follow if he demanded it. Brastigan knew what he should do, what he wanted to do. He also knew that if he did it, he might never see his brother again. Brastigan's own words trapped him. He'd told Lottres, "I'll back you up." He hadn't realized he would be backing himself into a corner.

BRASTIGAN lay awake, restless. His bunk felt hard as rock, which was what it was. At least it was long enough to stretch out his full length. Most inns were not so suited. A part of him knew he should appreciate being indoors, out of the icy wind, but all around him were the snorts and snores of sleeping men. Even after so many days on the road, the unfamiliar sounds disturbed him. It was as if the echoing halls had breath of their own.

Time and again he turned over, looking at the single candle left burning on its antler rack. The walls of the chamber were adorned with more mosaics, but no amount of decoration could relieve the gloom of the windowless chamber. The lonely stub of candle burned as low as his spirits.

The fight at the Dead Donkey, the mysterious knife—those events seemed a lifetime ago. Yet they were why Brastigan was in this weird place. He rolled over and punched the rolled up cloak that served as his pillow. He should have been in Harburg, working with Eben. The assassin might have been caught by now, and Lottres needn't have these delusions. Then Brastigan would be able to defend Crutham Keep, instead of larking off on Yriatt's fool excursion.

Even more troubling was the blind obedience of Pikarus and his men. Pikarus should have supported Brastigan, as the older prince. Instead, by saying nothing, he lent his weight to Lottres's position. Javes and the rest held mum. Were they just too well trained to wonder? Or maybe he didn't know Pikarus as well as he thought. Brastigan couldn't believe he was the only one to doubt the witch's motives, but nobody else was asking any questions. They went along with her and Lottres like a pack of hounds on leashes.

Brastigan's thoughts chased each other in circles, like a dog biting at its own tail. Their yapping kept sleep at bay for a long, dark time.

* * *

Therula came out of a nightmare, thrashing and moaning. She wanted to run, as she had in the dream, but something trapped her feet. She kicked and struggled. Her fist struck a bedside table. The crash and the pain of impact brought her fully awake.

It was only the bedclothes that tangled her feet, Therula realized. She stood up to loosen the clinging fabric of her nightgown. Instantly her head began to reel. Her body was bathed in icy sweat, and her jaw vibrated with chills. She sat down abruptly to keep from falling.

This vertigo was becoming all too common. She had felt it the day she encountered Oskar near Eben's chamber, and again during that awful breakfast meeting. Therula rubbed her aching hand and tried to dismiss the connection from her mind.

Sickened by the gamble Oskar had pushed her into, she had been doing her best to avoid him. After this latest nightmare, she could no longer deny the depth of her fear.

Therula stood up again, carefully. When she was sure she wouldn't faint, she began to pace her darkened bedchamber. Something was terribly wrong. She felt it as strongly as she had before her meeting with Eben. In her mind, Therula recited a list of odd incidents: Oskar and Eben being so friendly, an unusual attitude for both of them. Oskar knowing Unferth was dead before anyone had told him. Eben departing, having told no one but Oskar his intentions. The addition of new palace guards, strangers Oskar had hired to replace Pikarus's squadron. And her repeated dizzy spells, which occurred only when Oskar was present. Or during nightmares; Therula couldn't remember exactly what her dream had been about, but she was sure Oskar had been in it.

By themselves, these things seemed innocuous, yet Therula was sure there was a pattern. She groped toward understanding, but it slipped from her mind just as the nightmare had.

Clearly, however, Oskar was the connecting piece to this puzzle. If she questioned his relationship with Eben, then she must also question Unferth's death. But Oskar was her brother. No, her king—supreme and untouchable. That was the true nightmare.

* * *

Hours later, Brastigan's stomach woke him. The air of the caverns now held a musty, sweet odor: porridge. Though his head felt heavy and his eyes burned with sleeplessness, the teasing scent of food wouldn't let him rest. He turned over and saw Lottres's bed lying empty. That did rouse him.

The moment he sat up, Pikarus's eyes were open. Brastigan looked away from his wary, calm regard. He was sick to death of wondering where that one's loyalties lay. He got up and turned his back, kneeling to pull fresh clothing from his duffel. If Pikarus put his game face on this early, why, Brastigan would, too.

Others stirred, hearing him move. Soon the room was full of soft sounds of men packing up to move out. Brastigan dressed quickly and left.

Back to the long hall, then, where the hearths blazed and cauldrons steamed. Lottres was seated next to Yriatt, their heads close together. The pale girl was with them, too, her bewildered stare fixed on the nearest fire. Brastigan scowled at them as one of the Urulai women handed him a horn and a wooden bowl.

Sitting close to Yriatt was near the top of Brastigan's least favored things, but the line was backing up behind him. He walked stiffly toward Lottres. Strange, how the things he took for granted had suddenly become thorny issues. Still, there was no need to flaunt his humiliation by sitting alone, and it would steady the men if the two princes at least attempted to show unity.

Lottres eyed Brastigan as he approached. His tense face showed a mixture of resentment and relief. He shifted just enough to permit Brastigan to sit. The dark prince bit his lips to keep back a sarcastic thanks for the privilege of his brother's company. Lottres's bowl was already empty, he saw. A map was spread between him and Yriatt. Fortunately, the witch had turned away, tipping a spoonful of gruel into the girl's lips.

Brastigan's horn held cider, slightly sour in his mouth but pleasantly hot. The bowl contained thick porridge with dried berries scattered on top. Brown rolls were neatly stacked on the table. There was comfort in the familiar meal. His head began to clear after the first few bites, and he ate with real appetite. It was good to feel his accustomed energy. Or maybe he was just too tired of fretting to worry any more.

The meal was brief and mostly silent. The soldiers ate quickly, knowing they must move soon, yet there was a current of suppressed excitement among them. Maybe, Brastigan thought suddenly, Lottres wasn't the only one who craved adventure. Pikarus's squad would gain more glory as a small group, moving behind enemy lines, than as one unit of the larger Cruthan army. Of course, they were more likely to die that way, too. Brastigan turned his head, eyeing their sergeant. If, as it seemed, there were some connection between Pikarus and Therula, maybe the risk seemed worthwhile. A man who returned as a war hero stood more chance of gaining a princess' favor.

Brastigan put his spoon in his mouth and found it empty. He was still hungry, so he stood up. Beside him, Lottres seemed to jump. Brastigan felt his lips curl in a sneer as he strolled back toward the kettles. Even when he gave way, he could still make his brother flinch.

He sauntered back to his place, fragrant steam curling upward from his bowl, but before he could sit down, one of the female archers hurried into the chamber. Brastigan hadn't seen them since their arrival. He watched curiously as she bent her head to speak softly into Yriatt's ear.

Yriatt, in her turn, told Lottres, "It is time we moved."

They both rose from the table, Lottres telling Pikarus, "Sergeant."

And Pikarus said, loudly enough for all the men to hear, "Eat up and let's go."

Along the table, men gulped the remains of their meal in great bites even as they stood. Brastigan, who had just bent his knees to sit, straightened with an exasperated sigh. He downed the dregs from his horn in a long pull and followed Lottres with his bowl in his hand. Nor was he the only one to eat as he walked. They had all missed having warm meals during the past strange days.

Passing wooden bowls from hand to hand, the men armed each other. Unasked, Lottres assisted Brastigan. He returned the favor. The silence was thick with things unsaid. With the last bits scraped off the side of his bowl, he stacked it with the others beside the door. Then, with Victory belted at his side, Brastigan swept his duffel over his shoulder.

The mules were waiting in the large chamber where they had entered Hawkwing House. Someone had groomed the beasts, and bulging saddlebags showed they had been re-supplied. With them... Brastigan stopped, feeling a sudden tightness in his chest.

Two tall beasts, ghostly gray, stood near the head of the line. Urulai horses—he knew them at once. Sturdy blankets covered their backs, instead of saddles, and a familiar falcon stood on one of those. The proud beasts wore no reins, but their pale manes and tails were braided and decked with beads.

Memories crowded Brastigan's mind, things half forgotten, and a sudden longing. Who would want a bulky Cruthan charger, having seen one of these lissome beasts? The line was backing up behind him again. Reluctantly, he spurred himself forward, making for the mere mule that awaited him.

He tore his eyes away from the horses long enough to lash his duffel behind the saddle. In doing so he noted that the mule's bit and the buckles on its tack had all been darkened with charcoal. The two gray horses wore wooden beads, which wouldn't reflect sunlight. A wise precaution, maybe, for skulking behind enemy lines.

Across his beast's back, he saw a cluster of the female archers. Yriatt was at the center, identified by her horned head-dress. She had removed the veils and gewgaws, but the upstanding horns remained. Why she retained those escaped Brastigan. They seemed impractical for travel. Not that he cared for her comfort.

The low voiced discussion was unintelligible, but it sounded serious. No doubt the witch was coaching the archers to guard the walls in her absence. With their men gone, the women had no choice but to defend the keep. Brastigan still found it slightly perverse that women took up arms.

The witch turned from the circle of archers, who melted into the shadows of the antechamber. Together with Lottres, she helped the girl-ghost onto the falconless horse. And Brastigan made a quick decision. He swallowed his pride and took up the reins, leading his mule toward the front of the line. He might have no love for his aunt, but in the interest of solidarity, he would ride close to his brother.

Lottres was at the head of the column. Yriatt's horse was to his left, the girl's pack-tied behind it. Pikarus, seeing Brastigan, fell back at once. This left open the spot behind Lottres, beside the girl. At least Brastigan was near one of the Urulai horses, he thought sourly.

A moment later Lottres mounted his mule. Brastigan and the others did the same. Sitting on her horse, Yriatt raised her hands above her head. Lottres watched, tilting his head slightly as if he listened to something. The mules began to whicker nervously, and candle flames fluttered. Brastigan felt his muscles tighten. After a short while, the witch lowered her hands. Nothing else seemed to happen.

Yriatt called a single word into the shadows. A low, mechanical groan echoed in the chamber and a sliver of light appeared high along the outer wall. It widened swiftly as the gate was let down. Cold air blew into the room and made the candle flames lean over, as if they would flee.

Brastigan shook himself, trying to relieve his tension. What was that performance for, anyway?

It was light outside, but foggy. The wind pushed mists from the heights into the chamber. As the near half of the bridge descended to level, the column moved forward. Hooves made hollow thumps on the planks as they approached the fog-shrouded wall. The dense mist hid the defenders even from knowing eyes as they passed beneath the outer arch. Then came the scrape of cobbles under hooves, and they were back on the stony field.

No path was marked, but Yriatt led them sharply to the left. The fog might hide them from enemy eyes, but any foe with hearing still could find them. Nor could they hurry, lest a beast lose its footing and fall. Bits of sound hinted at the surroundings: the chatter of the brook fading behind them, and the airy whisper of wind over the rocks. The farther they went, the more Brastigan wished the fog would lift. He badly wanted to know where the edge of the hanging valley was. The fog clung to them, damp and slightly sticky, like an overlarge garment.

It was a great relief to see the stunted spruce trees loom out of the mist before them. A narrow game trail led down toward the valley below. The hillside was steep, though not as bad as the stony track of the day before. This time, at least, the fog provided shelter from hostile eyes. As they descended, the trees grew thicker and the mist finally thinned out.

Through the branches, the Cruthans glimpsed a deceptively peaceful scene—rugged peaks above pine green slopes, with the white streak of a cascade here and there. A brisk breeze sent dark-tinged clouds scurrying across the sky. It stirred the treetops, so the branches murmured like people talking about them after they had passed. Occasional bird calls punctuated the susurrus.

The falcon soon rose from Yriatt's saddle. It glided above them as it had done before, playing the spy. Time and again, Brastigan turned in the saddle. He saw no hint of danger. By all appearances, the land was deserted. Perversely, that made him more tense. If the land had been invaded, as everyone said, there should be some sign of the enemy. Yet he saw only treetops and mountain peaks and swift moving, gray tinged clouds.

In a way, Brastigan was disappointed. Bad news had come after bad at Hawkwing House, too fast to really follow it. His body felt tight with frustration. He needed a good fight to clear his head, and an enemy he could kill without remorse.

Instead, he had too much time to think about what might be happening in Crutham. Unferth, Therula, little Cliodora... News of the invasion might not even have reached them. Would they reach the safety of Crutham Keep before the attack came?

It was so hard to judge the danger. He would have to see the enemy army to judge its power, but Sillets had a fearsome reputation. Would even Habrok's prodigious strength be enough to keep them safe? More than that, why didn't Eben answer Yriatt's call? Crutham would need his powers to counter the sorcery of Sillets. They had better hope nothing had happened to him.

* * *

Other men might relax on the ride down, or keep a watch for danger, but Lottres was too busy. His training had begun in earnest the night before. Yriatt's physical presence wasn't necessary, as Lottres had learned when she spoke to him from across the holding.

First had been a series of tests—if he could hear her, or make her hear him—that left him exhausted but exhilarated, although Yriatt had deflated Lottres's pride at being able to hear Brastigan's thoughts by pointing out that their long friendship made it easier. Before leaving Hawkwing House, she had assigned him to practice hearing other men, as well.

"You are to listen only," Yriatt told Lottres with daunting strictness. "Do not speak to anyone. Do nothing else until I show you how. Our enemies know I must come. They will be watching for any hint of my power. I am able to conceal myself, but you may yet betray me."

"I will never do that," Lottres had vowed.

He meant to keep his word, so while the soldiers rode through the dim woodlands he used the first form. Relaxing, Lottres located the riders around him. Focusing on one after the other, he picked out the hum of their thoughts. Lottres reveled in his secret abilities. It was fun to eavesdrop, especially since no one else could catch him.

Lottres listened to Javes wondering if Egger had reached Glawern in time, and if he was on his way to Carthell yet. He sensed Pikarus's focus on guarding the princes and Yriatt. To Lottres's surprise, the source of Pikarus's calm assurance was a woman—Therula! Pikarus believed that Therula loved him. Lottres would have loved to whisper this into Brastigan's mind, but his promise restrained him.

Besides, Brastigan was still grousing. In fact, Lottres soon discovered that most of the men did nothing but complain to themselves. Yugo was hungry. Aglend's back hurt from his mule's rough gait. Roari was bored. As time passed, the novelty of eavesdropping wore off. Lottres itched for something more interesting to do.

Tentatively, he reached for Yriatt. *"Noble lady?"*

He sensed Yriatt's disapproval, though her back was to him, but she didn't lecture Lottres for breaking silence, as he expected.

"You may address me as maess," she answered crisply. *"You shall be my* thaeme."

"Not eppagadrocca?" Lottres asked.

"We do not keep slaves," Yriatt replied with asperity. *"That is what eppagadrocca means—a mind slave. When my father and I take a student, he is*

thaeme, a child of one's heart. We seek to create bonds of affection, not servitude."

Lottres was silent, relieved and slightly flattered. Though he admired Yriatt, he couldn't have hoped she felt any affection in the short time she had known him.

Yriatt went on, *"You are improving,* thaeme, *but there is another skill I must teach you. This is the third form, which is a defense. You must learn to guard your own thoughts."* She continued darkly, *"Soon enough, we will encounter* eppagadrocca, *or worse — their master. You must be able to block them, lest you yourself become a danger to me."*

"I would never..." Lottres protested.

"Do you think you would be given a choice?" Yriatt retorted, not unkindly. *"You mean well, but you have barely begun to learn. Now,* thaeme, *hold your breath."*

Chastened, Lottres did as he was told. He immediately felt a tightness in his throat as muscles, accustomed to working on their own, abruptly ceased. It was amazingly difficult to hold them still.

"Breathe," Yriatt told him.

Lottres breathed, trying not to gasp like a fish out of water.

"Again," Yriatt said.

Lottres held his breath. His chest ached with the effort to keep his diaphragm stiff.

"Now feel," Yriatt said, *"how your will forms a barrier between the body and its functions. This is what you must learn to do. Breathe."*

Gratefully, Lottres obeyed.

"Try it now," Yriatt urged. *"Make your will firm, just as your muscles were."*

Lottres did. He could feel Yriatt prodding, almost as if she turned around and poked him with a stick.

"Relax," she instructed. Then, *"Again."*

"Noble... maess," Lottres stumbled over the unfamiliar word.

"You may breathe while we do this," Yriatt said with a suggestion of dry humor.

Lottres chuckled softly. He didn't think he laughed aloud until he felt Brastigan's suspicious thoughts. Lottres stiffened his mental barrier, trying to shut his brother out. Then Yriatt jabbed at him. It felt a little like being punched in the stomach. Lottres closed his mouth to keep back a grunt of pain.

"Ignore him, thaeme," Yriatt said sternly. *"I am the one you must guard against."*

"Yes, maess," Lottres whispered back to her.

"We will continue, then. You will hold your barrier. I will test it. If you wish to avoid further pain, concentrate only on your lessons."

"I understand," Lottres said, though a part of him resented Brastigan for the interruption.

"Begin," Yriatt said crisply.

* * *

Though the steep terrain lent some speed, the descent from Hawkwing House seemed to take all day. In reality, it was just after noon when the trail leveled off. They took a hasty meal in the dense shade of a fir grove, where a waterfall tumbled down a sharp incline. The lower limbs had been cut away from some of the trees, creating a cavelike space. The packed earth of its floor suggested people often rested here. Neatly trimmed logs provided seating, but there was no hearth, so this wasn't a permanent camp. It could be a staging area for pack trains preparing to mount the steep trail.

This was the first sign of habitation, besides the trail itself. Yet Brastigan couldn't imagine the Urulai consenting to live at Hawkwing House, no matter how much Yriatt resembled her dead sister. Everything Joal ever taught Brastigan had to do with the mountains and forests. It wasn't normal to dwell in tunnels and darkness. There ought to be a village somewhere, exposed to the natural rhythm of the sun and seasons.

Brastigan chewed on trail bread and frowned as his eyes fell on the strange girl. Speaking of unnatural things... Lottres and Yriatt were seated in a close conference, as Brastigan guessed would become usual, and the men gave them as much space as the small tree-cave permitted. The girl sat beside them, forgotten. She seldom did so much as blink, let alone ask for food or drink. Neither had she made any effort to defend herself against stray branches whipped back by those riding before her. A red weal crossed her cheek, seeping crimson, as evidence of her apathy.

Brastigan frowned again. He didn't expect Yriatt to show much kindness, but this was a human, of whatever sort. It wasn't right to ignore her. He jammed the last of his trail bread into his mouth and went to retrieve a waterskin from his saddlehorn. Both Lottres and Yriatt turned sharply as he approached them.

"Yes?" the witch asked coolly.

He ignored her, kneeling before the nameless girl and offering the waterskin. She didn't respond, of course. Well, he'd fed water to injured men on the trail before. He cupped her chin, pressing with her thumb and middle fingers on her cheeks to press on her jaw joint. She responded by parting her lips slightly, and he trickled a few drops into her mouth.

Lottres asked irritably. "What are you doing?"

"What?" Brastigan snapped back. "We're watering the beasts, but the people go without?"

The girl swallowed the liquid, and even licked her lips afterward. Taking that as an expression of interest, Brastigan tipped his skin to give her more.

Lottres opened his mouth to protest, but Yriatt gave a curt laugh. "It doesn't matter," she said, turning her shoulder toward Brastigan to show her lack of concern for his opinion. Lottres closed his mouth, the words unsaid, and did likewise.

Brastigan gave the young girl several drinks and then took a close look at her face. Crusted blood brushed away beneath his fingertips, and no fresh blood appeared. The welt was only superficial, it seemed. Two or three smaller cuts were visible, none as serious as the one. The girl gave no response to his crude medicking.

Most of the soldiers had finished their meals and were walking back toward their mules. Hastily, Brastigan snapped off a corner of trail bread. He rubbed it gently against the girl's lower lip, as he'd seen his sister Estarra do when teaching her babes to eat solid food. The girl obediently opened her mouth. She chewed slowly, as if it took great concentration. Brastigan stuffed more bread into her mouth as quickly as she would take it. Still, most of the wafer remained in his hand when Pikarus called, "Saddle up!"

He found the girl would stand when he gripped her elbow, so he led her to her horse. The animal turned its head, clearly recognizing Brastigan as a stranger. He would have loved to probe its intelligence, but the troop was forming up. Since the girl couldn't mount by herself, Brastigan lifted her by the waist to set her in the saddle. He nearly tossed her over the horse's back. The girl weighed nothing. She might be no more than cobwebs and air.

By now Brastigan was the only one not mounted, so he pushed the remainder of the trail bread into her hand and trotted to his mule.

As he passed, Javes leaned over and tapped his shoulder. "You make a fine nursemaid," he muttered.

Brastigan scowled at the jest. "I was taught it's wrong to ignore one who's in your care," he retorted, loudly enough for Yriatt to hear. To Javes, he added, "Anyway, it's her horse I like, not her."

He stalked on, the soldier's answering laughter ringing behind him. Still, the joking nettled. Until now, only Lottres had been so bold, but Lottres rode ahead of him with two strange women between them. Everything else was different. Why not that, too?

The land still sloped downward, but more gently now. The path from the tree-cave roughly paralleled the watercourse. The cataract soon joined a larger creek and the path bent to follow.

This was ancient forest, grown thick with massive trees whose overlapping branches created a dense shade. Off the path, the ground was hoof-deep with fallen needles and branches. Even the occasional percussion of armored men did not ring far. Moss covered the tree trunks and forest floor, and it drank up sound as a thirsty man drinks water.

The path was free of large obstructions and well beaten into the forest floor, yet a layer of fallen needles suggested it hadn't seen much use of late. It skirted the largest trees, but still stayed close to them. The lowest branches of these forest giants were high above, and little brush grew in the green dusk, so no branches whipped their faces now. Even the witch had room for her horns under the natural vault. This forest was a far grander hall than any men could make, in Brastigan's mind.

The tame groves of the lowlands were often raided for timber and hunted for game. Not so this wild land. Humans were strangers here. Brastigan tried to relax, breathing in the earthy scent of the forest. He found he couldn't. Instead, the hollow feeling grew in his heart. After all, he was not the Urulai he had thought himself. For the first time, he felt like a stranger in the wilderness.

Water ran downhill, as it must, and their path followed. Spears of light slanted through gaps in the canopy here and there. At times they skirted meadows where beaver ponds drowsed in the bright sun, but the path stayed under the trees.

They made a good speed on the winding trail, changing from a trot to a gallop at intervals. The earth was damp enough to raise little dust, but there would be no more fresh mounts, so they had to spare the beasts. The spears of light had changed their angle when bright flashes came to them through the trees. Lottres slowed to a cautious walk as they approached an edge to the woods. The troop stopped, blinking against the unaccustomed daylight.

On their right, the creek they had been following roared down toward a wide lake whose waters seemed twice as blue as the sky above. Another rocky vista was mirrored in the glassy lake. To their left was a broad semi-circle of bank grown with tall grass and wildflowers. Brastigan's mule wheezed eagerly at the smell of it, but something else caught his eye. The green skirts of the trees ended well above ground, and at a uniform height. That wasn't natural. The clearing was ringed with tree-caves.

"It's perfectly safe," Yriatt said, when Lottres sat still too long. "No one is here."

"Is this an Urulai village?" Lottres asked.

"It is. The villagers came to stay with me after Shaelen warned them on her way to Altannath. No one has been here for two months."

Lottres seemed to relax, but Brastigan swung down from his mule. "If it's all the same to you, let's scout it out first." He waved at Pikarus, and three others dismounted, following him. Brastigan didn't think he needed permission to scout, but it did feel good to be listened to for once.

Brastigan moved quietly through the woods, blessing the craftsmen who made his harness. Only the occasional squeak or heavy step betrayed them as they came up behind the settlement. First they passed a large dung heap, and then an oval of packed earth suggesting a rudimentary stable. Beyond that was the first of the tree-caves.

A long, rectangular hearth had been raised up of earth and river stones. It was much like the one of Hawkwing House, except smaller. Beside this was something new: a long granite stone. Its surface was pocked with mortar holes for grinding grain. Leather thongs dangled from the branches overhead. Those must attach some kind of roofing. A series of holes along the rear of the space suggested that tent pegs might have been driven into the soft ground.

It was well enough to shelter under the trees in summer, when the weather was warm, but the mountain winters were harsh. There had to be some other sort of dwelling for winter. Maybe the tribe wintered at Hawkwing House.

The troopers followed Brastigan through four of the shelters. All were alike except for trivial details. Tucked between the trees, they found a trio of light canoes concealed by branches. Brastigan felt like an intruder. This could have been his home, but now he didn't know if he had the right to step up to his ancestors' hearth.

There was no time to wallow in self-pity. He glanced at Javes and the others, confirming his opinion there was nothing significant to be discovered. They tramped back to their waiting fellows.

It galled Brastigan to say it, but he did. "She's right. There's no one here."

Pikarus asked, "Do we stay the night?"

Lottres seemed to think about that. "There is free fodder for the mules."

The animals were looking thin, it was true, and the tree-caves were safe enough, but Brastigan knew he couldn't sleep here.

"If there's daylight, I say we move on. We have places to be," he said

Yriatt said, "Brastigan is correct. Let us go."

Before anyone else argued, Brastigan strode to his mule. As he passed the girl, he stopped. There, in her hand, was the trail bread he had given her. It hadn't been touched in all their hours on the road. What kind of creature was she? With a disgusted snort, he took it from her unresisting hand and tossed it into the brush.

The line was already starting to move as he swung into the saddle and kicked his beast into motion. Yriatt led off, following the curve of the meadow and keeping them under the eave of the trees. Brastigan felt strange as they passed the row of empty shelters. He was glad they weren't staying, and yet he felt that he was leaving something behind, as well. He stiffened his back and rode on.

CHAPTER TWELVE
PLAYING PEEK-A-BOO

THEY didn't just leave the Urulai camp behind. It seemed they left daylight behind as well, for the path clung stubbornly to the forest's green gloom. Were his ancestors so afraid of the open sky, Brastigan wondered. It seemed unnecessary. What was there to fear?

Again, the trail roughly followed a watercourse, this one the broad stream that was the lake's outlet. Glancing at the sky, when he could see it through the tree canopy, Brastigan realized the sun was setting over his left shoulder. The waters flowed northward, and not just for one stretch. Every stream the troop crossed went that way, running along narrow valleys and foaming through clefts in the rocks. They had crossed the spine of the mountains. Crutham lay behind them. Before them was the unknown and hostile land of Sillets.

On the other hand, it was hard to feel too nervous. So far, Sillets looked exactly like Crutham. Still they rode, keeping under cover, until at last the leafy twilight dimmed into a true dusk. It was almost too dark to see when Yriatt led them down a steep bank. She reversed direction to head upstream, beside the water, and called a halt in a deep oxbow. Huge logs, left by some long ago flood, lay scattered about like jackstraws. The falcon perched on one of these, looking smug. Beside it was a gap just wide enough for the mules to skin through.

Beyond the ready-made barrier was a level patch of sand and gravel right up against the bank. This place bore no sign of human shaping, so it wasn't another Urulai redoubt, but that didn't seem to matter. A pit was dug, and once they were sure no water seeped in, a fire lit. The log dam provided plenty of dry wood for fuel.

Brastigan helped tether the animals against the barrier. He did his part willingly. Just for one moment, one of the Urulai horses leaned over as if it might stand on his foot, but he brushed the two horses well, and they suffered the attention.

Brastigan was gathering the long, coarse grass from the steep dark bank when a sound stopped him. It was a kind of falcon's cry, starting high and descending in short barks, but this was much deeper. After the falcon, it sounded like a man's voice compared to a boy's. Brastigan crouched, making sure his long form wasn't exposed. That was no enemy, condor or crow, crying alarm at the sight of them. It came from high above, where the rocky peaks merged into the rusty sunset sky. He couldn't see the creature, but he knew what it was.

Brastigan stayed low, plucking up grass by its roots in the failing light. A griffin! How could he forget those miserable beasts, scourge of the high peaks? He'd seen them from a distance while hunting with his brothers in Begatt, but never had to fight one. Eagle wings and a cruel, curved beak together with a panther's claws—it was an absurd combination, and frightful. They weren't terribly smart as animals went, but they didn't need to be. Their fearsome strength was dangerous enough.

This explained the Urulai compulsion to stay under cover of the trees. Being big creatures, griffins ate big: elk, mountain sheep—and horses. Brastigan hurried down with his burden, adding it to the piles Javes had already accumulated along the picket line. Any horse was a precious resource in this wild country, and the Urulai horses were exceptional. He completely understood the need to protect them.

More shrieks came echoing down on them as Brastigan approached the fireside. It sounded like more than one beast. The soldiers sat tense, looking over their shoulders at the dark crags above them.

"Easy," Javes was saying as Brastigan sat down on an exposed rock. "They're just talking to each other. It's how the prides defend their territories."

Someone muttered, "They come in packs?"

"They're just beasts," Pikarus answered calmly. "No worse than bears. We've nothing to fear."

"Bears can't fly," Yugo retorted.

Yriatt, at the fireside, answered serenely, "They will not attack us. They killed yesterday."

How did she know that? Brastigan turned his face away, hiding his sneer for the sake of unity. The griffins went on screeching. Their cries made a poor accompaniment to a poor meal of dry bread, dry meat and sour cheese. The men ate hunkered down, as if one of the creatures might stoop upon them at any moment.

When Brastigan was finished, he sat up tall and looked over Lottres's back. Yriatt had gone to kneel beside the fire pit as soon as she had eaten. No feminine tasks for that one. She now sat unnaturally still. The flickering red light played over the angles of her face. It gave her a mask-like seeming, remote and inscrutable. It was well enough that she left menial tasks for the soldiers, but Lottres seemed to feel he was free of chores, too. He watched Yriatt with an intense focus, though Brastigan saw nothing worth seeing. Meanwhile, the moon-pale maiden sat behind Yriatt, shadowed and ignored.

Brastigan stalked over to the girl. "Here," he ordered curtly, extending a parcel of dry sausage and cheese. She didn't acknowledge him. How could anyone be so mindless? He dropped onto a nearby stump and kicked the rock she sat on.

Finally, when her seat rocked beneath her, the girl did blink. Her head moved in slow jerks, turning over and downward. Like a babe, he thought—a suckling child that couldn't control its own body. The smooth brow puckered slightly, and she stared at his boot as if she had never seen such a thing before.

After she'd had a good look, Brastigan abruptly put his foot down. Then he raised his other foot, and set it on the other side of her rock. A long moment passed, and then, again, her face twitched over to regard the new and amazing presence of a different boot. His sister's brats did the same thing when they played peek-a-boo. Was that what this girl was, a babe in mind despite her adult size? Yriatt had said people sometimes came to her for healing, though he couldn't imagine the witch doing it out of charity alone. Yet what other purpose could the girl serve?

This game continued for several minutes, first one foot and then the other. When Brastigan had enough, he set both feet down and leaned forward, offering a bit of cheese. Now the girl did stare, turning jerkily from one side of the rock to another. Finally her pale eyes moved outward, finding his two feet braced on the ground. She looked upward next, and seemed perplexed to see his knees.

"Come on, eat." Exasperated, Brastigan stuck his hand under her nose.

The girl leaned back, giving his fingers and the bit of whitish cheese the same confused examination his feet had gotten. He sighed aloud, and leaned closer to rub the food against her lower lip. The girl opened her mouth and he shoved the cheese in. She seemed startled when he lowered his hand to pick off another bit of cheese. His movements were too quick for her to follow. She chewed even more slowly than before, as if she couldn't remember how it was done. Or maybe the taste of the cheese bothered her.

"Okay, it's a bit sharp," he growled. "It isn't that bad."

The girl continued eating as he gave her bits of cheese and meat. Brastigan sighed over the chore. She seemed so helpless, and that was an impediment to the speed that was so crucial. He really couldn't see what Yriatt brought her along for. It was necessary, the witch had said. Or did she? Brastigan couldn't recall her exact words.

Of course, there was little use in challenging Yriatt's judgment. The stars would fall from the heavens, most likely, before that one explained herself. Not that Lottres would ask a sensible question to begin with.

Brastigan turned his head, and saw that his brother was actually moving. Yriatt sat stiff and still, but Lottres turned his head from side to side, as if his neck had cramped. Then his brother turned toward him. Like the girl, Lottres seemed startled by Brastigan's presence.

Before he could turn away, Brastigan asked, "What are you two up to?"

He spoke neutrally, to avoid giving offense. Which, for Brastigan, was an unnatural event in itself. Lottres frowned warily.

"No, really," Brastigan said. "I want to know what you're trying to do."

"We're listening," Lottres replied. He waited. When Brastigan didn't laugh, he went on, "Listening for the enemy. Any noises that might tell us where they are."

"Sounds useful," Brastigan admitted.

Lottres shrugged and turned away, muttering something under his breath.

More time had passed than Brastigan thought while he tended the witling waif. The sky above was strewn with a splendor of stars. Pikarus was telling out watches, and those men not on duty demonstrated how the sand was loose enough to dig out shallow trenches for sleeping. Lottres joined them. Brastigan shifted his own shoulders and thought sleep did sound appealing.

The girl had stopped eating as soon as he didn't push food at her. Brastigan wondered momentarily if she wanted a bed dug, or needed a trip to the latrine first. He quickly decided his duty didn't extend so far. He left her staring at the space where his feet had been.

Brastigan walked past Yriatt, who remained as still as one of the logs behind her. He took the first available bed, with a nod of thanks to Roari, who dug it. Javes took the next one over, but Brastigan was in no mood to talk. He lay down and pulled his cloak over his head. Despite the discomfort of sleeping in harness, he fell asleep at once.

As the days passed, Lottres had but two tasks: listening to those around him and blocking Yriatt's probes. She tested him constantly. The only respite was when they worked together, searching through the fire for any sign of the Silletsians. Yriatt had an evil instinct for knowing when Lottres was tired or distracted. Most nights, he went to bed with a throbbing headache from her painful strikes.

"Remember, *Thaeme*," she would say if he protested, "this is what you wanted."

Then, like as not, she would probe again to see if he had kept his defenses up. More and more, Lottres did just that. He was learning to sense an attack coming. Some of the time, he even blocked them without accidentally holding his breath.

His eavesdropping skills had improved, as well. Lottres was able to focus on any of the men, whenever he wanted to. Only the nameless girl continued to resist his probes. And Yriatt, of course. Lottres didn't quite dare eavesdrop on his *maess*.

Still, it bothered him that he couldn't hear the girl. Lottres sensed only emptiness in her. It was like listening for voices at the bottom of a well. He didn't understand it, and that made him wary. He reminded himself that it was Yriatt's business, not his.

Maybe that was why Brastigan wouldn't leave the girl alone. In his perversity, he insisted on interfering with her. Brastigan didn't like Yriatt, and he wanted to bother her. Bother Lottres, too, if he could. Then there was the basic attraction of a female. He had seen Brastigan charm enough girls with his roguish grin, just to pass time. As long as the two of them weren't alone, Lottres supposed it was all right. After all, he had more to worry about than his brother's petty games.

In a way, Lottres felt sorry for Brastigan. He wasn't pretending to be affected by the news that his mother hadn't been born Urulai. The pain was sincere. Still, Lottres kept his sympathies to himself. Brastigan wouldn't want his pity.

Besides, it was such a refreshing change that he, Lottres, got to drag Brastigan along where he didn't want to go. He rather enjoyed doing it. Lottres admitted to himself that he wasn't ready to yield the upper hand. Not yet.

* * *

The days fell into a routine of hard riding and snatched meals. The land was no friend now. The mountains on every side were as jagged as jaws full of teeth, and they no longer had smooth Urulai trails before them. The falcon scouted out game tracks that kept them in the woods, scurrying to cover when they must cross open land. Every dawn and dusk they heard griffins calling, and it wasn't only the falcon that kept its eyes on the sky. Yet every night the bird found them some secluded place to camp.

Every night, too, Brastigan found himself tending the silent girl. It became a part of the daily pattern to lift her up and down from her horse and offer his arm while she stretched her legs. If the men looked askance, Javes had been the only one to speak of it.

Despite her witless seeming, the girl came to recognize Brastigan. At first it was just his feet she knew, and then his hand holding some bit of bread or cheese. On the second night she insisted on feeling his hands. Soft fingers glided over his calloused ones, probing and puzzling. He could hardly feed her.

"Just don't chew on my knuckles," Brastigan told her. That was what Estarra's babes usually did.

On the third day, the girl picked his face out from whatever mist she saw before her. She gazed at him, and her eyes were no longer quite so empty. Brastigan felt his heart turn over. He had never been looked at this way before. The court women were worldly, knowing. None of them were innocent, not even little Cliodora. This girl, Yriatt's pathetic baggage, didn't chatter or invite or suggest. She just looked at him as if he was wonderful.

Nor was she, in truth, the mindless creature she appeared. The girl did perceive what went on around her. The others were just too busy to see the slight reactions that made up her unspoken vocabulary. When camp was set and Brastigan must leave her, the girl kept her eyes on him wherever he stepped. Sometimes, when he spoke, her lips twitched as if she were trying to smile but didn't know how. For the girl did remain silent, despite her new responsiveness. She sat like a dream, as perfect and lovely as a sunbeam or a drop of dew.

By the fifth day, the Urulai horses were forgotten. Brastigan was the girl's willing servant. What man could resist such flattery? Brastigan couldn't, and he knew it. Once, long ago, Lottres used to look at him the way the girl did now. Being a proud thirteen-year-old, he hadn't appreciated what it meant. Not that any girl could replace his brother's friendship, but it soothed his wounded pride to be regarded with unqualified admiration.

Besides, he now knew Yriatt was wrong about the girl. That alone was enough to cheer him. Despite a strong desire to rub it in his brother's face, Brastigan held the knowledge close. If it were Yriatt who made this pretty girl into a nothing, she might put her back that way. If that happened, Brastigan would have to kill her, and Lottres would never forgive him.

If Brastigan was content, his brother wasn't. Just as the girl was really blossoming, Lottres appeared at Brastigan's shoulder while he was tying up the mules.

In a harsh whisper, Lottres asked, "What are you after?"

Brastigan had been aware of his brother's agitation when he cared for the girl. Yriatt didn't seem to care, but Lottres obviously did. Now Brastigan's mind was crowded with things he couldn't say: that he felt so isolated from the men, so alienated from his brother, it felt good when someone, however strange, seemed to need him.

He swallowed these thoughts and answered, "I'm working." Brastigan lifted the bundle of mules' reins in demonstration. "Which, by the way, you haven't been helping with since."

"Don't give me that," Lottres hissed. His eyes fixed on the girl, who sat waiting at the fireside. "You've never been one to concern yourself with a creature like that. Why do it now?"

Brastigan rebelled at the slighting description of the girl as a creature. He shut his mouth on that, too. Lottres would run to Yriatt in a heartbeat if he knew the truth.

"It gives me something to do, all right?" he answered sharply. "In case you hadn't noticed, I'm not exactly in charge around here."

Lottres stared at him, narrow eyed, and then said, "You're hiding something."

Brastigan stared back, wondering if Lottres really knew his thoughts. Then he sneered. "So that's what this was about. You're jealous."

"What?" Lottres frowned.

Well, Brastigan wasn't about to be lectured. If this was a fight, he would give worse than he got. Lottres had had this coming for days now.

"There's something magical about her," Brastigan said. Had to be, for her to touch him so. "You don't know what it is, but you can't stand for me to be near it, because magic is supposed to be just for you. Not lowly, insensitive me — only for you."

"No, it's..." Lottres broke off, and tried again. "That's not it. You're tampering with something you don't understand."

"And you do?" Brastigan challenged.

Lottres's thin lipped silence gave the answer to that.

"Well, for your information, I'm not tampering with anything." Brastigan knelt to tie off the reins with a hard jerk, releasing the anger his brother always seemed to provoke these days. "It just gives me something else to think of besides the invasion."

When he straightened Lottres was merely staring at him, doubting and wondering. "That's all?"

"What else?" Brastigan snorted.

At this moment Javes appeared, leading the rest of the pack mules. Brastigan took the reins and indicated, with a jerk of his chin, that the man should find other duties. Which, being a good soldier, he did.

The moment he was clear, Lottres started again. "I just don't want to see you turn that poor creature into your doxy."

Now it was Brastigan's turn to stare in disgust. It was true the girl was pretty, and it had been weeks since he had a woman. He couldn't deny the need, but to think he would vent it on someone so helpless... How could his own brother think of such a thing?

"Not every woman I spend time with is my *girlfriend*," Brastigan answered coldly, emphasizing the polite word. "She is a nice girl. She does everything I tell her. It's so refreshing. The rest of you don't listen to a word I say, but she does. In return, I treat her like a human being."

Lottres released an exasperated breath. "But she might not be a human being. She might only look like one."

"And your witch," Brastigan retorted. "Is she human?"

Again Lottres was silent, unable to answer him.

Brastigan tied the mules' reins with the others. He began yanking on cinch straps, dropping laden saddle bags to the ground. He deliberately let one fall near Lottres's foot, forcing him to step back.

"Don't try to tell me about relationships when you're after *that* one," he snapped.

"I'm not after her." Lottres stuttered, flustered.

"Sure," Brastigan sneered. He straightened, looking down on his shorter brother. "You chase your woman and I'll chase mine."

Lottres stood a moment longer, too insulted to speak. Then he let out a hiss of breath between his teeth, and stalked off.

Brastigan glared at his brother's retreating back. If Lottres didn't like the truth, too bad. It was only what he deserved. Now he knew how it felt to have his advice ignored. Turn the girl into a doxy, indeed! Brastigan continued dragging saddles and bags off the tired mules. As he worked he glanced around the latest camp, where the men made busy with such comforts as they could have. Was that what they all thought, that he would use the girl and abandon her?

A shrill cry caught his attention. Brastigan looked up to see a screeching flurry in the evening air, beating wings and tearing claws. The falcon was fighting a raven! It wasn't a fair fight, since the raven bulked larger, but the falcon showed no fear. The two birds tumbled toward the ground and vanished into the treetops.

They reappeared moments later, wings beating upward again. Black feathers spiraled down, but the raven showed no sign of weakness. It gave a harsh shriek of hatred, and the falcon screamed in reply. Once again they dove at each other with talons outstretched.

Brastigan tore his eyes from the aerial battle. In the bags he was moving, he'd just seen... There! He yanked at the twine, tearing free a short bow from its wrapping of oiled canvas. These weren't weapons of war. The men had used them to hunt rabbits, in the leisurely days before they reached Hawkwing House. With one eye on the feather fight above, Brastigan strung the bow and grabbed a pair of arrows.

Pikarus must have had the same thought, for he appeared beside Brastigan. The dark prince stepped back, giving him room to find his own weapons. Then he planted his feet and nocked an arrow. Just as he drew the bowstring back to his ear, the raven and the falcon tumbled into the treetops again.

Brastigan waited, though his arms ached and his fingers burned where the cord dug into them. Branches waved wildly. Then a single winged shape emerged. Brastigan glimpsed black feathers, saw the raven's blade shaped beak. He loosed his arrow. Pikarus's bow snapped a heartbeat later. The raven swerved, but too late. The first arrow sent it spinning into the path of the second. It cartwheeled into the treetops, and then no movement was seen.

Pikarus and Brastigan shared glances, but with little triumph in them. The falcon hadn't reappeared. In a rare display of urgency, Yriatt picked up her skirts and ran into the forest. The two men jogged toward the center of camp, where the soldiers had gathered into a murmuring huddle.

Brastigan shouldered his way to Lottres's side, and demanded, "Does this mean what I think it does?"

Still clinging to his anger, Lottres answered with a terse nod. Brastigan felt his gut grow tight. The enemy they had been dodging had spied them out at last.

Pikarus was all business. "What should we do now?"

Lottres shrugged. His eyes were fixed on the shadowed trees. "Wait."

Pikarus didn't seem to like this evidence of his prince's dependence on the witch. Nor did Brastigan. They were soldiers, and didn't need some female telling them what to do.

While Lottres delayed, Brastigan looked around them. The evening's camp was in a shallow dell between two rounded hills. Large chunks of shale had broken away from the exposed faces, giving each a skirt of stones. Before them was a small meadow, where the tethered mules tore at tall grass. There was water, a tiny spring in the meadow, but it was very exposed. That could be a problem if an enemy force trapped them. The day was growing late. If they were going to move away from here, they didn't have much time to do it.

The men suddenly stopped talking, and Brastigan turned. Yriatt emerged from the trees, a bundle of bloody feathers cradled in the crook of one arm. Several men moved aside to let her pass, for she walked with her face downward, seeming not to care what lay before her. When she reached the place where the fire pit had been dug, she sank to her knees. Jarred by the motion, the falcon gave forth a pathetic creak of pain.

Despite himself, Brastigan felt pity to look on the once-proud thing. It panted and trembled. Deep gouges on its neck and breast poured real blood over the false gold of its feathers. Its wild mystique gone, it was just a wounded and helpless creature.

Surrounded by silent troops, Yriatt spoke no word, but gazed upon her wounded pet with a terrible calm.

Lottres knelt beside her to ask, softly, "Maess, is there nothing you can do?"

The witch's face seemed suddenly pinched and old. "Of course I could, but I must not."

Lottres straightened slightly. Brastigan shook his head. The falcon was obviously dying, and the witch didn't seem to care. Yet she hadn't taken her eyes from the stricken bird, either. Gently she stroked its stained feathers, ignoring the blood on her hands.

Both Pikarus and Javes shifted restlessly, and Lottres bent forward to try again.

Anticipating the question, Yriatt said, "There is no need to flee. We are not in immediate danger."

"Are you certain?" Pikarus asked.

"They will not be upon us so quickly as that," she answered in a flat voice. "They, too, require daylight to move."

The soldiers around them looked relieved to have even that much of a clear answer.

"Very well. We'll carry on here," Pikarus declared.

At his words the men began to disburse, returning to their duties with a haste borne of anxiety. Brastigan lingered a moment near the fire, where Lottres murmured something to Yriatt.

"I dare not reveal myself," Yriatt said in that same cold voice. "With my father held captive, Ysislaw's slaves will be watching for me to aid him. They may now suspect I am here, but since the raven was killed by arrows rather than magic, they will not be sure. Therefore Ysislaw will not turn from his course. If I were to act openly, with all my powers, he would sense it. It is not often he finds me with so few defenders. He would come at once to take me while I am vulnerable."

So all the witches and wizards could sense each other? They had to take her word for that, of course. Her concern seemed real enough, though fixated on herself. That must be why Yriatt sent her student, Shaelen, to Altannath: to shield herself from discovery.

"And if I were to act?" Lottres asked.

Yriatt shrugged. "The *eppagadrocca* would not recognize you. This would make them curious, but since they are already busy, they might not be able to investigate soon. I, however, would be known at once." Implacable eyes fixed on Lottres. "Above all, Ysislaw must not suspect I am here."

She turned back to her pet, and gave a kind of start. The falcon no longer panted, but lay limp in her arms. Its fierce gaze was fixed on emptiness. Just for a moment, Brastigan saw Yriatt's fingers tighten. Head bowed, she leaned forward and placed the falcon on the sticks that had been laid for the fire. She knelt close, as if for a kiss. The witch blew a soft breath into the kindling. There was an answering hiss, and the whole burst into flames.

Brastigan stepped backward. He was surprised to feel a genuine emotion for the falcon. For all it had turned his life upside down, he had to admit it had been useful in the past days. Then he told himself it was just one less problem, and turned away. With that on the fire, it would be a while before any cooking was done.

Brastigan strode back to his own duties, unloading the mules and staking them closer to the camp. As he carried in the baggage, he saw Yriatt methodically adding wood to the blaze. The horns on her head looked crooked as dead snags against the firelight. Lottres sat beside her, loyal in her loss. The girl was there, too. The faintest frown creased her forehead as she watched Yriatt. Brastigan wondered how much she understood of what had happened.

Above them, a sooty plume rose like raven feathers against the sunset sky. That could serve as a marker, bringing the enemy to them all the sooner. Seeing the rigid set of Yriatt's shoulders, Brastigan decided not to mention it. He gave the two horses an extra rub down.

After a cursory meal, for Yriatt maintained her vigil and no cooking got done after all, Brastigan took the girl over where his bedroll was laid out. The braids Yriatt had put in her hair were getting fuzzy, so he took them out and put in new ones. This time, he used the Urulai style.

Braiding the hair was a social ritual, a time to talk over past events and plan things to come. Or, as Brastigan recalled, for Joal to warn him against repeating some infraction or other. The girl was no talker, but at least he had the pleasure of stroking her silken hair. Brastigan used a set of spare beads from his pack, red ones. The girl seemed entranced.

Then, defying his brother's disapproval, Brastigan laid out a place for the girl beside his own bedroll. No matter what anyone thought, he wanted her nearby. He was troubled by the sense that she might be snatched away just as abruptly as the falcon. Or he might die. After all, they were at war.

The girl seemed excited to be resting beside him. She wouldn't lie still, but insisted on feeling over his face and hair the way she had done with his hands a few days before. First she fingered the beads in his hair, and then the ones in hers.

This was something Yriatt might notice, so Brastigan brushed her hands away. "Lie down," he growled. "Go to sleep."

She obeyed, and then he felt sorry for himself.

* * *

"Mother?" Therula hesitated in the doorway to Alustra's chambers. She blinked in the darkness.

The curtains were drawn, leaving the room dimly lit, and the air had a faint, musty odor. Therula shuddered, reminded all too clearly of the last time she entered a darkened chamber at mid-morning. Yet she also knew it was wrong for Alustra to immure herself here, as if she had died, too.

"Mother, where are you?" Therula called anxiously.

"Here," Alustra's voice answered faintly.

Therula should have felt better hearing her mother's voice, but she didn't. Anger made her heels pound harder as she swept across the room and wrenched at the draperies. The heavy brocade fabric seemed to actively resist being pulled aside. Once she had the curtains open, Therula turned the window latch and pushed the pane outward. She could fairly hear the rush of stale air leaving the room.

Blinking against the brilliant daylight, Therula turned back to the room. Alustra sat up in bed, still wearing a linen nightgown. The fine, white fabric only emphasized the redness around the queen's eyes. Her dark hair, too, was spun through with a lacework of silver.

"Are you all right, Mother?" Therula dragged a chair to the bedside and sat in it.

"I am fine," Alustra answered. It didn't sound as if she meant it.

"Then what are you doing, lying in bed?" Therula demanded, more sharply than she intended. "Just because Father is gone doesn't mean your duty is over. The people need to see you."

Alustra's eyes veered away. Therula swallowed what she meant to say next. Instead, she caught her mother in a fierce hug.

It wasn't just mourning that kept the queen shut up in her apartments. At least, not for Unferth alone. Two days ago, another terrible blow had fallen. Alustra's most faithful retainer, Tarther, was dead. He had been knocked from his horse during a training exercise and broken his neck. His body was being returned to Tanix on a fast galley, as of yesterday's tide.

It was a stupid accident, really. Coming so soon after the loss of Alustra's royal station, Therula knew it made everything much harder. No one had ever had cause to think there was anything more between them than servant and master, yet Tarther had been closer to Alustra in some ways than Unferth himself.

The queen's silent decline was evident in the pitiless daylight flooding the chamber. Even the rich furnishings seemed to have lost some of their luster. The handmaidens who waited on a queen's every breath had drifted away. Perhaps that was to be expected. It still seemed unfair. Alustra had lived in Crutham for more than thirty-five years. Despite countless indignities, she steadfastly ministered to a nation she often despised. After all this, she was left alone.

A rustling in the doorway announced the arrival of Alustra's lone remaining attendant. Margura bowed briefly to Alustra and Therula, then carried a covered tray to a small table near the bed.

"I have brought your majesty a light breakfast." Margura spoke gently, as if she addressed a child. "Will you take it now?"

Alustra nodded. "Bring it here."

"And your highness?" Margura looked to Therula.

"No, thank you."

Margura uncovered the tray, revealing sliced bread, soft cheese, and smoked fish. She poured tea for Alustra and deftly laid fish and cheese over the bread.

Seeing that Therula watched her, Margura murmured apologetically, "The queen sleeps often. I try not to disturb her during these difficult times."

"Don't let her sleep all day," Therula said curtly. She didn't like the implication that her mother was growing frail. Margura regarded her with innocent surprise. Therula told her mother, "You are still a queen. You must act like one."

Alustra regarded her dully. "My dear, I must be realistic."

"Realistic?" Therula bit back. Never had she heard her proud mother sound so tired, so... defeated.

Alustra ate what Margura gave her and didn't answer. Oh, what Therula wanted to say! Especially to Oskar, who never deigned to visit and console his own mother. But Therula knew she was little better. Far from confronting Oskar with his neglect, she could hardly bring herself to sit in the same room with him.

"You do have the right to request your own residence," Margura murmured consolingly. "Someplace quiet, where you can take time for yourself."

The words startled Therula from her distraction.

"Leave Harburg?" Therula fairly shouted. "Absurd! A queen doesn't leave her capital."

"It is her majesty's right." Margura looked wounded, as if she couldn't believe Therula misunderstood her loyalties. "Hasn't she earned a bit of privacy?"

Therula merely glared at Margura. How could this... this strumpet pretend to be faithful, all the while trying to isolate Alustra further?

"A small manor would be nice," Alustra mused, as if she hadn't heard what Therula said.

"It is beautiful in Firice," Margura quickly suggested. "Have you seen the waterfalls along the River Tharow? They are lovely. In spring, when the orchards are in bloom—"

"That's much too close to Carthell," Therula argued. With war likely, what could the girl be thinking?

"There are other places," Margura demurred. "Your majesty must have seen many restful places as you traveled through the countryside."

"*Gerfalkan*," Therula thought. She couldn't help it. Let Alustra choose a new home in Gerfalkan, and Therula would beg to come with her. Anything to be farther from Oskar and her own guilt.

A rapid knocking interrupted her thoughts. Margura went to the door, leaving Therula to gaze at her mother and hide her dismay. Surely Alustra couldn't be serious. It sounded like she intended to banish herself from public life. How could she, after so many years of service? What would Therula do without her?

Just as Therula began to wonder what was keeping Margura, the handmaiden hurried back to the bedside.

"Your majesty, the king has sent for you." Margura spoke softly, urgently. She glanced at Therula. "Your highness as well, I'm sure. If you would finish that, your majesty, I will prepare a gown for court."

"Why?" Therula demanded.

Margura had already turned away to open Alustra's wardrobe. Therula nearly missed the gleam in her eye of some strong emotion, perhaps fear.

"A messenger has arrived," Margura said. She drew one dress out of the cabinet, shook her head, and pushed it back in. "He rode day and night from Glawern. Crutham has been invaded."

"Carthell?" Alustra rapped out. For a moment, she looked like her old self, self-assured and indignant at the treachery. Margura continued shaking her head.

"No, your majesty. Sillets."

Therula heard herself gasp. "Sillets? I thought they meant to negotiate for trade." And Lottres's voice echoed in her memory, saying that Hawkwing House was in the north, near the Silletsian border.

Alustra sighed deeply and rose from the bed. It seemed to take real effort. "Sometimes, my dear, there is little difference between an ambassador and a spy," she said. "Clearly the Silletsian was seeking information, not trade, but don't worry too much. Crutham has faced this before. We have always prevailed on the battlefield." She clasped Therula's hands briefly, then turned away. "That one is fine, Margura. Don't fuss about it. I'm coming."

"Yes, but..." Therula stopped. She swallowed heavily and murmured, "Yes, Mother. Excuse me."

A familiar sense of gloom closed over Therula as she hurried to her own chambers. Pikarus was in the middle of something terrible after all. Somehow, she felt she had known this would happen.

CHAPTER THIRTEEN
THE BONE MEN

BRASTIGAN dreamed of the girl. Her cold fingers touched his eyes, his neck. He turned away, but still she was there, gently feeling his forehead, his nose. He awoke feeling exasperated, his groin hard and tight. Even as he rolled over, scolding words on his lips, he realized his mistake. The girl wasn't touching him. She lay still, wrapped in whatever dreams she might have. It was raining, and he needed to use the latrine.

When his head had cleared enough to walk without stumbling, he went there. Returning, Brastigan yawned hugely. He knelt to get Victory and strolled toward the dim swath of the meadow.

It was very early morning. Compared to the bite of a mountain sunrise, the air was mild here. Fading stars and layers of shadowy gray described the predawn world. The whitish clouds which had birthed the rain glided southward, trailing wisps of fog behind them.

The sky soon stopped its spitting, and the eastern horizon took on a hint of purple. The griffins began their morning concert. It sounded farther off today. As the clouds blew off, mountains appeared, squat and rounded against the sky. A broadening of the land to the north suggested lowlands rather than more mountains. Altannath lay before them, and whatever power held Master Ymell prisoner.

Of course, they had to get there before they worried about him.

Soft stirrings told Brastigan the griffin serenade was rousing the men. He moved back through camp, taking care not to step on anyone. The faint light showed Yriatt and Lottres both lying near the fire ring. It was good to know they actually did sleep, though why he should worry over his brother, Brastigan couldn't say. However, they both sat up as he approached.

Lottres was not one to wake quickly, so Brastigan didn't speak immediately. He prodded the fire into life. Yriatt and Lottres watched sourly, as if the flames crackled especially to annoy them. Both their faces had a stiff and crusty look, like a wet rag that has been dropped and allowed to dry where it fell.

Through smoke that made the morning air shudder, Brastigan slanted a look at his brother. "Did you get enough sleep?"

"I'm fine," Lottres grunted. He ground the heels of his hands over his eyes in a way that made Brastigan doubt his words.

"And you?" Brastigan asked of Yriatt. She wore her horned headdress even when sleeping, he noticed. Crazy female.

She shrugged the irrelevancy aside. "Enough to serve."

Her eyes lingered on the fire. Remembering what last burned there, Brastigan stared at the coals suspiciously. He was glad to see no shape of feather or bone remained among the ashes.

Before he could think better of it, he muttered, "I'm sorry. About the bird."

Lottres blinked over his crooked fingers, as if he couldn't credit his hearing. Yriatt regarded Brastigan with something akin to respect. She nodded slowly.

"As with all beasts, I knew he must die before me, but this was unexpected." Her voice was slightly hoarse. "From here, the land changes. We will have no more trees to shelter us. I was counting on his eyes as our defense." Lottres moved closer, offering comfort, but she shrugged him away. "What's done is done. We shall go forward, as we must."

"Could you take another?" Lottres asked. "Or, could I?"

Yriatt smiled wryly. "It is too soon for that, *Thaeme*." Lottres nodded, downcast.

Brastigan cleared his throat. With an effort at nonchalance, he asked, "So, you were listening again last night. Hear anything interesting?"

Where is the enemy, he meant. Yriatt seemed to understand that.

"They come," she said.

"Soon?" Brastigan asked. She nodded.

Brastigan glanced over his shoulder. The mules drowsed in the meadow and wisps of fog rose from the springs in the gray light. There was nothing here to help them if they were set upon.

"If we move, we may avoid them," Lottres suggested.

"Let's move," Brastigan decided.

He tossed more wood onto the fire and rose. Looking over the whole camp, he called out, "Everyone up!"

A kind of collective groan arose from the sleeping men, but training compelled their obedience. The camp was soon busy with men sitting up, stretching, shuffling to the latrine. Returning to his own spot, Brastigan gently shook his companion awake. She smiled up at him with eyes more blue than the lightening sky. It made him remember his dream.

He scarcely fed her two bites when Javes walked by with his duffel over his shoulder. "You ready? I could use a hand."

"Be right there," he answered. Brastigan rolled the blankets that served as his bed and stuffed his cloak into his own duffel. Then he turned to the girl's bedroll. She watched his hurried movements carefully, so he told her, "I'll be right back. Stay here."

The caution wasn't really necessary. She had never moved on her own before. Brastigan saddled mules for the soldiers and brought them into line, while Javes loaded the pack beasts. By the time Brastigan led the girl's horse to her, Pikarus was burying the fire. To his surprise, Brastigan found she had eaten the rest of her cheese without him telling her to do it.

While the men huffed and hurried, Yriatt stood still, horns high, facing north. Brastigan looked over his mule's ears, where Lottres sat in the saddle, watching his mistress with rapt attention.

"Something?" he asked.

Lottres nodded, a quick jerk of his chin. Before he could speak, Yriatt hurried to take her horse's reins.

"I've found Shaelen," she announced to no one in particular. "Evading the enemy is well and good, but we must not be cut off from her. Come, we've little time."

They crossed the meadow quickly. The mules left a trampled path. That would provide a handy marker to any who followed, but there was no help for it.

They found their familiar stream and a shallow spot to cross it, then struck east toward the nearest line of hills. The riders now passed beneath trees which seemed like spindly saplings compared to the forest giants they had seen a few days ago. This land had an open feeling, with sparse cover. It made them vulnerable. Brastigan wasn't the only one who glanced upward, watching for the black wings of spies above them.

They crossed as much rock as dirt now, level sheets like coarse mud gone dry. At least they didn't raise much dust. All the hills were crowned with weathered stones. Unlike the sharp gray granite of the high peaks, these were low and blunt, the color of bleached bones. The odd bloody stripe added color. Stone fins and fangs thrust this way and that, like a madman's castle. Penetrating such a prickly barrier seemed impossible, but Yriatt remained confident.

"We cannot cross the valley," she said when Lottres asked. "The land is too open. There is a pass before us, and then we circle to the south."

With the broadening light, Brastigan kept his vigilant watch. Even the girl's adoring gaze couldn't relieve the tension in his gut. Higher they climbed, risking exposure with every mule's step. Looking back and downward, he could see winged things moving in the treetops. Black things. The rocks loomed above them. From a distance they had seemed solid, like the scales on a lizard's back, but close up there were many breaks and crannies between them. Yriatt led a sharp turn, and they entered a cleft in the rocks. That would give them some cover. Brastigan relaxed, a little.

Even as he did, a sound echoed among the rocks. It wasn't a raven's gargle, but the shrill rasping of a crow. Two long caws and a short coughing sound. The men reined in, looking around. Only rocky spires stood above them. There was no sign of their winged betrayer. Farther off, there came a faint echo. Word was being passed.

Yriatt kneed her horse forward, and the others hurried to follow. Some strung bows and rode with heads cocked, ready to silence the spy. Mocking caws followed as they wound upward on the knees of the rocky hill. They scratched at Brastigan's nerves. Hooves grated on solid stone with a din that announced their presence as much as the crows did. Then came a new sound, through the riot of hooves over stone: the belling of hounds.

Yriatt paused often, listening. She might continue ahead, or take a turn away from the cries. The way the rocks echoed, those ominous sounds could come from anywhere. Now they mounted a ridge, feeling the sun's heat reflected from the pale stones. As they topped that rise the baying came suddenly clearer, and all too near.

Brastigan spurred forward, momentarily drawing even with Yriatt. "We're being tracked like wild game. If you know this area, find us a place to stand."

Because he bestrode a mule, the shorter of the steeds, Brastigan had the disconcerting sense that she, with her horned hat, was now taller. He didn't like it.

The witch merely said, "Perhaps you're right," and urged her horse forward. Impatiently, he fell into place behind her.

The way down was steeper than up had been, and chancy over the smooth rocks, yet they didn't dare take it slow and cautious. They rode for the scant tree cover. Then it was too late for hiding. Brastigan saw movement through a gap in the rocks—men on foot, running up the slope toward them.

"Hold!" Brastigan reined in, and the racing mules piled up behind him, jostling and squealing.

"We're found!" Pikarus echoed, struggling to control his startled mount. "Circle up! Get the pack beasts in the center! Soldiers to the outside!"

As the men frantically sorted themselves out, Brastigan stood in the saddle, counting the oncoming enemy. Racing at the fore were a trio of black dogs. These were no floppy-eared, fawning hounds. They had the heavy shoulders and docked tails of fighting dogs. A few yards off, they skidded to a halt and stood bristling, cropped ears pressed flat to their skulls. They showed no fear, but stared with the utter intensity only a dog can possess.

Impressive as they were, the more serious problem was the oncoming file of soldiers. He counted eight, twelve, seventeen, twenty. Gangly fellows, wearing leather caps and carrying swords, but with little body armor. They came at a good pace despite the cant of the hill. A mounted man followed them, armored and wearing a surcoat with the dragon of Sillets. An officer, no doubt, commanding the footmen.

Brastigan turned his mule to see the soldiers form a rough crescent between the mules and the onrushing foe. He looked twice, and then he was sure. The dogs weren't staring at him. Their malevolence was fixed on Yriatt.

That was as good a reason as any to spur to her side. Lottres was there, of course, looking like he had no idea what to do in this situation.

"It's you they want," Brastigan said to Yriatt. "Do you fight?"

"I will shoot," Yriatt answered. "Anything else is only at greatest need."

He lowered his head for a moment, gritting his teeth. What was the point of having a witch along if she didn't use her powers?

Lottres looked torn. Combat had never been his skill, for all he had Joal's teachings. Yet it was a man's place to fight. There were only nine soldiers on the Cruthan side, Brastigan included, to twenty of the enemy.

Beside them, the girl looked alarmed at the confusion around her. Much as he wanted to, Brastigan knew he couldn't stay with her. And Lottres still held mum.

"Stay here, then," he told his brother. "Protect the women."

Lottres looked both relieved and guilty, and Yriatt coolly put in, "He can calm the animals, if that would help."

"It would help a lot," Brastigan told her. The mules were hardy, but they were still just beasts. The soldiers couldn't fight while controlling them, and it was no good if they panicked and ran off. Brastigan grabbed Victory, his helmet and shield, and swung down from the saddle, tossing the reins to Lottres.

"Take care of the girl," he told his brother. "The witch says we need her."

Lottres frowned, maybe objecting to the rude classification of his teacher, but Yriatt ignored it.

"Come, *Thaeme*, I will show you how," she said. The girl turned in the saddle, trying to keep Brastigan in sight as Lottres led her horse away. He watched her a moment more, and then turned back to business.

Which was drawing nearer by the moment. Brastigan strapped on the helmet and shield, and stamped to loosen his saddle-stiff legs. Around him, men were stretching, shrugging, cutting the air with swords. Brastigan checked their line and found it troublesome. With so much space to cover, they couldn't stand as close as he would have liked. He located Pikarus, directly on his right, and Javes, four men down on the left. Turning, he focused his vision over the rim of his shield and fixed his attention on the approaching foemen.

They were a sorry lot, not the kind of force he expected from an empire of Sillets's reputation. Their swords were of crude workmanship, and they had no shields or body armor. Threadbare clothing in mismatched patterns hung over angles of bone. Their sole uniform was a scanty red tabard.

Aglend, on his left, muttered, "This is an army?"

Brastigan had to agree, except his initial impression that these were youths had been wrong. Brastigan knew skinny—he was skinny. These men weren't skinny. They were gaunt, shriveled flesh corded over their bones, and with them came a peculiar odor like that of something long dead. What he didn't understand was how starving men could mount the rocky slope at such speed.

He answered, "Don't take them lightly. If they serve the black magicians, they may be more than they seem."

Still they came on, silent except for the tramp of ill fitted boots. No war cries to rouse the blood, no warrior's scowl. No expression at all.

The bone men were scant yards away, now. Brastigan drew deep breaths, full of waiting. His muscles felt tight, coiled. Unlike his brother, Brastigan had never been afraid of a fight. He flexed his fingers eagerly, shifting their grip on sword and shield.

"The black tower will never fall!" Brastigan shouted.

Farther down the line, Javes cried, "Cut them down!"

A roar went up from the Cruthan line, then a crashing as steel met steel. Brastigan stepped between two of the foes, blocking to the left with his shield and to the right with Victory. Right away, he knew this wouldn't be easy. Brastigan had always been faster than the heavy set Cruthan men, able to avoid their clumsy blows. He had no such advantage now. The bone men were just as fast, and very strong. He blocked two blows that left his sword hand tingling, then lunged in return. He twisted Victory, forcing the enemy blade aside, and jabbed at the gap in the bone man's defense. The point struck exactly where he aimed it—and stuck!

It was like stabbing into a chunk of wood. Victory's tip scarcely penetrated the leathery skin. But there was no body jerk, no cry of pain, no blood. The enemy brought his weapon around, ready to retaliate. Brastigan managed to wrench Victory free and fell back a pace, reassessing. Maybe he'd struck a rib?

The first cries of pain went up along the Cruthan line. Pikarus was crying, "Stand fast! Let them come to us!"

Brastigan tried again. He blocked right with Victory, then turned as the man on his left raised his weapon. He lunged at the exposed throat, this time, and saw the blade strike true. The enemy's blade descended, but Brastigan raised his shield and pushed closer. As he felt the punch of Victory shearing through the man's throat he shoved with his shield and turned again, blocking an enemy strike from the right.

Even as he raised his shield and positioned himself to guard against the right-hand foe, he realized the one on the left hadn't fallen. He blocked automatically, staring at the black line, angled slightly upward, across the bone man's leathery neck. This time he knew he'd struck true. The man should have fallen. But still there was no blood.

Brastigan fell back again, glancing toward Pikarus. The sergeant was hard pressed, his face a snarling mask of war. Brastigan knew his face bore the same distorted expression. He aimed a cut at the neck of the bone man pressing Pikarus back. Again, he struck clean and hard. Again, there was no reaction.

Over the irregular beating of swords, he called to Pikarus, "What do you think? I got a clean thrust to the throat, and nothing."

"They're not men. They don't bleed." Pikarus grunted back as he swung his sword. Brastigan could tell he'd struck one of the bone men in the chest, but it did no more good than Brastigan's throat slash. "They don't die!"

Well, if finesse was out, brute force would have to do.

"Chop off their sword arms!" Brastigan yelled to anyone who could hear. "Cut them down like trees if you have to!"

Of course, that was easy to say. The bone men's withered skin was so tough, he could see why their masters didn't bother with mail. But any strategy was better than nothing. Brastigan and Pikarus stood shoulder to shoulder. Working in turn, blocking for each other, they managed to sever the wiry limbs. First one, then another, then a third wizened arm fell to the dusty rocks.

Still the bone men stood. Still they fought. With just one arm they grappled and grabbed, dragging shields down or holding back sword blades with fingers that felt no pain.

"Try the legs?" Pikarus called. After much hacking, they managed to hamstring two of their four foes. Even then they tried to come back, pushing themselves forward on their hands. Brastigan kicked one off by itself and straddled its skinny body. He chopped its head off before it could turn over. You couldn't say it truly died, but it finally stopped moving.

Pikarus turned aside, aiding Yugo, who struggled against three bone men. Brastigan worked his way toward Javes. Beheading was easier from the unprotected rear. Of course, it meant he was by himself and vulnerable, too. Brastigan stopped thinking for a while, just chopping and dancing away from crippled enemies. Others didn't fare as well. One man was pinned down by two one-armed bone men while a third stabbed him. Another wasn't moving at all.

"The black tower will never fall!" Brastigan cried as he charged to that man's aid.

It was a long, ugly, exhausting battle. Brastigan had been in fights before, barroom brawls and bandit raids, but those were against men—bleeding, feeling pain, just as desperate to survive as he was. This one was different, so brutal and quiet. The bone men suffered in grisly silence, as if they didn't feel their arms being hacked off, their legs cut from under them. How could any creature suffer such wounds and not notice?

At the end of it, his sword arm burned with exhaustion. His shield hand was numb from the power of his grip. Brastigan gulped in dusty air, felt the gambeson beneath his armor sodden with sweat. The ground was strewn with body parts: bone men writhing like enormous worms. Even now, the crippled, crawling things tried to come at them. Most disturbing was the complete absence of blood. There should have been blood. Brastigan, who had never shied from battle, felt his stomach turn at the cleanliness of this carnage.

Only when he stopped to breathe did Brastigan understand the true horror. For beneath the leather caps were falls of stringy matted hair. Black hair, just like Brastigan's.

It was Pikarus who put his outrage into words. "Can those be Urulai?"

"They would never serve Sillets!" Brastigan snarled.

But hundreds of warriors were missing in Urland, their fates unknown after twenty years. Somehow they must have been enslaved by sorcery. That would explain their poor condition, for who would concern themselves over an army of slaves?

For years, Brastigan had heard stories about Sillets and its evil magic. He had never truly understood. Now, he loathed Sillets and its undying king with an intense, personal feeling. Whoever created such monstrous beings deserved to die.

Brastigan needed something else to look at. He glanced around. The mules had been backed up against a fin of rock and stood in a huddle, heads down, ears hanging slack. Lottres sat in the midst of them, the reins loose in his hand. His face, oddly calm, gazed into nothing. Yriatt sat tall and alert with a hunting bow across her lap, an arrow ready. The three dogs lay in heaps of black fur. When did that happen? Brastigan hadn't heard her bowstring snap.

Behind both of them, the girl sat on her horse with an expression of horror. He strode to her side, wondering if the fragile creature understood what was happening. He hoped it was just the noise that made her look that way, not the grisly work he had been doing.

Brastigan patted her knee. "I'm fine." It seemed to calm her.

Finding his own mule, Brastigan got a waterskin. He took two deep gulps, and added, to his brother, "Thanks for all your hard work."

Lottres didn't respond, but Yriatt said in a brittle tone, "This is not over."

She was looking past the girl, past Brastigan. He spat another mouthful of water onto the stones and turned. Pikarus helped a limping Roari toward his mule, while Javes methodically struck heads off bone men. Then, beyond Javes, came noise and movement. A pair of black dogs burst over the hilltop. Yriatt's bow sang, and one of them tumbled over with a shriek. Behind them, a full squad of bone men crested the hill.

"Get back in line!" Pikarus shouted. Javes leaped to obey.

Brastigan dropped his waterskin and sprang forward. His heart hammered in a way it never had before. At least one man was dead, and it was a miracle that was the only loss. Two others needed help to stand. That made seven on the Cruthan side, if the injured men could fight, against creatures harder to kill than cockroaches. And they were already tired.

But giving up wasn't possible. Javes and Pikarus called orders. The soldiers scrambled for their places, kicking dead bone men out of the way. Yriatt's bow sent arrows terribly close to their heads, trying to remove the second howling mutt. Brastigan took his place at the end of the line.

"For the black tower!" His voice was a hoarse bark. Victory felt heavy as a log of wood. His speed was gone. But he didn't feel afraid. He just had a job to do.

This time Brastigan hardly had the chance to strike a blow. Something else struck first, grabbing his leg as he stepped forward to swing his blade. He struck hard, then looked down. One of the bone men had escaped Javes's reckoning. It held him by the knee. Brastigan kicked, tried to pull away, blocked an incoming blow, and tried to cut off the creature's arm to get free.

He lost his balance and fell awkwardly. The flat rocks made for a hard landing, and a shaft of pain ran up his arm. Biting back a cry, Brastigan curled inward, covering himself with his shield as best he could.

When the pain cleared enough to think, he raised his head. He was nose to nose with the one-armed bone man. He drew a lungful of its fetid odor, stared into the shriveled pits of its eyes. Brastigan jerked back from the unpleasant proximity, tried to lift Victory and found he was lying on top of it. More bone men had both his legs, dragged at his shield, rained blows on his back. His armor did its job and kept the dull edges at bay.

Through the thumping of blows on his helmet, he heard Javes bellow, "Protect the prince!" But Brastigan knew with cold clarity that the other soldiers were all in bad spots. It wasn't likely anyone could help him.

He kicked again, struggling to free himself. When that was no use, he rolled onto his back enough to free Victory and jab upward. It was awkward, but it was all he could do.

Vaguely, behind the Cruthan line, he heard strange, barking cries. Then came a loud snarl, like water poured on a pan of hot grease. After that, a rush of hot wind. The air boiled and churned above him. Bone men went flying like rag dolls. Cruthan men were shouting and swearing.

At last, Brastigan could move his legs! He rolled over, finding Javes above him. The soldier relaxed a little, seeing him still moving, and offered a hand up. He took it gladly.

"It's about time she did something," Brastigan grumbled.

"What did you say?" Javes yelled, as if he couldn't hear himself speak.

Bone men and dead dogs were everywhere. Most lay broken, though a few picked themselves up and came on again. Pikarus was calling to his troops, trying to get them in order. Brastigan heard a racket behind him, and turned to look at the new trouble.

The noise had shaken the mules out of whatever spell held them. They rolled their eyes and danced, squealing in terror. The girl was the source of the weird barking cries. She stared at him and shrieked again and again, unable to put real words to her fear.

Meanwhile, Yriatt struggled to guide her horse through the turmoil. Reaching the girl, she roughly grabbed her shoulder. All composure gone, the witch's voice was high and hard. "What are you doing? Stop!"

"Hey! Let go of her!" Brastigan shouted. That was his girl the witch manhandled. Javes shouted beside him, and he had to turn to face the foe again.

It wasn't easy to watch both situations at once. Mostly he fought, parrying blows and giving back as many as he could. In snatches, he saw Yriatt raise her hands. The beasts stopped their skittish prancing. When he next looked, Lottres was talking urgently, in a grieved tone. Telling tales on Brastigan, no doubt. Both their faced turned to Brastigan, and he spared a moment for a mocking wave.

Most important, between bone men and sword blows, was the girl. She clutched her horse's mane and stared, her face drawn and anxious. She must have had quite a scare when the bone men pulled him down, to make her do... whatever it was she did.

Because he knew it wasn't Yriatt who made the air boil. It was the girl. She wasn't perfect and pure at all. Some kind of witchery touched her, just like Lottres.

Frustration gave Brastigan new strength. He hit the bone men harder, faster, wanting to cut them, beat them, because if he looked at his brother now he might do something much worse. Save his sword for his enemies; that's what he had to do. It wasn't easy.

The first battle had seemed to take forever. This one was over too quickly. When the last bone man fell, Brastigan stood aching all over and cold as the grave.

Javes hadn't left his side. Now he asked, "Your highness, are you all right?"

"Get the men up," Brastigan snarled.

Javes jerked back, and threw a hasty salute. Brastigan prowled the field, looking for a moving enemy to lop something off of. Those who didn't move, he stomped on with vengeful kicks.

When no further targets offered themselves, Brastigan looked over the battlefield. Javes was helping bandage Yugo's bloody shoulder. Pikarus rolled a fallen man over and knelt beside him. It was Aglend. As Brastigan watched, Pikarus took up the dead man's sword. He pulled a ring from Aglend's hand and cut a lock of his hair, placing these in a small leather bag. He drew it tight and tied the ends about the haft of the sword.

Brastigan's fury turned cold. Numbly he cleaned Victory and sheathed her. Aglend and Roari, both dead. Their bodies would have to be left behind. He knew that. The battered Cruthan force had no way to care for them. And Brastigan knew full well how lucky he was to live out the battle. If not for the girl, it could have been him staring sightless into the hostile sky.

He trudged back to his mule, and finally looked up at the distraught girl. She gazed down, joy lighting her face through tear tracks and dust. Her lips moved, but she no longer tried to speak. Cursed thing that she was, Brastigan had to hold himself back from kissing her. Too many eyes about, judging. Instead he clasped her hands, forgiving her already.

Yriatt wasn't so tolerant. She stared down at Brastigan from her horse, eyes dark and terrible beneath her crooked horns. "What have you done?" she demanded.

"You're the witch," Brastigan snapped back. He loosened the girl's hands and swung into the saddle. "You tell me."

Lottres made a coughing sound. "This isn't the time for games, Brastigan."

"I'm not playing," he answered. "I'm no magician. If she doesn't know what's going on, how should I?"

Yriatt's dark hair crackled with the energy of her anger. Lottres tensed with fury, hands balling into fists. Before either could speak, Pikarus shouldered his mule between them.

"We cannot stay," he said with quiet urgency. "Everyone is upset, I know, but we must move on. Please."

"My thoughts exactly," Brastigan responded cheerfully, baiting Yriatt. "Do you lead, or shall I?"

Yriatt stared at Brastigan, relenting not a hair in her rage. "This is not over," she said.

She turned her horse, and they were away.

CHAPTER FOURTEEN
SHADOW WOMEN

TRUST Brastigan to ruin everything, Lottres thought fiercely. He and Yriatt had had everything under control. Especially the mules. Lottres had felt what Yriatt did. He had copied her and held the mules all on his own. Even if they were merely beasts, Lottres had reveled in his power— until Brastigan turned his triumph to ashes.

He and Yriatt had been so careful to conceal their magic. There might have been a chance to beat back the assault and keep the *eppagadrocca* from sensing their presence. But no, Brastigan had to play the hero and nearly get himself killed, and the girl went mad with fear. How she got such power, Lottres didn't know, hollow as she was. What mattered was that the enemy knew for certain there were wizards approaching who weren't *eppagadrocca*. Whatever danger they had faced before, it was doubled now.

The Cruthans made the best speed possible, tending southward when they could. Through gaps in the stony palisades, Lottres caught glimpses of Altannath. It wasn't a friendly sight.

The valley below was broad, shallow and bare of trees. Clumps of tawny grass and heaps of crumbled stone were scattered around a green lake that shimmered beneath the sun. Near the center of the barren vale was a jutting butte, easily taller than the hills ringing in the valley. At its knees were a cluster of tents and a makeshift corral. Weather had dulled the crimson cloth, but there was no mistaking the standard of Sillets.

Along the lake-shore, patterns were scratched into the dry ground: a grid work of paths between blocks of flattened grass. This had been a much larger encampment until recently. Of more immediate concern, however, were the plumes of dust swirling above the valley. Lines of bone men crept beneath them, patient and mindless as worms.

Lottres could feel the *eppagadrocca,* too. He heard bits of their talk, and felt them probing, seeking. His rage against Brastigan could be a weakness, Lottres knew—something the enemy might detect. He kept his guard up while Yriatt shielded both herself and the girl. Whatever Lottres had to say to Brastigan would have to wait.

* * *

The riders descended quickly, losing themselves in the rocky warrens. Anger and confusion rode with them, filling the air like the dust the mules raised. Mostly it was the girl that tangled Brastigan's thoughts. Whenever he turned toward her she was looking back, anxiously, as if he might vanish from her sight.

When she looked at him like that, he knew exactly what she wanted. It was the same thing he wanted of any female he kept company with. Brastigan had never waited for any woman. If she wasn't prepared to get physical, he moved on. Now he wondered if he had been waiting, after all. Waiting for the girl to be ready.

And yet, this one was worth waiting for. She was like a flower, opening from a tightly closed bud, so perfect in her innocence and silence. Her growing awareness of the world around her was a kind of revelation. Brastigan saw himself, through her eyes, as a supreme figure, admired and adored. Whatever his relationships with women had been before, none of them had ever made him feel worthy of such regard.

Rocks served to conceal the Cruthan force, and they held no tracks. Perhaps that was why they were able to outpace the enemy. Yet no one was in the mood to take it slowly. They pressed the animals hard, until even the Urulai horses were flagging.

Brastigan called to Lottres, whose mule lagged behind Yriatt's horse, "If we don't take pity on these beasts, we'll be walking!"

Over his shoulder, Lottres gave Brastigan a look of supreme irritation. He nodded, but didn't speak. Brastigan shrugged to himself. Let Lottres go ahead and ignore him. He'd soon find out what happened when you overtaxed your steed.

A while later, though, Yriatt turned aside. Soon they came to a sluggish stream, its banks thick with scrubby willow trees. They halted at last, and crowded the mules beneath the trees.

It wasn't easy getting down from the saddle. Brastigan's muscles had grown cold as he rode, leaving him stiff and sore all over. The others seemed to feel little better. Javes had his hands full keeping the beasts from guzzling the tepid water. Pikarus got the wounded men down to rest under the trees. Both Henrick and Yugo seemed lucid, though Yugo's blood had soaked through his bandages. Brastigan reminded himself to speak with them soon. They deserved to be thanked for their efforts.

Considering recent events, however, Brastigan didn't want to leave the girl alone for long. Limping like an old man, he went to get her down from her horse. She practically fell into his arms, drawing fresh complaints from his many bruises. It hardly seemed to matter. For a moment Brastigan couldn't move. It felt so good to have a girl clinging to him that way. He gazed into her trusting eyes, knowing she would gladly give him whatever he wanted. Whatever a man wanted.

He swallowed hard, and gently moved her back.

Then came Yriatt's imperious voice. "Give me the girl."

Brastigan turned, confronting the witch in the shifting shadows of the willow trees. Yriatt was haughty with anger. Lottres was at her shoulder, harried yet smug. Like Oskar preparing to bully someone, Brastigan thought, and that was a comparison he had never thought to make.

Brastigan attempted a pleasant tone. "No, I will not. But I will talk to you about it."

"She is under my protection," Yriatt replied. Her lips hardly moved as she spoke. "Give her to me."

"I said, no," Brastigan answered. "She isn't a thing to be handed around."

"You act like she is," Lottres interrupted. "Like she's a toy." His eyes gleamed. Brastigan thought he must be enjoying that he was right, and his brother wrong.

It grated, but Brastigan knew his brother was partly correct. The girl had been the witch's creature to begin with, but no force on earth was going to make him walk away from her now.

"I told you, it isn't like that," Brastigan said, holding to his temper. "I'm trying to consider her feelings."

In a choked voice, Yriatt said, "She is not supposed to have feelings. If she does, then you are to blame."

"Not have feelings?" he scowled. "Everyone has feelings. Even you."

Yriatt ignored the jibe. "I permitted you to care for her because I thought you could do no harm. I was wrong. You cannot be trusted with her."

The girl herself had been crowding closer to Brastigan with every harsh word spoken. As Yriatt stepped closer, she slipped completely behind him. He could feel her breathing hard as she clung to his grubby surcoat.

"I don't think she likes you," Brastigan smirked.

Yriatt drew herself up, her eyes blazing with anger. Whatever she might have done was interrupted as Pikarus suddenly stepped between them.

"You cannot argue here." Pikarus's clipped voice was a surprise. No polite phrases and deference now—his blue eyes were stern as steel. "These are wounded, tired men. Your quarrels will destroy their spirit when they need it most. If you must disagree, then move out of our hearing."

"Fine with me." Brastigan glared a challenge to Yriatt.

"Very well," hissed the witch. "Let us walk."

The four of them pushed their way upstream. Lottres had to help Yriatt get her horns through the tangled branches. They stopped in a hollow among the crowding willows. The amber glow of sunlight through the branches seemed to come from very far away. There was scarcely room for Brastigan to stand straight, but he found a twisted root for the girl to sit on. Then he stood in front of her, facing Lottres and Yriatt.

Pikarus came as well, to Brastigan's surprise, placing himself between the two sides. Ready to jump in, if he had to. What Brastigan didn't know was whose side Pikarus would take.

"All right," Brastigan began, "before you land on me about what I've done, why don't you tell me what you've done?"

"I?" Yriatt said. The single word was sharp enough to cut leather.

"You," he answered. "You told us you try to help sick people. It's obvious she's not right in the head. So is she sick or under a spell? What are you doing to help her?"

"She is not under a spell," Yriatt bit out. "She *is* a spell. A shadow, to be precise."

"A shadow?" Brastigan asked. "What's that supposed to mean?"

Even Lottres looked confused, but the witch regarded Brastigan as if he had asked the most stupid question possible.

Coldly, she explained, "We had not been able to learn my father's fate for weeks. Shaelen offered to investigate. Yet a sorceress would be captured or killed before she learned anything. Sillets has many ways to find out its enemies."

"You mean the dogs," Lottres supplied eagerly.

"And others. That is why I must take such care."

Carefully, Pikarus asked, "Could no one else go?"

"Only a sorceress could understand what she saw," Yriatt told him, "or I would have asked the Urulai to do it. I could not come myself, and so I was forced to accept Shaelen's offer. To make her safe, I divided her temporarily from her power. That," she looked to the cringing girl, "is merely a shadow. A vessel to contain Shaelen's power until she reclaims it."

While Brastigan stared at Yriatt, trying to wrap his mind around what she'd said, Lottres gazed at the girl with stunned admiration.

"Amazing," he breathed.

The object of all this scrutiny seemed to shrink in on herself. She turned her face away, like a babe too overcome by emotion to even look at what she feared.

Pikarus said, "Surely some other..."

Yriatt shook her head. "It must be a living thing, and I could not bestow such power on an unthinking beast."

"So you made your own unthinking beast," Brastigan managed. "You made her, full grown, from nothing?" How could she have such power, he wondered.

"I did," Yriatt said. Her dark eyes narrowed with utter contempt. "And *you* took her for some peccadillo."

Now this, Brastigan knew. He could understand and answer an insult. "I don't know why you should assume that about me," he said, with some of her coldness, "but it isn't a peccadillo. It is friendship, no more."

"It didn't look like friendship to me," Lottres retorted.

"Things change," Brastigan thought. Until today, he hadn't known the girl had the feelings she did. He wasn't going to say that to his brother, not when he sided with Yriatt.

"That's because you've had your head in the clouds," he snapped back. "You don't see men dying around you —."

"I shall take your word," Yriatt interrupted, "as to the nature of the relationship, but you have placed me in a difficult position. The shadow was not supposed to awaken. I didn't think it could. I would very much like to know what you did to cause this."

This was the first time Brastigan had ever heard Yriatt admit any uncertainty. "If you must know," he drawled, relishing the moment, "we played peek-a-boo. And I guess I have to remind you that we're only having this conversation because of her. There were twenty of those bone men to eight of us, and the two of you sitting up there, not stooping to get your hands dirty."

"You are lucky she didn't kill you," Yriatt answered fiercely. "She has no control of her power."

"Well, she didn't kill us. She saved us," Brastigan retorted, "and I consider my friendship well repaid."

"I am not interested in your judgment of my actions," the witch said. "Do not forget, it was I who summoned you, to aid me and do my will. In doing so, you act in the defense of Crutham. In defying me, you place all in peril."

"She's right," Lottres reasoned, exasperated. "Saving our home is what's important, isn't it?"

"Maybe so," Brastigan snapped, "but we're not servants to send here and there. She treats us like Sillets does the bone men, using us for her own convenience." Yriatt stiffened angrily at this comparison. Brastigan spoke on. "These men are under my command. I'm responsible for their welfare, and I won't have their lives thrown away."

Pikarus shifted, as if he would say something, but Brastigan narrowed his eyes and stared straight at Yriatt. "What's incredible to me is that you made this girl without thinking about what it means. She is alive, just as if you gave birth to her, yet you expect her not to live." He swallowed an angry knot in his throat. "Living things live. It's what we all do. Why would you think this girl is any different?"

Softly, terribly, she answered, "Not every life is equal. This one was always intended to be brief. The shadow was not supposed to exist in its own right. Whatever you have done to her, she holds within her the essence of another person. That must be returned to Shaelen."

Brastigan stared at Yriatt. There seemed no appropriate response to such arrogance. Even Lottres looked taken aback.

Finally, Brastigan managed, "How can you create a life, just to destroy it?"

"When one has lived as long as I have, one develops an impartial perspective," Yriatt said.

Brastigan found himself scrambling in the face of her callousness. "Well, I hope I die young, then."

"You may get your wish," she warned softly.

"Just give the power back to your friend and give the girl to me," Brastigan demanded. "I'll take care of her."

"I shall consider it," the witch said, in a way that made him think she wouldn't consider it at all. "But you cannot expropriate what is rightfully Shaelen's. I will not permit it."

Brastigan had never liked Yriatt. From the moment they met, he hadn't liked her, all the more because she said they were related. Until this moment, he had not truly hated her. Somehow, his loathing gave him a kind of calm.

Yriatt's flat black eyes fixed on Brastigan, as if she knew his thought. "I caution you not to interfere further."

"Or what?" Brastigan gave a bark of laugher. "You'll do nothing. Someone might know you're here." He clapped a hand to his cheek, feigning alarm, and then sneered, "Don't threaten me when I know you don't mean it."

Clearly it galled Yriatt to admit he was right, so she didn't. "I suggest you enjoy the time you have left."

Brastigan turned and took the girl's hand, drawing her to her feet. He led her through the tangled thicket, toward the mules.

"Don't you worry," Brastigan told the girl. "I won't let her hurt you." He hoped that promise wouldn't be as empty as Yriatt's threat.

Lottres stayed behind, of course, heeling to his new master. After a moment Brastigan heard footsteps behind him. He turned with a jerk, then relaxed.

Pikarus fell in at his left shoulder, murmuring, "Your highness, is it wise to quarrel with her?"

"Someone's got to," Brastigan growled back. He felt an absurd relief that Pikarus had chosen to follow him today, not Lottres. "Look where it got us, following her blind."

"We are also following your father's orders," Pikarus pointed out.

"Orders?" Brastigan gave another harsh laugh. "Is that all you can think about?"

Quietly, Pikarus told him, "Orders are all a soldier has. We speak or stand silent, strike or withhold, based on our orders. It's difficult for us when the orders aren't clear."

"I know, I know, but that witch controls everyone I care about. I can't just let her do whatever she wants." Brastigan stopped, facing Pikarus. "We lost two men today, good men. You heard how she talked about them, like it was nothing. We can't count on her. We have to protect ourselves."

"Attrition may become a problem, your highness," Pikarus answered with mild irony.

"Don't remind me." Brastigan clapped the officer's shoulder briefly, feeling the rigid metal beneath his hand. "We'll hold it together somehow. We have to."

The girl clung to Brastigan's arm as they wound through the willow thicket. This time, he didn't try to make her let go.

* * *

Brastigan snatched a moment to speak with Yugo and Henrick. Then it was time to hoist them back up on their mules, without so much as a word from Yriatt for their pain. She should have been able to do something for them, Brastigan thought bitterly. But no, she protected herself at their expense.

The stream was shallow, so they rode under the patchy shelter of the willow trees, moving slowly to spare the mules. The water would disguise their scent, if more dogs hunted them, and shade was welcome as the sun rose higher. They stopped often, too, but no one questioned that. Not when every man could see ravens and crows criss-crossing the sky. Brastigan knew he wasn't the only one who noted a steady spiral of condors in one particular quarter.

At the bottom of a hill the stream veered north, running toward the lake Brastigan had glimpsed earlier. The rutted road into Crutham ran beside it. They urged their mules out of the water and waited for a raven to soar another way. Also for the water to run off their beasts' hooves. When Yriatt deemed it safe, they cut across the Crutham road and up toward yet another fantastic rocky spine. Luck was their friend, this time. They crossed without incident and hid in the rocks on the far side.

Still they listened for sounds of pursuit, straining their ears into the quiet afternoon. Hooves on stone sounded very loud. No crows called now, but many scrub jays. Listening to the shrill rasping, Brastigan wondered if Sillets tolerated only birds with ugly, grating voices.

Yriatt stopped abruptly. After a moment, Brastigan realized she was listening to the strident bark of a ground squirrel. The witch turned aside, toward an arch weathered into the pale rock. Beyond that was a narrow canyon, all but closed at its top. The interior was cool and dark. The riders stopped when Yriatt did.

"We wait," she told them.

They didn't wait for long. Within moments, Brastigan heard hooves. They sounded soft, as of a horse not shod. An Urulai horse? Even as he made this guess, a horse and rider were silhouetted against the light from outside. Tall, slender—even as she merged with the shadows of the canyon, Brastigan knew the rider was an Urulai woman.

Yriatt rode back along the line, Lottres following closely. "Shaelen," she assured them as she passed.

The stranger drew closer, appeared from the darkness at Yriatt's side. Briefly the two women clasped hands. They exchanged a few words in Urulai. Yriatt introduced Lottres, and he took the stranger's hand as well.

Brastigan stared at the shadowy figure, looking for some reason to despise her. He soon found one: this was another of Yriatt's female warriors. Shaelen wore dark trousers with a leather jerkin above them. She carried a bow, too, and a quiver of arrows across her back. Her horse was gray, a glimmering phantom in the dim light.

Shaelen's body might look Urulai, but her face was the wrong shape. Too round, the mouth too full, the skin too brown. Her eyes were dark enough for an Urulai, and two braids dangled beneath the flaps of a leather cap. But that hair was red—Silletsian red. So she was a child of the war, a half-blood like Brastigan. The slight similarity made him like her even less.

Those dark eyes swept the Cruthan line, seeking, and finally settled on the girl. A kind of calm seemed to come over Shaelen. She showed a quick interest, too, as her eyes fell on Brastigan. Looking back to Yriatt, Shaelen murmured something. The witch answered with quiet scorn. It was plain who they were talking about.

To Brastigan's surprise, Shaelen spoke softly, in a passable Cruthan. "That was rude, to speak a foreign tongue in front of you. I apologize." She bowed her head toward Javes, who was the nearest officer to her.

He glanced back at Pikarus and Brastigan before answering, "Accepted." Then he spoke the question uppermost in Brastigan's mind. "Now what?"

"We must take time to plan," Yriatt answered. She asked Shaelen, "Do you know of a place where we can be hidden, yet overlook the valley?"

"This way, *Maess*." Shaelen turned her horse.

Shaelen led them under cover of the jutting rocks. As shadows lengthened toward evening, they followed a line of sharp plates which stood precariously slanted. The trail angled down, the rocks leaned over them, and just as it seemed they would be crushed, they emerged into a spacious cavern with a level, sandy floor. At the rear, a spring yielded cold drips of water. Scattered stems of dry grass and mounds of manure suggested a resting place for Shaelen's horse. Large rocks were laid out for a fire ring, with wood neatly sorted by size. However, there were no ashes within it.

A broad opening on the western side was screened by pine trees. Beyond those was a sweeping view of the valley, washed with sunset's bloody glow. The hill Brastigan had seen earlier stood directly before them. Now that he wasn't riding for his life, he recognized its smooth, conical shape.

That made three of the enigmatic mounds they had seen so far: the Dragon's Candle near Harburg, the Dragon's Tooth at Rowbeck, and this one. Its presence made him wary.

The soldiers began to set camp, but Brastigan didn't want to leave the girl alone, so she held the reins while he and Javes tended the mules. One by one they stripped saddles, watered them, and gave each one a well deserved rub down. They fed the beasts what they could of grain.

Pikarus made sure all injuries were properly cleaned and bandaged, while another man distributed packets of cold food. The men ate in silence. Exhausted, maybe, or fearing what was to come. Remembering Pikarus's words, Brastigan wondered if they were really just waiting for someone to tell them what to do. For orders.

Meanwhile, Brastigan saw Yriatt talking with Lottres and Shaelen. The sky was getting truly dark when they emerged from their huddle. If they had a plan, they didn't mention it. Yriatt went to the spring to drink, while Lottres and Shaelen collected their meals.

Then Brastigan heard Pikarus ask, "Noble lady, I have been wondering. What were those creatures we fought today?"

In the quiet chamber, you could fairly feel the men straining to hear the answer.

Somberly, Yriatt replied, "Someone called them bone men. That is as good a name as any."

"Those are no men," Pikarus objected.

"But once they were," she said. "There is a place in Sillets called the Valley of Walking Bones. Criminals and enemies, any who resist Ysislaw's power, are sent there. It is a prison of starvation. There are no animals, no growing plants, not so much as an insect to eat.

"When the captives are reduced to the point of death, they are fed from a foul brew. Only the strongest spirits refuse it. Others, who are desperate to live, drink. But they do not live. They are changed."

Her voice left a terrible silence in its wake. Brastigan thought he wasn't the only one who shuddered at her words. To imprison an enemy was one thing, but deliberate starvation... What kind of man was this Ysislaw, to order such a torture?

"Can nothing be done?" Lottres asked, subdued.

"To cure them? No." She shrugged. "Your soldiers handled them well enough this morning."

Easy for her to say, when two men were dead and two more wounded. Brastigan kept his peace, sharing a quiet meal with the girl. It was an unpleasant surprise, then, when he heard a soft footfall and looked up to see Shaelen approaching. The younger witch seated herself directly in front of Brastigan, where he couldn't avoid looking at her.

The newcomer had removed her cap, releasing a tangle of ruddy curls behind the two braids in front. At least she had no horns, he thought. A whiff of pine came with her, as if she had used the powerful scent to disguise her body odor from enemy trackers.

Brastigan scowled. "What do you want?"

He could see the details of her garb now. Rows of stitching showed where something had been sewn into her jerkin to stiffen it. From the spacing of the stitches, it was most likely elk rib bones. A dark blue *jeup* hung at the base of her throat. Its design was invisible in the failing light.

Her face, above it, was thinner than he had first thought. Dark hollows ringed her eyes, and her cheek-bones stood out below. She looked at the girl with a kind of hunger.

"Answer me," Brastigan growled.

Shaelen's dark eyes were faintly sad now. She nodded toward the girl, who made herself small against Brastigan's side. "*Maess* said you took good care of my shadow. I came to thank you."

"I didn't do it for you," Brastigan answered curtly. Yriatt's student didn't seem to have the same egotism, but it would take more than a soft voice to placate him.

"Even so, you did a kindness when you didn't know me." Shaelen broke off a piece of bread and offered it to the girl. She took it hesitantly, and held it in her lap.

Brastigan looked between them for a moment, the witch with smoldering hair and sun-toned skin beside the girl as blonde and pale as the weathered stones above them.

"If she's your shadow," he snapped, "why doesn't she look like you?"

"I don't know why *Maess* chose that form," Shaelen answered frankly. "Perhaps to isolate her, so she wouldn't bond with those around her."

Sardonically, Brastigan smiled. "It didn't work."

Softly, Shaelen said, "But you must be a man of rare perception to see beyond her affliction. I think that's what angers *Maess*, you know. That you saw, when even she did not."

"Don't give me too much credit," he mumbled around a bite of dry bread. All he'd perceived was an opportunity to embarrass the haughty Yriatt. Only later had his purpose changed.

There was a flicker in Shaelen's dark eyes, as if she knew what he was thinking. "I understand how you feel," Shaelen said quietly.

"So you know all about me and how I feel?" Brastigan mocked her presumption. "Well, I'm glad someone does."

"I didn't mean..." Shaelen began.

He cut in, "All I know is, your witch took my brother away. Now she's going to take my friend away." He gestured to the girl. "What will I be left with?"

"You will not lose your brother," Shaelen protested.

"Oh, no. Of course not," Brastigan answered sarcastically. "I didn't lose him. He left. Turned and walked away—to her."

He glared across the dark cavern, where Yriatt and Lottres were speaking with Pikarus and Javes. He would have liked to know what they spoke of, but his unwelcome companion persisted.

"Do not be afraid of your brother," Shaelen said. "You must have been close friends for a long time. Now he is changing. Perhaps that is what frightens you. But his love for you will not change. Try to trust him as you once did."

"Mind your own business," Brastigan barked. She didn't know him at all, and yet she talked about his life.

Shaelen shrugged, and tore off a bite of jerky. Brastigan wished she would leave. He didn't want to like her. She tried again.

"*Maess* once told me," Shaelen began, "that all who come to her are desperate. Were you desperate?"

"Nobody was desperate when we left Harburg," he drawled scornfully. Although, that might not be true of Lottres. He'd used the same word himself, that his brother was desperate. He had to admit, "By the time we got to Hawkwing House, Crutham had been invaded. Maybe we were all desperate, then."

Shaelen smiled at the wry jest, and added, "As she is, for her father."

Brastigan was silent, rejecting any sympathy for the heartless witch. "Were you desperate?" he asked, goading Shaelen.

"Oh, yes." She seemed to feel no shame in admitting it. As she chewed another bit of jerky, she went on. "I was hearing things no one else did, and I wanted it to stop. That's what I asked of her."

Brastigan glowered, wondering why she was telling him this. He certainly wasn't interested in her reminiscences. Because she seemed to expect it, he asked, "Well, did she?"

Shaelen smiled faintly. "No."

"Sounds like her."

"She didn't do it for me," Shaelen amended. "She taught me to do it myself. By then, I understood what I was hearing and chose to listen, instead." Her dark eyes gleamed in the dusk of the cave. "Now, I want those voices back."

There it was at last, in her eyes. The desperation she spoke of. A hunger for power, Brastigan called it. She was just trying to make friends so he would give her the girl without a fight.

"I knew it," he growled. "You and that witch, you're just the same."

Shaelen straightened slightly, anger narrowing her eyes. Her smile was forced, now. "I'll take that as a compliment."

"Don't."

Suddenly she leaned forward, took his hand. Her fingers were as hard and calloused as a man's. "Have you ever been injured, so you couldn't walk?" she asked urgently. "That is how I feel now. I bear you no ill will, but I must be whole again."

"Don't touch me." Brastigan twisted his hand out of Shaelen's grasp. He put his arm around the girl's shoulder, pulling her close to him. "She isn't property. You can't trade her around like a horse."

Then, from behind him, came the voice he wished least of all to hear.

"Yet it is wrong to take for yourself what belongs to another," Yriatt said coldly. "That would be theft. Don't you agree?"

He looked right up into her face. "We don't keep slaves in Crutham."

Exasperated, Lottres knelt beside him. "Brastigan, be reasonable. We need Shaelen at her full power, so *Maess* can free Master Ymell. If we can't do that, Crutham is as good as gone, and then what have we come all this way for?"

Brastigan hesitated. Lottres was using the same word for Yriatt as Shaelen had. Was this some kind of secret language?

"Hear me out, prince of Crutham," Yriatt said. "I cannot deny the shadow has its own life. If you cooperate, I will try to preserve it." She spoke these words as if she were committing herself to a great indignity. Brastigan stared at her, unwilling to trust.

Lottres tried again. "You don't have to stay and watch."

"Don't try to get rid of me!" Brastigan snarled.

"Your presence is not required," said Yriatt.

"My shadow trusts him," Shaelen put in. "I will trust him."

Brastigan glared at her, wondering if she meant it.

"Very well," Yriatt nodded.

CLIODORA leaned over and whispered, "Can't we leave?"

"We have a right to be here," Therula answered brusquely. The younger princess squirmed in her seat.

Therula understood why Cliodora felt uncomfortable. Emotions were running high. Not the least of them her own. It had been less than a day since the exhausted Duale arrived with his grim message. Voices echoed slightly in the grand hall, where a cadre of courtiers stood by, observing. Their constant whispers of speculation scratched at Therula's nerves.

Alustra continued her self-imposed isolation. She had been invited to this council, but declined. Oskar knew all she had to teach him by now, she said, or if he didn't, it was too late to learn. This left the duty to Therula, who was tired of being spoken to like a child whenever she asked a question.

True, this was a council of war. Without training in such matters, Therula couldn't understand some of what the men said. Even so, she refused to leave her position as an observer. Alustra had a favorite axiom, "If you want to know what is really happening, you must sit in council." The truth of this had never been more evident.

Oskar sat his throne, above them all in more ways than one. There had been no official comment on his failure to recognize the Silletsian representative as a spy. However, Therula was aware of many whispers in private. The courtiers wondered why Oskar still wore the tall Silletsian hat, rather than returning to a traditional Cruthan style. In Therula's opinion, Oskar would see the change as an admission of error. This he would never tolerate.

Only three other of Unferth's sons were present: Habrok, Eskelon and Sebbelon. The rest of the princes and noblemen had left the capital mere days ago, after Oskar's coronation. Messengers were rushing to recall them, but even Calitar and Axenar wouldn't arrive from Begatt for a day or two more. The assembly seemed incomplete without them.

Not that their absence had stopped anything. Oskar had summoned all his commanders, including Captain Ingewald of the Harburg town guard and his most senior sea captain, Addonnas. The seaman wore leather armor and the guardsman wore steel, but their faces were much alike, seamed with years. Each line suggested an experience they had survived—a good recommendation, as Therula believed. By contrast, Garican, the newly appointed captain of the castle guard, looked like a stripling. He appeared ill at ease among such company. Luckily, Oskar hadn't had time to replace Habrok as Champion of Crutham. Habrok's familiar, calm presence inspired confidence, at least.

A good part of the day had been spent in seemingly endless discussion of troop levies and how soon they might reach Harburg. Now they were debating where the Silletsians were likely to strike. Sebbelon and Eskelon, who had spent some of their youth in Verelay and knew the mountains well, suggested the invaders would make for Carthell first.

"Carthell is more powerful than either Verelay or Daraine," Sebbelon reasoned. "It will have to be secured or the Silletsians could be caught in a pincer between Daraine, Harburg and Carthell."

"Do you think so?" Oskar drawled. He smiled, but wasn't amused. "Johanz has not sworn fealty to me."

"The duke may be restless," Eskelon admitted, "but he won't love the conquerors. They are outsiders even more than we are."

"If he were overwhelmed by invaders and we rode to his aid," Oskar mused with some irony, "do you suppose it would help him resolve the question of his loyalties?"

There were chuckles through the Great Hall. Watching Oskar, Therula couldn't tell if he really intended to punish Carthell's tardiness by leaving the province undefended. But Addonnas and Ingewald had offered an alternative approach.

"By your leave, I have researched the previous invasions," Ingewald said. "In the past, Sillets has passed over the mountains to Rowbeck, and thence down the valley of the River Ogillant. It is the most direct approach to Harburg."

"Yet they have always been defeated in Daraine," Habrok rumbled. He gave Sebbelon a little smile. "In a pincer between Carthell and Harburg."

"Indeed, your highness," Ingewald agreed. "Yet I fear there is more. Captain Addonnas?"

The ship's captain bowed low. "Your majesty, in the days since your coronation I have received multiple reports of strange vessels in the northwest. As you know, Sillets controls Urland, where there is a plentiful supply of timber. I fear what we have seen are Silletsian warships, most likely slave galleys."

"Have you confirmed this?" Oskar interrupted, frowning.

"I have assigned scouts to investigate, your majesty," Addonnas replied, "but you must realize a sea invasion could be upon us even before they return. If my suspicions are correct, Sillets will come through Rowbeck and attempt to catch *us* in a pincer between its land and sea forces." There were fresh whispers among the court. "They also may bring troops ashore somewhere along the coast. For example, you have already sent for soldiers from Begatt. If they stage a landing there, Duke Culbart would be hard pressed."

"You don't know they have any such plans," Eskelon protested. "Carthell..."

"We must consider every possibility," Habrok countered.

"We have only so many soldiers," Sebbelon said. "You were just telling us it will take weeks to raise our forces. Crutham can't be everywhere."

"Alas, that is true, your highness," Ingewald said. The old warrior's face was grave and sad. Listening to him, Therula felt cold with panic. Beside her, Cliodora was trembling. "Yet Addonnas is my friend. I give his opinion great weight."

"Since the Silletsians's previous strategy has failed so often, we must expect they will try something else." Habrok addressed Oskar formally, making no claim on their relationship. "A sea assault is one likely alternative. If it is your majesty's command, I will ride out to meet the Silletsians at Rowbeck, or perhaps at Caulteit, leaving Captains Ingewald and Garican to defend Harburg. I can also order Firice to move toward Carthell. This would allow us to respond quickly to Carthell, if need be. Or, we can await the return of Addonnas's scouts, and move based upon that information. Your majesty, it is your decision."

Therula and everyone else in the Great Hall gazed at Oskar, looking to their king for courage and hope. He sat silent a long while, under his tall hat. The very style was a mockery to all of them.

"Waiting is difficult for all of us," Oskar finally said, "yet that is what we must do. We must wait for what Addonnas's scouts can tell us. We must wait for our armies to gather. Most of all, we must wait for our brothers." Therula leaned forward, watching intently. Was this a long awaited acknowledgment of their extended family? Oskar concluded, "For today, we will do nothing else."

A profound silence fell over the hall. All around her, Therula saw the shocked expressions of the assembled noblemen.

Carefully, quietly, Habrok asked, "Is that your majesty's intention? That we do nothing?"

"What about Verelay and Daraine? Do we leave them to the wolves?" Sebbelon demanded.

"If Captain Addonnas is correct, we will need every man here." Oskar spoke with exaggerated courtesy, as if Sebbelon had committed a terrible faux pas. Therula could see both Eskelon and Sebbelon clenching their fists in rage at his tone. "I will send no soldiers until I know where the enemy is. Therefore, Habrok, you will gather our armies here, in Harburg. Do nothing more for now."

"Yes, your majesty." Habrok bowed low, perhaps concealing his own feelings.

Therula sat stunned by the import of Oskar's decision. Do nothing more? He couldn't mean that. Unlike Carthell, Daraine and Verelay were old and trusted allies. They had been among the first to pledge their loyalty to Oskar as Crutham's new king. How could he turn his back on them?

Even so, Therula's duty was clear. It fell to her to speak for those who would otherwise be forgotten in the emergency. Therula tried to produce a steady, calm voice as she called out, "Brother, may I speak?"

"Of course, dear sister," Oskar murmured. His slight smile reminded her of her regrettable pledge.

"If it pleases your majesty," Therula began, "I would ask a favor of

Captain Addonnas. A number of our younger siblings are here in Harburg." Therula let her hand rest on Cliodora's shoulder, and felt her little sister cringe from the eyes upon her. "Many are still children. I would ask for a ship to take them to safety while we still have time."

"What, leaving?" Oskar smiled again, openly baiting her.

"Not I, your majesty," Therula answered. "I would suggest that our mother accompany the children. She..."

A muffled snicker interrupted her. Therula frowned as Eskelon asked mockingly, "Send the queen with children who aren't her own?"

"Mother is accustomed to that," Therula answered coolly. "As it is her own brother, Telamar of Tanix, who is most likely to grant our kindred shelter, it is logical for her to lead. In addition," Therula turned back to Oskar, "Mother has served the public all her life. Now her hands are idle, her life empty. It would do her good to have a task, even one such as this."

Oskar regarded Therula with a familiar, calculating expression. "Your kindness does you credit, dear sister. Yet I love each of our little sisters and brothers dearly. I wish to care for them myself. I could never exile them to live among strangers."

Therula willed herself to sit calmly and not respond to the open falsehood. Care for them? Oskar didn't care a wit for his half-siblings.

"These children may be our future," Therula said in a quiet, strained tone. "If we wait too long, it will be too late to save them."

"Trust me," Oskar answered negligently. "We will speak of this again, if we must."

"Very well, your majesty," Therula said with reproachful formality. "I thank you for listening to my request."

"You may always speak your mind to me, dear sister," Oskar assured her. "However, I see it is now dark outside. I will release all of you to prepare for supper."

With so little ceremony, Oskar stood up and the conference was over. The soldiers hurried off. The courtiers broke into whispering clusters. Therula led Cliodora from the great hall, hardly seeing which way she went.

She shouldn't have been surprised that Oskar paid her no attention. He never listened to anyone, these days. Even with her limited experience of war, Therula felt that his plans were madness. It was bad enough to be contending separately with Carthell and Sillets, but to abandon his own provinces? The dukes wouldn't forget this breach of their trust. There would be a price to pay when the fighting was over — a high price. Surely Oskar knew that.

And yet he pursued his bold folly. Therula honestly felt that she didn't know her brother any more. After all, he was her mother's son. She couldn't believe he would give up even an inch of what belonged to him.

"Big sister?" Cliodora asked timidly. "What should I tell my mother?"

Therula somehow found herself at the door to her own chambers. She didn't remember walking there. Cliodora gazed up at her anxiously. Therula squeezed her little sister's hands.

"Tell Casiana I tried," Therula said softly. "I will keep trying. I promise."

Cliodora nodded and bolted down the corridor toward her mother's apartments. Therula entered her own chambers. She suddenly felt very tired, and she had little appetite for supper. No one was watching, so she slumped on the settee and let her head hang over her knees.

How could Oskar have changed so much? That was what she couldn't understand. It was as if he had turned into a completely different person since his coronation.

That thought wouldn't leave Therula's mind. It ached like a rotten tooth. All her vague doubts and fears came into clear focus. It was, indeed, as if Oskar had turned into someone else. He looked like Oskar, sounded like Oskar, but he didn't act like Oskar. Not to someone who knew the king well.

It seemed absurd, impossible. A fireside story, not something that could truly happen. Yet Sillets was a land of black magic. And Oskar had been so hospitable to the Silletsian representative. Could the man have bewitched him? Were they controlling Oskar somehow?

Therula's heart beat faster and yet her fingers felt cold as she twisted them in her lap. So little was known about Silletsian magic. Eben might have had information, but he was gone. Yet if Sillets was involved, that might explain Unferth's sudden death. Removing a strong leader could have been the first step in their scheme. It could also explain why Oskar still wore the tall hat. And his refusal to aid Verelay, Daraine or Carthell — a decision that could tear Crutham apart. But that wouldn't be a problem for Sillets. It might be exactly what they wanted. A fragmented Crutham would be easier to subdue.

Partof Therula felt she was being silly and overly dramatic, letting her fears play with her mind. The other part felt utterly convinced. She knew she couldn't go making any hysterical accusations. Not yet. Not even to her mother, although she was frantic to tell Alustra what she thought. She had to know more, much more.

That meant she could no longer avoid her brother. She must face him and his ugly bargain. In fact, Therula would have to be with Oskar as much as she could, watching for some clue about what had happened to him.

More immediately, it meant she had to hurry up and get ready for supper.

✳ ✳ ✳

Brastigan felt stiff all over, from sitting down on the sand or maybe just from being so angry for so long. The day had been waning even before Shaelen and her unwanted company. Now the sky outside was the color of a wet dog, with only hints of daylight hues in its inky pelt.

It was darker still beneath the stone shelter. The only light came from a lantern in Yriatt's hand. The shutters were closed, but amber streaks found their way between the slats. Faces stood out in that faint glow when little else could be seen.

"We have no time for bickering," Yriatt said. Her horns, above her, were like ripples on the night. "Move away from the shadow, Brastigan. For your own protection, stay at a distance."

Brastigan stared at her, wishing for something to say. There was nothing new; nothing he hadn't already said. With intentional slowness, Brastigan scooted away until he was just beyond arm's reach of the girl. Lottres settled beside Brastigan, on the opposite side from her. Shaelen composed herself, hands on her knees and eyes closed, while Yriatt loomed behind her.

The girl watched with dismay as a circle cleared around her. She still held the bit of bread Shaelen had given her, as if she didn't know what to do with it. Blue eyes fixed on Brastigan, full of urgent questions.

"No, stay there," he growled when she leaned toward him.

The girl stared at him. Her lips parted and she made a squeak of fear.

Then came a metallic creak as the lantern snapped open. Brastigan tensed, shielding his eyes against the sudden glare. Squinting, he saw Shaelen in a stark silhouette. Every hair stood out, blood red against the lantern's white glare. Her shadow flowed out before her. It rolled across the sand like hot tar and swallowed the blinking, blinded girl. Her bird's cry of panic was suddenly cut off.

Brastigan couldn't help himself. He lunged into the darkness, hands seeking the warmth that had been at his side.

"Come back!" he cried in the blackness.

For the merest instant Brastigan's groping hands felt something as insubstantial as a cobweb or a dream. Then a lurch, and he fell right through it. He should have struck the floor, but he didn't. He fell and fell and fell, and thought he would drop into that blackness forever.

Something grabbed his shoulder. Then vertigo had him and he landed on packed sand. He fell on his right elbow and lay gasping. His bruised arm throbbed as if it would burst. But that wasn't what really pained him.

"What were you going to do?" Lottres raged beside him. "You idiot! If you weren't my brother..."

"*Thaeme*, be quiet," came Yriatt's stern voice.

Brastigan managed to sit up. Clutching his elbow, he saw that Shaelen was down too. The curly crown of her head faced him. The half-blood moaned as Yriatt rolled her over.

Brastigan didn't want to look at them. His eyes saw only the empty place where someone had been sitting and no longer was. For Shaelen's vivid black shadow was gone, taking with it that other pale, unwanted one. Among the kick marks in the sand was a bit of bread, dropped in the confusion. He stared at it and wondered how such a small thing could be all that was left of someone's life.

The world blurred around him. His head pounded, and his eyes burned. Somewhere nearby he heard a barking cry that became spastic coughing. It was only Shaelen.

"Brastigan." Lottres shook his shoulder. "Answer me."

Brastigan refused. He didn't trust his voice, and anyway, there was nothing to say. Or maybe there was.

"Get away from me," he muttered, and turned just enough to shove at Lottres. The traitor who tore away everything he held dear. His own brother.

"Hey!" Lottres lost his balance and fell on his backside. It should have been funny, but Brastigan couldn't bring himself to laugh.

Across the sandy floor, Yriatt helped Shaelen to sit up. Her coughing had subsided. Yriatt bent close to Shaelen, who croaked, "Maess, you must hurry."

For a moment the witch's cold face softened. "You are right, *Thaeme*." Brastigan thought he must have imagined something like warmth in her voice. Then she straightened, resuming her imperious nature. "Sergeant, prepare your men."

Behind them, Pikarus's voice echoed faintly. "Aye, lady."

As Yriatt vanished into darkness, Lottres tried again. "It isn't her fault, Bras. You shouldn't have jumped in like that. Say something."

Oh, now he used the familiar nickname. Well, it was too late to be making friends. Brastigan clenched his fists in the sand, feeling the harsh grains under his fingernails. He barely restrained himself from tackling Lottres and pounding that innocent, injured expression off his face.

"She tried," Lottres persisted. "It just didn't work."

"Let him be, Lottres. Let him have time." That was Shaelen, sounding stronger now. Her compassion turned Brastigan's stomach. "You have wounded men here. I'll be tending them, if you want to see how it's done."

Lottres hesitated, and then stood. "Yes, I do." He sounded angry again, as if he had any right to be.

Brastigan closed his eyes and drew his knees tightly against his chest. Two pairs of feet went crunching away over the sand. Let them go. Shaelen was right about one thing. He didn't want to see anyone.

He heard, though, with half an ear. Javes directed the men in dumping out their duffels and saddle bags and filling them with sand from the cavern floor. For a makeshift barrier, it seemed. He could hear Shaelen speaking, her words indistinct, and a question from Lottres. Then came a muffled cry—Henrick's voice—followed by soothing words.

Just like them, Brastigan thought. Healing would have to involve pain.

Hissing and crackling told him when a fire was kindled in the stone ring. Light reflected from the pale ceiling, flooding the shelter. Only Brastigan remained in darkness. Though his right arm ached, the rest of him felt numb and cold. All day he fought and hated and hung onto that girl, and still she was snatched away. Without even one kiss. Just that fast, the love he had been waiting for was lost. And now, so was he.

Footsteps came shifting back over the sand, together with a rhythmic tapping of demi-greaves. That ended in a squeak as the man knelt beside him.

"Your highness," came Pikarus's quiet voice. "We're going to need you soon."

"I'll be there," Brastigan mumbled between his knees. He was intensely grateful that Pikarus did not touch him.

Now that Yriatt had revealed herself, the bone men would be coming at them again. Or maybe something even worse. It would be an ugly fight, probably a losing one. It just didn't seem to matter.

Why couldn't he sit this one out, Brastigan wondered. After all, Lottres and Yriatt withheld their power during the first battle. But he knew he wouldn't really do that. He owed the men his duty, whether he had anything left to live for or not.

Pikarus waited, but Brastigan didn't move. Finally he said, "Aye, your highness."

Pikarus was just standing when the men laboring at the front of the cave gave out with startled curses. Javes's voice rang higher than the others. "What's that?"

Pikarus jumped up, and Brastigan raised his head incuriously. Over the tops of his greaves, he saw movement on the night's dark surface. Something black crossed the darkness, just where the crown of the hill would be. Then, from nowhere, a column of burning gold poured out of the night. It struck the Silletsian camp and spattered back upward, outlining an immense shape. Details came and went in the flickering blaze. Black leathery wings broad as ship sails. Spikes and spines to rival the rocky hills. An eye larger than the sinking moon gleamed above a hot orange maw that poured out ever more fire. Horns, black and twisted as old tree trunks, were wreathed in smoke and sparks.

Sounds reached them next. The beating of those enormous wings. A roar that sounded like tempest waves crashing to shore. Brastigan stared, its sheer size diverting him from his grief. Where did this thing come from? There was nowhere in the valley for a creature that size to hide.

"A dragon," Pikarus said with foreboding.

Someone asked, "Do we fight that?"

"No," Shaelen answered as she added wood to the bonfire. "She is on our side."

"Thanks for small favors," Javes responded ironically.

Nobody asked how Shaelen knew the monster was friendly, let alone that it was a female, but her matter-of-fact attitude seemed to break the spell that gripped them. The soldiers hurried to throw up the last saddle bags into a low wall partly blocking the shelter's open side. Pikarus went to join them, leaving Brastigan alone.

The serpent beat its wings, fanning the flames that engulfed the enemy camp. Then the black sails furled and it glided downward to vanish into the inferno.

The dragon's appearance made Brastigan's mourning seem pointless. He got up and hobbled to where he left his duffle. In its place he found a heap of crumpled and soiled laundry. His baggage had been emptied along with the rest. Brastigan extracted his sword, shield and helmet from the pile. Then he strolled forward to join the Cruthan line. There seemed no reason to rush.

Lottres and Shaelen were at the fireside. She had her bow out, and they were doing something with the arrows. Brastigan heard more of their gibberish—exciting the air, of all things—and passed without speaking. The soldiers lined up along the wall of sandbags and stared into the night, waiting. Counting their armored backs, he could see the two wounded were back in ranks. Shaelen was good for her word. Too bad her mistress couldn't say the same.

Brastigan stopped at Pikarus's side, wondering if the bone men would come. With their camp in flames, they might turn back. Still, they seemed pretty single-minded. Brastigan didn't feel fear. He was just very tired. For a moment he closed his eyes, letting them adjust to the darkness. Behind his eyelids something gleamed. A human form, pale as a wisp of smoke, the after-image of a life now gone.

He felt his throat close up with grief and jerked his eyes open, banishing that ghostly image. Then he saw the bone men coming. Not so fast this time, for the hillside was steeper. Or maybe their speed just didn't surprise him any more. Firelight, from behind the Cruthans, brought the foemen into high relief against the night. Conversely, the enemy would have the fire's glare in their eyes. Not that it was likely to bother them much.

"Here we go again," Brastigan breathed through his teeth.

On they came, with haggard faces at once pathetic and deadly. Their blank expressions, so like what the girl had been, filled Brastigan with horror. Then rage ignited, hot as the fires down below. How dare these monstrosities be up and walking around when his girl was gone? All his hate and grief, the punishments he wished he could inflict on Yriatt, found a focus. Around him, men began to shout, waving their swords and pounding their shields. But they were behind the wall, seeking its doubtful shelter. They still wanted to live. Brastigan didn't care if he lived or not. He gave a roar of his own and charged.

"Wait!" Pikarus cried, but Brastigan plunged into the first rank. He was soon surrounded, but he felt no fear. He trusted to instinct, letting his body dodge and parry and strike in the deadly dance he knew so well. Victory hummed through the air, singing her own song of power. Bone men fell like cut hay. Let the witches try their wishy-swishy spells. This was Brastigan's magic: sword magic.

Arrows came whistling over the battling throng. Some fell around him in booming flashes. Others, like lightning, seared the very air with a lesser form of the girl's blazing attack. Bone men fell, twitching, or burned as they stood and fought. So the wizards gave some account of themselves at last.

Brastigan's rage gave way to a strange exhilaration. For the first time in days, he felt relaxed and powerful. The enchanted arrows only added excitement.

But the bone men were endless in their numbers. However many he cut down, yet more came on. Brastigan lost track of time. It could have been hours later, or just a few minutes, when a powerful wind whipped sand into his face. He looked up to see the endless black expanse of a dragon's belly. Ebony claws gripped the top of the slanted rock that roofed the shelter, and an eye the exact color of flame blazed down on him. With a toss of its crooked horns, the dragon indicated he should get out of its way.

Under that malevolent regard, some vestige of self-preservation returned. Brastigan dispatched his current opponent and ran toward the rock shelter, stumbling over pieces and parts of the fallen. Bone men swarmed after him, but even as he cut around the makeshift wall, a deafening roar made the very earth tremble.

Once more fire came from the sky, blasting the enemy back down the hill. The dead on the ground were set alight. Black billows of smoke rose to join the night. Over the sheet of dancing gold, Brastigan saw a second dragon gliding on the air. It, too, bellowed out a blazing breath to scour the hillside.

Pikarus appeared at Brastigan's shoulder, raising his voice to be heard over the roaring flames. "Your highness, you could have been killed!"

Brastigan shrugged. "So what?"

He brushed past Pikarus to join his fellows as they all eased back from the heat and fumes. The soldiers regarded him with a kind of horrified awe. He cared no more for their regard than he did for the boot-lickers at Harburg. Farther back, he saw Shaelen and Lottres at the fire. Shaelen stood poised and confident, an arrow ready to pull. Her eyes roved restlessly, seeking any other targets. Lottres knelt, panting, a sheen of sweat on his face in the fire's unsteady light. Strangely, he looked happier than Brastigan had seen him in days.

Looking at his brother, Brastigan felt his energy desert him. His head was suddenly heavy, shoulders burning with exhaustion. His bruised elbow throbbed in time to his heartbeat, the minor injury inflamed by too much hard use. Brastigan glanced at Victory. The blade was clean, of course. He gratefully slid her into her sheath.

Aimlessly, then, he shuffled to the rear of the shelter, circling wide around the two witchlings. What was the point of all this, anyway? He'd laid dozens of the bone men low, giving them the clean death they deserved, but all the bloodletting in the world couldn't bring the girl back to him. If you could even call it bloodletting, when the victims didn't bleed.

He found his way to the Urulai horse that had been the girl's. The shadowy gray pricked its ears, recognizing him. Brastigan let his shield and helmet drop to the sand. He leaned on the dumb beast, longing to sit down but knowing if he did he might not have the strength to get up again. He felt the prickling of its hair under his cheek, and the hard round shapes of beads woven into its mane. The horse turned its head. Brastigan felt the warmth of breath as a soft muzzle brushed his hair. He let go a harsh breath.

There was a stirring, as of swords suddenly drawn, and Javes barked, "Who goes there?"

"I do," a familiar voice answered. Brastigan looked around to see Yriatt stride into the shelter. Just behind her came a man who looked Cruthan except for the high, wavy horns on his head. Shaelen and Lottres fairly ran to meet them. Pikarus advanced more slowly.

"My father, Ymell," the witch said with a curt gesture. "Make him welcome."

Ymell bowed to the soldiers with such grace they might have been standing in a royal court rather than a crudely fortified redoubt. "I am indebted to you all," he said.

Brastigan held his place and watched. He could see no mark of Ymell's imprisonment, though Yriatt commended Shaelen for discovering how it was done. There was little resemblance between the dark haired sorceress and her blond father. Ymell looked like a man of Crutham, with a blocky build and yellow hair falling to his shoulders. Only his horns set him apart. Oddly, he seemed no older than Yriatt. You'd think her father would be older than she was.

This was Leithan's father, too. That made him Brastigan's grandfather. He shook his head with an angry jerk. He couldn't think of this stranger in such intimate terms.

Ymell was undeniably charismatic. Brastigan could sense that, and the man hadn't even spoken to him yet. Still, like Yriatt, he had a reserve as well. After all, they weren't really humans. What was it Lottres had said about the girl? Oh, yes. That she only looked human.

Yriatt and Ymell might look normal, but Brastigan knew better. Yriatt had said it herself, that humanity was just a shape she wore. Brastigan hadn't understood what she meant, then. Now he knew. Father and daughter didn't have to resemble each other. They could make themselves look like whatever they wanted. They weren't wearing hats with dragon horns attached, either. They had horns because they were dragons.

Legend told of dragons, the most powerful creatures in the world. Brastigan would have bet that Ysislaw was a dragon, too. Who else would Yriatt fear but another dragon?

And what did that make Brastigan? Not really Urulai, not really Cruthan, but no horns on his head, either. He was nothing but a patchwork of a man, and none of the pieces matched.

Yriatt turned toward him, saying something to Shaelen. Her eyes met Brastigan's across the chamber. For a moment he saw an expression that might have been guilt, but more likely was contempt. Lottres, beside her, mirrored her expression. Then Brastigan was glad he had no horns, because that would have meant he was like Yriatt, a creature without conscience or compassion. Someone who would take an innocent life without a second thought.

The night continued to burn behind Yriatt, but if she sensed his hate she gave no sign. She turned toward Ymell, and her cool voice came to him faintly across the sand. "Oh, yes, Father. Leithan's boy is here."

Ymell turned as if she'd bitten him. "Where?"

The witch gestured and his eyes followed, finding Brastigan among the other dumb beasts. Ymell's stunned expression was not unlike Unferth's when Brastigan last spoke to him.

Brastigan couldn't face that searching gaze. Instead, he looked to Yriatt. He might despise her, but at least she was familiar.

"So, are we done now? Do we stay here, or go on?"

His harsh voice brought a lull, during which Yriatt's dark eyes took in the exhausted men around her. And, maybe, the amount of packing to be done before the troop could move anywhere.

"We stay," she said.

She spoke as if she were granting some special favor, but you took what you could get with Yriatt. The battle lines quickly dissolved as soldiers put their weapons away and fell to talking among themselves.

Ymell was still staring at Brastigan. He took a step forward, raising one hand, but let it fall as Brastigan turned away. It wasn't as if he felt anything for the man. He wanted no more of witchery. What Brastigan wanted was to lie down. To get out of his harness, too, but mostly just to lie down.

Before he reached the pile of clothes where his bags used to be, Pikarus strode over to join him. "Do you want a hand?" His quiet tone suggested he would back away if Brastigan wanted it that way.

"You don't have anything better to do?" Company was not what Brastigan wanted, but his elbow hurt enough that he wouldn't refuse the offer.

"Nothing that can't wait."

Soon Pikarus was easing off the mail hauberk. Without it, Brastigan felt as light and insubstantial as the girl had been. There wasn't a proper rack, so the two men laid it flat on the ground, where the dry sand could absorb some of the sweat.

"You could have been killed, your highness." Pikarus said, so calmly he might have been discussing the weather. "That would have been disastrous."

"Disastrous for whom?" Brastigan retorted wearily.

"All of us."

Next was the quilted gambeson, slimy and stinking like a patch of toadstools. Brastigan closed his mouth on a grunt of pain as Pikarus twisted his sore elbow. Fortunately, the rank odor of sweat dissipated quickly in the open air.

"Because your orders were to protect me?" the dark prince mocked.

"No," Pikarus answered patiently, "because the men depend on you. Prince Lottres may be intelligent, and he is often correct, but he doesn't fight like a soldier. You told me earlier today, we'll get through this. I still believe that."

Brastigan remembered the conversation only vaguely, as if it had happened months ago. He made a bitter sound that might have been a laugh. "I was kidding myself."

"Your highness..." Pikarus was silent for a moment. "We all saw how you fought just now. I've never witnessed the like." He quickly added, "Please, don't ever do it again."

"No promises." Brastigan shivered as the cool air met his sticky, damp skin.

"You may be feeling low now," Pikarus said. "Nobody blames you for that. But you really are the greatest swordsman in Crutham. I know you will survive this."

The unexpected repeat of his habitual boast made Brastigan swallow a lump in his throat. He forced a smile. "The greatest in the world, you mean."

Pikarus chuckled, but his gaze was steady. "Could be."

"Maybe that's my problem," Brastigan said, almost to himself. "No one gave me any orders, except to get out of Harburg."

The soldier surprised him with a dry chuckle. "The only one who can give you orders is King Unferth, and he only sometimes."

Pikarus went off to organize something. Brastigan's arms trembled as exhaustion really set in. He jerked on the first clothes he could find, not caring what they looked like, and kicked open his bedroll.

It wasn't easy to get comfortable on the hard ground. Bruises mottled his skin, like spots on rotten fruit, and each one had a pain to go with it. But that wasn't what kept Brastigan awake. It was the absence of the girl.

Was it really such a little while ago he fed her bread and cheese? Her last meal, as it turned out. Brastigan felt he had known her forever, but it was really just a handful of days. Such a short time to be the whole of someone's life. It seemed impossible that she was gone.

* * *

The fire burned low and the floor of rock shelter was paved with sleeping men. A sentry was still awake, and so was Lottres. Yriatt and Ymell sat near the fire. He could feel them communing on a level much deeper than he was capable of. Even though he was exhausted, Lottres was far too excited to sleep.

The evening battle had been exhilarating, even better than the afternoon's. For one thing, Lottres had done more. It had felt so good to act without hiding, and Shaelen, his fellow *thaeme*, gave so much encouragement. She had showed him how to make fire follow his arrows. It was so simple! Lottres had never been able to fight this way before. For the first time, he understood why Brastigan liked it so much.

"I am worried, heart-kin." Shaelen's voice came from the darkness in a thread so fine Lottres wasn't sure if she spoke aloud or directly to his mind. *"Will Brastigan be all right?"*

"I don't know," Lottres answered with his mind. Any mention of Brastigan irritated him, these days.

"Can't you do something?" Shaelen persisted. *"He is your brother."*

Lottres raised himself on his elbows just enough to see the glint of Shaelen's eyes in the darkness. He didn't understand why Shaelen even cared, after the way Brastigan had treated her.

"No one can do anything for him," Lottres said. *"You've seen how he is."*

Shaelen seemed to sigh in the darkness. Lottres sensed her affectionate dismay.

"You listen to fire and wind, heart-kin," she said. *"You hear condors, mules and crows. But do you listen to your own brother?"*

"It would be nice if he listened to me," Lottres retorted. *"Anyway, I've heard what he has to say."*

"Then listen to what he doesn't say," Shaelen answered gently. Her mind-touch slipped away, leaving Lottres suddenly alone in the darkness. He eased back down.

All the men had been talking about how Brastigan went berserk in battle. Brastigan was grieving, and that anguish was real. Yet his brother had brought this on himself. Lottres was tired of running after Brastigan, picking up his messes. It was past time for Brastigan to do his own dirty work.

Lottres turned over, trying to get comfortable. Then he sighed, knowing that Shaelen was right. He couldn't turn his back on a brother, however much he felt like it. Lottres had to clean up this one last mess, make it right between them.

But not now. Not while the stench of the bone men's burning made the night air heavy as a woolen blanket. Not now, Lottres told himself. Tomorrow.

CHAPTER SIXTEEN
DARK REFLECTIONS

BRASTIGAN woke up and muffled a groan in his bedroll. A faint glow suffused the rock shelter. Dawn was coming. He didn't greet it gladly. Brastigan's eyes burned, his head felt thick, and there was no part of his body that didn't hurt.

The bitter scent of smoke wafted past. Moving slowly, he sat up. The sky outside was gray as a ring-necked dove. His sluggish mind registered the pine trees, ranged in a black overlay against the frosty glow. Someone stood in silhouette at the cave mouth, crooked horns jutting above. The general form wasn't slender enough to be Yriatt. It must be Ymell.

Even as Brastigan thought this, the man turned toward him. "Good morning," Ymell remarked. He didn't speak loudly, but it was so quiet that his voice easily carried across the shelter.

Brastigan got up, though he wanted to lie back down. The men had fought hard yesterday. Even Brastigan wasn't selfish enough to wake them before their time. He walked unsteadily to join Ymell at the cave mouth, where sand-filled baggage still stood in a makeshift wall. It appeared even less stable in the daylight. The scorched hillside dropped away on the other side. Only a swath of trampled earth showed where the bone men had come up the slope. No trace remained of the enemy army. The ground had been burned clean.

Beyond the line of blackened trees lay the empty valley of Altannath. The mound rose above it, half dark as soot and half pale as gold. Wisps of smoke still rose from the ruins of the Silletsian camp. Even the emerald lake wore an ashen pall. At least no black wings defaced the lightening sky.

"I don't want to sleep, either," Ymell said, talking almost to himself. "I spent three months asleep, thanks to Ysislaw and his *eppagadrocca*. I think I shall enjoy standing for a while."

Even exhausted and discouraged as he was, Brastigan was too proud to ask how Ysislaw's spell had worked. Most likely, he wouldn't have understood the answer, anyway.

"What did you dream about for three months?" Brastigan asked disinterestedly.

"I don't remember," Ymell confessed. Then he asked, "And you?"

"Nothing," Brastigan mumbled. No dreams he wanted to remember, anyway.

Not to be put off, Ymell said, "I heard about what happened with the shadow child. That was very unfortunate. I am sorry for your grief."

Brastigan felt his guts tighten with fury. He knew good and well that Yriatt hadn't told her father the story. She considered the girl's life of such low importance. These wizards had no respect for privacy. Always picking out people's thoughts, they were.

"As a rule, I do not spy on others," Ymell corrected gently. "Shaelen told me about it. It wasn't easy for her, being divided from a part of herself. I only wish the circumstances permitted her the time she needs to heal, before we must fight again."

Ymell glanced at Brastigan, perhaps suggesting Shaelen wasn't the only one who needed healing.

"Poor Shaelen," Brastigan mocked. Maybe she was still human enough to feel remorse, but that didn't excuse Yriatt.

"My daughter has her pride, I fear," Ymell went on quietly. "Had I been there, I would have counseled her not to take such a drastic step. But," he shrugged, "it was my very absence that brought them to this. Alas that we cannot change what is past."

Brastigan stared across the charred valley, rejecting the implied defense. Excuses wouldn't bring the girl back.

"There is one thing I must tell you." Ymell's grave voice interrupted Brastigan's bitter thoughts. "I must warn you to beware Ysislaw."

"Really?" Brastigan widened his eyes in a pretense of surprise. "The king of our enemies, the leader of the invasion—you think I should be worried about him?"

"You misunderstand," Ymell said, though he smiled faintly. "I have foreseen..."

"Stop!" Brastigan clapped both hands to his ears. "Don't tell me."

Ymell regarded him with brows raised in surprise. When Brastigan was sure the wizard wouldn't speak, he lowered his hands and prowled along the wall, restless.

"You gave my father that "gift" years ago," Brastigan said over his shoulder. "It changed his life—and not for the better." Indeed, it seemed to Brastigan that Ymell's foretelling had set Unferth on a long road which led only to grief. "I don't want your prophecy. I'll make my own decisions, not be sent here and there because someone says it's my destiny."

"Perhaps you're right," Ymell replied. If Brastigan's rebuff upset him, it didn't show. "But do heed my warning. Ysislaw will go out of his way to take you if he can. You must be cautious."

"To hold me hostage?" Brastigan retorted. "Good luck. I'm, what, thirteen in line for the throne of Crutham? I don't think he'd have much use for me."

"Not to hold you," Ymell answered seriously. "Merely to slay you. There is reason for him to hate you especially."

Brastigan's mouth twitched. "I've never even met him. I haven't had time to annoy him properly."

"But your mother did."

That did make Brastigan turn and look at him. Leithan had been so quiet and gentle, bearing every insult her life offered without a word of complaint. How could she have angered anyone?

Of course, Brastigan had never truly known her. All he had was a child's adoring memory. Only now, having met Yriatt and Ymell, did he recognize the aloofness in Leithan's bearing, the isolation even from her own son.

Ymell looked back at him, perhaps waiting for permission to speak.

"Mother wouldn't slap at a flea that bit her." Brastigan snapped.

"She would reject an unworthy suitor," Ymell replied. Now it was he who looked away from Brastigan.

So Ysislaw had been Leithan's suitor? Brastigan tried to picture a man wooing his mother. Then he tried to imagine the exalted dragons doing anything so earthy as courting. Both times, he failed.

"Was that before he conquered her country, or after?" Brastigan asked wryly.

Ymell chuckled, but his mirth was bitter and terribly sad. "Yes," he said.

"Yes, what?" Brastigan was forced to ask.

"We dragons have always been divided about the reason for our existence," Ymell said. "I, and the majority of our kind, believe we have a noble purpose, to guide and protect humans. If we can, we will lead you to greatness." His voice swelled with sudden vigor, and Brastigan felt his blood quicken in response. Then Ymell's voice dipped and darkened. "Others have held that the only true purpose of any living creature is self-interest. Because of their mighty powers, they believed they had the right to do whatever they wished, even to rule over humans as tyrants."

There was no need to guess which side Ysislaw was on, but Brastigan didn't see what this had to do with Leithan. Why, he wondered irritably, could these wizards never say things plainly?

"These latter ones," Ymell droned, like a tutor lecturing a pupil, "warred against each other and humans. Fortunately, they exterminated each other over time. Of all this evil brood, only Ysislaw now survives. His domain is made up of lands seized from his fellows. The irony of his success is that, despite his vast power and endless life, Ysislaw has no real future.

"It's said that we most desire what we cannot have," Ymell went on. "Ysislaw dreams of a dynasty, eternal conquerors with power enough to bring the world to its knees. He wants the very thing your father has in such plenty: sons."

"Well, why not?" Brastigan asked with deliberate callousness. "You seem able to make yourselves into whatever you want. Surely Sillets has women who are willing to be its queen."

"We can change ourselves, yes," Ymell said, a forefinger raised in emphasis, "but only so far. Our horns, you have noted. Those do not change. They are the source and the symbol of our power. If we change our horns, our power is also changed."

Well, that explained why Yriatt took such pride in her horns, dressing them up with jewels and finery. Brastigan cast a skeptical eye on Ymell's horns. From a distance they seemed a smooth, uniform dark brown. Standing so close, he could see streaks of darker and lighter matter. Tiny ridges and grooves followed the curved surfaces in a complicated pattern. Still, they seemed ordinary enough, except that they grew from a man's head.

Then the obvious struck him, and he blurted without thinking, "Mother didn't have any horns."

"She did when she was born," Ymell corrected in a soft, careful tone.

"But?" Brastigan pressed. Despite his distrust of all things dragon, he had to know what had happened.

"Returning to your previous question," Ymell said, "Ysislaw can make himself into a human man, and he can enjoy human women, but he can get no offspring on them. Only another dragon could serve that purpose. Our kind are not many, and there are even fewer females. Those there are despise Ysislaw, as my daughters do... did. If he wants an heir, he must capture a bride and keep her. That is what he sought to obtain in Urland. He wanted my Yrien."

Brastigan sucked in a breath, understanding now why Ymell went on at such length about dragon politics and breeding. Leithan had been in the thick of both.

"Yriatt dwelt in Verelay, near to me," Ymell continued, "but Yrien dwelt in Urland. She was born there and had vowed to protect its people. We did not realize how isolated she was, how vulnerable." His voice trembled with remembered emotion. Brastigan said nothing, but listened and waited. "Ysislaw had massed his troops in several locations. Some were near the border of Urland and Paltey, but the larger group was just to the north of here. We thought that my mound was his target, and the troops in Paltey were merely to keep Yrien's Urulai from riding to my aid."

"It wasn't," Brastigan prodded. He felt anxious to hear more, and yet dreaded the tale.

Ymell nodded slowly, sadly. "Ysislaw waited until Yriatt joined me here, then swept into Urland. Too late, we realized we had been deceived. Even with Yrien's power, the Urulai were overwhelmed. She was forced to flee. That was a long and terrible war." Ymell trailed off, then said briskly, "I shall not bore you with minutiae. Though she defied him to the end, Yrien was trapped. Ysislaw vowed to make her his bride. At last, when she had no other choice, she did the unthinkable."

"She changed her horns," Brastigan whispered.

Once again, the horned wizard's voice was dark. "My beautiful daughter gave up her great heritage, her horns and her power. All that she was, she put aside. She changed herself completely and became an Urulai woman. Because of Ysislaw," he hissed with bitter hate. "Thus she denied his desire."

For once, Brastigan was left speechless. What could he say to such a tale — what could anyone say, who was merely human? Only now did he understand, very grudgingly, why Yriatt had been so afraid Ysislaw would find out where she was.

The silence went on too long. Brastigan couldn't bear it. He made himself ask, "What did Ysislaw do?"

"He tried to kill her, of course," Ymell said. "Not quickly — he wanted her to suffer in the form she had chosen. He flew with her to a high mountain glacier and threw her into a crevasse. He left her to die in an icy tomb."

"But she didn't die," Brastigan said. Obviously, or he would never have been born.

Ymell nodded. "Although Yrien had given up most of her power, she did not lose all. She was able to warm herself and call out to us. I returned her to her people. She was given a birth ceremony and a new name, Leithan. So I have been told. I was not there."

Brastigan could imagine not. Ymell would have been out looking for Ysislaw, the beast who had maimed his daughter. Any father would, no matter the species. Under his hauberk, Brastigan felt the flat lump of Leithan's *jeup*, hot and sticky against his skin.

"I think I know the rest," he said.

Brastigan had heard it all his life, how the exiled princess led her people to safety in Crutham. Now he saw the paradox, that Leithan had given the lecher king Unferth what she refused Ysislaw: her body, her son.

Reluctantly, Brastigan asked the question that had been biting at him from the moment Yriatt said she was his aunt. "What does that make me, then?"

"You are not a dragon," Ymell said quickly, perhaps sensing his need for reassurance. "There can be no cross breeding. You are human. An exceptional man, perhaps, but no more than that."

"Exceptional is right," Brastigan replied, lifting his chin in a caricature of his usual vanity. "I'm the greatest swordsman in the world!"

"As to that, I do not know." Ymell smiled gravely. "Do you understand, now, why you must beware Ysislaw? In his eyes, you should be his son. He wishes to destroy you, the living symbol of his humiliation."

"He can try," Brastigan retorted amiably. Inside, he felt his heart harden with anger. All that had happened—losing his home, his brother, his love— was Ysislaw's fault even more than Yriatt's. Ymell's tale only gave Brastigan a more compelling reason to destroy the evil dragon. Unexpectedly, he found himself casting about for any rumor of a poisoned spear or some other trick that might bring the mighty dragon low.

Of course, it was Lottres who could have told him that.

"Do not think of it," Ymell interrupted. "Ysislaw forced my dear daughter to make a terrible choice. Indeed, he deserves to die. It is my right, mine alone, to pass judgment on the evil of my kind."

"If you say so." Brastigan shrugged, putting this aside as a pointless argument. If Ymell wanted to take the risk, he was welcome to it. But if Ymell wasn't there and Brastigan was, why, that might be a different story.

They stood in silence for a time, Brastigan and the wizard he had to force himself to think of as his grandfather. Some of the tightness had left Ymell's face. The relief of having finished his sad tale, maybe.

But the tale wasn't really over. Everything Ymell had said made that more clear. All it had done was make Brastigan feel worse. Even his grief for the girl seemed trivial, and he resented that. A man should have a right to mourn without being upstaged by the events of years past.

The bitter scent of smoke drifted past him again. Voices, vague as the dawn light, echoed under the rock shelter. Brastigan glanced over his shoulder, feeling doubly tired now that the tension of Ymell's tale was fading. Yriatt was awake—he could tell it was her by the horns. She had a fire burning in the fire ring. Its cheery crackling mocked Brastigan's exhaustion. Javes set a blackened kettle on the stones. He measured water and crushed oats together, and began to stir. All around them, soldiers were getting up. No few of them groaned over their aches and pains.

Brastigan glanced at Ymell again, and then away. For what seemed like the tenth time in a day, he felt that he should say something but didn't know what. He barely knew Ymell, and that was Ymell's own choice. With his powers, the dragon wizard could have come to Harburg whenever he wanted. He could have spent time with Leithan and her boy, Brastigan. Would it have hurt him so much to make the effort? Yet he waited until now, when everything was happening at once and no one had time to think.

Brastigan glanced back to the fireside. Pikarus crouched there. His hands were busy feeding the fire, but he was watching Brastigan and Ymell warily. Waiting for an argument to break out, maybe.

"Let us call council," Yriatt announced from the center of the gathering. Her clear, calm tone made Brastigan feel even more lethargic.

Ymell, in turn, had been watching Brastigan. His pale eyes glinted with emotion. At his daughter's voice, he sighed to himself. Brastigan felt a lump rise in his throat. There was so much to say, yet his mind was a blank. So many words, he couldn't sort them all out. Ymell was turning away.

"Thanks," Brastigan managed, before the horned wizard could go. "For telling me the truth, I mean."

Ymell smiled with real warmth unshadowed by past sorrows. "You're welcome."

Together they walked back into the shade of the rock roof. The men were busy dressing, some of them shaving before they armed up. Still, Brastigan felt the eyes on him. He knew he didn't look good, and that was unusual. Brastigan wasn't vain, but he did make the most of his dark good looks to stand out from the crowd. No matter what happened, he came back with a sarcastic retort, confidence intact. Today he walked with a shambling gait, his proud hair tangled, and he didn't care what he looked like or who saw him. The long journey had stripped away such pretense.

The soldiers were sitting down in two ranks, Pikarus at their head. Javes, at the fireside, passed bowls of steaming mush along the lines. Brastigan murmured a greeting and dropped to the sand beside Pikarus, just in time to receive a bowl of his own. It was their first hot meal in days. Brastigan looked at the creamy porridge, smelled its musky warmth. He set the bowl down beside him. The ache in his middle had little to do with hunger.

Yriatt, Shaelen, Lottres and Ymell sat facing the soldiers. Once Javes had his own meal, Shaelen served for the wizards. While she did so, Yriatt declared, "Let us begin."

"Very well," Ymell said. "Although I am grateful for the efforts that restored me to myself, we now stand at a crossroads. Crutham has been invaded by her old enemy, and mine. We must choose where to spend our efforts to best effect, to turn back the invaders and destroy their tyrant ruler."

Pikarus followed this ringing challenge with a simple question: "Do we know where the emperor of Sillets is now, or how far the invaders have advanced?"

Ymell looked to Yriatt, who answered for him.

"On this morning's wind, Lottres heard sounds of battle. Glawern still holds, though hard pressed. We can conclude that neither Ysislaw nor his *eppagadrocca* are there. Such a small fortress could not have resisted them."

Shaelen added, "I have seen the Urulai warriors in place on Carthell Cleft. They have made a landslide and blocked the road. It will be long before the invaders cross there."

"The cleft isn't the only way into Carthell," Javes pointed out.

"True," Shaelen agreed, "but my people know these mountains and the Silletsians don't. We must trust they will be delayed in seeking another pass. If our warriors aren't spread too thin, they may be able to hold them back entirely."

"Even if they are," Pikarus said, "Mistress Yriatt told us at Hawkwing House that the main force is moving south toward Harburg. Wouldn't their ruler be with them?"

"Logically, yes," Ymell replied. "He will want to bring Harburg low with his own hand, and see for himself when the king must cry mercy."

"Although the mountains will have slowed them, I fear Rowbeck has already been taken," Yriatt went on. "They had no real means to resist."

"If they follow the pattern of past invasions," Lottres said, "they will divide forces again at Caulteit. One column will strike for Carthell, while the other rushes on to Harburg."

"If that strategy failed before, would they use it again?" Pikarus asked.

"It is still the most logical approach," Ymell answered. "To take Crutham, they must take Harburg. Moving toward Carthell serves to keep those forces from coming to Unferth's aid."

Brastigan sat silent, listening to all this and wondering why it didn't seem to matter. Yet something did bother him about what the wizards were saying. They were dancing around Pikarus's question. That's what it was.

"Wait," Brastigan interrupted. "Are you saying you don't know where Ysislaw is? You're only guessing?"

The four wizards glanced among themselves. Reluctantly, Ymell answered. "Correct. We know he is in Crutham. We do not know his precise location."

"We have overheard the reports of his *eppagadrocca*," Shaelen explained. "These are given each day at sunset. That is why we waited until last night to strike, and also why *Maess* was careful to silence them before she released *Maen* Ymell. We can act freely until sunset tonight. Then he will know *Maen* is free."

"You can't tell where he is from the reports?" Brastigan pressed.

"No, he conceals himself," Lottres answered impatiently.

Brastigan blew out a sigh. What good were wizards if they couldn't do something as simple as finding the enemy? Then he felt a nudge at his side. Javes frowned sternly at Brastigan, then nodded toward the bowl of porridge that sat cooling on the ground. Brastigan sneered back at him, but he did take a bite. The tepid mush tasted surprisingly good, after days of cold rations. He took another bite, and another.

"It is more than that, I believe," Yriatt said with steely softness. "I have already explained that we can sense nothing from Harburg. We cannot see into Carthell, either. I had not realized this because there was no one there I needed to speak to. Shaelen can sense the Urulai in Carthell Cleft because she knows them well. The rest of us cannot hear beyond Glawern."

"What would cause this?" Pikarus asked.

"We do not know," Ymell admitted. "Most likely, it was part of Ysislaw's invasion strategy. He may have sought to hamper Crutham's defense by preventing Eben from perceiving what happens in the provinces."

"Then do we know for certain if Egger and Duale were able to give our warning?" Pikarus asked. "Are Harburg and Carthell defended?"

"I do sense troops moving toward Harburg," Lottres said, "so Father must know. What concerns me more is that none of us can reach Eben. With rumors of war, he should be trying to contact us, but there has been nothing."

"I agree," Ymell said. "This is of great concern. Eben was my *thaeme* for many years. I should be able to reach him even in his sleep."

Brastigan took another bite of porridge and kept his opinion to himself.

"Could Ysislaw have sent one of his underlings ahead to Harburg?" Javes asked in a dry, pragmatic tone. "Maybe they already got rid of Eben."

"It would be like Ysislaw to place an agent in Harburg, to provide information that would aid in his plans," Ymell said.

Lottres looked at Brastigan, his brown eyes intense. Brastigan thought of their brothers who had died, and how this might have distracted Eben and Unferth at a crucial time. But to think that Eben was dead?

Shaelen asked quietly, "*Maen*, could Eben have fallen under the same spell that held you in thrall?"

"Ysislaw knows the value of a hostage all too well," Ymell said. Yriatt shifted suddenly in her place, and Brastigan saw her dark eyes were narrowed with hate. It was obvious who Ysislaw would have used Ymell to bargain with. Ymell continued, "No one would concede a point for Eben, I fear. It is more likely he is dead."

Brastigan swallowed the last of his breakfast in a hard lump. No warmer than his daughter, Ymell. He simply acted more civilized.

"Then we are left with three goals," Pikarus said. "One is to stop the Silletsian advance. The others are to learn what has become of Eben and Carthell. Which of those is most important?"

"Carthell is closer," Javes responded.

"Destroy Ysislaw and the invasion will collapse," Ymell countered.

"What if Ysislaw is already in Carthell?" Brastigan asked. "Maybe that's why they're blocking you there."

Yriatt and Ymell exchanged uncertain glances.

Lottres asked, "*Maess*, how is it possible to kill Ysislaw? For us, I mean."

He gestured to take in the soldiers, who were only men despite their weapons and harness.

"You cannot," Yriatt answered decisively.

"This is my task." Ymell's tone was softer, yet more terrible. "I have confronted Ysislaw many times, always to no avail. I would like this to be the last time I must duel with him."

"I shall aid you," said Yriatt. Something in her voice said she expected this request to be denied.

"Only if I fall," her father answered sternly. "The risk is too great, my daughter. To you most of all."

The two dragons traded eye-darts, ignoring the mere humans who sat around them. Yriatt bowed her head at last, but her lips were set in a thin line of anger.

Brastigan's mind had cleared as he ate, but his stomach churned as he listened to the worthless debate. Fighting a dragon didn't interest him. He wanted to get away from the ones he was already with. Yriatt had destroyed any reason he had to linger in her company.

Javes cleared his throat. "Do we pursue the invaders, then?"

"You're forgetting something." Brastigan answered before Ymell could. "Our duty was to serve her —" he jerked his spoon at Yriatt "— to her satisfaction. Her goal was to free her father. Well, he's free now." Brastigan looked to Yriatt. "Are you satisfied? Because if you are, we have a duty to our king and homeland, and they're in Harburg."

The witch gave him a long stare. "Perhaps that would be best." Her voice was taut, as if he had insulted her for no reason at all.

"We can't leave now!" Lottres protested.

"Why not?" Brastigan snapped back. "Let the dragons deal with their own. The rest of us would just get in their way."

"But..." Lottres choked.

Ymell considered the two brothers. "Perhaps both ends can be served by dividing our forces," he suggested. "Those who wish to return to Crutham may accompany Brastigan. The others come with me."

"I go with *Maess*," Lottres announced petulantly. As if there had been any doubt.

There was a moment's silence, heavy with the discomfort of choosing between the two princes. Maybe no one would follow him, Brastigan thought. He couldn't let it stop him. His desire to be away from Yriatt was so strong now, he could hardly breathe around it. Every time he looked at her he felt his loss again, sharp as Victory's blade.

Slowly, carefully, Pikarus said, "Our orders are to protect both princes, not just one. However, we are soldiers. As Prince Brastigan says, our king is in Harburg. We have fought the bone men and know how to defeat them. This information will be vital to Prince Habrok.

"Further," Pikarus went on, "I agree with Lord Ymell that the four of you will be able to move more quickly without having to watch over us." And, though he tactfully didn't say it, the troop's morale would improve without the constant arguing of the two princes. Pikarus concluded, "I believe Prince Lottres will be safe with Lord Ymell and Lady Yriatt. Or as safe as a man can be, in wartime. If we do divide forces, our squad will follow Prince Brastigan."

Yriatt and Ymell regarded each other silently, and Brastigan knew some kind of communication was passing between them. Lottres stared at Brastigan, his features lined with guilt and relief, triumph and accusation. The dark prince said nothing.

"Even if we all agree to that, the Silletsians have a long start on us," Javes pointed out. "How will we get to Harburg before them?"

"There is a way," Ymell answered quietly. "You can be in Harburg by noon, if that is what you want."

Brastigan glanced along the lines of soldiers, already fewer by two than when they started. As Pikarus had reminded him, these men depended on Brastigan for leadership. Whatever Ymell's way was, it was worth it if it got them all back to Harburg and something like a normal life.

"Yes, it's what we want," Brastigan said.

"Then," Ymell said, his voice betraying no emotion, "we wizards will go first to Carthell. Javes is correct—Carthell is within easy reach, and Ysislaw could indeed be hiding there. The possibility should be investigated."

"Very well." Brastigan gathered himself to rise. "Let's get packed and get moving."

Pikarus nodded. "Yes, your highness."

Returning to the improvised wall at the cave mouth, Brastigan located his duffel and yanked it out. Three others came down with it. Gritty dust billowed into his face as he poured sand out of the canvas bag. Then a soft breeze carried the dust away. Brastigan didn't bother asking who he had to thank for that.

Other men soon joined Brastigan. While they emptied the rest of the bags, he returned to his bedroll and began stuffing his things back where they had been. His right elbow no longer hurt, he noticed. Brastigan wondered if Ymell had healed it while they were talking. He hadn't asked for help.

Brastigan worked with renewed energy now that he had a goal more to his liking. Yet he felt no pleasure in it. Shame had joined the grief that weighed on his heart. Maybe he'd found a valid excuse, but he knew he was running away. Just like a dog, tail between his legs. Running home to daddy, and wasn't that a joke? With Crutham at war, it wasn't likely Unferth would have time to console his broken heart.

He punched down the last of his clothes and yanked on the drawstring with more than necessary force. From where Brastigan stood, there was only one thing he could salvage now. He left his duffel and stalked across the shelter, through the scurry of men packing and preparing to move. Javes was bringing the mules into line, but Brastigan continued on past them.

The Urulai horses raised their heads at his approach. The newest of the three, Shaelen's mare, regarded him warily. Then the gray mare, the girl's horse, stepped toward Brastigan. Gratefully, he took the reins. Maybe he deserved to be called Urulai and maybe he didn't, but he had never forgotten these magnificent animals. It felt like a morbid validation that the mare came forward to meet him.

"Who's that?" Shaelen stepped from behind her own horse. When she saw Brastigan, she murmured, "Oh."

They traded stares, the two half-blooded Urulai, and a sarcastic retort died on Brastigan's lips. Shaelen had found time to comb and braid her hair. With a sick start he recognized the beads she had used to tame her fiery locks. Red beads, the same ones he'd given to the girl on that last morning.

Shaelen gazed at Brastigan silently. Her round face was so like the girl's, and her lips moved, as if she wanted to speak but didn't remember how. Brastigan wound the reins around and around his hand, pulling so tight the blood throbbed in his fist.

Shaelen blinked first. "I'm so sorry," she faltered.

"Save it," Brastigan choked. He pivoted away, unable to face this dark reflection of his perfect lover.

A part of him raged that he should demand those beads back, tear them from her hair if she wouldn't give them freely. He didn't have the heart, not when she looked at him like that. Anyway, it didn't matter. He could never wear them himself. Brastigan forced himself to walk slowly, leading Shadow—well, what else could he call her?—back to his bedroll.

Of course, the problem with Urulai horses was they were broken to a light blanket, not the heavier Cruthan saddle. Shadow's blanket had a horn of carved antler, and he could hang Victory from that, but there was no place to tie baggage on. He'd have to think of something. Brastigan knelt with his knee on his blankets to roll them into a tight coil, an outlet for his frustration and grief.

As he worked, he heard footsteps approaching over the sand behind him. Brastigan turned, expecting Pikarus had come to tell him the troop could move out. It wasn't Pikarus. Brastigan turned away, shoulders hunched.

Lottres knelt beside him and laid a tentative hand on his shoulder. "How do you feel?" he asked.

Feel? Brastigan closed his lips against the withering rejoinders that came to mind.

"Don't ask me that now," Brastigan grunted.

For once, Lottres didn't retreat. Leaning closer, he asked, "What's wrong with you, Bras?" Brastigan raised his head to glare at his brother. Lottres flushed. "Okay, wait. I know what it is *now*, but you haven't smiled since we left home. It isn't like you."

Brastigan stared down at the bedroll he was crushing beneath his knee. How to explain it? He'd hated Yriatt from the moment he heard her name, because her summons had turned his life topsy-turvy. He had never wondered if his feelings were justified. But Lottres was waiting for his answer.

"Well, the falcon, to start with." Brastigan felt his hackles rise, remembering the bird's thin little voice. "Showing up out of nowhere, acting like it knew us, and then just dragging us off. It would ruin anyone's sense of humor."

"The falcon is dead," Lottres said gently.

So was the girl, Brastigan thought bitterly. Of course, the falcon had been

Lottres's talisman, a physical symbol of deep need, just as the shadow girl was to Brastigan.

"Then you started acting that way," Brastigan hurried on. He felt defensive, and didn't like it. "Your fire-gazing and all that. What was I supposed to think?"

Brastigan expected Lottres to stammer, just like old times, but his voice held steady.

"I was so excited when Eben said I could be a wizard, but I was afraid to tell you. I thought you would laugh." Lottres's gaze wasn't on his brother now, but focused on something within himself. Then he smiled with a trace of sadness. "I just wanted to do something nobody else could. Not our brothers, and not even you."

"You don't have to compete with me," Brastigan scowled.

"Easy for you to say," Lottres parried without malice. "I was trying so hard to hear through the fire, the way Eben said I should. When I finally did, I was really happy. I wanted you to be as glad as I was, but you weren't."

Because, Brastigan recalled, the farther they got from Harburg, the more his fears grew. It seemed the quest would cost him the only person he could count on in the ferment of Crutham's royal household. But, after all, it wasn't Yriatt who did that. It was Brastigan's own stubbornness, his cruel words, that drove Lottres away.

He shrugged awkwardly. "I was a fool. I know it. We've always been friends, but all of a sudden you were changing. You weren't who I thought you were." Brastigan gave a low, harsh laugh. "Neither am I. My mother wasn't even a human being."

"Did Ymell answer some of your questions, at least?" Lottres asked tentatively.

"He did," Brastigan said. But knowing the story of Leithan's travails wouldn't bring his lost love back. Brastigan straightened and kicked his bedroll over beside his duffel. Sounds of the camp breaking up suddenly closed around them, and the moment of privacy evaporated like dew in the sun.

"Then let me help another way," Lottres offered.

Brastigan's gambeson lay where it had been set the night before. Lottres picked it up, and Brastigan could see the padded garment had dried as stiff as wood. Lottres shook it lightly and then gave it a vigorous snap. Shadow snorted uneasily. A cloud of fine particles drifted around Lottres, and the gambeson hung limp from his hands.

"Shaelen showed me that," Lottres reported with pride. He handed the gambeson back to Brastigan.

"Thanks." Brastigan took off his shirt and pulled the gambeson on over his head. While not exactly clean, it was certainly more pleasant to wear than it had been. Lottres bent down to retrieve the hauberk. He helped Brastigan into his harness, just as they had done so many times. It was strange to think they would be going in different directions now.

"I'll tell Father where you are," Brastigan said in a level tone. "He'll want to know."

"Let him know *Maen* is going to Carthell," Lottres added. "It might help him to plan."

Just as Brastigan stuffed the last of his clothing into his duffel, Javes approached. Brastigan gave the bag and his bedroll to Javes.

"Just tie these on my mule and put it in the pack train," Brastigan said.

Javes nodded. "Aye, your highness."

"Well," Lottres began.

"Go do what you have to do," Brastigan told him. "You can't be half a wizard—even I know that. You've got to finish what you started. Just remember, we're still at war. No more daydreaming. Mind you watch what's going on around you."

Lottres summoned a weak smile. "And you."

Brastigan punched his brother's shoulder lightly, and watched as Lottres went to join Yriatt and Shaelen at the fireside. He saw his brother for the last time, and felt as if it was the first. Lottres moved with real confidence. No longer the gawky pup, Brastigan had to admit.

He donned his helmet and took up Shadow's reins. For the first time in weeks, Brastigan led his horse to the head of the column. But this time he would ride alone.

CHAPTER SEVENTEEN
THE WIZARD'S GATE

NO sooner was Brastigan in the saddle than Ymell appeared beside him. "Ride to the top of my mound, and I'll meet you there."

"To send us home?" Brastigan asked wearily.

"Yes. I removed a part from the apparatus some time ago, as a precaution," Ymell explained. "I must restore this before it can be used."

"If you say so," Brastigan shrugged. He turned in the saddle, scanning the line of riders behind him. Pikarus nodded to indicate all was ready. Brastigan said, "We'll be there."

He sat a moment longer, watching as the horned wizard strolled off toward the rock shelter's side entrance. At a slight pressure of his knees, Shadow moved forward. Brastigan blinked against the daylight as they left the shelter. Shadow's hooves kicked up black char as she crossed the seared earth of last night's battlefield.

A trampled path led straight down the steep slope. The bone men must have taken the most direct approach in last night's assault, rather than the safest. Since the last thing he needed was an accident, Brastigan turned left to make a long, slanted descent between the rocky fins of the hillside. Shadow moved slowly, picking her way, and he didn't hurry her.

It felt strange to ride boldly in daylight, after days of clinging to tree cover. Looking skyward, Brastigan saw no black feathered birds in the air. Of course, they hadn't seen the raven before it killed the falcon. There seemed little alternative, in any case.

Brastigan had just turned a switchback to the right when a shadow passed over them. The rush of wings followed. Shadow snorted, and muffled oaths came from behind him. Brastigan knew he wasn't the only soldier whose hand sprang to sword his sword hilt.

The dragon looked smaller in daylight. Perhaps its dark hide had blended with the gloom of night, thus giving an impression of greater size. Ymell's back and flanks were a deep red-brown, shading to tan on his belly and chest. Brastigan didn't remember seeing the paler colors, which would have stood out in darkness. It seemed Ymell could change his colors on a whim, just as he did the rest of himself.

The horns, talons and serrated back-ridge hadn't changed, nor the great sweep of wings which carried Ymell forward. Here and there, scales glinted as he moved. Under him, Brastigan saw, the dragon supported a long, gray stone in his four huge paws. It must be the very one he had noticed missing the day before.

Ymell swooped down toward the top of the mound, raising clouds of dust as his wings beat the air. When he could see through the haze, Brastigan watched Ymell turn the stone until it stood on end. Then he folded his wings and dropped to the ground, where he sat up on his haunches like a hungry dog. Ymell seemed to be rotating the stone, setting it just so.

The riders came to a patch of scree at the base of an old rock slide and Brastigan had to concentrate on urging Shadow onward. When he looked back up, the dragon had vanished, though the stone was still visible.

By now the Cruthans were moving past Ymell's fire-blackened mound. Between the jutting rocks, Brastigan could see a great dark hole in the northern flank of the hill. A ramp of packed earth rose toward it. There was no such colossal doorway in the Dragon's Candle. Brastigan wondered what lay beyond it.

It seemed they had been picking their way down switchbacks for hours, though the sun had scarcely moved when Brastigan cocked an eye at it. At last they reached the base of the slope. Crossing a gentle saddle, they began to angle up the grassy mound. Brastigan urged Shadow higher, avoiding the ruins of the Silletsian camp. He felt no need to look on what was left of the occupants after last night's conflagration.

Instead, he thought about what awaited them at the summit of the mound. Half remembered words teased at Brastigan's memory as Shadow kicked up black swirls of ash. The old man, back in Rowbeck, had spoken of something. A stone that sang, wasn't it? No, it had been too long. He couldn't remember.

The wizard's mound had an easier slant than the rugged hills. Shadow and the mules kept a good pace. They didn't take switchbacks now, but circled ever higher on the conical mound. Soon enough they reached the top, and the familiar oddities resting there.

The oval pool glinted among the parched grasses like a diamond in a band of gold. Beyond that was the upright stone, black blotched with green and yellow lichen. Only a slight disturbance of the earth hinted that the stone had ever been moved. Another thing was new: a series of enormous gouges in the soil at the edge of the mound, overlooking the burned camp. Yriatt had left her footprints on the dry turf.

Ymell stood waiting beside the tall stone. He stepped forward as Brastigan drew near.

"So what's this one called?" Brastigan asked blandly. "There's a Dragon's Candle and a Dragon's Tooth."

Ymell seemed genuinely confused. "Who calls them by such names?"

"We do," Brastigan answered. "I'll call this one the Dragon's Chimney," he decided.

"That name will do as well as any," Ymell answered, amused.

"What happens now?" Brastigan asked warily.

Before Ymell could respond, Pikarus cried, "Your highness!"

Pikarus kicked his mule and rushed to Brastigan's side, sword drawn.

Following his gesture, Brastigan saw movement to the east. There among the rocks was the black scar where they had fought the night before. A tiny figure stood atop the great stone slab that roofed the rock shelter. It looked like Yriatt, arms extended skyward. And descending toward her... Brastigan caught his breath. Griffins!

There was no mistaking the long bodies and dark gold wings. Around him, mules scuffed their hooves anxiously and the men muttered in their ranks. Leave it to Yriatt, Brastigan thought, to find herself a creature just like the falcon, only bigger and meaner.

"Fear not," Ymell soothed the men, who had drawn into a protective huddle around Brastigan. "My daughter has tamed griffins before. We haven't time to ride over land. Shaelen and Lottres must have such steeds if they are to keep pace with us."

Lottres would ride a griffin? Absurdly, Brastigan had to quell his envy. What a ride that would be! If you could trust your steed not to rip out your throat, of course. Brastigan squinted across the distance. Yriatt lowered her hands and confronted the two fierce beasts which paced restlessly before her. Griffins—tame? Those two words didn't even belong in the same sentence. Maybe, after all, Brastigan was happy enough astride Shadow, with her four hooves on solid ground.

"What about us?" Brastigan prodded. "What do we have to do to get home?"

"Be patient," Ymell said, though he regarded Brastigan thoughtfully. Whatever he had to say, he kept it to himself.

Feet hissing through the dry grass, the wizard strode toward the tall stone. Without fanfare, he placed both hands on the stone. Nothing seemed to happen. That was the problem with these wizards, Brastigan thought. There was never any thunder, nothing to tell you magic was happening except their own say-so.

Then he felt a tickling in his ears. Brastigan clapped a hand to his helmet, but it didn't ease the sense of pressure. The deep, pure note went on, like the fog horns they sounded on the great bay in winter.

The sound came from the stone. It wasn't so very loud, yet the vibration made Brastigan's bones itch. Ymell lowered his hands, but it didn't stop. Then a wavering light came up from the pool. Waves lapped at the banks, though there was no wind to tease the water—nor to cool the sweat collecting under Brastigan's helmet. Streaks and sparkles lit the dust in the air. That was what the old man of Rowbeck had said, he remembered: that there were lights in the water.

Ymell stepped behind the stone. He must have done something they couldn't see, for the rock began to move. It rotated forward in a controlled motion, not falling. The weathered stone lowered slowly to make a kind of bridge across the shimmering pool. As its tip touched the far bank, the foghorn hooting died away. The lights in the air made a constantly moving cloud of brilliant, gleaming particles.

"Come." Ymell beckoned. His face was fixed on the sparkling mist with intense concentration. "This is your way, now."

Brastigan paused, staring at that shimmering haze above the pool. Reluctantly he tightened his knees. Shadow moved forward. The soft thumping of hooves sounded behind him as Pikarus and the others followed.

"Simply ride across the bridge." Ymell said. He stepped backward, giving them space.

"Right." That was all? It sounded too good to be true, but this spell was what Brastigan had asked for. He couldn't back down in front of the soldiers.

Pikarus suddenly drew even with him. "Your highness, let me go first."

"No." Brastigan waved him back. "This was my idea. I'll do it."

Pikarus might have argued, but Brastigan looked away to find Ymell gazing at him. The horned wizard was calm, yet sad. Brastigan wondered what Ymell saw in him. Was it the ghost of his lost daughter? Or just a human who happened — impossibly, tragically — to be related to him? Brastigan squirmed inside, uncertain what he wanted Ymell to see. Or what he wanted this stranger, his grandfather, to mean to him.

Ymell clapped Brastigan's knee briefly. "I'm glad to have met you," was all he said.

Brastigan could find no words to express all he was thinking. Yet he couldn't bear all this grim foreboding.

"It won't be the last time." Brastigan urged Shadow forward with a swagger he didn't feel. Pikarus followed close behind.

Brastigan could now see that the column wasn't completely round. The upper side was slightly flattened, creating a better surface for riding. The dull thud of hooves on soil turned to crisp clicks as Shadow stepped onto the stone bridge. The mare moved cautiously, neck extended and ears twitching side to side. Brastigan didn't rush her, and soon enough she moved into the mist.

A weird sensation passed over him, like a breeze caressing his skin. Brastigan felt it even under his armor. Daylight dimmed within the cloud, yet he could see his way easily enough. Hoofbeats echoed strangely around them. After the full sunlight on his helm, the air was pleasantly cool and damp.

The bridge should have been just a few paces across, yet Shadow didn't come to its end. Brastigan was just beginning to be concerned when the mist suddenly cleared. Shadow pricked her ears and raised her head, and trotted into daylight.

Brastigan kept the horse moving to make room for others following, but he looked around sharply. Gone were the dry valley and bone-pale rocks. Farm fields lay on every side in a patchwork of green and gold. The king's highway was clearly visibly, lined with inns and cottages.

They were back in Daraine, and no mistake. In fact, Brastigan knew exactly where they were. This was the Dragon's Candle. He drew Shadow up and watched Javes lead the last of the mules out of the mist. Already the dancing motes faded from the air. The low sound they had heard at the Dragon's Chimney began again as the stone slowly rose toward a vertical position. This time, Brastigan thought its groaning sounded like a rusty gate swinging shut.

In fact, that was what it must be. Some kind of wizard's gate, secret to all but the dragons and their friends. They could skip around the countryside at will, bypassing days and weeks of travel. It didn't seem fair.

"That was strange," Pikarus murmured close on his left.

"Yeah," Brastigan muttered.

His attention was caught by another familiar sight. Crutham Keep was majestic, frowning over the city at its knees. The massive fortress always had looked best from a distance. Brastigan felt a moment's vertigo, as if he had done Lottres's trick and fallen asleep in the saddle. Emotions surged within him. Home-sickness. Weeks' worth of loneliness. The aching losses of his brother and the girl. The new knowledge of his mother's sacrifice, a sickening weight on his heart. After all that had happened, the citadel on its promontory seemed small and irrelevant.

The men were lined up, awaiting Brastigan's order. He gave it, and they started the long ride down from the Dragon's Candle.

* * *

The soldiers rode off, with Brastigan leading. Lottres watched them go. He couldn't decide what he felt. Relief, to be sure. At last, he could relax and learn without his brother's tantrums to distract him. Oh, the glory! To be surrounded by sorcery, breathe in magic and feel it grow within him!

Perhaps he felt some regret, as well, but he wasn't the one crying. Lottres glanced toward Shaelen, unsure of what he had heard. Her lovely face was white and strained in the dim light. Tear tracks glinted on her cheeks as she watched the last mule vanish down the slope.

Frankly, Lottres couldn't understand why Shaelen should miss Brastigan. He was only kind to women when he wanted something from them, and there was only one thing Brastigan ever wanted. Surely Shaelen could sense that.

His fellow *thaeme* flicked a glance toward Lottres and suddenly knelt by the fire. Her back was to the exit now, her face in shadow. It looked like she was breaking up the coals, but Lottres could tell that was just an excuse.

She had sensed that he was thinking about her. Maybe even knew what he had been thinking. Lottres wondered for a moment if living among wizards might be more complex than he had thought. Did they always feel what the others were thinking and react without a word being said? It seemed unfair. People thought all kinds of things. Lottres had learned that from listening to the men. Mostly, they kept those things to themselves. Even Brastigan did. It was what you said out loud that counted. If no one actually spoke, how could you know what to respond to?

Regardless of that, Lottres had no intention of passing judgment on Shaelen. He went to join her at the fireside, leaving enough room that she could back away if she wanted to.

"I talked to Brastigan," Lottres told her. "We patched things up, a little."

Shaelen shrugged. A new suspicion dawned, but this time Lottres was careful to guard his thoughts.

"Did he say something to you?" Lottres probed.

"No," Shaelen said.

Lottres hesitated, trying to think what else he could say. Finally he offered, "It wasn't your fault."

"It wasn't your fault, either," Shaelen answered with a tired smile. "I was split in two. I had no power. I was... nothing." As she spoke, Shaelen shuddered with remembered horror. "But she had her own experiences, her own feelings. Now that we've rejoined, I have two sets of memories. I'm not sure who I am."

"I can't imagine," Lottres said frankly. "I'm still getting used to hearing thoughts." That was an apology, if she wanted one.

"Don't worry about me." Shaelen assumed a brisk energy. "It will take time for me to adjust, but I will. And there's no time for self-pity now. Shall I show you how to extinguish the fire?"

"Yes, if you want to," Lottres said. If she didn't want to say any more, he would have to accept that. "Should I wait for *Maess* to show me?"

"She didn't say I shouldn't," Shaelen replied. "You are part of our family now. Each of us will teach you in our own way."

A family? Lottres couldn't help smiling. Four people hardly seemed enough to call a family.

Shaelen was saying, "Now, this is almost the opposite of the fire arrows you made yesterday. Watch me first."

Lottres sat back and released a breath to relax his shoulders. He let his eyes slip partially closed, feeling rather than seeing as Shaelen extended her control over the fire. He felt her power growing heavier, like an invisible hand closing into a fist. The yellow coals in the fire ring flickered and grew dim.

"Now you try," Shaelen said.

He did, clumsily at first. He could feel the fire's energy with his mind. It fluttered, like a small animal held in his hand. Carefully, he squeezed. He saw the coals begin to smother out.

"Good," Shaelen approved. "If you can finish this, I will release our horses."

Lottres nodded, concentrating on the fire. He could hear Shaelen moving around, speaking softly to the horses. He called over his shoulder, "Will they seek their home pastures?"

"I don't know." Shaelen sounded as dispirited as Brastigan had at breakfast. "I suppose I could order them to find Hawkwing House. The Urulai at home might still need them."

Then Lottres thought of something. "What will we ride?"

Before Shaelen could answer, Lottres felt a jab at his mind. He tried to block. Too late. Lottres winced and hissed with pain. Shaelen gave him a sympathetic glance.

"You must keep your guard up, Thaeme." Yriatt's voice came brisk and clear. *"Just because there are no eppagadrocca here doesn't mean there are none anywhere. Do not take it for granted that Father and I will protect you."*

"I won't, Maess," Lottres mumbled. He sounded as sulky as Brastigan. With an effort, he made himself sound more willing. *"I will try harder."*

"See that you do. Shaelen," Yriatt went on with a trace of gentleness, *"hold the horses there for a time. I have summoned the griffins, and I don't want them distracted."*

"Yes, Maess."

Shaelen had been just about to remove her horse's bridle. Now she slumped by the cooling ashes, the reins hanging slack from her hand.

"Griffins?" asked Lottres, who had been concentrating on his breathing.

"For us to ride," Shaelen said. "If *Maess* and *Maen* both fly, we must fly, too. We couldn't keep up, otherwise."

"Oh," Lottres said.

Inside, he felt a thrill of joy. Riding griffins? None of his brothers had ever done that! Lottres grinned. Oh, yes — this was why he wanted to be a wizard.

"There will be no pack beasts," Shaelen went on, "and we can take very little with us. Go through your things, heart-kin. Bring only what you must have. We will replace the rest in Carthell, if we can."

Lottres did as he was told. In truth, there was little he considered essential. His sword and armor, he already wore. The maps, he no longer needed. He rolled one change of clothing into a tight bundle and strapped it across his back. Shaelen did the same, except that she was armed with bow and arrows rather than a sword. Lottres was sorry he had returned the bow he borrowed from Javes. He wondered if he could make his sword blade flame.

Shaelen spoke softly to the horses. With her fingers, she gently combed the mane of her white mare. Lottres had helped calm animals before, but he had never summoned one. He held his breath for a moment, checking his mental guard. Then he extended his senses, trying to feel what Yriatt was doing.

She was aware of him at once. He felt a quick probe against his shields. When they held, Yriatt seemed to accept his presence.

"Come up, if you want to see more," she told him.

"I'm going up top," Lottres called to Shaelen.

Without waiting for a reply, he strode from the rock shelter through the narrow crack where they had entered. Lottres picked his way over the tumbled rocks, climbing eagerly. He emerged onto the wide, flat stone that formed the cave's roof just as the first griffin landed.

Lottres had never seen a griffin this close before. A stylized, heraldic likeness certainly didn't do them justice. The griffin had a long, feline body and great paws tipped with savage claws. It had a huge, hooked beak with a ruff of black tipped feathers behind it, almost like a lion's mane. Its broad span of dark gold wings was also edged with black.

The magnificent creature prowled before Yriatt, tail lashing and crest flared erect. Its beak opened for a hoarse screech. The second griffin circled above, clearly undecided about whether to alight. For a moment Lottres thought the one on the ground might charge Yriatt, but she lowered her hands. Lottres felt her power around him, a choking cloud. He struggled for breath, and knew the pressure on the griffins must be even more intense.

The first griffin shook its head, an almost human gesture. It folded its hind legs to sit, golden eyes bewildered. The bristling feathers relaxed and lay smooth against its neck.

Yriatt approached confidently. She passed her hands over the cruel curve of beak, letting the griffin take in her scent. As she did so, the second griffin landed quietly. This one was slightly smaller, its markings not so dark. It was still looked intimidatingly large compared to Lottres.

"These are males, young ones," Yriatt explained calmly. "They are old enough to leave their pride in search of new territory. I have persuaded them to do so today."

"How much do they understand?" Lottres asked. "Do you speak to them in words?"

Yriatt shook her head. "In essence, I have convinced them we are a new pride of griffins. Once Father and I assume our true forms, they will be more submissive."

"I'm sure," Lottres chuckled. He couldn't help laughing as he recalled how large the dragons were. Any creature with sense would be submissive.

Unexpectedly, he felt another sharp mental probe. He held it off.

"That is better," Yriatt said. "You may approach, *Thaeme*. Familiarize yourself with them, and let them know you."

Lottres took his time, for he felt nervous about the wild steeds. The amber eyes of the smaller griffin regarded him warily.

"I am a griffin," he projected.

The griffin responded by folding its wings and flopping on its side, for all the world like one of the cats in Crutham Keep's stable. Its tail made lazy loops on the stone. Lottres touched the griffin experimentally. To his surprise, its coat was made up of feathers rather than fur. They were short and stiff, not downy. The griffin's wings gave a restless snap. Lottres stepped back to avoid being knocked over.

From a safer distance, he looked at the griffin carefully and tried to think how he would ride it. With a horse, you straddled the back right up against the shoulders. If you did that on a griffin, its wings couldn't work freely, yet if you sat across its haunches, your weight would be too far back and the creature couldn't keep its balance.

Ymell's voice came to them. *"I will be with you in a moment."*

"Very well, Father," Yriatt replied.

Lottres turned to look toward the mound. With a pang, he saw the last mule disappear. He felt Ymell close the gateway and saw the stone begin to rise.

"I have released the horses, *Maess*," Shaelen said.

Her voice startled Lottres. Turning, he saw her scramble up to the stone roof by the same path he had used. Some of the strain eased from her expression as she gazed upon the two griffins.

"Magnificent creatures," Shaelen marveled.

"Indeed," Yriatt said, but her gaze was fixed on Shaelen, and it didn't take magic to guess her concerns.

Lottres felt something shift. He looked toward the mound again. Ymell had resumed his dragon form. He sat up on his haunches, wings partially open for balance, and began to work the standing stone loose. Moments later, he winged overhead with his huge burden, only to drop behind the rocky bones of the ridge and vanish.

Lottres blinked as if waking from a dream. Yriatt wouldn't like it if he failed another of her painful tests, so he turned back to the griffins and the problem they presented. Both creatures had turned their heads, watching warily as Ymell passed above them. Lottres considered them.

Really, the only place to sit was over the haunches. Perhaps he could do that and lean forward, stretching his length along its back to help balance his weight. If he held onto its neck with both arms, the wings should be able to move freely.

Since the griffins were still on the ground, Lottres approached the smaller one. *"I'm a griffin,"* Lottres thought at it.

Speaking softly, he stroked its flank with his hands. Lottres crouched against the griffin's side. He gradually leaned forward, taking care not to slide over its wings in a way that might break any feathers.

"I'm your friend," Lottres said.

He continued moving around, stroking the griffin gently and leaning against it briefly, until finally he stretched full length along its back.

Abruptly, the griffin turned and snapped at Lottres's head. He froze, not daring to breathe. The griffin pulled at a lock of hair that fell below Lottres's helmet. It mouthed the brown strands, released them, and took up another clump.

"He is preening you," Yriatt said, amused.

"I'm sure I need it," Lottres answered. It had been days since he last washed.

Lottres was still afraid to move, so he lay there and let the griffin comb his hair with its terrible beak. He had seen stable cats groom each other, but hadn't expected wild griffins to share the same behavior. Still, if it kept the creature from attacking, he would endure it.

A silent call alerted them a moment before Ymell's shadow darkened the sky.

"Father is ready," Yriatt announced. She stepped away, toward the edge of the rock slab. Then, with swift economy, she assumed her dragon form. Her body swelled and expanded, fair skin flushing dark. Robes became wings, hands turned into enormous talons. Her neck extended, and a long tail slid out behind to balance the weight. The dragon shook herself, like a cat rousing from a nap.

The change was so quick, Lottres could hardly follow the swirling energies that charged her flesh. What must it feel like, he wondered, to have such complete control over your body? Could a human like himself ever do that?

"Time to go," Lottres said to his griffin, though it couldn't understand. He moved to the side, gripping the griffin's neck with his arms and its waist with his knees. The griffin rolled to its feet easily, as if his weight were nothing. Lottres felt a slight pressure against his ribs as his steed opened its wings. Then with a leap, a rush of wind and dust into his eyes, they were airborne.

Lottres closed his eyes for a moment, fighting his dizziness. When he opened them again the rocky hills were dropping away below. Great, leathery dragon wings cut the air. Smaller, feathered griffin wings whistled after them. The lake glittered as they banked for a turn, and Altannath was gone.

This kind of riding would take some getting used to, Lottres discovered. You didn't ride a horse while lying on your belly! He looked around to see where the others were, and felt a twinge in his neck. Lying still, he shut his eyes, not in fear, but to experience the world as the griffin saw it.

Lottres felt the strokes of its powerful wings as if they were its own. He read the many scents of the air. He saw, with stunning clarity, the details of the land passing below them. Only one thing tempered his joy in flight. Somewhere to the south, a pillar of smoke rose black against the sky. Despite the distance, he heard faint screams. It told the griffin nothing, but Lottres understood its meaning all too well.

Glawern had fallen at last.

* * *

There was no need to wonder if his warning had reached Harburg. All the land was preparing for war. The king's highway, at the foot of the Dragon's Candle, was thick with traffic. Enemy soldiers meant looting and murder outside the town walls. The peasants from the countryside sought shelter in Harburg. For others, safety lay in flight to the south. Anyone who could get away from the war was going, and whatever they valued most went with them.

The soldiers followed Brastigan as he bypassed the jostling crowd by riding through fields beside the road. Hay wagons, loaded with people and possessions, struggled along beside them. Drovers wrangled herds of sheep, horses, and even geese. The smell of fear was as thick as the dust in the air.

On either side, farms and cottages stood shuttered and abandoned. Soldiers toiled in the green fields now, not farmers. Carrots and turnips were being torn from the ground at half their usual harvest size. Grain had been cut before it was ripe. It wasn't what you called a soldier's work, ordinarily. But they all knew a harsh truth: the invaders would make free with whatever they found outside the city walls. These soldiers would leave nothing that might help the enemy. No, not even the turnip greens. Whatever couldn't be carried into the city would be burned.

It was well past noon when Brastigan's troop approached the gates of Harburg. His stomach pinched with hunger as they joined a line of folk waiting to enter the city. A familiar banner hung over the massive gate. It snapped in a brisk breeze, scented with the stale-salt smell of the harbor. Brastigan regarded the walls of Harburg with a newly critical eye.

The battlements looked in good condition, at least. Boom cranes, borrowed from the wharves, extended over the walls. Sections of wooden hoarding were being raised up to the towers. Other workers dragged garbage from the dry moat or checked the grates over the sewage outfalls. A series of locks connected the harbor to the moat, which likely would be flooded soon.

That, Brastigan had seen before. It was done once or twice a year, when the sewers needed flushing. Every time they did it, the cellar at the Dead Donkey flooded, too. The memory provoked a sour grin.

As they drew nearer the gate, Brastigan realized not everyone was being admitted to Harburg. It seemed the aldermen had forbidden camping in public squares, and the inns were already full. Refugees who didn't have a place to stay were being turned away. This caused a storm of cursing and argument. A full complement of the city guard were on hand to stop fights and help get the bulky wagons turned around.

Brastigan felt almost guilty by the time he finally reached the gate. Since he was a recognizable figure, his party was quickly admitted. They rode through the Butcher's Gate and into Bloody Square. Livestock could only be brought into town through this one gate. Here the butchers of the city did their work. Only a faded odor now remained of those tradesmen. Their market stalls had been replaced by row upon row of barricades.

Barriers nearly blocked the streets leading out of Bloody Square, too. Around the courtyard, Brastigan saw archers in the shops laying out quiver upon quiver of arrows. If the gate was overrun, this would be a bloody square, indeed.

All these brave preparations should have lifted Brastigan's heart. They didn't. He remembered all too well the forces Yriatt and Ymell wielded so casually. Why, the dragons were big enough to stand up against the walls. A simple breath, and the city would be in flames. That didn't even consider their ability to fly, or their magic.

Brastigan shook his head, scolding himself for these fancies. Trouble enough was coming without him inventing any more in his mind.

Pikarus caught the motion and spurred up beside Brastigan. "Your highness?"

"Nothing," Brastigan said.

Jitters before combat, that's all it was. Ysislaw wouldn't come at the walls himself. He had an army of bone men and *eppagadrocca*. They would do the menial work for him.

Once past Bloody Square, the troop moved more quickly. The city's cobbled streets were quiet. Not surprising, with the populace being shut out. Many shops were closed. A few commoners hurried along with shoulders hunched, starting at shadows and strange travelers. The inns were busy, but not noisy. The only crowds were at the wells, where women drew water. They would hoard it, if they were smart.

They reached the ramp leading up to Crutham Keep. After answering another challenge, they started the ascent. Hoardings were up here, too. Wooden faggots were stacked beside barrels of oil, with great cauldrons in place to be used. Brastigan's sense of disorientation grew as they turned switchbacks and passed beneath spyholes. He knew these walls well, yet they seemed strange now, as if they had changed during his absence.

He didn't think he was the only one who was worried, either. The

Cruthan forces seemed to be in good order, proud in their polished harness, but these men weren't sure of themselves. They were too quiet, not strutting and bragging as warriors should. Their eyes, under helms of steel, were shadowed and afraid.

Then they were back under the yawning portcullis. Brastigan's return was the opposite of his dramatic leave taking. In fact, it was distinctly anti-climactic. Grooms scurried from the stables to meet them, but the keep's grand courtyard was empty otherwise. It seemed that they and their noble quest had been forgotten.

Pikarus moved up beside Brastigan. "It seems quiet," he observed, not quite asking the question Brastigan was sure he had in mind.

"I know what you mean," Brastigan answered. "Get the mules unloaded. Then take your gear back to the barracks. My things to my quarters as well, please. Let the men wash up and find their families. I'll go to Father, or he'll send someone for me. You go see Tarther, or... whoever it is you report to." He let his lips twitch into a grin, remembering Pikarus's fond farewells to Therula.

The man-at-arms didn't acknowledge the jest. "Very good, your highness."

"Oh," Brastigan paused, remembering. "Let me know if Duale's a daddy yet."

Pikarus did smile at that. "Of course. I'll send word."

A groom stood near Brastigan. He was a skinny adolescent with a pronounced Adam's apple. The lad stared at Shadow as if he had never seen her like before. Maybe he hadn't.

"This one is mine," Brastigan told him. "I'll see to her, and I don't want anyone else fooling with her. Got it?"

"Yes, your highness." The lad's voice cracked, and he ducked his head with humiliation. Except for the pale hair, he reminded Brastigan of himself at the same age.

"But you can send someone to let my father know I'm here," Brastigan added as he led his horse toward the stable.

The groom tore his eyes away from Shadow to stare at Brastigan. His Adam's apple bobbed as he swallowed nervously.

"Yes, your highness," he squeaked.

The groom walked off. A moment later, he glanced over his shoulder and broke into a run. Brastigan watched after him, unable to understand his reaction. Then he led Shadow into the stables. He watered the mare and rubbed her down well. Shadow accepted his attentions with a regal bearing, as if this were her natural due.

Brastigan didn't hurry at his work. He was measuring grain for Shadow when the stable boy scuttled back in. Shortly afterward, a page approached Brastigan.

"The king will receive you, your grace," the man said in a soft, neutral tone.

Brastigan eyed the fellow as he washed his hands in Shadow's trough. This wasn't a mere page, as he had thought, but a court gentleman. Rodrec, that was his name. He wore a sober robe of dark blue velvet, its shoulders puffed up in the Tanixan style. A very tall hat with a square crown perched precariously over his long yellow hair.

"Lead on," Brastigan said.

He let his helmet dangle from his hand and gave Shadow a final brisk pat before following his guide. Behind Rodrec's back, he made a face. If the hat represented a new style, he was glad he'd been gone for a while.

Down the courtyard then. Brastigan longed to wash up, as Pikarus's men must be doing by now. But even more, he wanted to see Unferth. It was ironic, Brastigan thought. This was probably the first time he ever went gladly to see the king. It was a shock to think he truly needed Unferth. Of all people in the world, only a father would listen to Brastigan's tale without arguing, and sympathize with all his woes.

They approached the great hall, and Brastigan felt a stroke of disappointment. He had been hoping for a private conversation. Well, it wouldn't do for people to think he was getting sentimental over the old man, anyway. So what if he went before the king in dirty harness? Call it a reference to his past misdeeds. Unferth would recognize the jest. Alustra wouldn't approve at all, of course, which made it all the better.

They passed by windows as big as the queen's ego and turned into the ornamental archway. It was crowded inside. The air smelled sweaty. Everyone but Brastigan was dressed in their most fine and formal, but a lot more of the Tanixan puffery was showing these days. Lots of the new, tall hats stood up from the crowd. They made it harder for Brastigan to see over heads, as he was used to. When Rodrec stopped, his hat blocked most of Brastigan's view into the room.

He quickly realized he wasn't the only armored man in the hall. No merchants and supplicants came before the court today. These were military men, even the ones in velvet. Before the throne, an aide was reading a summary of the troops gathered to defend Crutham's capital.

Brastigan frowned as he picked out faces in the watching crowd. There was Habrok at the base of the steps. Not unusual, with battle coming, but he didn't so often see his other brothers, Calitar and Axenar, Leolin, Eskelon and Sebbelon. Brastigan hadn't seen so many of his older half-brothers together in years. In fact, almost all of Unferth's adult sons were here. The invasion had turned into a family reunion.

Rodrec shifted in place. He gave Brastigan a brief bow. "I'm sure the king will be with you momentarily," he murmured. Then he slithered away.

"Thanks." Brastigan didn't bother to lower his voice.

When he could see past the obnoxious hat, Brastigan's eyes fell on something that banished all trivial speculation from his mind.

The canopy was draped over the dais, gold stitched with black towers, just as it always was. Only, there were no longer two thrones beneath it. There was just one. Alustra's throne was gone. Unferth's throne sat alone at the center of the dais, but Unferth wasn't sitting on it. Oskar was.

CHAPTER EIGHTEEN
THE TRAITOR'S TRAP

FOR a few hours, Lottres virtually was a griffin, but in the time the thrill of flight gave way to monotony as the green-and-gray mountains of Verelya rolled beneath him. They were like waves of the sea, Lottres thought. Supposedly no two were alike, yet there was little to distinguish one from another. Only the tiny mountain lakes had any individuality. Lottres counted them as a way to pass time. Riding along on his stomach meant that his neck hurt whenever he tried to look ahead. He could only look down, and play games to pass the time.

It was quiet, high in the air. Perhaps that was what made the voice seem so loud. Lottres tensed. It wasn't so much words he heard, but a kind of shout. Someone had sensed their approach. An alarm was being passed.

Slowly, taking care not to unbalance his winged steed, Lottres raised himself on his elbows. Just ahead of him, Shaelen was doing the same. Her griffin angled its wings, dropping back to pace Lottres's mount.

"You heard that?" Shaelen called across the air.

"Yes," Lottres called back. "It looks like Brastigan was right."

He understood why she spoke aloud, rather than directly to his mind. Yriatt hadn't mentioned any wizards waiting for them in Carthell. If there were sorcerers ahead, they must be *eppagadrocca*.

"Keep your guard up," Shaelen cautioned. Then her griffin beat its wings and surged ahead.

Lottres could feel more probes now. Subtle touches, as Yriatt did before one of her assaults. He held his breath and stayed calm. No need to reveal himself with panicked bleating. After a moment more, the seeking passed. The two dragons flew onward, unhurried and unconcerned. Lottres reminded himself that he was their *thaeme* now. They would protect him. He kept his defenses up and scanned the passing mountains. Far below, a little lake winked at him, but he had lost interest in that game.

The land below was changing at last. The mountains fell away abruptly, in broad terraces. It looked as if the rocks had been shaped into steps for a giant to tread. A huge lake lapped at the base. In some places, rocky cliffs fell straight to the water. In others, pebbled beaches lined the shore. Ymell and Yriatt turned southward, following the water's edge.

Lottres had never seen it before, but he knew this must be the Sea of Carthell. It was a freshwater lake, vast and deep. Strange peoples lived on the opposite shore in cities too far off to see even from the air. Reeds clad the Carthellan shore, but farther out the lake was glossy and still, so dark it was impenetrable even at midday.

Even Lottres, with his weak human senses, could smell the water. He sensed his griffin's restlessness. It had flown hard and wanted to drink. Lottres was thirsty, too. He hoped they would land soon. Mindful that hostile wizards might hear, he quieted his thoughts.

Instead, he looked below for signs of habitation. He first saw small boats, some of reeds and some of wood. Fishermen gaped upward as the two magnificent dragons winged past. Lottres saw no nets in the boats. Instead, he glimpsed something that resembled a lobster pot.

Boats became more numerous. Soon houses and piers stood along the shore, and wagon trails wound among the trees. The shoreline bent sharply. When they glided around the curve, a city lay before them.

Carthell was smaller than Lottres had expected. The city lay in a natural bowl beneath the terraced mountains. Protective towers ranged along the step above. These, and the town walls, were built of an unusual, reddish stone. Lottres could see no such tint to the mountains behind Carthell, so the stones must have been imported. As they drew near, he could see that the buildings had rounded roofs, some of wood and others of weathered metal.

Carthell Keep stood on a small island, connected to the city by a heavily fortified bridge. Its walls were laid in alternating courses of red and gray stone. The striking pattern was a navigational marker as well as a symbol of prestige. As Lottres recalled, his brothers, Rickard and Albrett, had always been quick to point out that Carthell was once an independent state. They claimed their uncle's capital was far older and grander than Harburg. Lottres had never had time to search the archives and refute these assertions. After seeing Carthell, he had to admit a good argument could be made for the grandeur.

Yriatt and Ymell swooped low across the water as they approached the keep. Their presence had definitely been noted. Horn calls echoed from the keep and city walls, like angry bulls confronting an intruder. Lottres could feel his griffin's agitation. The clear air was muddied by city smells, and the beast didn't want to be so close to people.

There was a small landing just at the base of the keep's walls. Lake waters lapped at the sides of a large and ornate barge moored there. Something for the duke's private pleasures, Lottres assumed. The dock wasn't large enough for all of them to land at once. Ymell glided in while Yriatt and the two griffins circled over the lake. When Ymell had shrunk to his human form, Yriatt landed.

Lottres could see men running in the courtyards as his griffin folded its wings to follow Yriatt. The dock was in easy arrow shot of both the walls and bridge, he noted, though there was no sign of hostility. He sensed plenty from the *eppagadrocca*, however. Lottres had felt no more probes as they drew nearer to Carthell, but he could feel them now. They must have some way to conceal themselves, for he could hear only indistinct murmurs. Some came from the castle and some from the town. There were at least three *eppagadrocca*. Too much talk was going on for just two men.

The griffin's talons gouged the wood as it alighted on the dock. Lottres rolled off, landing in a crouch. His former steed flung itself skyward with an angry shriek. Lottres stood slowly, recovering his sense of balance after so many prone hours. With regret, he watched the two griffins retreat. They deserved thanks, but he didn't dare speak to them now.

"I have sent the griffins to the mountains," Yriatt said as Shaelen and Lottres joined her and Ymell. "They will wait a few days in case we need them again."

"We will wait, too," Ymell added with a wry smile. "Someone will come to collect us, I'm sure."

Lottres opened his mouth, but Shaelen spoke first.

"You heard the *eppagadrocca?*" she asked.

"We did." Ymell wore a hooded expression. "I believe it would be best, Lottres, if you did not reveal yourself. Maintain your barriers, and let them think you a mere man."

"They will know of Shaelen as my *thaeme,*" Yriatt added. "They may not know of you."

Lottres nodded. He could see that the element of surprise might be useful. He said, "With the two of you to worry about, they might not pay much attention to me at all."

Both wizards smiled.

"What do you plan to do, *Maen?*" Shaelen asked. "Surely they cannot hope to ambush us. We are all aware of each other."

"Why, we will bring Duke Johanz our warning," Ymell said. "What happens after will depend on his response."

"It's possible he does not know the *eppagadrocca* are here," Yriatt said. "Perhaps he will help us defeat them."

From her tone of voice, Yriatt didn't think this was likely. Lottres agreed with her. Unferth wouldn't have tolerated such people in Harburg without his knowing about it. There was no reason to think Johanz was any less vigilant. Lottres felt his heart grow cold. If Carthell was an accomplice, it cast the invasion in a much more treacherous light.

"Do not think too far ahead, *Thaeme,*" Yriatt said. "Remember to guard your thoughts. You are still inexperienced. The *eppagadrocca* may strike at you first, seeking to learn what you know of our intentions."

"Don't worry about me, *Maess,*" Lottres answered stoutly.

At the end of the dock, a small tower guarded a flight of steps up to the fortress. Its gate now opened with a rattle of chains. The boards of the dock quivered in time to marching feet as a column of soldiers emerged. Their surcoats were purple and white, the colors of Carthell. Their captain wore stiff plumes of the same hues on his helm. When he stopped, with his men ranged behind him, his eyes darted nervously, taking in the four of them.

"Halt in the name of Duke Johanz," the captain said, although no one was moving. He spoke a dialect of Cruthan, somewhat nasal but easy enough to understand. "State your names and your purpose."

Somewhere in the keep, Lottres could feel strangers straining to hear their reply.

"I am Ymell, a wizard," Ymell replied smoothly. He made a half-bow to the wary captain. "I have with me my daughter, Yriatt, and her companion, Shaelen. We are escorting Prince Lottres of Crutham, who comes bearing grave tidings. Duke Johanz will want to hear what we have to say. Will you please lead us to him?"

The captain's eyes had been fixed on Ymell and Yriatt. At the mention of Lottres's name, his head turned sharply. Their eyes met, and Lottres had the impression of some strong emotion. However, the man's face gave nothing away.

"Then, we are kinsmen," the captain said. "I am Dietrick, son of Johanz. Well met, cousin Lottres."

Lottres stepped forward, extending a hand in greeting. "I thank you for your courtesy, cousin. I only wish the circumstances were different."

So this was Johanz's own son? Now that he said it, Lottres did see some suggestion of Albrett in Dietrick's square jaw and deep-set eyes. Dietrick's nose hadn't been broken, as Albrett's had, and he was far too young to wear such a pinched, weary expression.

To Lottres's surprise, Dietrick took his shoulders in a brief, strong hug.

"I was sorry to hear about your father," Dietrick said. "He was a good king."

Lottres staggered a little as Dietrick let go. "My father?" he repeated blankly. "What do you mean?"

Now Dietrick's face was all too easy to read. With stunned pity, he asked, "What, did you not know?"

Lottres shook his head. "We've been traveling for several weeks. What has happened?"

"King Unferth passed away some ten days or more gone," Dietrick said quietly. "King Oskar rules Crutham now."

"No!" Lottres murmured. It couldn't be true. Ymell stepped up beside Lottres, steadying him with a gentle hand.

"These are evil tidings," Ymell said. "Please tell us more, Lord Dietrick."

Dietrick stepped back. His voice was tense now. "I think my father should explain what has happened since then. Please come with me. I will bring you to the duke."

The two lines of soldiers edged backward, making room on the narrow dock. Their captain strode back between them. Lottres cast a panic-stricken look at Yriatt as he followed Dietrick. Soldiers fell in on either side of them, silent except for the rhythmic tramping of feet.

The stairway was long, and wider than it had looked. There was plenty of room for the soldiers, but they stuck close anyway. Lottres followed Dietrick beneath one of the rounded towers and directly into the keep. Servants stood aside, pretending not to stare as the horned wizards passed.

Lottres hardly noticed where they went. His mind was still whirling. Surely this talk of Unferth being dead was a mistake, or some ghastly joke. Dietrick was clearly hiding something from them. Was it his father's treachery, or something else?

The great hall of Carthell Keep was a vast chamber, nearly circular even to the weathered bronze arches overhead. Round windows in the dome sent bars of daylight to pierce the gloom. The feeling of magic was thick in the air, like incense burned to cover a foul odor. Between that and his grief, Lottres felt he must struggle to breathe.

The hall was crowded, as daily court was in session. The ducal throne stood on a dais, just like Unferth's. The man sitting in it had to be Duke Johanz. He seemed to ignore the newcomers, concentrating on the petitioner before him. Loitering nearby was a group of young men who might have been his sons. Lottres glimpsed Albrett among them. These men stared openly, raising hands to cover their mouths as they whispered among themselves.

The banner over the dais told Lottres more of what was wrong in Carthell. There should have been a Cruthan flag there, either side by side with Carthell's or sewn in quarters on a single banner. Lottres could even pick out hooks on the plaster where such an emblem might have hung. It wasn't there now.

Dietrick stopped, and Lottres nearly ran into his back. All soldier now, Dietrick murmured to Lottres, "We must wait just a moment, cousin."

"Of course," Lottres said.

Dietrick's eyes stayed on Lottres's face. Again, there was a gleam of emotion in Dietrick's eyes. Sympathy, perhaps, or just plain curiosity. Lottres badly wanted to know what his cousin was thinking. Only the memory of Yriatt's warning restrained him from plundering Dietrick's memory. Lottres tried to school his features and show less emotion himself.

Shaelen shook his resolve when she slipped up beside him. Her fingers were cold as she clasped Lottres's hand.

"I'm sorry," she murmured.

"Your grief is as our own," Yriatt added softly.

Lottres felt his throat tighten, his eyes sting. Yet a part of him wondered how his mistress could say such a thing. She and her father were dragons. They wouldn't die, would never face such a loss as this.

He must have been broadcasting his feelings, for Ymell smiled sadly. "But we have," he said quietly. "Even a dragon can be killed. My own wife and one of my daughters are both gone."

Yriatt added, with hurt sharpness, "To live so long is all loss, *Thaeme*. It is our burden, seldom our joy."

"Forgive me, *Maess*," Lottres stammered.

Perhaps all of them were glad when a loud voice called, "Who comes before this worthy court?"

There was a great stirring and muttering in the hall, as everyone was free to stare at these strangers with their horned heads. Dietrick moved forward and Lottres followed again, with Ymell, Yriatt and Shaelen coming after. The soldiers remained where they were. At the base of the platform, Dietrick stopped and saluted.

"Noble father," he intoned with what seemed to Lottres like an excess of formality. "This day I present to you our cousin, Lottres, son of Unferth. Cousin

Lottres brings us news which you must hear. With him are Lord Ymell, a wizard, his daughter, Lady Yriatt, and her companion, Lady Shaelen."

They all bowed in turn. Lottres understood now why Dietrick kept calling him cousin and not prince. With Unferth gone, all titles were uncertain. Albrett didn't seem worried, though. He smirked when he caught Lottres's eye. Albrett had gained weight since he left Harburg. The tight collar of his tunic pushed his jowls up against his face, giving him a bloated look.

Dietrick went on, "Our cousin has only now learned of King Unferth's passing."

"We mourn with you, noble cousin." Yohanz spoke in the same nasal accent as his son. Cautiously, Lottres looked up into the duke's face.

Johanz of Carthell was much like Unferth, though a decade younger. Both had light hair and eyes and thick beards, though Johanz's beard was cut off short and square. They shared a certain girth, the result of days spent sitting in council chairs. Even their royal robes were similar. Lottres noted the Carthellans wore plain, close-fitting garb in darker colors. Ironically, they looked more Cruthan than most Cruthans did these days.

Yet there was no mistaking the shrewdness in the duke's eyes. He looked on his guests with deliberate calculation, something Unferth had always tried to conceal beneath a jovial facade. The silver coronet he wore was set with many amethysts. It gleamed with newness.

"I thank you for your kindness, your grace," Lottres replied. He couldn't quite bring himself to call the duke cousin, when so many questions hovered in the air. "I fear we have no time to mourn. The news I bring is dire. Crutham has been invaded. We come to warn you of Silletsian soldiers who even now attempt the Carthell Cleft."

Then Lottres fell silent as Johanz raised his hand.

"This is no news to us," Johanz said. "I believe it was one of your brothers who dispatched a messenger to bring us warning. He reached us some days ago."

"I am glad to hear that," Lottres said. "We didn't know of his fate. Is Egger here now, and safe?"

"Alas, he came to us sorely wounded," Johanz answered. "He did not live long beyond his arrival. We honor his sacrifice by taking his warning to heart, and are well prepared for war."

Egger, dead? Lottres did his best not to show his suspicions. Johanz's tone implied something more than what he said aloud. Considering the absence of a Cruthan banner and the duke's new coronet, Lottres thought he knew what it was.

Carefully, Lottres inquired, "Then, you ride to the defense of Crutham?"

Johanz smiled tightly. "That is a more complex question."

"Oh?" Lottres asked, as if he didn't understand. "What is complicated about duty to your king?"

Albrett fairly snickered at that.

"It is true, I swore loyalty to King Unferth," Johanz said. He spoke slowly and precisely, as if this changed his betrayal. "Yet we of Carthell have always felt this arrangement was one-sided. It is an unfair burden, with little reward to us. With King Unferth's passing, our duty too has passed away."

Johanz paused, and murmurs of support rumbled through the great hall. Lottres tried to ignore Albrett's cruel grin.

"Will you abandon past loyalties?" he asked directly.

Johanz maintained his smile. "It is simply that we wish to renegotiate some of the terms before we swear allegiance to King Oskar. The time is not yet right to open discussions."

Meaning that Johanz planned to wait until Crutham was in real trouble and Oskar was desperate before he started talking.

"Shall I convey that message to my brother, King Oskar?" Lottres asked. He couldn't keep the strain from his voice. Albrett chuckled again. Lottres didn't look at him. Albrett always had enjoyed watching someone else squirm.

"A generous offer," Johanz said. "In due time, perhaps, I will ask you to carry my terms. I wish you no ill, cousin, but I cannot permit you to travel at this time. It is far too dangerous," he added sanctimoniously.

"Not at all dangerous, for us," Ymell interjected, speaking for the first time.

"No, you must remain as my guests," Johanz replied, pretending not to hear the wizard. "I assure you, every comfort will be provided. You will come to no harm in my house."

Egger must have thought so, too, Lottres said to himself.

"Dietrick, escort our kinsman and his companions to their chambers," Johanz concluded.

"Yes, Father," Dietrick answered. His voice held undertones of bitterness and reproach, but he turned stiffly and marched away.

The soldiers of Dietrick's squad stepped forward. They were clearly prepared to use force if Lottres didn't go with their captain. With two wizards at his back, Lottres wasn't afraid of them, but he didn't need Yriatt's compelling stare to remind him that they, not he, would decide when to act. Lottres bowed curtly to the duke, and followed.

Dietrick strode ahead with long, angry paces. Lottres had the absurd sensation that he was back in Harburg again, trying to keep up with Brastigan. A lump rose in his throat. Without his father, nothing in Harburg would ever be the same.

Dietrick led them up stairs and around corners. By the time he stopped, Lottres had no idea where they were. That must have been part of Johanz's plan. The corridor ended in a blank wall. Four doors stood open, two on either side.

"Cousin Lottres." Dietrick made a curt gesture, indicating one of the rooms. He spoke on, in clipped tones. "Master Ymell, Mistress Yriatt, Mistress Shaelen."

Lottres stared at Dietrick for a moment. He still couldn't believe what was happening. Instead of welcome and shelter, they were imprisoned! It was little consolation that Dietrick couldn't meet his eyes.

"Forgive me," Dietrick said, still speaking with strained formality, "but I must ask for your weapons, Lady Shaelen. And your sword, cousin."

Silently, Lottres and Shaelen complied. Each of them entered their assigned room and soldiers closed the doors. Lottres found himself in a windowless, cramped chamber. A bed and small dresser nearly filled the space. He dropped his small bundle on the bed and slumped beside it, at a loss. Johanz's betrayal was infuriating. His imprisonment was humiliating. No one would dare treat Unferth's son this way if he were still alive! But he wasn't.

In a way, Lottres was surprised Johanz had found four rooms to use as their prisons. Even in a large keep, every inch was dear. The traitor duke must mean to keep them apart, unable to make plans. This really was no impediment to communication, but if they spoke mind-to-mind the enemy would surely hear.

Perhaps, he thought gloomily, that was the *eppagadrocca's* plan: force them to use telepathy, so they could be spied on more easily. Lottres wondered exactly what the Silletsian magicians were doing here. He could only assume they encouraged Johanz's rebellion as a way of weakening Crutham for their own conquest. He hadn't been able to tell who they were, or where, among the press of the Carthellan court.

The door opened, and Lottres straightened with a jerk. Dietrick stood framed in the wooden arch.

"Cousin, I am truly sorry." Dietrick spoke furtively. "Not all men of Carthell are renegades and cowards. I hope you will remember this, when times change."

Before Lottres could respond, Dietrick stepped back. He closed the door. The bolt turned with a note of finality.

* * *

Brastigan felt his chest contract. His throat tightened as if someone were choking him. His mind grappled with this impossible sight. He couldn't seem to understand what it meant.

Oskar wore a robe of black brocade with big, pointed shoulders. On his head was a high, black hat. A crown clasped its base, balancing the ridiculous height of the hat. Oskar wore the crown of Crutham with poise, listening to the emergency preparations with focused intelligence. As if he thought he deserved the crown. But where was Unferth? Was the king ill? Maybe Oskar had taken his place temporarily.

Even as he thought it, Brastigan knew in his gut that was wrong. Unferth was dead. He had to be. Alustra would never suffer her precious throne to be removed. Nor would Oskar tolerate such an insult to his mother under any other circumstances.

Unferth, dead? It was impossible, so wrong. The old man had said... He had told Brastigan... "Stay away just for a while. Keep yourself safe..."

Unferth, dead! How dare the old man die before hearing what Brastigan had to tell him? About Lottres, about the girl, even about Leithan. This wasn't what Brastigan had agreed to, not at all!

Now Brastigan was aware of a nearby courtier watching him. Cold, uncaring eyes analyzed his reaction. Brastigan held back the impulse to punch the man. All the way through town they came. Every guard who stopped them must have known Unferth was dead. Even the groom had known. And not one of them saw fit to mention it?

Brastigan eased back toward the doorway, seeking the cover of shadows as he had done on so many previous visits to the great hall. His dark eyes narrowed, focused on Oskar with all the rage he couldn't express. Look at him up there, posing like a leader. Big shoulders, big crown, big head—that was Oskar. Oskar was no king. He was an over-dressed idiot.

Then Oskar looked up sharply. His pale eyes found Brastigan through the throng. With a curt gesture, he interrupted the speaker.

"Brastigan," he called with a kind of grandiose benevolence. "Why do you hide? Come forward and join our company."

Still playing the kindly sibling, was he? Brastigan couldn't refuse a royal command, but he could obey in his own style. The court shifted nervously, clearing an aisle. Slowly Brastigan strolled between the ranks. He greeted each of his brothers in turn, some with a brief handshake, others with a friendly punch on the shoulder.

"Nice to see you again," he murmured to Sebbelon. And to Axenar, "It's been too long."

In the corner of his eye, Brastigan could see Oskar frowning at his slow progress. Inside himself, he grinned. It was a familiar boyhood ritual, tweaking his brothers. In truth, he didn't know how to talk to half of them without it.

Calitar must have seen Oskar's displeasure, too. He quietly growled, "Quit fooling around."

"What fun is that?" Brastigan smirked back at him.

He stopped when he came to Habrok. Of all the sons, Habrok looked most like Unferth, so square and solid. Their eyes met, and Brastigan felt his jaw tremble. Habrok pulled him close in a crushing hug, pounded his back with numbing force. For some reason, Brastigan breathed easier afterward. He turned to face Oskar with a confident showing of teeth.

"I have returned, my good brother!" Brastigan trumpeted, taking up Oskar's own words on their parting. The new king didn't seem to recognize the satire.

"Welcome, Brastigan," he said, a smooth purr of satisfaction. "Well met, indeed. You have been away too long."

Brastigan might have agreed with that, but he couldn't bring himself to take Oskar's side in anything. Instead, he bowed with a mocking snap and spoke the words he couldn't avoid.

"It looks like there have been some changes. Where is our father, pray tell?"

Oskar's face, under the crown, twisted in an exaggerated display of surprise. "Alas, did you not know? Our dear father is gone. He passed peacefully in his sleep." Oskar bent his head for a moment.

It was a convincing show, and yet... Brastigan felt his throat tighten again.

He knew Oskar too well. Alustra's son felt no grief over his father's death. No, he was well pleased with this turn of events.

Brastigan forced a similar expression of sorrow. "My deepest condolences to Queen Alustra."

That slight should have sent Oskar into fits. It certainly sent a flurry of dismay among their brothers. Yet, again, Oskar didn't seem to notice the barb.

"I shall tell her of your sympathies," he answered smoothly. "But you have been carrying out our father's wishes as well. Tell me, Brastigan, how fared your quest? What did the Lady of Hawkwing House seek from you?"

There was so much to say, but those were all confidences he had meant to share with Unferth. Maybe he could tell Habrok or Calitar about Lottres, about the girl. Never Oskar.

"If you want the whole story, I'll need ale," Brastigan said with humor he didn't feel. "*Lots* of ale. The short of it is, we went to Hawkwing House. We met the witch. We ducked griffins. We went to Altannath. We fought the Silletsian army. They're all cursed, by the way. We..."

"Cursed?" Habrok interrupted.

"Just the kind of tale I'd expect from you, Brastigan," Leolin snorted.

"I'm not making it up!" Brastigan told him. "We called them bone men. They look like men, but they're not. They're some kind of monster."

Leolin snorted again, rolling his eyes, and Sebbelon said, "Brastigan's no liar."

Brastigan nodded gratefully to Sebbelon, who was only a little older than he.

"Tell us more," Habrok said.

"As near as we could tell, they're what's left of the Urulai," Brastigan admitted reluctantly. "Tall and straight and dark, like me, but so skinny they were like walking bones. They're dead, you see. Yet they walk. They're pretty fast, abnormally strong, but not too smart. Luckily, they have lousy weapons and no armor to speak of."

"Black magic?" Calitar asked grimly.

"The evil of Sillets," Brastigan agreed. "They don't die. You have to hack their arms and legs off to stop them coming at you. We lost a couple of men figuring out how to handle them. Oh, and they do burn. Problem is, there could be thousands of them. Nobody knows how many warriors were captured in Urland."

The soldiers in the room stirred restlessly, glancing among themselves to see who believed Brastigan's tale. The princes looked worried, but Oskar didn't seem interested in the enemy forces.

"You said you went to Altannath," he asked with quiet intensity. "What did you do there?"

"Oh, we set the dragon free," Brastigan said with mocking good cheer. "That was what Yriatt wanted us for."

"Indeed," Oskar murmured. He sat back, eyes lowered in thought.

More nervous glances passed among the men, and anxious murmurs. Brastigan grinned tightly, remembering his own reaction.

"Don't worry, he's on our side. The dragon, I mean," Brastigan told them.

"They headed for Carthell, to see if Johanz needs help. Our squad came home, soon as the witch said we were done."

"Is Lottres with them?" Axenar asked.

"Oh." Brastigan rolled his eyes. "That's another long story, but, yeah. He's with the witch and the dragon. There are also some Urulai—live ones," he smiled without humor, "holding Carthell Cleft against the enemy. We had to give up on Glawern, I'm afraid."

As one, Unferth's sons relaxed. Brastigan realized they had been waiting to hear if another of their number was gone.

"I thank you for this crucial information," Oskar said smoothly. "We shall use it well. It is good to know you carried out our father's commands on your journey."

Brastigan frowned at his condescending tone. As if Brastigan had known Sillets would invade and taken it upon himself to go jaunting off anyway. It was just like Oskar to dismiss what he had done. After all, you couldn't have anyone else in the spotlight.

"It wasn't my idea to go on that fool quest," he snapped. "I did what I was told because I'm loyal. Loyal to my home. As long as I have breath, I'll fight for Crutham!"

"Hear, hear!" Calitar cried.

A spontaneous cheer went up in the hall. Brastigan was left feeling the fool, but he raised his hands in mockery of Oskar's grand posing. Then Brastigan turned to Habrok. He laid his hand on Victory's hilt.

"You just tell me where to go, and I'll be there," Brastigan proclaimed. "We'll chop those bone men to bits, and feed them to our hogs!"

Habrok returned a crooked smile. "Now I know our kingdom is safe."

"Well spoken," Oskar interrupted. Brastigan noticed he hadn't been clapping as loudly as many others. "Well said, indeed, Brastigan."

It had to gall Oskar to flatter him. Oh, he made a good show, but Oskar hadn't missed that Brastigan offered his sword to Habrok first. Oskar was good at hiding his malice, but Brastigan knew they still loathed each other as much as they ever had. In a funny way, it was almost comforting. Lottres was gone, and Unferth was gone, but he could still rely on Oskar's hatred.

The new king smiled through his teeth and said, "You must be weary from your long journey. You may retire now, and rest. I will provide you the ale another time, and you will tell me all about your adventures."

"I await the day," Brastigan lied with great sincerity. He bowed, covering his disgust.

He continued bowing, turning in a circle to acknowledge each of his brothers. Some smiled at the display, some frowned, and Sebbelon aimed a mocking kick at his backside.

"Go on, you fool," Sebbelon chuckled. "Get out of here. You smell like a horse."

Brastigan did as he was told, but he didn't hurry. In a way, he felt he was leaving the last of his father behind.

Unferth was dead. No longer would he sit on the throne and wear the golden crown. A despised sibling had taken his place. No amount of ale could ease the bitter sting of that knowledge.

Chapter Nineteen
The True Gold of Crutham

DESPITE her resolution, Therula didn't attend court, but it wasn't because she feared the stranger Oskar had become. Rather, she sought out her half-sisters and their mothers, hoping to learn what they knew about it. Without raising any questions about herself, of course. She did this by feigning a deep concern for Oskar.

"Rulership must be such a burden, at a time like this," Therula sighed, over and over, for most of the day.

She learned nothing relevant except that Leoda's mother, Jenne, a seamstress, had made the first Silletsian hat Oskar wore. Eben had ordered it from Jenne two days before the coronation. Jenne grumbled that she had had to stop working on Leoda's coronation gown and make the hat instead. Now Eben had left, and she hadn't even been paid for the work.

Therula returned to her own apartment, puzzling over this morsel of information. Eben had always helped protect Crutham. It seemed unthinkable, but could his absence be a defection?

A knock came at the chamber door. Cliodora burst in without waiting for permission. The younger princess was pink-cheeked, panting.

"Sister, sister!" Cliodora squealed. "They're back! Brastigan is back!"

Therula managed a weak, "Oh." If Brastigan was here, then Pikarus had returned as well.

Cliodora didn't seem to notice Therula's reaction. She was too busy bouncing on her toes. "Will he come to see us?" the girl asked eagerly. "Oh, I can't wait."

"Of course he will," Therula said, more primly than she intended. How she longed to have feelings as uncomplicated as Cliodora's! "Stop your dancing. I need you to do something for me."

"Go find Brastigan?" Cliodora demanded happily.

Therula hugged the girl to conceal her annoyance. "Later," she said. "First, find Pikarus. Say that I must see him immediately."

Cliodora's mouth made an O and then she giggled. "Pikarus?"

"Yes, Pikarus," Therula answered irritably. "Before he reports to Oskar or Garican or anyone else, he *must* speak to me. Understand?"

"Yes!" Cliodora squeaked. Therula realized she was squeezing her little sister's shoulders with a fierce grip.

"I'm sorry." Therula hugged Cliodora again, trying to mean what she said. "This is terribly important. You must tell Pikarus exactly what I said. And don't let anyone stop you. Remember, you're a princess, too."

Cliodora's shoulders hunched. Her young face grew shadowed. "No, I'm not. Not any more," she whispered.

"Don't say that!" Therula exclaimed. She let go of Cliodora's shoulders so she wouldn't shake the girl. "It isn't true. You are the daughter of a king."

"But he's dead!" Cliodora wailed suddenly. "Papa's dead, sister. Everyone looks at us differently now. All the courtiers sniff, and some of the servants ignore us. Orlyse and Frella and Leoda—we all think so."

"Who are the servants to decide?" Therula retorted. She hated to admit, even for a moment, that Bettonie's haughty attitude might prevail. "It's not all about them, apple blossom. It's about you, too. This is your birthright. You mustn't let anyone take it from you."

Cliodora straightened her back and summoned a wobbly smile. She lifted her chin and marched out the door with the intensity of a soldier going to battle.

When she had gone, Therula let her knees go soft. She sank into her chair and stared at the burned out ashes in the fireplace. Cliodora's fragile smile tore at her heart. What must it feel like, to be so afraid and so young? Therula had to acknowledge their situations were very different. No one was going to repudiate Therula, a full sibling to the reigning king. But Cliodora? Oh, the poor girl was so young to be facing such things!

Yet Therula had her own fears. The mere mention of Pikarus's name made her feel as if she had eaten something horrible. She could neither swallow it nor spit it out. Of course she was glad to know he was safe, but guilt tarnished her joy. How could she tell him what she had done? She knew she couldn't hide it. Oskar would make certain of that.

She had summoned Pikarus to her, but she had no idea what she would tell him. The waiting dragged at her, a crushing weight on her heart. It seemed hours since Cliodora left her chambers. Therula told herself not to be silly. It took time to carry a message across a castle as large as Crutham Keep. But soon the passing minutes told her it really had been a long time.

Therula jumped up from her chair, pacing the room. Her own anxiety mocked her. What if Cliodora was too late? Oskar could be questioning Pikarus even now, taunting him with her lack of faith in him. What would he think of her?

The door latch rattled. Therula froze, her fingers tied in a nervous knot before her. She wrenched them apart, held her hands at her sides... But it was only Cliodora who slipped through the door.

"I gave him your message," Cliodora hurried to say, "but I had to wait to see him. Two of the men didn't come back. Pikarus was talking to their families." Her voice trailed off on the mournful news.

"I see," Therula murmured. "Thank you, sister."

Without thinking, she resumed her pacing. So Pikarus had to comfort grieving relatives? That would put him in an even worse mood. Then Therula shook her head, chiding herself for being selfish. Pikarus had to do his duty. He had things to worry about besides her.

Cliodora was at the door, half the time watching Therula pace and half the time peeking out. At last she gave a delighted squeak.

"He's coming!"

Therula froze again. As before, she had to force herself to relax. Cliodora seemed to have forgotten her troubles, for she was bouncing on her toes again.

"Can I hide in your room and listen?" Cliodora teased.

"No!" Therula had to make herself laugh. "Go on, silly. There won't be much to hear."

"Oh, really?" Cliodora giggled.

"Just go!" Therula said. She opened the door to push the girl out, and Pikarus was there.

Time seemed to stop as Therula looked into his face. So did her breathing, her heartbeat. Somehow she had forgotten how blue his eyes were. Pikarus looked tired, but his soldier's reserve softened into gentleness at the sight of her. Therula trembled. She nearly turned and ran. Pikarus stepped back, allowing Cliodora to leave, before he entered the room and closed the door.

"You wanted to see me?" His voice held a special meaning for her alone.

Therula she stepped forward and hugged him fiercely. She wanted to kiss him, but she couldn't bring herself to try. It was such a relief to feel Pikarus's strong arms around her. Familiar scents of dust and horses clung to his surcoat. If only this sense of peace could last.

When she didn't speak, Pikarus asked, "Has something happened?"

Therula shook her head. "No, but it could."

Reluctantly, she stood away. Therula led Pikarus away from the door, in case Cliodora had decided to eavesdrop after all.

"While you were gone, I..." she faltered. "That is, Oskar..."

Pikarus watched quietly. His military stiffness was back, watching for nuances as Therula floundered.

"I'm sorry. I'm babbling." Therula stopped talking. She felt like an idiot instead of a princess. Taking a deep breath, she tried again.

"A few days after the coronation, Oskar sent for me. He knew about us. It's hard keeping secrets, I suppose. He said... He thinks..." She swallowed, forcing the odious words out. "Oskar thinks you only love me for my position. I said he was wrong, that I didn't believe it, but he..." Therula spoke in a rush now, but when she looked at Pikarus he was all soldier, as silent as the settee which stood between them.

Miserable, unable to face him, she went on, "Oskar wanted to test your love. He offered a wager. He said you wouldn't be faithful to me on your journey. He said..."

"He would have lost that bet," Pikarus cut in, calm and sure.

"Of course, I know that," Therula said desperately. "I never doubted you, not for a moment. But he insisted on it."

Now came the moment she had been dreading. Pikarus's jaw tightened as he realized she had taken Oskar's wager. His fingers, on the back of the settee, grew white.

"I never should have listened to him." Therula was babbling again.

"You're not a race horse! But he said... He promised he wouldn't interfere with us. I thought, when you won... If you were true to me... It seemed worth it, to get his blessing. I..." The torrent of words slowed at last. Therula faltered, "I'm so sorry."

She couldn't bear to look at Pikarus any longer, to see the hurt and disappointment in his eyes. Therula turned away, biting her lip to keep back tears. Her fingers were knotted in the air before her, and she couldn't make them let go.

After much too long, Pikarus spoke.

"I'm glad I heard this from you," he said, too quietly. "You are right, I don't appreciate being gambled on. It was a cruel demand that Oskar made of you. But..." Therula dared to look around, saw his fingers relax their grip on the settee. "You did win. If your brother honors his bargain, perhaps it will bring us peace in the end."

At once, Therula found she could breathe again, though her chest still ached.

"Now I must ask you about something else," Pikarus went on. "Please try to think clearly."

Therula nodded, swallowing against her tension. What could Pikarus mean? Did he want to know about Unferth's death? Or where Tarther was? Or Oskar's leadership?

"I've noticed the new style in hats since we returned," Pikarus said.

The irrelevance surprised her into laughter. "I'm sorry," Therula apologized. She was well aware her mirth was tinged with hysteria. "Yes, the Silletsian representative wore a hat like that at Oskar's coronation. They've been all the style since."

"Sillets?" Pikarus asked.

Therula nodded. She didn't wonder at his frown.

"An ambassador attended the coronation, talking about increased trade with us. Oskar was quite taken with the idea. Or perhaps, simply taken in." Therula didn't try to hide her irritation. She wondered if she should tell Pikarus what she suspected. No, her suspicions would only add to the tension between them. "No one seems to see the paradox, that they've invaded our country and we still wear their styles. Oskar hardly ever takes his off."

"Oskar?" Pikarus repeated, more quietly still.

Now it was Therula's turn to ask, "Is something wrong?"

She winced at the awkward question, but Pikarus didn't seem to notice. He stood silently, hands clasped behind him and eyes nearly closed. Finally he said, "I must speak to Brastigan. Do you know where he is?"

"No," Therula said. "Cliodora is probably out looking for him, but..."

"I will search for him, too. If Cliodora finds him first, you must send him to me." Pikarus went to the door, lecturing Therula like captain to soldier. At least he wasn't looking at her the way he had before.

"But I wanted to tell you..." Therula said, following him.

"This can't wait." Pikarus paused with his hand on the latch. With a trace of his old warmth, he said, "I'll see you again soon."

The door closed. Therula stood helplessly, feeling terribly alone. When her beloved was with her, she could hardly think what to say. Now a hundred words crowded her mind. She leaned backward, slinging to the back of the settee for support. The wood was still warm from Pikarus's hands.

Therula had thought, earlier, that she could never be repudiated. Now she wondered how she could have been so wrong.

* * *

He had left the court for his own rooms, but the chambers seemed small and stuffy after so long away. Once Brastigan was out of his filthy harness, and in control of his emotions, the baths were the first place he wanted to go. Not even the wonderful sensation of cleanliness could lift Brastigan's spirits. Bathed and washed and famished, he prowled his quarters, waiting for the meal he had ordered.

The bath had been empty by the time Brastigan got there. It was too bad. He had hoped to find Pikarus, or even Javes. It seemed they had something more to talk about, after all.

Oskar's taking the throne did explain a few things. Like why the men on the walls seemed so bewildered. Losing your king on the eve of battle would do that. Oskar was well known, but he had always kept himself to Harburg, letting Habrok handle the bloody stuff. The soldiers didn't know Oskar as a battlefield commander.

Well, maybe they didn't have to. It looked like Oskar planned to keep Habrok on as Champion of Crutham. That was basic good sense. Good politics, too, making a point of family unity by summoning their brothers during the crisis. Then Brastigan snorted to himself. It also brought a convenient force to hand, if Oskar needed someone to do his fighting for him. Unferth's sons were a small army in their own right. The risk was that one of them might make a hero of himself—a potential rival.

Still no supper. Frustrated, Brastigan found a comb and dragged it through his damp hair. He smiled without humor. Oh, Alustra had to be furious with Unferth for widowing her! A dowager queen was nowhere near the same as a reigning monarch. The fact that Oskar had removed his mother's throne told that tale. But he had to do it, of course. A man couldn't rule when he was ruled by another, not even a doting mother.

Absently, he began to braid his hair. Transitions of power were always a time of vulnerability. Brastigan had to wonder if Sillets was somehow involved in Unferth's passing. The timing of their invasion seemed a little too convenient.

A tap at the door distracted Brastigan from his brooding. He turned to call, "If you have food, come in! Otherwise, go away."

The door opened softly. Margura entered, balancing a tray loaded with covered dishes. A delightful aroma came with her as she glided to the table where Brastigan sat. Despite the welcome presence of food, he felt his stomach drop. Why Margura? Why now?

The contrast with the shadow girl was like a blow to his gut. Maybe it wasn't fair to compare them, but he couldn't help it. They were both blonde beauties — the true gold of Crutham, as poets would say. That was the only thing the two women had in common. Margura seemed brazen and sensual after the silent, gentle girl-child. Only now that he'd been away from her did he understand how much more there could be. It was hard to believe she had ever attracted him.

As always, Margura smiled coyly. She bent forward to slide the tray onto the table.

"I wanted to see you," she murmured softly.

Brastigan cleared his throat uncomfortably. "I'll bet."

Margura hadn't changed a bit, but her gown had. It was deep green velvet, still low cut but the shoulders and waist puffed out more. A delicate golden chain dangled a fiery yellow gem into the garment's plunging neckline. Although she was still lovely, her face had a sallow tone beneath the cosmetics.

A slight frown puckered Margura's smooth brow when Brastigan failed to greet her as she must have expected. He glanced toward the door.

"Shut it," he said. "I need to talk to you."

It wouldn't be easy to tell Margura he had no interest in her any more, especially when she had a romantic reunion planned. Still, he didn't want to alienate her too soon. She might be useful.

The courtier's blue eyes glinted with suspicion, but she dipped in a curtsey. Her gown rustled as she went to the door, which creaked as it swung closed. Brastigan didn't watch her. He took lids off dishes, revealing half of a cold roast chicken, buttered bread, baked apples drizzled with cream. The bread tasted wonderful, though his stomach still churned with tension.

Margura slid another tray onto the table. This one held a flagon and a short brown bottle. Ale!

"Ah, that's what I need!" It wasn't so hard to smile now.

His companion poured smoothly, raising little foam. Her measuring gaze was fixed on Brastigan as she gave him the glass and sank into the chair opposite him.

"Was it a difficult journey?" she asked.

"Frustrating." Brastigan took a long, bitter draft. "A lot of time wasted running hither and yon, when I really wanted to be here." For a moment, Margura's expression lightened. Brastigan decided to prepare her for disappointment. "The last few days have been tough. We fought hard, and I'm dead tired."

Margura glanced aside momentarily. "It's been difficult here, too." She spoke defensively.

"Yeah, tell me about that." Brastigan fixed his dark eyes on Margura. "We came all the way through town, and no one bothered to mention that my father had died. I had to walk into the hall and see Oskar sitting on the throne." It wasn't her fault, but Brastigan couldn't keep the anger from his voice.

"An unpleasant surprise, I'm sure." Margura smiled with sympathy, but also, he thought, a trace of mockery.

"It was." Brastigan swallowed his bread and took another long drink. Then he started picking the roast fowl apart. "So when did he die?"

"Seven days after you left," she answered, "give or take a day."

"And he just died in his sleep?" Brastigan tried to keep the suspicion from his tone. "No reason whatsoever?"

"I heard that he complained of indigestion to his valet, Jesprey," she said. "He retired early. Princess Therula found him the next morning."

Brastigan winced. Therula must have taken it hard. "Who examined his body?"

"Eben was summoned, but the king had already been dead for several hours." Margura seemed to study him. "At his age, it didn't seem unusual."

"What's he been doing since then?" Brastigan remembered Yriatt complaining that she couldn't contact the wizard.

"Eben?" Margura seemed surprised by the question.

"Yes, Eben. The king's own wizard," Brastigan retorted. "What does he say about the invasion?"

Margura frowned, as if she had to think hard about this. "I haven't seen him," she finally said.

"You haven't seen him?" Scowling, Brastigan took a bite from his chicken leg. He wasn't paying attention, and bit his own finger. "Ow!"

"What's wrong?" Margura asked, all concern.

"Nothing." Brastigan brushed her worries away. "So you haven't seen Eben at all. Since when? Before or after Father died?"

"After. He was at the coronation." From Margura's expression, she had no idea why Eben was so important.

Maybe he wasn't, but Yriatt and Ymell seemed to feel he was. Rather, his silence was. Brastigan wished, now, that he had some way to reach the two dragons, if only to let Lottres know what had happened. The pup shouldn't have to walk into the shock, as Brastigan had.

Margura was looking at Brastigan oddly. He waved a chicken bone at her. "So Oskar stepped right into the gap, did he?"

"He has, indeed," she answered with a hint of emotion he couldn't identify.

"How's Alustra taking it?" Brastigan asked with some irony.

"The queen is devastated," Margura answered sadly. "She supports Oskar, of course, but it is difficult to interest her in anything."

"She misses the old man?" The sarcastic question went down with another draft. "Me, too."

"Really?" she murmured. "I didn't think you were close."

"Not as close as we should have been," he muttered, and took another drink. "It wasn't my decision."

"I am sorry, Brastigan." Margura briefly laid her hand over his. Her touch felt heavy and sweaty.

It was the first overt expression of sympathy he had received from anyone.

For a moment, Brastigan's grief threatened to choke him. He managed a smile. "Thanks." Then he took his hand away and reached for more ale.

"The coronation was three days later," Margura remarked with honeyed tartness. "It was quite interesting with all your brothers and sisters here at one time."

Brastigan grunted. The details of Oskar's fete were of no interest whatsoever. What mattered was the count of days in Harburg as compared to his journey. Had Sillets invaded before Unferth died, or after? He was too tired to figure properly, but it nagged at him.

"The relay rider arrived from Caulteit a few days after." Margura unknowingly answered his question.

He asked, "Are all of them still here? My brothers, I mean."

"Only the oldest sons," Margura said. "The king... That is, King Unferth, had sent some of the princes away for training just before he died. Kesper is in Praxium, Imric is in Fanglith, and Bartole is in Maduras. Tellek and Gorthar were both in Firice. I don't know if they will return to fight."

Brastigan nodded. This accounted for the younger lads, and it held with Unferth's plans to spread his sons around for their safety. But it did leave out one brother.

"What about Alemin?" he asked. "I saw most of the older ones in the hall today, but not him."

"Prince Alemin left suddenly. A sea voyage, they say." Margura paused, fire in her eyes. She added in a brittle tone, "I heard he got a girl pregnant and had to get away from his wife's brothers."

"Fool." Brastigan shook his head and rolled his eyes. He never had thought much of that particular half-brother, but he hadn't realized Alemin was a coward. A man and a woman might part ways, but he should never abandon his child. It was probably the only thing Unferth had taught Brastigan that was worth anything.

Margura startled Brastigan by placing her hand over his. She pressed hard this time, and her mouth was thin with tension.

"Tell me the truth," she said.

"What do you mean?" he asked, distracted by too many memories of Unferth, of his brothers.

"Did you think I wouldn't notice?" Margura accused. She leaned forward, and her nails dug crescents into the back of his hand. "You won't look at me or touch me. There's someone else, isn't there?"

"Yeah." Such a small word, surprisingly easy to say. With a bleak elan, Brastigan added, "She's dead."

Margura sat back then. Her lips trembled with anger and hurt, but she didn't try to hold Brastigan's hand any longer. He lifted his flagon and drained it.

"And my father is dead." Brastigan stared at the foam on the bottom of his flagon. "And Lottres..."

"Lottres is dead?" Margura interrupted.

"Might as well be. He isn't here." Brastigan glanced at the leavings on his plate. He pushed it away. Loneliness made a painful band around his chest, but even now he knew better than to tell Margura anything so personal. "I'm alone. Maybe that's the way I want it."

"Just for a while?" Margura held onto her composure, but the yellow stone glittered in rhythm with her angry breathing.

"I don't know."

That was a lie, of course. Brastigan could never desire heavy flesh and hot blood, not after a girl made of cobwebs and shadows.

"I understand," Margura said. "Really, I do." But there was that brittleness in her voice again, and Brastigan was pretty sure she didn't understand anything at all.

Proving him right, Margura continued, "The living can't compete with the dead."

"You don't have to," Brastigan told her with something like tenderness. "Don't be waiting for me to change my mind. Someone else will come along, and he'll be better for you than I am. Believe me, that won't be hard."

He lifted his flagon again, but then remembered it was empty. Brastigan looked into its emptiness and sighed. All the weight of his grief and exhaustion returned, redoubled by Margura's disappointment. His head felt heavy with drink, yet he was too upset to just go to sleep. And he was out of ale.

Margura leaned back, watching Brastigan. She put on a smile as tight as the bodice of her gown. "You really have changed," she said. "Next, you'll be telling me you aren't the greatest swordsman in Crutham, either."

Brastigan's head snapped up, a reflex of his warrior's pride. Margura laughed at his reaction, thought it had a ragged edge. She leaned forward slightly, and produced a bottle from under her skirt. It was smaller than the ale bottle, a murky green with darker contents. Margura set it on the table between them.

"I was saving this for our reunion," she said. "It will do for you to toast the dead."

She stood up and stacked the two trays, then gathered the dishes. Brastigan lifted the bottle. It was warm from Margura's body heat, heavier than it looked. The cork squeaked as it came out. Margura carried the trays toward the door.

"You do know the way to a man's heart," Brastigan said to her back. Liquid gurgled into his flagon.

Her voice trembled again. "If only I did."

The latch rattled, and the door swung open. It closed hard. Brastigan was left in a silence ringing with regrets. He raised his flagon to no one.

"To the king!" he said, and drank deeply.

Margura's brew wasn't ale, as Brastigan had thought. Powerful sweetness burned its way down his throat. Apple brandy. It wasn't Brastigan's favorite, but he wouldn't refuse it. Anything that made him drunk would be good enough for this wretched day.

He raised his flagon again. "To the girl."

A pleasant burning began in his stomach. Relaxing heat pulsed outward with every beat of his heart.

"To absent friends." He drank once again, and thought of his brother. They should be in Carthell by now, Lottres and his mentors. Someone there must have enlightened them about Unferth's fate. Maybe he didn't need to worry about the pup after all.

That took care of the first round of toasts, but Brastigan had a lot of brandy left. He was about to salute the king again, when someone rapped at his door.

"Brastigan," came a childish, muffled voice.

Margura's brew was strong, all right. Brastigan had to think past the fumes before he recognized the voice.

"Come in," he called. The words were slurred and strange in his ears. Brastigan started to stand up, but the door flew open. A lithe blonde girl raced toward him.

"You're here!" Cliodora shrieked. "You're really here!"

Her enthusiastic greeting was almost too much. Brastigan stumbled backward as she crashed into him. He fell into his chair and hugged his little sister to him.

"Whoa!" he laughed. "Slow down!"

Cliodora threw her arms around Brastigan's neck. He kissed her bright gold hair. Then she stood back and wrinkled her nose at him. "Your face feels all scratchy."

Brastigan rubbed his stubbly chin. "It was a long journey. Don't you like me with a beard?" he teased.

"You're no town elder," she scoffed. Then Cliodora's eyes were downcast as she slid into the chair Margura had recently occupied. "Did you hear about Papa?"

Brastigan felt a surge of fresh grief, to hear Unferth described with such childish affection. "As a matter of fact, I have just been drinking to his memory."

He raised his flagon to his lips in demonstration, tasted its sweet fire.

"I miss him," Cliodora said softly, sadly.

Brastigan swallowed against the ache in his throat. "So do I, princess," he said hoarsely.

Her fingertips drew an idle pattern on the table top. "Mama thinks we might have to leave soon."

Brastigan frowned. "She does?"

"She says it's awkward for her, without Papa. We shouldn't be an embarrassment to the new king." Cliodora pouted momentarily. "But Therula says I shouldn't give up my birthright."

Brastigan blew out a breath. He would miss Cliodora if she left, but he had to admit Casiana might have a point.

"There's a war going on," Brastigan said. "If your Mama knows someplace safe..." Cliodora regarded him so unhappily that he stumbled. "You have to do what you're told, princess." And a strange thing that was for him to be saying!

Cliodora folded her arms on the table and sulked. Brastigan took another pull from the flagon. The brandy was stronger than he had thought. He was no stranger to drink, but his head was reeling. Which didn't matter. He was bone tired, sick inside with grief. He needed something to make him sleep, and sleep hard.

"I told Therula you're here, but she wanted to talk to Pikarus first," Cliodora said, still petulant. Then she perked up. "Can I hear some of your stories?"

Stories? Brastigan wouldn't know where to begin. Still, Cliodora and Therula might be the only friendly audience left for his tales of woe.

"Not now," Brastigan said. His voice was sounding slurred again. "I'm done in, princess. But later. Later, I promise."

"You'd better," Cliodora huffed as she jumped to her feet. Then she smiled again. "I'm so glad you're back. I missed you a lot."

"Thanks, princess." Her words brought warmth to Brastigan's heart, as none of Margura's had.

He walked with Cliodora as she pranced out of the room. Once she was gone, his smile vanished. Brastigan locked the door. He made it back to the table and emptied the bottle of apple brandy into his flagon. Once again he raised his cup to the vacant room.

"To the king."

There was no one to notice if his tongue got tangled.

"To the girl."

In fact, Brastigan thought, he might not even make it to bed before he passed out. It didn't seem to matter.

"To absent friends."

Brastigan kept repeating the same three salutes. Soon enough, the brandy was gone. And so were his wits. And so was the world.

CHAPTER TWENTY
ESCAPES

HOURS passed while Lottres lay in his windowless room. It felt like days. He tried to think of something useful to do, some way to use his powers and set everyone free — without giving them away. All he really thought of was how little he knew. Despite the powers he took such pride in, Lottres was helpless, trapped and alone.

Then he felt the tickle of a mind probe. It wasn't like Yriatt's sharp force, but he was sure someone was trying to insinuate into his thoughts. He held his breath for a moment, then forced himself to relax. Instead of blocking, Lottres concentrated on his emotions, showing what the spy would expect to see: shock and indignation at Carthell's betrayal, self-pity, grief over Unferth.

Nor was his mourning all for show. How could it be? He would never see his father again. A part of Lottres didn't want to believe it, though he knew he should. Johanz of Carthell certainly seemed to think it was true. He wouldn't have launched his rebellion if he didn't think Unferth was gone.

Lottres lay on the narrow bed and let his heart ache. What else was there to do?

Just as he was getting truly maudlin, the cool thrill of Yriatt's power brushed the unseen eavesdroppers away. Lottres sat up on the bed. The bare wall was rippling, like water when a stone is thrown in. Fascinated, Lottres watched, trying to feel how Yriatt did this. As he stared, she walked through the solid stone.

"Are you ready to leave, *Thaeme*?" she asked.

"Yes, but..." Lottres stammered. "*Maess*, won't they hear you?"

"I certainly hope so," Yriatt answered with asperity. "I did not rescue my father from Altannath so we could be shut up in this little hole. Come, *Thaeme*."

Yriatt approached the door. Her power went out before her. Lottres heard the bolt on the other side slide back. The door opened without her touching it. From beyond it, Lottres could feel Ymell doing something as well, though he couldn't tell what it was.

They were showing off their abilities on purpose, Lottres realized as he followed Yriatt. They were taunting the *eppagadrocca*, provoking them. She wanted them to come and confront her. Well, maybe Yriatt was right. Dangerous as it was, a wizard's battle would be better than sitting in a cramped tower, doing nothing.

They emerged into the corridor. Lottres blinked at the sight of an armored guard lying flat on the floor. He hadn't realized Dietrick left a guard, although it did make sense. Lottres felt a surge of panic, until he saw the man's peaceful expression. His chest slowly rose and fell. The guard wasn't dead, but deeply asleep.

Ymell opened Shaelen's door. He casually stepped over the prone watchman and asked, "Shall we go?"

"Yes, Father," Yriatt said.

"Where do we go?" Lottres asked. "What will we do?"

"We'll think of something." Ymell brushed past. Lottres must have been confused, for he thought he saw a spark of mischief in Ymell's eyes.

Lottres hesitated as the others set off down the corridor, remembering how helpless he had been feeling. Gingerly, he tugged at the sleeping man's sword. The guard showed no reaction as his weapon slid free.

Thus armed, Lottres hurried after the others. No plan, just going. It was exactly what Brastigan would have done. Lottres found himself laughing out loud.

"What is it?" Shaelen asked.

"Nothing," Lottres quickly replied. It would be cruel to remind her of Brastigan, and an unnecessary distraction.

Yriatt must have caught Lottres's thought, for she snapped, "Do not compare us."

"I never would," Lottres hurried to say. "But, *Maen,* what is our goal? Do we try to take Carthell, or simply break for freedom?"

"I wouldn't turn my back on Carthell," Shaelen said.

"We need no traitor knives at our throats," Ymell agreed. He spoke without even the smallest trace of humor now. "Even if Johanz did not detain us, there are others to be dealt with. I will not leave Ysislaw's creatures to do as they wish."

"We couldn't, anyway," Yriatt said. "If they follow the pattern, they will report our presence to their master at sunset."

"He will know *Maen* has escaped tonight," Shaelen said, "when the *eppagadrocca* at Altannath don't report to him and don't answer his calls."

"Even so," Yriatt said, "it would help us a great deal if Ysislaw did not know exactly where we are."

"Let him be the one to wonder, this time," Ymell added with grim satisfaction.

They came to a stairway. Without hesitation, Ymell turned downward. Lottres, following, wondered how Ymell knew which way to go. He certainly didn't remember which way they had come in. And that wasn't the only thing bothering him. The sensible side of Lottres's nature balked at Ymell's careless attitude.

"*Maen,* how will this work?" Lottres found himself asking. "We came here to warn Carthell of the invasion. We can't just denounce Johanz as a traitor and..."

"Even though he is?" Yriatt needled slyly.

"Of course he is," Lottres said, flustered, but he knew too much about governance to keep quiet. "Johanz is the duke. He rules here. How will you defeat his armies without devastating the land just as badly as Ysislaw?"

"We can do more than start fires, *Thaeme,*" Ymell said gently.

"I know that," Lottres said, "but even if you kill only the *eppagadrocca,* touching no one and nothing else, Johanz cannot sit still for that. He is the ruler here," Lottres repeated urgently. "He can't just let you do whatever you want. No one would respect his laws. Maybe you could convince him to expel the Silletsians first. That would avoid humiliating him. Or did you plan to simply overthrow his regime? Who would take Johanz's place? You, *Maen*?"

"You are indeed a king's son," Ymell murmured, but that answered nothing. Feigning injury, he said, "You think me unqualified?"

"You're not Carthellan," Lottres replied. "They will resent any outsider, no matter who he is."

"How do you know where we have lived?" Yriatt retorted. "Perhaps we have been Carthellan in the past."

"They didn't greet you as if they knew you," Lottres said. "Anyway, we have to get to Harburg."

Ymell chuckled, perhaps at Lottres's stubbornness. "Let me explain, first," he said, "that I am convinced Johanz is either a willing collaborator or he is the *eppagadrocca's* pawn."

"Or both," Yriatt put in with cool disdain. "Ysislaw has a way of using those who think they are using him."

"How do you know?" Lottres asked.

"I have been trying to probe Johanz's mind," Yriatt answered. "Someone is protecting him. Why would they do that, if he isn't involved with their plans?"

Ymell went on, "Whether Johanz is a fool or a schemer, we cannot leave him as he is. He must be deposed. I believe you should be able to speak for your brother Oskar on that account."

"I suppose," Lottres replied a little stiffly. He was being teased, and didn't like it. "Oskar doesn't appreciate people taking things upon themselves."

"Would he permit a traitor to go unpunished?" Yriatt spoke sharply.

"No," Lottres admitted, "but Oskar will want to make the decision himself."

They had descended two levels as they talked, passing closed doors and layers of red and white stones. Before them was another stout wooden door. With an angry flick of Yriatt's wrist, it swung inward toward them.

Beyond the portal, Lottres glimpsed blue sky above the blunted teeth of castle walls. He caught a whiff of musty lake air. Long shadows of afternoon ran across a cobbled courtyard beyond.

"*Maess*, wait!" Shaelen suddenly cried.

A violent gale flung the door wide open. Billows of dust surged in, blinding them. The wind shrieked like an angry cat. Then came a boom that made the stones quiver underfoot. Lightning snaked in at the door, twisting in patterns too bright to look at.

Lottres stumbled backward up the stairs. He blinked the stinging grit from his eyes and cursed his own folly. What a fool he had been—so intent on arguing, he made everyone forget the dangers ahead of them.

Yriatt and Ymell stood firm in the stairwell. Their robes flapped against their bodies, but the white-hot serpents forked to pass harmlessly around them. Shaelen retreated, joining Lottres on the stairs as the wind wailed and lightning snapped in the air. Through the wooden haft, he felt his borrowed sword vibrate with electricity.

The two wizards exchanged some communication too quickly for Lottres to understand. Yriatt nodded to Ymell. Then the floor rippled beneath her. Swiftly and surely she sank through the stones. Ymell strode into the courtyard to confront his foes. Lightning followed him like a swarm of angry bees.

Lottres coughed against the burn of ozone in his throat. Dust was everywhere: in his nose, between his teeth. The thunderous crash of electricity made his ears drum in protest.

Shaelen shouted above the screaming wind, "I thought this was going too easily!"

Lottres wiped sand and tears from his eyes. He yelled back, "What should we do?"

Outside, he could feel three *eppagadrocca* as dull, throbbing points of malice. Faintly, he felt the panic of castle residents as they heard the erupting battle. He couldn't sense Yriatt at all, and that frightened him.

"Look, watch me," Shaelen said. The wind still rushed into the stairwell, but it suddenly stopped beating at them. A stray bolt of lightning streaked in the door. It deflected from the shield of Shaelen's will.

"Can I..." Lottres began.

Shaelen was already nodding. She spoke quickly. "Make a fist. Feel how tight your shoulder gets? Just do that to the air in front of you."

Lottres closed both hands, but all he felt was his fingertips pressing into his palms. Nothing happened to the air.

"Try again," Shaelen urged. "I can't cover you, heart-brother. *Maen* needs my help. You must learn to do this for yourself."

"I'm trying," Lottres said. He squeezed his fingers until his wrists ached, but still nothing happened. When his chest began to ache, he realized he was holding his breath. He sucked in air with a gasp. Lottres's mental shields were rigid as steel, but what he wanted to happen wasn't happening.

"Make a picture in your mind," Shaelen said with forced patience. "You have trained with sword and shield, haven't you? Think what a shield feels like. Then make a fist."

She left him on the stairs, darting down to the open doorway. Buffeted once again by the wind, Lottres closed his eyes and tried to shut out the noise and rough gusts. He pictured the first shield Joal had given him to train with. It was wood covered with leather, round and flat and heavy. He raised his left hand, his shield hand, as if to guard himself. Lottres remembered the faint smell of leather, the way the straps cut into his forearm. He made a fist and willed the shield to be there.

The wind faltered. Lottres opened his eyes. Nothing was there. His will crumbled, and the cold air flung dirt into his face again.

Lottres sat on the steps, groaning with frustration as he rubbed his eyes. When he looked over his fingers, he saw Shaelen framed in the doorway. Her feet were set and her arm was braced as if she held a bow. She reached back, plucked nothing from the space above her shoulder, and drew back as if to shoot.

As Lottres watched, a fiery arrow leapt from Shaelen's hand. Then another, and another. Shaelen moved suddenly, and lightning flickered past her. She turned and fired toward where the lightning had come from.

"She can do it," Lottres thought angrily. "So can I."

He propped his elbow on his knee and drew the picture of a shield in his mind. He made it bigger this time, one of Habrok's great slabs that would cover a man from his knees to his chin. Lottres closed his fist. The wind stopped again.

"That's it," Shaelen called over her shoulder. "Well done!"

Lottres stared at the shield he held. It was translucent, glowing white-gold like distant sunlight. He loosed his fingers a little, but the image of a shield remained steady. No more dust in his eyes!

With renewed confidence, Lottres went to join Shaelen in the doorway. Over her shoulder, he could see the wide courtyard. Ymell stood a few paces out from the tower. His back was to Lottres. Lightning raged around him, surging from the three *eppagadrocca* half hidden in the wind-whipped dust. Their attacks didn't seem to bother Ymell in the least.

Lottres squinted, trying to get a clear view of the Silletsian wizards. What he could see was vaguely disappointing. The *eppagadrocca* looked like ordinary men, with sober robes and beards cut square. From the malevolence Lottres sensed, he had expected they would be abnormal in some way, that such distorted minds must be reflected in their bodies.

"We don't seem able to hurt each other," Shaelen said. She snapped off another fiery arrow. It flew straight at the left-hand *eppagadrocca*, but winked into nothingness before touching him.

"What can we do?" Lottres asked. Then he realized he was asking the wrong question. "What is *Maen* doing?"

"I think..." Shaelen said, then shook her head. "I don't know."

One of the enemy wizards was staring at them, Lottres saw. He had no doubt the man would have heard whatever Shaelen told him. A moment later, lightning streaked toward them. Lottres and Shaelen stepped back, shielding themselves. The burst slid aside.

Lottres smiled without humor. He had been right that the *eppagadrocca* would focus on Ymell and Yriatt and ignore him. Lottres looked again at Ymell, attracting so many strikes and yet doing nothing. Why didn't he retaliate? For that matter, where was Yriatt? Lottres couldn't sense her nearby.

In a way, Lottres thought, the dragons and *eppagadrocca* knew each other almost too well. None had a tactic the others couldn't anticipate. What they needed was to surprise the *eppagadrocca*. Do something they wouldn't expect.

His heart beat faster, but Lottres had an idea. He closed his eyes for a moment, gathering his courage. He didn't know enough magic to help, but perhaps his sword would be enough.

"I can't just stand here," Lottres said to Shaelen.

She turned, startled. "What will you do?"

"Surprise them, I hope." Lottres was pleased that Shaelen didn't argue. It buoyed his confidence. "Can you give me covering fire?"

"Of course," she said. "Good luck."

Lottres didn't run. He probably couldn't have. The wind was even fiercer outside the sheltering tower. Lottres strode out into the maelstrom, his shield deflecting the worst of it. He made for the *eppagadrocca* on his right. The man was focused completely on Ymell. His teeth were gritted with effort and hate. Lottres crossed behind Ymell. He was almost upon the man when he turned with a startled jerk.

"For the Black Tower!" Lottres yelled.

The *eppagadrocca* raised his hands. Lottres lifted his sword. Lightning flared. He caught the blast with his shield, as he had seen Habrok do many number of times in practice. The jolt forced him back a step, but Lottres quickly caught his balance. He lunged forward, within striking distance. His sword struck the *eppagadrocca's* own shield. It hummed with the impact.

The enemy skipped backward, a hasty retreat. Now Lottres felt his enemy's mind power, and this time it didn't tickle. He sucked in a deep breath, knowing he couldn't hold both the mental and physical shields for long. Fire arrows fell around them, Shaelen's promised aid.

Lottres tried again, leaping to the attack. There was a brilliant flash as his energy shield struck the *eppagadrocca's*. His whole left side ached with the shock. Lottres could see pain in his enemy's face, too. They both stepped back.

"Fool," the *eppagadrocca* snarled. "You are no more than a bother to me!"

The Silletsian struck again, with lightning and mental fire. Lottres felt his dual shields wavering, but he could also feel that his enemy was tiring. Shaelen continued firing her arrows, and Lottres had an idea.

"Crutham will never be yours," he grunted.

Lottres took a step back, tottering as if weakened, and he shifted his stance to the right. The *eppagadrocca* automatically turned to face him. Lottres moved again, and again. The Silletsian wizard grinned wickedly.

"What do you say now, whelp?" he crowed.

Lottres had made the *eppagadrocca* turn around. His back was to Shaelen, and the sorceress didn't let the opportunity go to waste. Her fiery arrow pierced the Silletsian's shield. He toppled with a howl of pain.

Lottres stumbled forward as the *eppagadrocca's* physical shield collapsed. "I say good-bye," he snarled. One hard thrust, and the Silletsian lay still.

Lottres turned away from the surprised expression on the dead man's face. He lifted his sword in thanks to Shaelen.

"Well done, *Thaeme*." Ymell's voice came to Lottres clearly through the gale.

"Thank you, *Maen*." Lottres tried not to swell with pride. There was too much still to do. Remembering that Ymell was supposed to be in charge, he asked, "What do you want me to do?"

"I was just letting them wear themselves down a bit," Ymell answered with a shrug. "Your way works nicely, too."

A crackling cloud of lightning surrounded Ymell, yet he seemed unconcerned. With a start, Lottres realized the dragon wizard was capturing all the power the three enemies threw at him.

While they were talking, the wind suddenly changed pitch. It was both deeper and louder. Lottres turned to see a cyclone racing across the courtyard. It was narrow, dirty gray with dust from the courtyard, and it writhed like a serpent. It was also heading right for him!

Lottres gasped for a moment, wondering how he could escape the sucking wind. Then he ran, circling to his right in the faint hope this newest enemy would make the mistake of putting his back to Shaelen. It didn't work. The cyclone snaked in front of Lottres, blocking his way. He stumbled aside, felt wind-claws even through his shield. The storm screamed with almost human fury. Lottres ran in earnest.

Then it caught him. Lottres felt himself lifted from his feet, spinning like a child's top. The wind sucked breath from his lungs. Lottres shut his eyes and clung to his shields, fighting for air, fighting the vertigo. Then a roar, a flash that dazzled even through closed eyelids. The cyclone vanished. Even with his shield, Lottres felt his hard jolt on the cobblestones.

Lottres struggled to his feet. Ymell came to help him up. No more lightning cloud around the wizard. Ymell must have released all the energy he had been holding. The second *eppagadrocca* lay twitching on the pavement. The last one turned and fled.

The *eppagadrocca* was heading for the huge, arched gate into the keep's inner ward. He didn't make it. Shaelen's arrow struck him squarely in the back. He fell with a yowl like a beast's. The *eppagadrocca* struggled onward, dragging himself with his hands. His legs trailed limp behind him.

Lottres sprinted toward him. The enemy couldn't be allowed to escape and warn Ysislaw. As Lottres caught up, a new voice rang out: "Hold!"

Lottres skidded to a halt. For the first time, he became aware of heavy running feet, the rattle of hauberks against demi-greaves. Soldiers poured from the keep. The wall above him was lined with archers. Lottres looked over his shoulder, knowing even Ymell and Shaelen couldn't help him against so many.

The only sound was panting and shuffling as the *eppagadrocca* struggled in the dust. Slowly, with a purposeful tread, Dietrick came down the steps from the gate.

"Good afternoon, cousin," he said.

* * *

"I thought you said he was here," Therula accused.

"He was," Cliodora insisted. "I just talked to him a little while ago."

"Then why doesn't he answer?" Therula gestured to Brastigan's stubbornly closed door.

The two princesses stood in the corridor of the men's wing. Passing servants cast curious glances at them. The fact that Pikarus and Javes escorted them was no excuse. Women weren't permitted here unless they were servants at work. Until a few weeks ago, Therula was certain this lapse would have been reported to her mother. She and Cliodora would both have faced the queen's censure. These days, Therula didn't think Alustra would bestir herself from her bed, even if someone did report them.

"He was drinking something." Cliodora made a face, remembering. "I could smell it when I hugged him."

Javes laughed curtly, and Therula leaned her forehead on the door. She groaned with frustration. Trust Brastigan to get blind drunk, just when they needed him.

"Why didn't you say so?" Therula demanded.

It wasn't fair to focus her anger on Cliodora, but Therula was angry and frightened. She had been feeling this way for days, wishing for Pikarus to come back and restore stability. Instead, everything was worse. Therula was no longer willing to suffer alone.

Then she saw the way Pikarus was looking at her. Therula turned from him, trying to swallow her shame. She pounded on Brastigan's door.

"Brastigan, open up!" Therula cried. "Brastigan!" She tried, really tried, not to shriek like a fishwife.

"Perhaps he's drunk himself to sleep?" suggested Javes, the only one not flustered.

"I didn't think that happened easily," Pikarus countered. He gently caught Therula's wrist. "Stop. There is one other place he might have gone."

"Where do you think he is?" Therula let him hold her throbbing hand. Too soon, he let go.

"In the stables," Pikarus said. "Let's try there."

"What's in the stables?" Cliodora asked fretfully as everyone trailed after Pikarus.

"He got a new horse on our journey," Pikarus said.

"You may be right there," Javes said cheerfully. "Brastigan could be walking around, looking for us, too. If you're for the stables, I'll take another pass through the barracks."

"Do that," Pikarus said.

The brief phrases gave Therula the impression Pikarus wasn't telling them something. She thought about it as they went down the stairs and into the vast courtyard. Javes trotted off, and Therula found she couldn't bear the silence.

"Where did he get a horse?" Therula asked. She liked horses.

The silence stretched, until Therula feared Pikarus wouldn't answer her at all. He cleared his throat.

"There was a young lady we encountered," Pikarus began awkwardly. "The horse was hers."

"A young lady?" Therula laughed. With Brastigan, there were always women around. It was so normal, she felt relieved.

Cliodora was less tactful. "He got a girlfriend?" she bubbled happily. "Ooh, that must be why Margura was looking so frosty! What's her name? What's she like? Where is she now?"

"Cliodora," Therula chided.

There was another long pause. Therula studied Pikarus's face. He was uncomfortable, she realized. Something was wrong, or complicated. Knowing Brastigan, it was both.

"I'm sorry, your highness," Pikarus told Cliodora. "I believe Prince Brastigan must be the one to tell you about her."

"At least tell me her name!" Cliodora begged.

Pikarus paused again. This time, he looked surprised.

"I don't know if she had a name," Pikarus said. "I never heard one."

"She didn't have a name?" Cliodora scowled, as if she was sure Pikarus was teasing her.

"Let it be, Cliodora," Therula warned. Pikarus had been using only past tense in speaking of this mystery woman. Something must have happened to her. For one thing, if she were still alive, Brastigan wouldn't have her horse.

Cliodora walked along, pouting. Therula heard her muttering that she would ask him about it herself. Walking like this wasn't exactly togetherness, but Therula had no intention of being alone again. Reminding herself that she wanted to enjoy Pikarus's company, the elder princess asked, "What kind of horse is it?"

"Urulai," Pikarus said.

"Really?" Therula demanded. For a moment, her love smiled into her eyes, just as in days gone by.

"It is a fine mare," Pikarus said. "I can understand why Brastigan is so attached."

They had crossed the courtyard at last. Therula pushed into the stables, eager for a sight of the rare breed. It was easy to pick out the Urulai horse by her height alone. Her coat seemed to gleam in the dim light of the stable, a gray as pale as moonlight. The mare had her nose buried in a pouch of grain, but lifted her head with a snap as they approached.

A groom appeared, bowing to both princesses. "Did you want to ride, your highnesses? I'm afraid Fire Rose still isn't ready to ride, but there is the bay..."

"Bring me an apple," Therula answered absently. Her full attention was on the beautiful horse.

The lad cleared his throat. "Your highness, Prince Brastigan didn't want anyone to be near this horse."

His Adam's apple bobbed nervously when Therula turned, frowning. Then she realized he was probably right. The Urulai horse had backed to the far end of her stall and fixed them with a wary regard. Strangers clearly made her uneasy, and a frightened horse was a dangerous horse.

"It's all right," Therula told the groom. She stepped back to give the animal room. It seemed she would have to be content with admiring the mare from a distance. She had an elegant, arched neck and dark eyes that reminded Therula of a wild deer. It was hard to estimate her height without getting closer, but the Urulai horse clearly overtopped the other beasts in the stable, just as Brastigan stood tall among men.

"She's beautiful." Cliodora sighed with longing.

"I can see why Brastigan wanted her," Therula agreed.

"Sergeant!" A call made them all look around. Javes trotted into the stables.

"No one's seen hide or hair of him," Javes reported, breathing lightly. "I don't like this."

"Nor do I," Pikarus said. He turned to Therula. "We may still have time before dinner."

"Time for what?" Therula asked. She had the feeling there was something she was supposed to know, something obvious, but she didn't know, and it chafed like a woolen cloak against her skin.

"To find Brastigan," Pikarus answered impatiently. "He must still be in his room. Can you summon the housekeeper to let us in?"

"Of course." Therula turned away before her face betrayed her, but her heart was a storm of hurt and rage. Why was Brastigan so important? Pikarus had had weeks to talk to Brastigan! He should have wanted to spend time with her, Therula. To reassure her there was hope for their love. Instead, he was obsessed with her rascal brother.

Pikarus had said that Oskar's wager didn't matter, but maybe that wasn't how he really felt. For the first time, Therula was willing to consider that Oskar, with his odious assumptions, might have been right.

* * *

Someone was knocking on the door. A man's voice came muffled from the corridor. It might have been Pikarus. Or it might not.

Brastigan roused just enough to realize that he didn't care who it was or what they wanted. His head felt too heavy to lift. He let it rest on the tabletop and waited for the noise to stop so he could go back to sleep.

* * *

Brastigan snapped awake as rough hands caught at his elbows. Reflex, honed by too many days spent at the Dead Donkey, moved him before his mind was fully awake.

Brastigan caught the edge of the table, where he had been sleeping. He pushed with his hands and kicked with his feet. Table legs grated over the floor as the force sent him crashing into someone on his right.

"Yoh!" the fellow yelled. There was a crash and a thud as Brastigan's chair and the man went to the floor together. Another man laughed coarsely.

Brastigan tottered backward, giving himself room. There were two men, one on either side of him. They wore the hauberks and helms of the palace guard.

"Who are you?" Brastigan demanded. His voice was thick with drink. "Get out of here—I'm sleeping!"

He was still in his quarters. Fading daylight in the window showed that he had been passed out for some while. His two visitors looked like Cruthan soldiers. There was the familiar black surcoat with the tower insignia on the breast. But that definitely wasn't Cruthan they were grunting at each other. They ignored his orders and advanced, grinning unpleasantly.

Unfortunately, Brastigan was still staggering drunk. At least, he hoped he was drunk. How else to explain the whirling black tunnel where the archway into his bedroom should be?

There was no time to think about that. The two men separated, coming at him from different angles. Brastigan had witnessed enough robberies to know what could happen next.

"Get out of here!" he shouted. Brastigan was suddenly furious at these oafs for barging into his peaceful binge. They didn't listen.

He lunged at the man on his left. He used his foot instead of his fist, a spinning kick that blended into his dizziness. He was too slow. The fellow caught his foot and pulled, dragging him forward. Brastigan fell, but he managed to twist his foot free. He landed rolling and would have come to his feet, but the other one swung Margura's bottle in a swift green arc.

Light and pain exploded in Brastigan's head. He lay twitching, desperate to move. His legs wouldn't obey him. He was kicked onto his face. His arms were jerked behind him. Then came the cold click of manacles. And the world went away again.

CHAPTER TWENTY-ONE
FREE AND YET TRAPPED

DIETRICK advanced down the steps, drawing his sword as he came. Reluctantly, Lottres raised his own weapon in response. From the moment they left their prison cells, this fight had been inevitable. Still, he wished it didn't have to happen.

"I don't want to fight you," Lottres said. He eased back, eyeing the archers on one side and Dietrick on the other. Ymell and Shaelen were striding across the courtyard, but they were probably too far off to help.

"I see you have discovered the rats in our cellar," Dietrick answered. "These vermin have infested Carthell for too long. I'm in your debt for destroying them."

Dietrick spoke almost cheerfully, and he wasn't even looking at Lottres. His gaze was fixed on the fallen Silletsian. The *eppagadrocca* stopped struggling as Dietrick approached. Lottres could see no sign of Shaelen's energy arrow, save for a small hole in his tunic and a dark blot soaking through the fabric.

"Get away from me," the *eppagadrocca* panted with shrill panic. "I have the Duke's favor! If you touch me, your father will..."

He suddenly fell silent. The point of Dietrick's sword was at his throat.

"I think not." Dietrick's voice was thick. Lottres felt his mind boiling with frustration. "For months, I have been forced to endure your blight upon Carthell. You offered my father victory, but you have only led him to dishonor. Perhaps to his death. I have had to stand by, watching, but now —" Dietrick drew back his sword.

"No!" shrieked the Silletsian.

"My lord!" Ymell called. "A moment, if you please."

Dietrick's shoulders trembled with the effort of restraining himself. "A moment only."

"Please allow me to handle this," Ymell said as he reached Lottres's side. "You must not bloody your sword, Lord Dietrick."

"Even if I wish to?" Dietrick smiled, showing his teeth.

"I can guess how this has troubled you," Ymell answered. "You, a man of honor, have been forced to cooperate with scoundrels. When you objected, your father sent you to command the walls rather than heeding your counsel. Is this not true?"

Ymell's words were soothing, all reason. He didn't use magic to compel Dietrick's obedience. As far as Lottres could tell, Ymell relied on logic alone. Dietrick nodded with an angry jerk, reluctant to concede the argument.

"Do not judge the duke too harshly," Ymell said. "The sorcerers of Sillets can entice a man to their way of thinking, even against his own will."

"That wouldn't take any great persuasion," Dietrick snapped back. "The duke's ambitions are well known here."

"Now we come, upsetting the apple cart." Ymell spread his hands with wry humor. "This is, indeed, a chance to reverse your father's unwise policies, but your sword must be clean, my lord, lest your motives be placed in doubt."

"Then what do you suggest?" Dietrick demanded. "As long as these sorcerers live, my father is bound to them. Only when they die can he see past their lies."

"You need not strike the blow yourself," Ymell reasoned. "If you permit me, I can assure that he dies quickly and painlessly, with no blame upon you."

"A painless death is more than he deserves," Dietrick said, but the moment of crisis had passed. Dietrick's sword point sagged toward the cobblestones. He would no longer strike in the heat of rage.

Then, from behind him, Lottres felt a surge of power—Shaelen's power. The *eppagadrocca* gave a choked cry and lay still, a pool of darker red spreading around him. Dietrick watched dispassionately, as if the man were no more than a rat caught in the storerooms of the keep.

Lottres couldn't help wincing, though he knew the man would gladly have killed him if their places had been reversed. If Ymell disapproved of Shaelen's deed, he gave no sign.

"It seems the question has been settled," Ymell observed. "Perhaps this is for the best."

Dietrick slid his sword into its sheath with an irritated motion. This may have been a signal, for the soldiers on the walls relaxed. The archers unstrung their bows and began to file back into the tower.

"All that remains," Dietrick said, "is to decide what to do about the three of you."

"We were just on our way to speak to the duke," Ymell answered mildly, yet with a hint of steel. "There are matters we have to discuss. Will you escort us? I'm sure he would feel safer."

"No doubt," Dietrick said, but he made no move to lead them anywhere. "One of you is absent. Your daughter was with you earlier, I believe. Did she remain in her chamber, while the rest of you stepped out for this adventure?"

"Not at all," Ymell replied. "Yriatt has gone to hunt the other rats beyond these walls. Fear not—my daughter is very discreet."

"Ah, that explains it," Lottres thought. While Ymell stayed in the keep, attracting attention to himself, Yriatt had gone to find the last *eppagadrocca*.

"In good time," Dietrick said, "I would like an accounting of those rats. For the moment, I will do as you ask. Please come with me."

Dietrick strode off, stiff-legged. Lottres waited until Ymell had passed, and fell in beside Shaelen. As they climbed the steps toward the massive gate, some of Dietrick's guardsmen emerged. At his curt motion, half of them continued into the courtyard. Glancing back, Lottres saw them preparing to remove the bodies from public view. The remaining soldiers fell in around Dietrick and Ymell.

Dietrick led them upward, into the heart of the keep, and this time Lottres watched carefully where they were going. Soon they approached a pair of big wooden doors, carved with figures of sailing vessels. The two guards there looked askance at Ymell, but they saluted Dietrick and allowed him to pass.

The room beyond was a large council chamber. Ruddy sunset light flowed in at a broad window. Beyond the glass lay a stunning landscape of mountains and water. Nearer at hand, a group of men were gathered around something on the council table. Lottres immediately recognized Duke Johanz and Albrett.

"Father," Dietrick said. "May I speak with you?"

"What was all that noise?" Johanz demanded, looking up. When he saw Ymell, he closed his mouth with a snap. Albrett, at the duke's elbow, stood straighter. His eyes narrowed as he stared at Lottres.

"I'm afraid that is my fault," Ymell said in a self-deprecating tone. "I must speak with your grace on an urgent matter. In my impatience, I left my chambers and was waylaid by those whom I know as my enemies."

Johanz put on an expression of concern. "As I feared. I cannot guarantee your safety, Lord Ymell, if you won't accept my protection."

"There is no need for any concern," Ymell answered with a stern gleam in his eye now. "The *eppagadrocca* will trouble you no longer."

Johanz couldn't quite hide his scowl at this news, but he turned his anger on Dietrick.

"And what do you say to this?" Johanz demanded. "Are chance travelers permitted to assault my invited guests?"

"How was I to stop them, Father?" Dietrick asked. His voice was strained and posture stiff. "The noises you heard were cyclones from the heavens and lightning they summoned to their hands. We are mere archers and swordsmen."

"If these guests couldn't defend themselves," Shaelen said quietly, "perhaps they were never as powerful as they claimed."

As one, the Carthellans bristled at her words.

"Please," Ymell interposed. "I have little time for nonsense, your grace, so I will speak plainly. My companion —" Ymell nodded to Lottres, who was suddenly aware of sharp eyes on himself "— has reminded me that you are a man of experience and not a callow fool. Therefore I will not insult you by suggesting you do not know who your guests were and what their purpose was. Nor will I bother to warn you that the Emperor of Sillets is a practiced deceiver. That many others before you have sat down at his table, only to find themselves and their lands as the main remove."

Johanz sat calmly enough, though his hands, folded on the table, showed his anger in their white-fingered grip. On closer viewing, Lottres saw his face was seamed with fine lines of age. Ymell, who must be far the elder, appeared youthful in contrast.

"Then what are you here for?" Albrett demanded. His fleshy face was red with anger.

"Merely to advise," Ymell replied. He didn't deign to look upon Albrett, but focused his mild regard on Johanz. "Those who were sent to foment rebellion are gone. No longer do they control you, or spy on you. If you choose, you may now reconsider this perilous alliance."

"Why should we wish to do that?" Johanz countered. "We who were once free..."

"Your bond with Crutham may be irksome," Ymell interrupted, "but the yoke of slavery to Sillets would be far worse, I promise. For this moment only, Carthell is free. Whether it remains so is your decision."

"What do you care for Carthell's freedom?" demanded one of the other young men at the table.

And Albrett puffed out his chest. "If Carthell is to be part of Crutham, why shouldn't one of us rule the whole? I have an equal claim to the throne of Crutham."

So that was it! Lottres couldn't help laughing. He shouldn't have been surprised by Albrett's claim. The Carthellans scowled at his mirth.

"Come, brother," Lottres mocked Albrett. "You couldn't stand up to Calitar or Axenar, let alone challenge Habrok in battle. Or did you think our cousin Dietrick would fight in your place?"

Even as he said it, Lottres felt Albrett flinch inside. The fat fraud must have hoped to avoid fighting for the throne at all. Perhaps Albrett hoped Habrok would simply die in the war, and spare him the effort.

"A king need not dirty his hands," Albrett said, in what he must have hoped was a lofty tone. Even Johanz's face showed a trace of disgust.

"On the contrary, young man," Ymell said, so kindly that Lottres flinched from the depth of the insult. "Above all else, a ruler must be willing to do what is needful, not only for himself but for the sake of his people." Then the horned wizard's eyes returned to Johanz. "Even if it means stepping back from his heart's desire. Your grace, I urge you to consider your position. An invasion has been launched, open war declared—but not by you. There is still time, if you have the wisdom to seize it. Put aside your pride. Lead your troops to Crutham's defense. If you aid him now, King Oskar may be willing to overlook your tardiness."

"If I don't?" Johanz did not flinch when meeting Ymell's gaze. "Will you summon your lightning to blast us all?"

"I will not apologize for defending myself," Ymell replied. Even now, Lottres was amazed that he didn't use his powers to force his will on Johanz. "Nor would I threaten you, your grace. What I offer is an honorable compromise. To accept would be the wiser course."

"Father." Yriatt's voice came suddenly, vibrant with excitement.

Ymell broke off, and both Shaelen and Lottres started at her call. No one else seemed to notice. There were gasps in the room, men cursing and hands falling to sword hilts. A huge, black form soared outside the window. Yriatt turned in the air, making a purposeful display of her wings and talons.

Two of the duke's advisors leaned forward, speaking into his ears. They meant to whisper, but Lottres heard them clearly.

"It's the monster we saw before," one said. "How do we fight such a creature?"

"Don't listen to the wizard, your grace," another was saying. "You have committed yourself to Sillets. You cannot step back, for the sake of our freedom."

While they murmured, Ymell asked, *"You disposed of the last eppagadrocca?"*

"I did," Yriatt replied. *"In dying, his mind was laid bare to me. I know where he is."*

Lottres felt his heart skip. He had no doubt who Yriatt meant.

"Return to me," Ymell said. Aloud, he said to Johanz, "If you wish to confer, your grace, I will be happy to wait for a moment."

"You are too kind," Johanz answered. His eyes were hot with resentment, but his manner changed as Yriatt banked outside the window. With leisurely power, the dragon glided toward the castle walls. Men murmured as she disappeared from view. Then the Carthellans drew into a tight huddle around their duke. Dietrick hesitated before going to join them.

Lottres and Shaelen followed Ymell as he slowly walked away from the Carthellans. They made their own cluster just inside the door.

Joined mind to mind, Lottres silently asked, *"Where do you think he is?"*

"I don't know," Shaelen answered quickly, *"but there's something else."* Lottres could sense her tension in the tightness of his own knees. Even before she said it, he guessed. *"Brastigan is in trouble. I feel it."*

"Brastigan?" Ymell asked with quick concern.

"Are you still linked to him?" Lottres asked. *"I thought..."*

"It must be because of her," Shaelen said. Lottres could feel her frustration. *"My shadow self was so connected to Brastigan, I — I just know something is wrong!"*

"My grandson should have been in Harburg for several hours by now," Ymell said. Lottres was surprised at the wizard's tone of affection and concern.

"I know," Shaelen said. *"I don't understand what could be wrong."*

"With Brastigan?" Lottres couldn't help smiling. *"It could be anything."*

Behind them, he caught rumbles from the Carthellan circle. "...I never touched him, Father," came Dietrick's set voice. Albrett whined something, and Johanz snapped, "That has changed."

"Brastigan should be safe," Ymell murmured. Lottres had the impression he was trying to reassure himself more than anyone else.

"No one in Harburg is safe," Yriatt cut in. Lottres could sense her in the corridor outside. *"For that is where Ysislaw is."*

Ymell responded with an almost physical jerk, restraining such a powerful hate that Lottres felt scorched by its fury. The door opened and Yriatt entered. Her face was composed, but her eyes blazed with emotion.

"Then we go to Harburg," Ymell said. Not that there was really any question, Lottres thought.

"And these fools?" Yriatt glanced at the murmuring circle of Carthellans.

"If we win, it will not matter what they do," Ymell responded.

But Lottres wondered if this was true. Now that Shaelen had spoken of her fears, Lottres did feel a lurking dread. He pictured Brastigan in his mind, seeking some sense of his brother, a way to convince himself all was well. He felt only emptiness. Just as when Yriatt tried to find Eben, Lottres thought. There was simply nothing. Only now, knowing that Ysislaw was in Harburg, did he guess the enemy wizard must have been blocking all probes in order to conceal his presence.

"We'll look for Brastigan as soon as we reach Harburg," Lottres said, speaking to Shaelen alone.

Her chin twitched in an unhappy nod. *"I shouldn't feel this way,"* she said, a resentful grumble. *"I don't even like him."*

"Sometimes I don't, either," Lottres confessed.

"Enough." The Duke's voice came clear and strong. He stood up at the table, while his advisors scurried back to make a united front around him. The four wizards, too, turned to give Johanz their attention.

"I thank you for your guidance, Master Ymell." Johanz spoke in a conciliatory, even obsequious, tone of voice. "Although Carthell is under no obligation to King Oskar, it is true we have historic ties. I shall send my army to Crutham. Perhaps, as you have said, gratitude will strengthen our position in later negotiations."

As clearly as if Johanz had spoken aloud, Lottres heard him think, *"And if Crutham is weakened by battle, we may be able to defeat them without the aid of any allies. Then Albrett will see his wish granted, and so will I."*

Lottres glanced at Ymell and Yriatt, but neither of them gave any indication they had heard Johanz. Ymell made a sweeping bow.

"You are indeed a wise and foresighted leader," Ymell said. His flattery was as obviously false as Johanz's had been. "Now I must take my leave. There is another pressing matter before me, but I will look forward to seeing the banner of Carthell on the field of battle."

"That you shall," Duke Johanz affirmed. "Dietrick, my son—see to this."

"At once, Father." Dietrick saluted and left. For the first time since they arrived, Lottres thought, he didn't look as if his teeth hurt.

The four wizards bowed as well and took their leave. Lottres watched Dietrick walking ahead of them. Dietrick didn't seem to suspect his father's duplicity. His thoughts were full of materials to be gathered and orders to be given.

Yriatt asked, *"Do we permit Johanz to do this, Father?"*

"I have done what I can," Ymell answered. His thoughts were remote, and probably focused on his old enemy, Ysislaw. *"The Cruthans will have to deal with Carthell. Even we cannot be everywhere, daughter."*

But Lottres wasn't certain Oskar could deal with Johanz, not while Ysislaw lurked in Harburg. This one exchange illustrated just how useful mind-magic could be—and how dangerous. Just as Lottres knew Johanz's intentions, Ysislaw could know his enemies' every thought and see their strategies before they took shape. How could Oskar, or Brastigan, or anyone else, hope to defeat him?

* * *

"Housekeeping," called Nerona. She knocked gently on Brastigan's door. "May I come in?"

There was no reply from inside the room. Nerona, the head maid, glanced anxiously at Therula. The princess nodded with an assurance she didn't feel.

The housekeeper turned the key in the lock. It creaked and then opened with a heavy snap. The lock worked as reluctantly as the housekeeper did, Therula thought. Not that she blamed Nerona. Brastigan wasn't likely to be glad of the disturbance.

The chamber beyond the doorway was dark. Undeterred, Pikarus pushed right in with Javes at his heels. Therula and Cliodora lingered in the doorway.

"Will there be anything else, your highness?" Nerona asked.

"No, thank you. This will do," Therula replied. Nerona bowed and walked away. Only then did Therula murmur to Cliodora, "Come on."

Feeling like an intruder, Therula led her younger sister into Brastigan's small suite. She could hear Pikarus's voice, muffled, from the bedchamber.

"You were right about the drink," Therula murmured to Cliodora. She waved a hand before her face to dispel the fruity aroma. "It smells like apple brandy in here."

Javes came out, carrying a candle. He lit this at the nearest cresset. The two young women waited until Javes had returned with the light before venturing past the doorway.

"He was sitting right there," Cliodora said. She pointed to the small table and chairs under the narrow window. The table stood at an odd angle from the wall, and one of the chairs lay tipped over in the corner farthest from the door.

"He isn't here now," Pikarus said as he returned from the bedchamber. "But I found this on the bed." Pikarus lifted his hand, displaying a sword in its sheath. Therula immediately recognized Brastigan's weapon, Victory. Like most men she knew, he seldom went anywhere without it.

Except for Pikarus's voice, the room was very quiet. It was also rather chilly. Therula had the impression no one had been here for a good while. She felt colder, wondering about Brastigan's absence.

"Where could he be?" Cliodora asked, sidling closer to Therula.

"Take a look at this," Javes said.

He set the candle on the table and knelt to reach under it. Javes straightened with a small, dark green bottle in his hand. Pikarus held the bottle near the candle. Glass gleamed as he turned it from side to side. Therula saw something on the bottle, a brown smear clouding the shining smoothness. A long black hair curled away from it.

The two soldiers passed a grim look between them. Therula swallowed heavily, and went to join the two men. Cliodora followed close behind.

Therula made herself ask, "Is that blood?"

Pikarus stared at the bottle, his eyes narrowed in thought. Almost absently, he reached out to draw Therula to his side.

"Yes, it is blood," he said quietly. "Someone has been here, and Brastigan is gone."

"Who would want to attack him?" Therula asked. "Why now, instead of while you were on the road?"

"I want to find him," Cliodora whimpered. "What can we do?"

The silent room was full of portent. Shadows, thrown by the candle flame, loomed on all sides of them. Therula could almost have thought the silhouettes were leaning closer, listening.

"There is only one person who can help us now," Pikarus answered softly. He looked into Therula's eyes. "We need to see your mother."

It looked like there was good reason for Pikarus to be worried about Brastigan, but Therula still felt confused. She didn't like not knowing what was going on.

"If we do," she asked, "will you explain what's happening?"

Reluctantly, he nodded. "I will explain it to the queen, and to you."

As best she could, Therula drew strength from her beloved's nearness. She straightened her back and lifted her chin.

"Let's go see Mother," she said.

He felt his head first, pounding like waves against the shore. Then he felt his stomach, churning in time with the spinning of his head. Brastigan came to himself by painful degrees, and wished every moment that he could return to oblivion.

He was lying down. The surface beneath him was too hard for any bed. His shoulders felt stiff and cramped. Brastigan tried to turn over, but he couldn't move his arms. He struggled, kicking and swearing. The burst of panic did nothing to help his situation. It did, however, bring him fully awake.

He was in chains, of course. In a small, dark room. The feeble light of a wall torch sent fresh torment blazing through his eyes. Brastigan squinted and blinked. As the pain faded he saw curved walls, a steel chamber pot, a straw pallet where he had been lying. A stout wooden door was opposite him, well beyond reach.

Brastigan twisted in place, trying to see the manacles behind him. Iron chains ran from his wrists to a fitting in the wall. These held his hands behind him. However, he was relieved to discover that his wrists weren't fastened together. The chains were merely twisted around each other. Rolling carefully, out of respect for the protests of his stomach, he managed to untangle them. With great relief, Brastigan stretched his arms to loosen his shoulders.

Reaching behind his head, he found a painful welt and a damp stickiness on his hair. The bump felt huge. No wonder his head was pounding. He was still wearing the same clothes he had had on earlier, including his boots and sword belt, but Victory was missing.

Whoever did this had been in a hurry, Brastigan thought. He felt his lips twitch in a dark grin. You could tell he had been attacked in the castle — on the streets of Crutham, his boots would have been the first thing stolen. Patting his chest, he determined that Leithan's *jeup* was still there, too.

The stonework looked familiar, so he was still in Crutham Keep. This wasn't the main dungeon, though. He must be in one of the tower rooms. From the size of it, probably Eben's tower. They hadn't moved him far — another suggestion of haste in his abduction. The floor was suspiciously dry and clean, and the links had the sheen of new metal. Someone had made all this recently, then. But why?

Brastigan sat up, straw crackling as he moved. He leaned forward and propped his head on his knees. His memory was patchy. He recalled talking to Margura, and something about Cliodora, and drinking until he passed out. Then there was a little bit of a fight. Which, obviously, he had lost.

He should have known better than to drink what Margura had given him, especially right after he broke off their relationship, but it had felt so good to be drunk. It was what he wanted most in the world, to just pass out and not have to think for a while. Margura's parting gift had seemed a miracle.

He'd let that need blind him. Now he wasn't feeling quite so good. Locked up, hung over, and a horrible taste in his mouth. Brastigan didn't doubt Margura had betrayed him. What he couldn't figure out was why. She didn't have the resources to construct a prison for the punishment of her former lovers, either. If she did, he thought, it would be a lot more crowded. Margura must have been acting for someone else. But who, and why?

The lock turned in the door. The quiet sound startled him. Brastigan didn't move, kept his forehead against his knees. His temples pounded in time with his anxious heartbeat as the door opened, admitting another painful stream of light. Through slitted eyes, he looked up.

A man swept in, silhouetted against the torchlight from outside. A heavily cloaked form followed at a careful distance. The man was Oskar. It had to be. Who else would wear that enormous hat?

Then Brastigan saw, really saw, the shape of Oskar's hat. In that moment, he realized several things. He understood the new fashion in headwear. He knew why Oskar hadn't seemed to care that he belittled Alustra. Why Oskar hadn't asked after Lottres. How Eben had vanished so suddenly. And Brastigan knew he was in even worse trouble than he had thought.

He also knew why Ymell couldn't find Ysislaw with his armies. The evil dragon wasn't with his armies. He was here, in Crutham, wearing another man's face: Oskar's face, the face of the king.

The door clicked shut. Footsteps drew closer, grating over the floor. Brastigan cursed himself for not recognizing the horns sooner. He was so tired, he'd let the shock of his father's death blind him. He shut his eyes for a moment, trying to think. What could he do now? If Ymell was right, Ysislaw might well kill him. He had no way to protect himself.

Brastigan let go a shuddering breath. He was a warrior. He would face his enemy, not hide. Brastigan opened his eyes.

To every appearance, Oskar strolled toward him. There were the rich mourning robes, the crown of gold and big velvet hat. It wasn't a bad imposture at all. Ysislaw looked every bit as pleased with himself as Oskar usually did.

"Well met, noble brother." Ysislaw's voice was rich with gloating as he tossed Brastigan's words back at him from earlier that day.

Brastigan gritted his teeth and made a decision. "No brother of mine," he answered, a flat challenge. He was sure he would regret speaking out. Didn't he always?

"So you know me?" The stranger who wore Oskar's face smiled. "Excellent. It saves me the bother of explaining."

"Glad to be of help," Brastigan growled sarcastically.

Ysislaw's smile widened with malice. "It would be too bad to think poor old Ymell had an idiot for a grandson."

Who said he didn't?

"You killed my father," Brastigan charged. He sounded calmer than he felt.

Ysislaw shrugged. "A mere trifle." His smile vanished, leaving Oskar's eyes cold and remote, utterly divorced from humanity. "Kings come and go, but we endure."

Brastigan knew all too well what he was referring to, and he was pretty sure his dubious birthright didn't extend to a dragon's immortality. Brastigan looked away, and his eyes fell on Ysislaw's companion, who had stopped well behind him. A voluminous black cloak concealed most of her face, but Brastigan caught the wink of a yellow gem in the cleft of her deep green gown.

It was Margura, of course. He'd never doubted her treachery, really, yet the betrayal stung. She was Cruthan. How could she ally herself with the tyrant of Sillets?

"You are ignoring me," Ysislaw said abruptly.

"So sorry," Brastigan retorted. "It's just that I could never keep my eyes off a pretty girl."

Ysislaw made a flicking motion of the wrist. Brastigan gasped against a sudden pain. It felt like a lightning bolt had entered through his eyes, passed through his skull, and ricocheted off the bump on his head. Brastigan gave a choked cry, and another. He felt he couldn't breathe past the agony.

"Never ignore me," Ysislaw told him with cold hate, "and never be so bold again. I may need you alive, but it does not have to be pleasant for you."

The pain seemed to go on for hours. Soon enough Brastigan leaned back, panting and trying to keep his gorge down.

"So I'm your hostage?" Brastigan managed to choke out.

"Do not forget it," Ysislaw said.

For the first time, Margura spoke. Her voice was low and submissive, her eyes downcast. "Your majesty, there was your pledge to me, also?"

Tensely, Ysislaw turned toward her. He smiled again, but carefully, as if he must remember how to do it.

"Oh, that?" He turned a sneering glance on Brastigan. "I don't know why you chose this mongrel."

"No other is suited to my need," she murmured.

Brastigan could hardly recognize the bold minx he had known. Margura's treachery was truly complete. She hadn't been duped into thinking she served Oskar. She knew who Ysislaw really was, or she wouldn't be so respectful.

"It means nothing to me. A bargain is a bargain, and I do appreciate all your efforts, Lady Margura." Ysislaw spoke indulgently, but then added, "This won't spare him, you know."

She sank in a deep curtsey. "I would never ask it. I am deeply grateful to your majesty's help. My only wish is to serve you in return."

Brastigan watched, feeling his headache ease. Better to concentrate on their conversation than on his pain. Any thought of escape or revenge would have to wait. Whatever he knew to save Crutham would have to stay buried, at least until Ysislaw was gone. Then Ysislaw turned toward Brastigan with narrowed eyes.

Brastigan quickly muttered, "I'm not ignoring you."

"Good." Ysislaw's grin was all teeth. "Then let me be the first to congratulate you."

Brastigan asked, because it seemed to be expected, "For what?"

"Oh, didn't your mistress tell you?" Ysislaw asked with cheerful malice. "You and Margura are to wed."

Brastigan stared at them. This was so alien to what he expected, he could do nothing else. Margura tensed, flushed with humiliation, and Brastigan understood a whole new set of things.

"Alemin," he managed. "You're the one who... And he ran out on you. That's why you were so friendly right before I left. You wanted me to think the babe was mine."

Margura merely glared at him, her eyes brilliant with rage and shame. After trying so hard to get pregnant and trap a prince, she had finally succeeded—but with the wrong prince. Alemin was already married. He couldn't make an honest woman of her. Margura must be desperate for a legitimate union to conceal her shame.

"Alas," Ysislaw went on mockingly, "it will be a brief marriage. Despite your boasting, Brastigan, I fear you will fall beside your brothers. The walking dead, in their vast numbers, will overwhelm you. Your widow will be left with your rank to console her."

His mock sorrow couldn't cover the chilling fact. Brastigan and his brothers had been gathered to destroy them. Ysislaw needed to get rid of Unferth's heirs even more than Oskar did. A conqueror wouldn't want legitimate successors challenging his supremacy.

"Can you at least untie me for the honeymoon?" Brastigan asked with a pretense of hope.

"As I understand it, the marriage has already been consummated." Ysislaw's mocking leer left his eyes hollow. Margura sulked, but didn't dare express her feelings.

"Where's the real Oskar?" Brastigan asked. He couldn't believe he cared, but he did.

"Oh, do not worry about him," came Ysislaw's bland reply. "He is alive and well, for as long as I may need to enforce his mother's cooperation. She hasn't figured it out yet, but that sister of yours, Therula, suspects something."

Good for her, Brastigan thought, but Alustra's cooperation might not be needed much longer if Brastigan understood Ysislaw's plan. He only hoped Ymell would be able to delay the Silletsian army until he got out of here and warned Habrok.

Ysislaw chuckled softly. Brastigan's stomach turned over at the sound of it.

"Dear old Ymell. He cannot defeat me," Ysislaw said. "I have had nothing but time to plan this campaign. Nor have I any lack of allies. Your own dear Oskar, for instance. Did you know, he asked for my help himself. That's right! He invited me here. And he was not the first."

Ysislaw began pacing, laughing at the dark jest. "It was Johanz of Carthell who started it. It seems some ancestor of his once ruled Crutham. He thought it time to restore his dynasty, and he had his nephews, Rickard and Albrett, make the claim for him. Johanz requested my assistance in removing the obstacles before Rickard, especially Prince Oskar."

Brastigan tried to stay calm, just put aside his feelings, listen, and later think about what it all meant.

"It was a rare opportunity," Ysislaw went on. "I did not fail to exploit it. Oskar was anxious to work with me when he learned of Johanz's plan. However, since I did not reveal exactly who had been cooperating with Rickard, he decided the time was right to dispose of all the extraneous heirs."

Brastigan sat silently, his heart pounding. He could easily believe in Rickard's ambition, and Oskar's duplicity was no surprise, either. Carthell's was. That was where Lottres was supposed to be.

He tried to bury that thought, hide it from Ysislaw by looking to Margura. "And her?"

"Oh, Lady Margura has been instrumental," Ysislaw smirked. "She knows everyone's bad habits. When her situation changed, I naturally wanted to help her." He patted Margura's shoulder, much as a man might pet a favorite dog. She flinched at his touch.

"Once the fighting is over, I am sure she will find another mate," Ysislaw said. "One more suited to her new station."

"Someone just as rotten as she is?" Brastigan retorted.

Margura flushed angrily, but Ysislaw said, "Oh, I hope so. I can always use more servants with her talents."

Margura smiled, preening at this praise.

"It was really Eben who helped put it all together," Ysislaw was saying. When he saw Brastigan's face, he chuckled. "Yes! Eben, of all people. He somehow learned of Oskar's role in the royal slayings."

Through the dagger, Brastigan guessed—the one that had nearly killed him. "Was that your doing?" he asked.

"Oskar handled those arrangements himself, I believe," Ysislaw answered casually. "Once Eben realized what he was up to, Unferth threatened to disown him. Suddenly, the noble prince was desperately in need of my help. I was only too happy to assist him."

Ysislaw glanced at Brastigan. He seemed to expect some reply.

"By taking his place," Brastigan guessed.

"Precisely," Ysislaw hissed with satisfaction.

"What did you do to Eben?" Brastigan asked.

"Oh, he's at the bottom of the bay. Unferth never suspected the replacement." Ysislaw smiled cruelly. "When his dear friend gave him a potion to help him sleep, he drank without question. That cleared the way for Oskar—and me."

So Ysislaw must have poisoned Unferth. Brastigan leaned against the wall for a moment, felt its cool solidity bracing his back. Some day he would learn not to ask questions when the answers were better left unknown. As he tried to shake off his morbid imaginings, Ysislaw suddenly knelt. He knotted his hand in Brastigan's hair and yanked his head up.

"As for your precious little brother," he whispered, "your *pup*, I'm afraid he will find a surprise waiting for him in Carthell. Johanz is still in my tent, you see. He blames Oskar for Rickard's death, and he thinks the throne will pass to Albrett when all is done. Johanz will do everything he can to assist my agents there, including laying a trap for Ymell and his paltry band."

Brastigan kept his face as far from Ysislaw's as he could, though the pulling of his hair stung. He could smell his enemy's breath, heavy with wine and food.

He found himself squeaking like the stable hand. "Why are you telling me this?"

Ysislaw didn't move his face, nor relax his grip. "Because," he said, as calm as ice on the mountaintops, "I want you to know there is no hope. I have won. For all your bragging, your brave heroics, you have lost."

"Not yet," Brastigan said, a feeble threat.

"Did you think I would not know where Lottres and Ymell are?" Ysislaw sneered. "Everything you think and feel is open to me. You can have no secrets. I shall kill your brothers and take my pick of your pretty sisters. None shall escape me." He bent even closer, though Brastigan leaned frantically away from his overwhelming presence. "You are doomed. Just like your mother."

"You did enough to her!" Brastigan cried. Fury overcame his sense of self-preservation. He kicked out at Ysislaw and had the satisfaction of seeing his enemy reel backward.

Then the pain returned, as sudden as a thunderclap. Lights flashed before his eyes, sickly greens and yellows. Brastigan fell to his side and screamed with the agony, with his rage and, yes, his hopelessness.

"Oh, shut up," Ysislaw said with casual spite. Brastigan's throat seemed to lock, robbing him of breath. "An exceptional female, Yrien. I would have grown fond of her," Ysislaw mused.

Behind Ysislaw, Brastigan glimpsed Margura watching them. Her eyes gleamed with the acquisition of new knowledge.

Panting, Brastigan rasped out, "I'll bet you thought Yrien couldn't escape, either."

To his amazement, Ysislaw was calm again, remote and alien. He knelt again and smiled, a terrible cruel smile. "But she didn't. Nor will you. Your homeland is mine, and all who you love are doomed. Think on that, "greatest swordsman in Crutham.""

Blue eyes, so like Oskar's eyes, bored into Brastigan's dark ones. In that moment he believed Ysislaw was right, that there was no safety anywhere. The fear gripped his stomach, twisted it into a knot of bile. Gagging, Brastigan had to turn from his foe. He lunged toward the chamber pot and barely reached it in time.

Ysislaw let him go. To Margura, he said dryly, "There is still time to find another bridegroom."

"Pathetic," Margura murmured scornfully, "but my time is short, your majesty. I fear I must decline."

Brastigan glared up at them through eyes blurry with sickness. He wanted to say something to Margura, something that would hurt her as much as her betrayal hurt him. He couldn't think of a thing.

The two were already walking away, tyrant and traitress together. The door swung open before they touched it, and shut behind them with a solid bang.

Brastigan was left alone in the pitiless prison room. His hair was soaked with cold, sticky sweat. His head pounded like smith's anvil. His knees, folded under him, ached against the hard stone floor.

Not until the last of his nausea passed did he move away from the chamber pot. Brastigan staggered back to the pallet and dropped onto it with a groan.

He had considered hiding his thoughts, maybe pretending to be frightened and seeing if Ysislaw would lose interest when he thought he'd won. In the end, there was no need to feign terror. That was real enough.

The pain dulled after Ysislaw left, but shame burned like a hot iron within him. Because he knew, just for that moment, that Ysislaw had truly beaten him. They locked eyes, and it was Brastigan who blinked. He gave way. Now he sat, cowed, and wondered how he could ever escape Ysislaw's prison.

CHAPTER TWENTY-TWO
COUNCILS OF WAR

I know what you are thinking, Father," Yriatt said with calm ferocity, "but I will not stay behind. I refuse."

The sun was sinking in earnest, casting its red glare over the walls of the keep and the town beyond. The Sea of Carthell had turned a strange, murky brown as it lapped at the duke's private pier. The four wizards had returned there to wait for the griffins, which Yriatt had summoned.

They had to get to Harburg right away, Lottres knew. Now that they knew where Ysislaw was, speed was of the essence. Just knowing his location didn't solve all their problems, however.

"You must stay behind," Ymell said, matching Yriatt's urgency. "I will not have you going anywhere near Ysislaw. He has already taken too many of my loved ones. Further, now that Carthell is mobilizing, someone must fly to Firice and assure their troops are marching. I cannot do it. You must."

"If you feel it is so dangerous, I will not leave your side," Yriatt answered with a fiery sweetness.

"The risk is too great," Ymell insisted.

"No, Father," Yriatt said.

Lottres watched with embarrassment as the two dragons clashed. He didn't know whose side to take. What he did know, with a wrenching certainty, was that Brastigan was in terrible danger. Like Shaelen, he couldn't bear to wait around while his brother was alone, suffering.

"Cousin!"

With relief, Lottres turned away from the confrontation. Dietrick had emerged from the water gate. Lottres strode back to meet him. Dietrick carried one large canvas bag over his shoulder and a smaller one at his side.

"Before you go, I must return these," Dietrick said. He set down the small bundle and rolled the larger one over his shoulder. Unknotting a drawstring, Dietrick presented Lottres's sword. Lottres accepted it, and passed back the sword he had borrowed. Then, with a small bow, Dietrick offered Shaelen her bow and arrows.

"It seems you didn't need them," Dietrick added wryly, "but we shouldn't keep what isn't ours. There is also this." He lifted the smaller bundle. "Food for your journey, since you haven't eaten with us and now must travel again."

"My thanks." Lottres accepted the package eagerly. His stomach gurgled in agreement.

"No, it is I who must thank you," Dietrick answered. "It will be good to have a clear purpose again."

Lottres found he had to look away from the emotion in his kinsman's eyes. It seemed impossible that a man of Dietrick's integrity could spring from the court of Carthell, where the duke had such slippery morals. Lottres wondered if Johanz understood what a prize he had in his son. Recalling how Ymell and Yriatt were locked in their contest of wills, Lottres thought perhaps some fathers never did fully appreciate their children.

"*Maess!* Why must we wait?" Shaelen cried. Her face was pale, her expression agitated. Shaelen, even more than Lottres, was attuned to Brastigan and aware of his distress. "He needs us!"

Lottres was sure he saw a trace of pity on Yriatt's face, but she answered with steely patience, "As we already have discussed, the gateways are no longer open to us. Ysislaw controls too many of them."

"He would know at once where we are," Ymell said. "We must surprise him, if we can."

"I know, *Maen,* but why can't we go?" Shaelen cut the air with an exasperated gesture, taking in Lottres and herself.

"Yes," Lottres said with quick excitement. "Why can't we?"

"You would face Ysislaw alone?" Ymell asked, aghast.

"I know how to keep quiet," Lottres answered defensively. "I did it all the way to Altannath, didn't I, *Maess?*"

Yriatt nodded, reluctant to agree.

"There's a gateway right near Harburg," Lottres went on. "It's called the Dragon's Candle. Yes, he'll sense when we come through, but he'll be expecting the two of you. Shaelen and I should be able to deal with whatever guard he has on it. And there can't be much—nobody ever goes up there, and a guard would be noticed." Lottres eyed the darkening sky. "We could get into Harburg before the gates close, if we hurry."

"Then the two of you could fly to Firice together," Shaelen said. "*Maess* wouldn't have to go by herself."

"Or you could simply fly to Harburg," Lottres added. "You both can change your eyes to see in the dark. Can the griffins do that?"

"I think this very ill advised," Yriatt answered sternly. "You are still inexperienced, *Thaeme,* and you..." She trailed off, regarding Shaelen.

"I'm all right," Shaelen answered stoutly.

Dietrick, standing forgotten, suddenly asked, "What are these gateways you speak of?"

"A magical construct," Lottres answered. "A kind of wizard's gate. It would look like a tall mound with a stone on top, and a large pool of water."

"Like that?" Dietrick pointed, and Lottres turned to follow with his eyes. To the south of Carthell's walls, a single hill rose smooth and dark against the ruddy sunset sky. "We call it the Dragon's Well. It's said if any man goes up there, he will never return."

"In a sense, that is correct," Ymell allowed. To Yriatt, he chuckled, "Where do they come up with these names?"

"Does it matter?" Yriatt snapped back. "We should not be using the gateways."

"But it's so close," Shaelen murmured, her eyes fixed on the distant mound. "Lord Dietrick, would we be able to borrow a pair of horses?"

"Of course," Dietrick said, although he looked askance at Yriatt.

Ymell eyed the two of them thoughtfully, Lottres and Shaelen, each driven by the same need. A human need, which the dragons, however well intended, could never fully understand.

"We must go," Lottres insisted.

"You are not our slaves," Ymell said at length. "We will not forbid you to do what you must."

"We can only hope you do not compromise our secrecy," Yriatt said with angry tartness.

A part of Lottres cringed from her displeasure, but he couldn't be swayed. Despite all their disagreements, Lottres knew that nothing would stop Brastigan from coming to his aid if he were the one held prisoner.

"*Maess*, it doesn't matter. Ysislaw has Brastigan." Shaelen's voice trembled, and her eyes gleamed with tears. Yriatt scowled. "Brastigan knew our plans. I can't think how Ysislaw would not acquire his knowledge."

There was a thunderstruck silence. Lottres hadn't thought of Brastigan's trouble in those terms. He should have.

"You are certain Ysislaw has Brastigan?" Yriatt demanded.

"We both feel it," Lottres said. "Even if he didn't, his *eppagadrocca* here won't answer when he calls them. I believe he must know where we are."

The two dragons glanced at each other, abruptly reassessing the whole situation. Once again, Lottres sensed a communication between them too deep and swift for mere words.

"In my experience," Dietrick said, "you should avoid doing the exact thing your enemy will expect you to do." The silence stretched on. When no one answered, he awkwardly asked, "Do you still need those horses?"

"Yes." Ymell spoke slowly, with quiet portent. "I believe we do."

* * *

In the fading daylight, Lottres and Shaelen trotted toward Harburg's south gate. The road was crowded with traffic, most of it going the other way. It was slow work to move against the tide, but Lottres pursued it with all the patience he could muster. They had to get inside the city before the gates closed with nightfall, and time was growing short.

"They're not letting anyone in," grumbled the driver of a passing ox cart. "The inns are all full."

Lottres glanced over, saw the hay wagon piled high with household goods. Half a dozen children, perched among the furniture, gazed back at him anxiously. The peasant farmer looked grim. His wife, seated beside him, was having a hard time holding back her tears.

As a royal prince, Lottres expected no difficulty gaining entrance to the capital once he reached the gate, but there was no way to say so without seeming arrogant or cruel—or both.

"I thank you for the warning," Lottres said.

Even this reply seemed inadequate to the upheaval in the peasant family's life. However, there was nothing he could do to help them. Lottres turned away, to see sunset gilding the towers and hoarding on Harburg's city wall. It was his second sunset in one day, a novel experience that somewhat diverted Lottres from his worries.

From the moment they passed through the Dragon's Well, he had felt probes. Ysislaw's awareness followed them, seeking. In response, Lottres had been keeping his thoughts placid as the pool beside the Dragon's Candle. Nor did he and Shaelen speak to each other. Ysislaw would have heard them, and guessed who they were. Only now, as they approached the noisy crowds of Harburg, did he think it safe to speak at all.

Nor could Lottres sense anything of the mysterious barrier blocking probes into Harburg. Of course, he wasn't using his magic. Neither did he or Shaelen know where Yriatt and Ymell were now. They had left Carthell in purposeful ignorance. If Ysislaw caught them, they couldn't tell where their mentors were because they didn't know.

All forward progress had stopped. The road into Harburg was solid with horses and riders, wagons and carts. Lottres stretched in the saddle, muffling a yawn. The slow pace had given them time to eat in the saddle, at least. They were near enough to see the gate guards now.

"Where will we go, once we get inside?" Shaelen asked. Her soft voice was nearly lost among the welter of angry voices at the gate. Lottres, glancing aside, saw trepidation on his companion's face. Lottres wondered if Shaelen had often been inside a town like Harburg. Carthell keep, though impressive, was a single structure with a limited population. A walled city was a different situation.

"We'll head for the keep," Lottres answered reassuringly. "Don't worry. I know my way through the maze."

Shaelen's wan smile hinted that Lottres had been correct in guessing the source of her anxiety. The line shuffled slowly forward.

"I have to tell you, I don't feel completely safe," Lottres confessed. "Eben and Brastigan lived in the keep, where they should have been secure, yet they both disappeared. I can't think where else to look for them, though. What do you think?"

Shaelen raised her head, staring at the keep over the gray walls of the city. She wasn't using her magic, only listening to whatever her heart told her.

"I feel," Shaelen said after a long hesitation, "that Brastigan is there."

"Then we have to go," Lottres said simply, "but we won't announce ourselves too loudly, if you know what I mean. Maybe we should look for Pikarus first and see what he's heard."

"I don't need Pikarus to find Brastigan," Shaelen said with astringent certainty.

"I know," Lottres said, "but we might need help to get him out of whatever mess he's in."

"My lord!" someone called.

Lottres looked up. One of the guards was waving him forward. A frustrated growl went up from the line. It followed Lottres and Shaelen as they squeezed through to the gate.

"Prince Lottres?" the guard asked, eager to please. "I thought I recognized you. Shall I sent a runner ahead to the keep and let them know you're coming?"

"That's not necessary," Lottres quickly assured him. "It looks like you need every man here."

"That we do," the guard chuckled in wry agreement. "Very well, your highness. You may pass."

"Thank you," Lottres said. He prodded his horse onward, into Harburg and the unknown.

* * *

"Good evening, your highness," Margura murmured, bowing Therula and Pikarus into the queen's apartments.

"And you," Therula answered. "Thank you for helping to arrange this."

"Certainly, your highness," Margura said.

Alustra's attendant seemed to be in a very good mood. Her eyes lingered on Pikarus as he entered behind Therula. Something in the woman's expression made Therula reach back, clasping her lover's hand. She wasn't jealous, Therula insisted to herself. It was just that Margura, with her clinging green gown, represented temptation. Even with the embroidered gloves she and Pikarus both wore, Therula felt she had to make a point.

"Good evening, Mother," Therula said, pulling Pikarus past Margura.

"Good evening, my dear." Alustra rose from a small dressing table. She crossed the room to greet Therula with a kiss and embrace. Alustra moved slowly, as if the effort was nearly too much for her. Pikarus bowed over Alustra's hand, and the queen barely summoned a smile. "Welcome back, Sergeant."

"Thank you, your majesty," Pikarus said.

Alustra wore a gown of black brocade with a black satin snood over her hair. Over the gown she wore ropes of pearls whose gleam was hard and bright against the somber fabric. The outfit was too lovely to be called a widow's weeds, even though it was. The gown drained all color from Alustra's face, leaving her gray and wan.

"Come, Pikarus," Therula exclaimed, "you must tell us all about your journey."

Therula felt her cheerfulness was a bit forced. And who could blame her? This meeting with Queen Alustra—for Therula still regarded her mother as a queen, no matter what Oskar might say—was disguised as a private supper. Only Pikarus and Therula were attending. Javes and Cliodora had had to be excluded, much to the younger girl's outrage.

"Very well," Pikarus said. "We left Harburg, as you know..."

He launched into a dry saga full of inconsequential details such as what the troop had eaten at every inn along the road. Therula couldn't understand it. Pikarus wasn't normally a dull speaker, and he'd hinted he had something important to talk about!

Despite herself, Therula found her mind wandering. The room was busy with servants, laying a small table with white linen and silver utensils. Others carried covered platters which wafted delicious aromas after them. Margura, Therula noticed, was edging toward the chamber door. She had lost much of her self-satisfied air, and now appeared rather pale.

"Margura," Therula said, glad for a chance to interrupt Pikarus's droning. "You don't look well."

"It's nothing," Margura demurred. "I'm simply a little tired." But her face had a chalky color and gleamed with sweat.

"Return to your quarters, then," Alustra said. "Lie down and rest. I won't need you for some while."

"Thank you, your majesty." Margura curtseyed with obvious gratitude and quickly left. Therula wondered if the queen's attendant was going to rest at all, or scuttle off to supper where she could ogle Oskar. Judging by her expression, though, Margura wasn't well enough to be around food.

"I'm sorry she's not feeling well," Pikarus said. Something in his voice made Therula look at him twice. Then she remembered how Cliodora had said she thought Margura had been with Brastigan earlier in the day. In fact, this was twice Margura had been with Brastigan and he had been late to meet Therula. Could Margura be involved with Brastigan's mysterious absence?

But Pikarus continued with his infuriating lack of communication. He seemed about to carry on with his exhaustive travelogue when one of the servants stepped forward.

"All is in readiness, your majesty," he said with a bow.

"Thank you, Walther," Alustra replied, so hastily that Therula knew she also wasn't anxious to hear any more about the weather three weeks ago in northern Verelay. "You may bring the plates. Then leave us."

The servants complied. As soon as the door closed behind them, Pikarus gave a sigh.

"My apologies," he smiled as he helped Therula into her seat. "I didn't want to bore you, but some of the servants might have been listening."

Pikarus stepped over to hold Alustra's chair, as well. The queen glanced up at him, puzzled. "Why would anyone want to listen? Nothing of any consequence happens here."

The table was set with platters of white fish covered in mushrooms, onions, and a white cream sauce. Steam rose invitingly from the dishes, but Therula set her fork down with an angry click.

"Yes, who?" Therula demanded. She wasn't sure what annoyed her more, Pikarus's silence or her mother's resigned self-pity. "You've been hiding something all afternoon. Now tell me what's going on. You promised you would."

Alustra looked between them, surprised out of her lassitude. "Eat, dear. You'll feel better," she advised Therula. Then Alustra prodded Pikarus, "Is something interesting happening? Please tell me. I've been bored to death, shut up in here."

Therula obediently picked up her fork to sample the delicious, creamy fish. Her eyes, however, were fixed on Pikarus.

"As you wish, your majesty," he said. Pikarus was all business now. "You know, of course, that Prince Brastigan and Prince Lottres were summoned to Hawkwing House."

"I was there when Unferth sent them," Alustra reminded him. She dabbed at her mouth with a cloth.

"We arrived there and discovered that Mistress Yriatt, the noble lady who had sent for us, is a dragon," Pikarus said.

"A dragon?" Therula repeated blankly. Surely the old tales about dragons were just that—fantastic stories, pretty to hear but empty of fact.

"A dragon?" Alustra asked sharply. She didn't seem to doubt a dragon's existence.

"Yes, your majesty," Pikarus said. "Are you aware what that means?"

"Legend says," Alustra responded softly, "that the two islands, Forix and Tanix, were once ruled by a dragon wizard. Her name was Yllest, and she was a dreadful tyrant. She could change herself into anything she wished, and she had other powers besides. The people never knew when she was nearby, listening to their lamentations, for it is said she delighted in the suffering of others." Alustra paused to sip her wine. "Yllest was overthrown by two brothers, Forix and Tanix, the namesakes of our lands. I cannot speak of Forixan custom, but to this day dragonkind are forbidden to cross the borders of Tanix. I didn't know such creatures existed here."

"It sounded as if Father knew," Therula remarked, recalling the night of Unferth's farewell to Lottres and Brastigan.

"He shouldn't have permitted them to dwell here," Alustra insisted. "Those who live so long cannot understand the feelings and needs of humans. Whenever they intrude upon our affairs, it is we who suffer."

Alustra spoke with something of her usual, vigorous disapproval. That alone heartened Therula.

"In that I fear you are correct," Pikarus said. "What I must tell you, your majesty, is that there is already a dragon in Harburg. One far less benevolent than Mistress Yriatt."

Both women stared at Pikarus. Therula put her fork down again. She had lost all appetite. Therula's mind raced. She had known something was different, even since the day Pikarus left. Now he said there was a dragon in Harburg? She was afraid even to think who the imposter might be.

"What makes you say that?" Alustra demanded.

The queen had suddenly regained some of her color. No longer aged and drab, she stared at Pikarus as she would a merchant she was negotiating with, or a servant who was about to be flogged.

"Partly, it's the hats," Pikarus said. He chuckled at the expression on Therula's face. "As I understand from Master Ymell, dragons can indeed change their shapes, but when they do, they must always keep their horns.

Javes and I noticed when we returned that everyone is wearing these new hats. They appear just the right size to cover a dragon's horns. Can you tell me when this new fashion began?"

Alustra didn't immediately reply. She raised her glass to drink again. Even in the queen's practiced hands, the surface of the wine trembled. Alustra knew the answer, Therula thought, but she couldn't bring herself to speak the words.

"With Oskar, of course," Therula whispered. She didn't want to say it, but someone had to.

"No." Alustra turned her fierce gaze on Therula now. "How can you say that?"

"Mother, it's obvious." Therula did her best to speak steadily under Alustra's gimlet eye. "Although, strictly speaking, we might say the new style began with Eben. Jenne told me Eben ordered Oskar's hat from her, just before the coronation. I don't know if you remember, but Eben was wearing that marvelous headdress at the ceremony, the one with the dragon horns." She raised her eyebrows at the significance. "I don't suppose it was really a headdress at all."

"Then Eben must be the imposter," Alustra put in, too quickly.

"Mistress Yriatt said she hadn't been able to reach Master Eben from Hawkwing House," Pikarus answered.

"And no one has seen Eben since the coronation," Therula said. "Oskar told me he had left. He made it sound as if he asked Eben to stay, but he refused."

"Was Oskar bare-headed at the coronation?" Pikarus asked. Therula nodded. "Perhaps Ys..." He stopped, changing what he had been about to say. "Perhaps the enemy impersonated Eben first. He would have had to remove Eben anyhow. As a fellow wizard, Eben would have given him away."

"Then he would have had a free hand," Therula said. "Eben had the king's favor. No one questioned him."

Pikarus nodded. "He must have changed places with Oskar later on. After Oskar had taken the throne, and he would have a king's power to use as he wished."

"Ridiculous," Alustra insisted. "Oskar would never surrender the throne. It was his birthright."

It had been at the center of Alustra's life as well, Therula thought. Hadn't she seen her mother devote every effort to assuring that Oskar rose above the pack of bastards and won the crown? Perhaps that was why Alustra had been so withdrawn since the coronation. With Oskar safely on the throne — as it had seemed — what else was left for Alustra to do?

"Think, Mother," Therula said gently. "Haven't you and Oskar always been close? Yet he's done nothing but isolate you ever since he took power. Taking your throne down, sending Margura in here every day to tell you how old you are."

"I—" Alustra began to defend Margura, but then closed her mouth again.

"I don't believe Oskar would do that," Therula pressed. "He respects you too much. But a stranger might, someone who regards you as a threat to his illicit scheme."

"Enough!" Alustra cried.

Alustra stared down at her plate, eyes closed. The soft skin beneath her chin trembled. For a horrified moment, Therula thought she might see her mother cry. What would she do then? If Alustra cracked under the strain, what could anyone else do?

Then Alustra straightened her back. Her eyes snapped open, fixed Pikarus with a calm and imperious stare. Alustra was a queen again.

"I cannot believe this. Yet I must," Alustra said. She sounded weary, but strong enough to face down a dragon herself. "Now I must ask you, Sergeant. Where is my son? Is he alive or dead?"

Therula swallowed hard. Pikarus must expect Alustra to lead them in defeating the impostor. Therula was certainly counting on it! But if Oskar was dead, Alustra had nothing left to fight for.

"Your majesty, I don't know," Pikarus answered. "I have heard that the enemy believes in holding hostages. Therefore, I think it likely King Oskar remains alive, but I have no way to know with any certainty."

"Are Habrok, or any of the others, involved in this plot?" Alustra asked.

"Not Habrok," Therula put in.

"I would be very surprised if Prince Habrok was involved," Pikarus agreed. Then he admitted, "With some of the other princes, it is harder to be sure."

Alustra shrugged. "Then the defense of Crutham may be left as it is, in Habrok's hands," she said. "You, Sergeant, will be free to search for my son."

Before Pikarus could respond, the door opened. All three of them jumped. Therula saw Pikarus's hand grip his sword hilt as two figures scuttled into the room.

"How dare you enter my chambers!" Alustra scolded.

"Forgive me," a familiar voice replied. Lottres closed the door furtively, and approached the table.

"Lottres!" Therula exclaimed. "You're back, too?" With a guilty start, she realized she hadn't even noticed his absence. She quickly added, "Thank goodness you're safe."

Pikarus, too, relaxed. "Your highness. I thought you were in Carthell."

"We were. It's been a busy day," Lottres answered with a wry smile. He bowed toward Alustra. "Your majesty, may we join you?"

"Please do," Alustra said. Her eyes were on Lottres, assessing him.

Pikarus joined Lottres in bringing two more chairs to the table. Therula found that her appetite had suddenly returned. Because, she realized, her mother was in command again. The burden of uncertainty had been lifted from Therula's shoulders.

As she belatedly began to eat, Therula eyed her half-brother and his companion curiously. Lottres had lost weight on his journey. His face was thinner and his beard was longer, but he walked with new energy. A woman was with him, tall and dark eyed, but so strangely dressed! Auburn hair was done in the Urulai beads Brastigan was so fond of. She wore a scandalous outfit, leather boots and trousers under some kind of jerkin that seemed to be stiffened with animal bones.

Did all Urulai women dress like men, Therula wondered? How odd! She couldn't help wondering what Brastigan thought of it. Despite his outrageous behaviors, Therula knew Brastigan had conventional tastes in women.

The strange woman seemed to flinch. She shot Therula a piercing look. Therula looked away, not wanting to acknowledge someone so unsuitable, but she couldn't forget the Urulai woman's hurt expression. It was almost as if she knew what Therula thought of her. No, that was impossible.

"Your majesty, this is Shaelen of Hawkwing House. She is a student of Mistress Yriatt's." Lottres spoke with careful formality.

Therula didn't miss the reproachful glance he turned on her. She pretended to, though she had the mortifying feeling this Shaelen might have known what she was thinking, after all.

"I see," Alustra murmured, her expression neutral.

"Shaelen, this is Queen Alustra and her daughter, Princess Therula, who is my half-sister," Lottres went on.

Shaelen nodded, saying nothing. It was going to be awkward if she didn't understand Cruthan. Or perhaps she was shy, Therula thought. If the stranger really was a sorceress, she would try to be charitable.

"Are you aware of all that has been happening?" Alustra asked. Her voice, as she looked at Lottres, was almost accusing.

Gravely, Lottres answered, "We did know that Sillets has invaded, and Duke Johanz was good enough to tell us that Father had died. I'm sorry." He seemed to mean it, too.

"We all miss him," Alustra answered briefly, brushing his condolences aside. "Now tell me, what else happened in Carthell?"

"Duke Johanz didn't make us very welcome," Lottres said. "In fact, he imprisoned us under cover of hospitality. Johanz intended to collaborate with Sillets in conquering Crutham. He thought Albrett would take the throne afterward and then he could rule through Albrett." Lottres made a face, giving his opinion of this scheme.

"This is no surprise," Therula said darkly, remembering the absence of a Carthellan representative at Oskar's coronation.

"But?" Alustra prodded. The news didn't seem to shake her grim purpose.

"Master Ymell and Mistress Yriatt destroyed a group of Silletsian spies in Carthell. Afterward, the duke saw his error," Lottres said with what sounded like a dry understatement. "He will march to Crutham's aid, though I must caution that Carthell is still unreliable. If the circumstances permit it, Johanz may yet attempt to place Albrett on the throne."

"Oskar is the king of Crutham," Alustra replied with fierce resolve.

"I agree," Lottres hastily answered.

"Did you also know that Oskar has vanished?" Alustra asked with a cold edge to her voice.

"No," Lottres admitted. "We knew the enemy was somewhere in Harburg. Until we heard you saying so, we didn't know he might have taken Oskar's place."

"What do you mean, you heard us?" Therula interrupted. "You weren't even here!"

Lottres gave Pikarus a surprised glance. "Didn't you tell them?"

"It hadn't come up," Pikarus answered.

"What are you speaking of?" Alustra demanded.

"I am also a student of Mistress Yriatt," Lottres said. "I'm learning to be a wizard."

"You?" Therula blurted incredulously.

"Why not?" Lottres gave Therula an exasperated look.

"Well, I —." Therula fumbled.

Lottres, a wizard? The gawky boy, forever with a parchment in his hands? It didn't seem possible he should do something so drastic. So...romantic. And yet, hadn't she just been thinking something was different about him?

"You are a king's son," Alustra said, cutting off Therula's jumbled thoughts. "One must wonder where your loyalties lie, with your ancestral domain or with your new masters."

"Since Mistress Yriatt was my father's ally, I don't see the conflict," Lottres answered. Therula could tell he was trying to control his anger, but the dull red in his cheeks gave him away.

"Then you will fight for Crutham," Alustra went on, ignoring his reaction. She glanced at Shaelen with cool question. "Both of you?"

"Of course," Lottres snapped.

"If we are permitted," Shaelen spoke for the first time. She had a slight accent, but Therula was surprised to hear that her Cruthan was quite good. "If our presence is too disagreeable..."

"No," Lottres broke in.

The two of them shared a long glance, and Therula could fairly hear the silent argument between them. Then Lottres looked squarely at Alustra.

"I accept your right to command me," he said. "You are the queen, and I will do as you order. But this is my home. I won't be driven out by superstition."

"Very well." Alustra didn't acknowledge his accusation. "As long as you do obey."

"Then," Pikarus hastily put in, "why did you return to Crutham, your highness? You might have remained in Carthell with... the others."

Shaelen shifted uncomfortably in her seat. Lottres was so careful not to look at her that Therula had to wonder what they were hiding.

"It's Brastigan," Lottres confessed. "We both sense he's in some kind of trouble."

"That's nothing unusual," Alustra sniffed, annoyed all over again by the reminder of her least favorite princeling.

"This time is different," Lottres said. "He's in real danger. Especially if Pikarus is right about Ys... uh, someone having taken Oskar's place."

"Your majesty," Pikarus said, "Javes and I have been searching for Prince Brastigan since we realized that our enemy must be here. We cannot find him."

"Compared to the fate of our missing king," Alustra retorted, "I fear that is of little consequence."

"Brastigan has a right to be here, just as I do," Lottres began with real heat.

"Mother, Lottres, please don't argue," Therula begged. "Not now."

Alustra turned for a moment, her brows raised in stern surprise. Therula held her own gaze steady. She knew Unferth's constant infidelities had hurt Alustra. Indeed, after her own doubts of the past few weeks, Therula understood better than ever how her mother felt. Yet the one good result was that Unferth's many sons were all highly motivated to keep Crutham free. This wasn't the time for Alustra to cling to past grievances, not with their kingdom teetering on the brink of destruction.

"Therula is right," Lottres said, though his arms were folded stubbornly across his chest. "If we get into family history, we'll be here until dawn. Perhaps we should concentrate on the matter at hand."

Alustra didn't acknowledge Lottres's rebuke any more than she had before, but Pikarus quickly picked up the subject.

"Her majesty has requested that my squad search for the king," he said. It was a careful choice of words. Only Oskar or Garican could issue orders. Alustra had to make requests. "Will you both assist us?"

"We have to be careful," Lottres cautioned. "He will sense it if we use our magic. Then we're all done for."

"There's no reason you couldn't accompany us," Pikarus said. "Your eyes are as good as any man's, and we may need magic to free them, regardless of the risk."

"If the same enemy has taken both of them," Shaelen ventured, "they may be held together. In finding one, we may find both."

"That would be a great good fortune," Alustra said. Therula was relieved to hear her make some effort at reconciliation.

"When do we begin?" Lottres asked. "Supper is still going on in the Hall downstairs, but it won't last forever."

"We must wait until high night," Pikarus said. "But I think we shouldn't remain here much longer."

"We need to rest, anyway," Lottres said. "We've been traveling all day. Where can we wait and not be seen? In the barracks?"

"No, you'd be noticed," Pikarus said. "Rumors would spread."

"Your own quarters are occupied, I'm afraid," Therula said. "Eskelon and Sebbelon needed a place to sleep, and I don't know where else we can put them. I don't think anyone is using Brastigan's room, though. He's supposed to be in it."

Lottres gave Shaelen another questioning look. She shrugged uncomfortably.

"That will have to do," Lottres said.

He and Shaelen rose, and Pikarus did, too. As they all trooped toward the door, Therula was left at the table with her mother, among the beautiful dishes and half eaten delicacies. She turned in her chair, watching Pikarus leave without touching her, without saying a word. Therula stared at her plate and stiffened her chin to keep it from trembling.

Alustra reached across the table to take her hand. She looked tired again, Therula thought. Perhaps the sparring with Lottres had reminded her of too many past conflicts, battles in a war which, truthfully, she had lost years ago. But a woman of Alustra's pride did not surrender, no matter what the situation might be. Though her skin was loose with age, her grip was as firm as ever.

"I have learned," Alustra said softly, "that a woman must never permit herself to be ignored."

"Oh, Mother!" The blunt advice startled a laugh out of Therula. She came around the table to embrace her mother with fierce emotion. "I'm so glad you're back with us."

Then she sprang to her feet and ran after Pikarus. Therula found the three of them in the corridor. Lottres was turned toward the door, as if he had known she was coming.

"I'm sorry about Mother," Therula said as she joined them. "She will come around. Expedience overcomes ego, you know."

"I wish she wouldn't always throw it in our faces. It's not like we wanted to be born out of turn." Lottres slouched down the corridor, still irritated. The others followed him around the corner and down the stairs toward the inner courtyard.

"I know," Therula soothed. She also knew Alustra wasn't the only one who ought to apologize. Therula turned awkwardly to Shaelen. "If you don't want to use Brastigan's room, you can borrow my bed. I don't think I'll be going to sleep early."

Not while Cliodora was likely to burst in with all her questions the moment Therula returned from dinner. Not to mention her own worries about Oskar and Brastigan and the future of Crutham.

"Don't be a prude," Lottres snorted. "Nothing will happen."

Therula felt her cheeks tingle as he misunderstood her concern. As if she didn't know Brastigan had had women in his bed before!

"Thank you," Shaelen murmured. "That is kind of you, princess, but I think we should stay together."

"I agree," Pikarus said. "You're both too vulnerable as it is."

"Shaelen can sleep in the bed," Lottres went on. "I'll sleep on the floor." Then he jumped, as if Shaelen had stepped on his foot, but Therula hadn't seen her move.

"We won't be in the bed at the same time because one of us must keep watch," Shaelen said. Strangely, Lottres was grinning at her.

They had crossed the inner courtyard and now descended the ramp toward the outer court. The sky was darkening above, and the towers of the keep were the color of a dove. Light from the windows of the grand hall spilled patches of color over the cobblestones. Vague forms moved behind the glass. Therula had the weird sense that she was an outsider in her own home. As if the evil being who impersonated her brother had walled her away from the true life of the keep. She found herself shivering.

"Are you cold?" Pikarus asked. He moved beside her, not quite touching, yet near enough that she felt his presence like a woolen cloak. "Perhaps I should escort her highness to her chambers."

"That's fine. I know where we're going," Lottres said. As they separated, Lottres added, "But you aren't fooling anyone, Pikarus."

Therula pretended not to hear him. She lifted her chin and marched off toward the women's wing. "I'm not sure I like him as a wizard," she grumbled as Lottres and Shaelen disappeared into the men's wing.

"I suppose he can't help showing off," Pikarus said. He sounded unperturbed. That bothered Therula almost as much as Lottres's teasing.

She should be glad, Therula thought. Pikarus wasn't purposely ignoring her. He had been distracted, and rightly so. His news—Oskar gone, a stranger in his place—was grave. Therula shouldn't have assumed his silence was sinister. She was a princess. She ought to know that everything wasn't always about her.

Candlelight inside the building made Therula blink. The flames seemed harsh and bright after the gray dusk outside. They walked in silence, though Therula's temples throbbed with tension. So many words, held in so long. She felt she must choke with the need to speak.

"Come in for a moment, Sergeant," Therula said when they reached her door. It was the same bland order she always gave, only now twisted by her tension.

"Don't let Lottres upset you," Pikarus said, accurately guessing some of her mind. He made sure the door was tightly closed before turning into the room.

"But he's right, isn't he?" At last Therula dropped her pretense, let Pikarus see the fear in her eyes. "It's what we've been doing all along—hiding!"

"We both agreed that privacy is best." Pikarus took her small, cold hands in his great warm ones.

"I just don't want you to think I'm ashamed of you," Therula blurted out.

"I never thought that," Pikarus scolded affectionately. He drew Therula into his arms. She clung to his strength and wished she could stop shaking.

"Everything has been so confused," Therula told him. "And I missed you so much! Father died, and then Oskar was acting so odd, and that stupid gamble of his. I was so afraid of what you would say."

"You couldn't have known it," he said, "but King Oskar must already have been replaced when you made your wager with him. The dragon has ways to make you agree with him, even if it wasn't what you wanted. Don't dwell on it, my love."

"I hadn't thought of that." Therula leaned against Pikarus, feeling a flood of relief. "Even so, I was afraid you would meet another woman on your journey. It seemed like Father did, every time he stepped out the door. I couldn't bear it if you didn't want me any more."

"Never think that!"

Pikarus bent toward Therula. She sighed with sweet relief and clung to him while they kissed passionately. Ah, this is what she had longed for all day. No, all week—all month! Soon Therula was warm from head to toe. She no longer had any doubt of her lover's feelings.

Even when their lips parted, Pikarus held Therula close.

"Our enemy has made you question yourself," he murmured. "You must be strong, for the danger is still great. Now I must go. Javes and our squad will need to prepare for tonight's work."

"I know." Therula nodded reluctantly. She stood on her toes to kiss him again. "Go. Send word when you've found either one of them. And be careful, my love."

Brastigan lay on the pallet, waiting for his emotions to fade along with the pain and nausea. Emotion, he thought with disgust. That had been his problem all along: emotion. Ever since he left Harburg on Yriatt's quest, he'd been so turned around, he didn't know what he was doing. Emotion drove Lottres away from him. Emotion made him turn to a girl who was only half there. Emotion over Unferth's death blinded him to danger.

It was time to remember he was a warrior. A great warrior, he reminded himself. If Ysislaw was vain enough to think this one skirmish meant victory over Brastigan, so much the better. He would teach the tyrant, in time.

Strangely, Brastigan found himself grinning. He no longer felt hung over. He was invigorated, alive with purpose. No more of this sitting around, waiting —as the girl would wait—for someone to tell him what to do. Brastigan knew what he had to do. It was a relief to have a clear goal, even if it was as simple as getting out of this prison.

Brastigan sat up, holding out his hands for a close look at the bindings. The single, long chain ran through a round steel eye in the wall behind him. It connected the two metal cuffs on his wrists. Ah, but the cuffs weren't solid metal bolted together by the chain. They opened or closed with a hinge. Each had a spring-catch, and the black slot of a simple lock.

Here was something he could work with. Brastigan grinned again, blessing the many days he had wasted at the Dead Donkey. He yanked off his empty sword belt. With the buckle's flat tongue, he set to work on those locks. It might take a while to worry them open, but he would manage. At the moment, he had nothing but time.

CHAPTER TWENTY-THREE
FINDING THE LOST

THE manacles came off easily enough, but Brastigan soon found escape wasn't such a simple matter. The door could only be unlocked from outside. Brastigan pressed his ear to the crack, but heard no voices or movement. When he knelt to peer beneath the door there was only blackness on the other side.

So Ysislaw had left no guards. He must not think he would need them. Well, he might be right about that. Isolation was an effective prison on its own.

Brastigan rested on the floor for a moment. Then he sprang to his feet, not bothering to move quietly. He should have known it was going too easily. Here he was, free! Yet still trapped. Free and trapped at the same time. Wasn't that the story of his life?

Brastigan prowled his small cell with restless energy for a time, then slouched down on the pallet. As soon as he sat still, he felt his eyes burning with exhaustion. His mouth opened on a yawn as wide as the plains of Daraine. Passing out drunk didn't count as resting—he was still worn to the bone.

Since he couldn't break out, Brastigan did the only other thing he could do. He stretched out and rolled over with his back to the door. Holding the steel cuffs, he curled his arms against his chest so that anyone who checked on him would think him still in chains. Then he went to sleep.

* * *

Brastigan's room was quiet and dark. Dark, because Lottres had put out the candle when all the occupants of rooms around them had settled into sleep. Quiet, because Shaelen was resting at last, and he didn't want to disturb her.

Upon reaching Brastigan's room, they had both spent a good deal of time examining the archway between the sitting room and the bedchamber. They both sensed residual energy there. Shaelen thought the arch could have been the center of a transportation spell, like the Dragon's Candle—or Dragon's Well, depending what side you came from. If Pikarus was correct that Brastigan had been abducted, it could have happened in this very room. As it was, the archway was more tantalizing than helpful.

Lottres shifted in his chair. He would have welcomed a pot of tea, but since that was denied him, he relied on his own thoughts to keep him awake. Certainly they were thorny enough to do the job.

Therula's harsh judgment, based solely on appearances, had bothered

Shaelen a great deal. Lottres didn't like it, either. He hadn't remembered Therula being so prissy. Still, Lottres tried not to hold it against her. Of all Alustra's children, only Therula ever went out of her way to be civil to the rest of the family. Yet she was always putting herself across as so worldly and sophisticated, when she was hardly more than a fluttering, frightened girl. The deception disappointed him.

Soon enough, Lottres got bored with fuming over small slights. He sat still and listened, as he had all the way through Altannath. It wasn't hard to locate Ysislaw, of course. His power and presence filled the main keep as light fills a lamp. Such enormous self-confidence made Lottres feel small. He wondered how they would ever fool Ysislaw, with his ages of cunning. They would just have to hope that whatever blocked magic from outside Harburg would conceal them, too.

Lottres yawned, then told himself he'd better stop doing it. Unlike him, dragons didn't even have to sleep. Yriatt said they found sleep pleasurable, and this was how the *eppagadrocca* had managed to ensnare Ymell, but it wasn't essential. The dragons could recover their energies through meditation. Shaelen had said she knew how, but that this wasn't the time for lessons. Lottres agreed. He could imagine Ysislaw up in the keep somewhere, listening for any hint of their presence just as Lottres listened for him.

Besides, Lottres's head felt so heavy, he probably would have fallen asleep if he tried meditating. He shifted in his chair again, trying to remain alert and focused.

Faintly, from the harbor, Lottres heard the moan of a fog horn. It sounded like a very large cow. Or voices in a dream. The mournful bellow came again. Lottres stifled another yawn. He was about to get up and see if Shaelen was ready to join Pikarus, when he heard a voice.

"Answer, slave."

The summons wasn't loud, but it startled Lottres into complete wakefulness. So smooth and reptilian in its cold force—that had to be Ysislaw!

A reply came almost instantly. *"I am here, master. Rowbeck is ours. The portal has been repaired, as you instructed."*

"Do not tell me what I already know." Ysislaw brushed the *eppagadrocca's* thoughts aside. *"My enemies are moving. We must act first. Awaken the handlers and get the walking bones moving. You will come through immediately."*

"As you say, master."

"Prepare yourselves. I go to open the way."

Ysislaw's voice cut off, abruptly as the slam of a door. The silence in its wake roared like thunder. No, Lottres realized, what he heard was the drumbeat of his own heart.

When the sense of Ysislaw's message penetrated his surprise, Lottres sprang to his feet. He no longer felt even a little bit drowsy.

Shaelen was already up, moving in the dark. "I think he's going to leave the castle," she said, a bare whisper in the inky blackness. "But if he brings the bone men through..."

"I know," Lottres breathed in return. It sounded as though the military situation was about to get tense. "Stay here. Keep listening. I'll go to the barracks and warn Pikarus. We need to wait until Ysislaw leaves before we do anything."

Sensing Shaelen's agreement, he turned toward the door. Lottres forced himself to move slowly. He'd better not make any noise. Ysislaw wasn't gone yet. Nevertheless, this was a priceless opportunity. With Ysislaw away, he and Shaelen could use their magic more openly. It was a stroke of luck they couldn't afford to let pass.

* * *

It seemed only a moment had passed when Brastigan snapped awake. It was sound that roused him. A key ground in the lock. The door groaned softly as it opened. Brastigan lay limp, listening to the sly whisper of shoes across the floor.

The lone torch on the wall was burning out. It gave only a sallow light. Brastigan's fists tightened over cold links of chain as the footsteps drew nearer. He narrowed his eyes to slits and forced himself to breathe deeply, feigning sleep. The footsteps stopped. A hand fell on his shoulder.

"Brastigan," came a man's voice, a coarse whisper. "I know you're awake—No, wait!"

Brastigan rolled over and tackled whoever it was. They both crashed to the floor together. Brastigan threw a loop of the chain around the man's neck and jerked it tight.

"Shut up, you," Brastigan snarled. "Just do what I say."

The fellow made some coughing reply. Brastigan stared at him, suddenly recognizing Lottres's curly beard, his face growing red over the constricting chain.

For a moment, emotion threatened to choke Brastigan. He could hardly believe his brother was here, just when he needed him most. After all their arguments, too. It must have been magic that called Lottres to him. Brastigan was so glad to see him, he didn't much care.

"Get off, you idiot!" Lottres's voice came clearly, though he couldn't really have spoken.

"Oh." Feeling stupid, Brastigan released the chain. He rolled off Lottres.

"Are you all right?" Pikarus called from the doorway. Another figure lurked behind Pikarus, someone Brastigan couldn't see.

"Yes," Lottres answered, though he rubbed his neck irritably. Then he smiled at Brastigan. "Remind me not to wake you up again."

"Welcome home," Brastigan smirked, summoning his old humor. He tossed the chains aside and stood up, offering Lottres a hand.

Pikarus approached, offering a familiar sword in a well-worn sheath. He also carried Brastigan's duffel over his shoulder.

"Your highness," Pikarus said, "you'll want these."

"Yes, I do. Thank you!" Brastigan seized Victory eagerly. He gave the bright blade a quick inspection in the faint candlelight. Then he took his duffel. By the weight, it had his whole harness inside.

"Let me help you," Pikarus offered.

"We need to hurry," Lottres said.

"Really?" Brastigan snorted with mocking humor. "You think so?"

Lottres shoved at him with friendly anger. "Cut it out."

Brastigan yanked at the duffle's laces. Metal pieces clattered down onto the pallet. There was no gambeson in the pile, so Brastigan dragged the hauberk on over his clothes.

"Do I need to tell you Father's dead?" Brastigan asked as he worked.

"No, I'd heard." Lottres shook his head. He helped Brastigan get his hair clear of the metal links. "Things were lively in Carthell."

"Rumor has it Johanz turned traitor," Brastigan said. He stood up, allowing Pikarus to fasten his demi-greaves and Lottres to work on the vambraces.

"Who told you that?" Lottres asked.

"Ysislaw."

"What?" Lottres nearly dropped the left vambrace as he buckled it to Brastigan's shoulder. Shaelen appeared from the hallway, silent as a ghost. Brastigan felt his heart grow cold at the sight of her. He forced himself back to the matter at hand.

"After I was jumped in my quarters, he came in here to gloat," Brastigan explained. He did his best not to look at Shaelen. "Ysislaw's been disguised as Oskar—did you know?"

"As we feared," Pikarus murmured. He had returned to his work. The second demi-greave was now securely fastened.

"Pikarus figured it out first," Lottres said. "Shaelen and I got here a few hours ago. He told Alustra and Therula, too, although I'm not sure what they can do."

"Her? She'll think of something," Brastigan snorted. He shrugged his shoulders and stamped his feet to settle his harness in place. Pikarus approached with a clean surcoat. While Pikarus settled the folds, Brastigan tightened his sword belt. "So, Carthell?"

Lottres shrugged. "Ysislaw had left some of his *eppagadrocca* there. They weren't prepared to face both Ymell and Yriatt."

Brastigan remembered the fires on the hillside about the Dragon's Chimney. "Is Carthell Keep still standing?" he quipped.

"Yes," Lottres said with a smile. "There, all done, and we need to get out of here. Ysislaw has left, but we don't know how long he'll be gone. We want to be far away before he comes back."

"Where did he go?" Brastigan asked as he stepped into the hallway. It was still dark, though Pikarus shielded a candle in a plain steel holder. The passage curved to follow the shape of the outside wall, and you couldn't see far. Anything could be lurking just around the bend.

"I'll show you," Shaelen said.

Brastigan didn't want to be anywhere near the witch. Reluctantly, he followed her to the nearest arrow slit. The night sky was black marbled with gray as the usual fog drifted in from the sea. He could see the torch-lit walkways of Crutham Keep below, and farther off the parallel line of the city walls. From the angle of view, Brastigan could tell he had been right: this was Eben's tower.

But something else dominated the dark vista. Out beyond the battlements, a column of brilliant green light stood in midair. The light flickered erratically. Brastigan narrowed his eyes, gauging the distance.

"It's the Dragon's Candle." Lottres answered Brastigan's question before he even spoke it. "The Silletsians have taken Rowbeck. I heard them say they fixed the Dragon's Tooth."

Brastigan didn't bother to argue. He could tell Lottres was right. Then he drew a sharp breath. The light meant the wizard's gate was open. Someone was coming through. That was what made the light waver. In fact, judging by the constant flickering, a lot of someones were coming through.

Brastigan couldn't help noticing that Shaelen wasn't looking out the window. She was staring at him. Even in so short a time, he had forgotten she carried in her face a fire-toned reflection of the girl's lost beauty. She even acted like the girl. Shaelen stared at Brastigan with exactly the dumbstruck expression he had seen so often in the shadow's eyes. The pressure came back to his chest, fiercer and harder.

"Ysislaw is bringing his army through," Pikarus said. His words made Shaelen blink. Brastigan could breathe again.

"So we've got a problem," Brastigan said. Not that he needed Pikarus to explain what was happening, but the distraction helped.

There was sure to be battle in the morning. Brastigan looked forward to it. He knew what to do in a fight. It was Shaelen he didn't know how to handle.

"Remember, we still have work to do," Lottres said.

"Like what?" Brastigan asked. Hadn't they come here to rescue him?

"Oskar is missing, too," Lottres told him. "Alustra wants him back, if we can find him."

Brastigan rolled his eyes. "I suppose she would."

"I think he's somewhere else in the tower," Lottres went on. "I just don't know where."

"You found me, didn't you?" Brastigan asked. A cold breeze was blowing in from the arrow slit. He stepped away from it and that baleful green pulse in the night.

"Ysislaw has some kind of spell over Harburg. It interferes with our senses," Lottres explained. "We know you too well for him to hide you from us, but I'm not as close to Oskar and Shaelen has never met him. Since Oskar is the more important hostage, it makes sense he's more heavily concealed."

We, he kept saying, like Shaelen had also been part of the search. Brastigan didn't want to accept that. Shaelen wasn't the girl. She didn't love him. And he sure didn't love her.

"We'll have to go room to room," Pikarus said.

"Good thing it's not a very big tower," Brastigan said.

The four of them hurried away from the arrow slit. Brastigan followed Pikarus, who still held the candle. Lottres came behind him, and Shaelen last, which was still too close for Brastigan's comfort.

Since Lottres was practically at his shoulder, Brastigan murmured, "So you know, Ysislaw claims the murders were Oskar's little project."

"Of our brothers?" Lottres quickly asked. His expression darkened. "I guess that's no surprise, but I think we'll both have something to say to him, before he gets safely home to his mother."

"Yeah," Brastigan grunted, "just a few things. Eben is dead, too. Ysislaw took credit for that."

"Ymell thought he must be," Lottres answered heavily. "I'll miss him, all the same."

They came to another door. It was wood clad with steel, just like the door to Brastigan's cell, but this one wasn't locked. Beyond it, stairs slanted up and down in gloom.

"Which way?" Brastigan whispered, so the sound wouldn't carry in the stairwell.

"Down," Lottres answered.

Footsteps echoed weirdly in the cramped stairwell. It made Brastigan think someone was following them. They soon reached a narrow landing and another doorway into the tower. As Brastigan recalled, this had led to Eben's personal quarters. Pikarus stopped there.

"You're sure he's in this tower?" Brastigan asked.

"He should be," Lottres replied. "Its the only part of the keep where you could hide a prisoner and be sure he'd stay hidden."

"The door is locked from the inside," Pikarus reported.

"I can get it," Brastigan said. He began to unfasten his belt, but Lottres laid a hand on his shoulder.

"Let Shaelen do it," Lottres said. "She's faster."

Though his heart boiled with rebellion, Brastigan stepped back. Shaelen slipped between him and Pikarus and knelt, placing her hands over the lock.

"The door is also barred from within," Shaelen reported.

"Can you get them both?" Lottres asked.

"Of course."

"How many guards down below?" Brastigan asked while they waited.

"Two on the landing below us," Lottres answered. "We left them sleeping."

"You shouldn't have," Brastigan answered irritably. A distinct click sounded as Shaelen sprang the lock. "The men who grabbed me were Silletsians, but wearing Cruthan uniforms. Ysislaw's managed to infiltrate the palace guards. Or maybe he just killed a few and replaced them with his own men."

Pikarus jerked back at this news. His mouth made a thin line. "I wouldn't be surprised if he did. I don't know if you heard, but Tarther also died while we were away. Garican is a weak replacement. It would be easy to bully him, especially for someone disguised as the king."

"You might be assuming too much," Lottres said. "I didn't notice any strangers—"

He was interrupted by a muffled clatter on the other side of the door.

"It's open," Shaelen announced, straightening, "but Ysislaw will have to return before sunrise, or risk being seen. Please, let's hurry."

"You don't have to tell us," Brastigan growled. He drew Victory, but Pikarus nudged him.

"Your highness, please let me go first."

Without waiting for agreement, Pikarus stepped up to the door. He put his candle holder on the floor, drew his sword, and shoved the door open. Brastigan almost expected shouts of alarm from inside, but there was only silence. Pikarus retrieved the candle and beckoned. One by one, the four of them slipped inside.

It was dark in the tower, and very warm. Even Pikarus's candle could hardly penetrate the gloom. The air was thick with a cloying odor. As Brastigan's eyes adjusted, furnishings emerged from the darkness: a simple bed, a writing desk, a shelf of neatly ordered scrolls, a chest of drawers with an ewer and basin on top.

These appeared unchanged, but there were some new additions. Two tall stands of twisted iron supported massive candles at either side of the bed. Their flickering light gave the chamber a funereal atmosphere.

Someone was lying on the bed. Oskar? Brastigan stepped forward. He froze as one of the floor boards squealed under his weight. Brastigan eased back.

"Are we sure there's no one underneath us?" he murmured to Lottres. The lower level held a sitting room, where Eben had given his rare consultations.

"It was empty when we came up," Lottres assured him.

"I hope you're right." Waving Pikarus to join him, Brastigan shifted to the side. They advanced more carefully, and managed to reach the bedside this time.

Oskar lay on top of the blankets. He was so still, he didn't even seem to breathe. Brastigan stared down at the face he hated. Oskar didn't look so handsome with his eyes closed and his features slack. His skin had an unhealthy, waxy texture except where an unaccustomed growth of beard furred his chin. He'd been lying there a while, all right.

"Shaelen, do you feel it?" Lottres murmured.

"Yes," the witch replied. Her face looked hollow as a skull's in the dim light. "If this is your King Oskar, I see him, but I don't sense his mind. Nor any of yours." Her gaze touched Brastigan with something like relief. He looked away from her.

"Whatever is blocking us must be in this room. We simply have to find it," Lottres said.

"I will meditate," Shaelen said. "Perhaps I will learn something."

She sat cross-legged beside the door, hands lying slack over her knees. Brastigan watched his brother walk slowly past the bed. Lottres looked from side to side, as if he searched for something.

"Don't touch anything," Lottres murmured as he passed.

Brastigan snorted at that. "How long do we wait?"

"I don't know," Lottres said.

Brastigan looked at Pikarus and rolled his eyes. Pikarus shrugged. He set his candle on the chest of drawers and folded his arms to wait. Brastigan prowled up and down at the bedside. In a moment, he remembered what Yriatt had said, that Ymell had been subdued by the scent of a poisoned flower. And here was this thick perfume in the air. It might be the same thing. Brastigan leaned over to the nearest candle. He inhaled deeply. His lips went numb.

Trying not to cough, Brastigan stepped back. "Hey, Pup," he sputtered. "I think it's in the candles."

"I'll be there in a moment," came the distracted reply. Lottres seemed rapt in his magical search.

Brastigan glared at the two candles as they burned, innocently spewing their venom. They were thick as small tree trunks, made to burn a good while before you had to replace them. That must be exactly what Ysislaw intended, to keep his prisoner helpless and not have to worry about him.

Brastigan gritted his teeth as he stared down at Oskar. The candles' overly sweet fragrance sickened him, but not as much as the sight of his half-brother's face. It was so tempting to leave the fool there. Let him suffer the penalty for his idiocy in making deals with Sillets. It was what Oskar deserved for turning on his brothers.

But it wasn't what Crutham deserved. Nor could Brastigan accept the idea of Ysislaw winning this war. Outside, the Dragon's Candle burned in the night. Ysislaw was out there somewhere. He might be coming back at any moment. Brastigan looked impatiently toward Lottres. His brother stood still, his back toward Brastigan and Pikarus.

It didn't look like Lottres would be any help. Frustrated, Brastigan bent over Oskar's bed.

"Hey, wake up," he hissed.

Brastigan jabbed at Oskar's shoulder. There was nothing there, yet the air around Oskar's body had a kind of icy solidity. It was like sticking his fingers into a snow bank. His whole arm tingled and throbbed. Brastigan jerked back.

"Ow," Brastigan complained. He shook his stinging hand.

"Perhaps we should wait for Prince Lottres," Pikarus rebuked him.

"What was that?" Lottres suddenly demanded.

All at once, the two candles shuddered. Their steadily burning wicks erupted into jets of crackling flame. Thick smoke billowed into the air. Both Brastigan and Pikarus jumped away from the bedside.

Lottres ran toward them. "What did you do?"

"I didn't touch it," Brastigan protested.

"Don't give me that," his brother snarled.

Smoke was quickly filling the chamber. The cloud spread in thick strands, gray as ash in the darkness. It burned in Brastigan's eyes. Coughing, he reeled backward.

"It must be some kind of trap," he said.

"Shaelen, open the door," Lottres cried. "We need air!"

"I can't," she called back. "It's sealed itself."

"Crouch down, where the air is clear," said Pikarus. His voice already sounded near the floor.

It wasn't hard to follow those instructions. The fumes were already making Brastigan light-headed. On his knees, he stumbled toward Pikarus's voice. Somewhere nearby, he heard Lottres coughing.

"I guess we should have expected something like this," Brastigan said.

"We can't leave the king here," Pikarus said. "Prince Brastigan, if you would please help me. Prince Lottres, help Shaelen get the door open."

"Right," Lottres said. His voice moved off toward the doorway.

Brastigan groaned inwardly, but he followed Pikarus. What other choice was there? They should have known Ysislaw would cast a spell to guard Oskar. He was too important a prisoner. Alas, he was also too important to leave behind.

Even with the two candles blazing, it was hard to see through the dense smoke. Brastigan rubbed tears from his eyes. Almost by chance, he found one end of the bed.

"Try to get a few good breaths," Pikarus said. His voice was near, but Brastigan couldn't see him. "We'll stand together and try to get him off the bed."

"Can I drop him?" Brastigan joked.

Pikarus didn't bother to answer that. "Ready? Go," he ordered.

Brastigan caught a last, deep breath and shut his eyes against the stinging fumes. He jumped up and hearly fell across the bed. Once again, it was like trying to reach through a snow bank. He gritted his teeth and grabbed what might have been Oskar's knees.

"Pull!" Brastigan shouted, wasting precious air. He suited words to action and hauled desperately at the prone man. Oskar's body half rolled, half fell off the bed. Brastigan staggered as the weight landed against his knees. He sat down hard, kicking to free his trapped legs.

"Well, we got him," Brastigan said. "Pikarus, did you hear me?"

Pikarus answered only with violent coughing. Gasping, Brastigan rolled over. He couldn't seem to get a breath of clean air. His whole body felt numb, and it was getting hard to think clearly.

"Pikarus?" Brastigan's voice came out a sickly wheeze. "Lottres, we could use a hand over here."

Lottres screamed.

"Pup!" Brastigan felt a rush of energy. He left Oskar for Pikarus to move— or not, as seemed more likely—and dragged himself over the floor toward the sound of his brother's voice. He didn't get far.

* * *

"Of all the idiots!" Lottres heartily cursed Brastigan, not caring if his brother might hear. "I didn't touch anything, he says. Did he think I wouldn't know?"

A bout of racking coughs interrupted his angry litany. Then he crawled on. The air was slightly clearer as he got away from the bedside. Not that it mattered. The chamber was filling with smoke so quickly, they would all smother soon if they didn't get out.

Lottres could sense Shaelen ahead of him, but something was terribly wrong. She lay still beneath the blanketing smoke. So still—and he couldn't sense her thoughts!

"Shaelen?" Lottres reached her side. He shook her shoulder. "Wake up, I need you."

Then, all at once, Ysislaw was in his mind. The attack was so sudden, so savage he didn't have time to shield himself. Like a sword-thrust, the enemy's thoughts shattered his defenses. Lottres screamed. He felt himself trapped in an instant, a mouse pinned down by a cat. Ysislaw absorbed his name and his innermost being. All that he was, all that he knew, was swallowed in the maw of his enemy's power, and then spit out with utmost contempt.

"So, another of Unferth's whelps," Ysislaw said. His words were like knives, slashing at Lottres's mind. *"And you think yourself a wizard. Pah."*

Lottres was too stunned to summon a response, but it seemed that none was needed.

"You thought you were so clever and careful," Ysislaw sneered. *"I merely allowed you to go free so that I could observe your movements."*

Lottres writhed on the floor, struggling in mind and body. Ysislaw's horrible, malevolent laughter filled his consciousness.

"And you, the loyal son, sought to rescue your brothers, including the very king who ordered you killed in Carthell. What a fool. But, if that is your wish, so be it. You sought poor, captive Oskar. I think it only fitting that you share his fate."

Lottres had the terrible feeling that Ysislaw enjoyed his helpless struggles. He lay still, panting.

"I'll send someone along to collect you," Ysislaw sneered. *"Or your bodies, at least."*

As suddenly as it had come, the evil presence was gone. The cessation of pain left Lottres limp, clammy with sweat. Exhaustion seemed to crush him to the floor, but the knowledge in his heart was worse. Ysislaw had set his trap with Oskar as the bait, and Lottres had led them right into it.

Lottres knew he should do something. If only he had more training, his magic might set them free, but he couldn't summon the strength to move. The smoke closed in around him, and with it, oblivion.

* * *

Hours had passed since Pikarus and Lottres went on their search. Hours, and still no word. Therula had tried to sleep, but it was no use. The more time passed, the more certain she became that something had gone terribly wrong.

It was dawn now. The maidservant had already been in to start her fire. Therula dressed herself in a formal gown, since she planned to be in court again after breakfast. She sat before the fireplace and stared at the flames without seeing them. Waiting. Just waiting. She had been doing this for weeks. It seemed much longer. Therula felt like a statue, stiff with the weight of lost time. A marble statue, with blue agates inlaid for her eyes and an elaborate dress painted onto the lifeless stone.

How ironic that Pikarus's longed-for return had made things worse, not better! No matter what happened, Therula had assumed she could rely on her status to protect her. Now she knew that for a hollow dream. If the king himself was a mockery, there was no safety for anyone. Therula's high rank was suddenly meaningless. She had only her wits to protect her. Now she knew how Brastigan felt.

If Brastigan still lived. Therula's mind swerved from that awful idea. If Brastigan was dead, Pikarus would be, too, and she couldn't bear to think of that. Therula didn't want to face life without him.

Yet she knew all too well she might have to, and not because of mere politics. No, there was a darker, more terrible possibility. Therula didn't know if Pikarus had considered it, but she must. If the Silletsians won, Unferth's daughters would be easy prey for the invaders. With Therula alone, Ysislaw could establish a regime with the appearance of legitimacy. She would be made a queen of ashes and rubble.

Such a thing must never be tolerated. And yet, what could she do? If this dragon had the black magic Pikarus and Alustra said, what hope of escape did Therula have?

Outside, trumpets echoed from the towers of the keep. As Therula heard their shrill command, her heart gave a sickening lurch. Soldiers were being summoned. The battle was about to begin. Therula couldn't understand it. How could the Silletsians be here so soon? It should have taken them days more to cross Daraine! Yet there was no denying the trumpets' cruel message.

Therula's knees creaked like a beldame's as she stood. With icy hands she lifted her cloak, tying it on as she strode along the corridor. Outside, it was a dreary, cloudy morning. A faint, foul odor rode a fitful wind from off the bay.

There was a controlled chaos under that gloomy sky. Men poured from the barracks, buckling swords as they came. Horses, catching the fever, neighed and pawed the ground fretfully. Therula had never seen such a sight before. Crutham had been at peace all her life.

Therula scanned the crowd, hoping against hope to see Pikarus or Lottres among the soldiers. She didn't, of course. She did see women running from the kitchens to bid their men farewell. The leave-takings had an element of hysteria, for the soldiers weren't merely going on a journey this time. They marched to war. Last time, Therula hadn't deigned to join them. She wished, now, that she had.

Miraculously, the confusion suddenly cleared into orderly ranks. Voices died away. Soldiers were looking toward the inner keep. Then, with a metallic whisper, the armored men knelt en masse.

Their king descended the ramp from the inner keep. His brothers came after in a solemn file, Habrok and Calitar and the rest in surcoats of black. Someone among them carried the battle standard, but Therula couldn't see who had been granted the honor.

Oskar wore a magnificent harness. Therula had never seen her brother wear armor, although she knew he must own some. She had to admit he looked every inch a king. Silvery steel blazed, even under the heavy overcast. The vambraces and demi-greaves were inlaid with towers of jet and gold. The sword of Crutham hung at his side. On the helmet, two dragon horns made a magnificent display. Except that she knew those were no mere decorations.

It was obvious this wasn't truly Oskar, now that she knew it. Therula could see the veiled laughter in the stranger's face as he received the homage of the assembled soldiers. He walked differently, too. Not strutting, as Oskar would, but almost prowling, like a snake that might strike at any moment.

A white horse was led forward, draped in livery of Crutham's black and gold. The pretender sprang to its back, a bold move Therula guessed was calculated to impress the soldiers with his vigor and confidence. The horse snorted and hopped, as if it sensed what kind of creature bestrode it.

"Men of Crutham!" the false king proclaimed. His voice echoed weirdly from the walls of the keep behind him. "How glad my heart is to see your brave faces. I have no fear of battle, for my dear brothers and you brave warriors ride with me. We shall be triumphant today!"

Habrok led the assembly in a deafening cheer. Therula winced. Oskar spoke the absolute opposite of the truth, and was acclaimed for it. She could hardly bear to listen to him.

"Come forth, Captain Garican!" cried Oskar.

"I am here, your majesty." Garican's voice cracked with nervousness. He stood straighter, as if that might conceal his lapse.

"To you, loyal servant," Oskar intoned, "I entrust my most precious loved ones, the flower of my realm. I leave them in your hands."

"I shall protect them with my life!" Garican vowed.

"Of that I am certain," Oskar responded. "Now we ride, men of Crutham. You know what we must do. Forward, my brothers. For Crutham, and victory!"

Oskar urged his horse forward, though he moved slowly enough that he wouldn't leave anyone behind. Habrok and the others were also mounting. The soldiers were surging to their feet. Therula watched with helpless rage as the impostor led her brothers away. How brave they all were, how strangely beautiful. Her heart ached for them, deceived into following a traitor's orders. Most of them didn't even like Oskar, yet they stood at his side in this crisis. They would do what was right for Crutham, and the likely reward of their loyalty was death.

"Are they really going?" A quavering voice startled Therula. She spun, to find Cliodora at her elbow. The youngest princess shivered in her nightgown. Her flaxen hair was unbound for sleep. Behind Cliodora were other shadowy figures. Unferth's daughters crowded the doorway with terrified curiosity.

"Yes, they're going." Therula extended her cloak to cover Cliodora, drawing her into a kind of embrace. Then she stepped back under the arch. The young women formed a circle around her.

"It seems the fighting has reached Harburg," Therula said. She did her best to sound calm about it. "The soldiers will go to defend us. Our own brothers lead them, so try not to be afraid. Now, all of you, go find your mothers. Get dressed and get into the keep. You'll be safe there."

"Can we bring a few things with us?" Orlyse asked. From her expression, Therula was certain she meant jewelry.

"A *few* things." Therula stressed the qualifier. "Then go to my mother. She will know what to do next."

The girls began to disperse, whispering among themselves. It was a sign of the crisis that they didn't argue about reporting to the queen. At any other time, this instruction would have brought a storm of protests.

"What about you?" Cliodora whimpered.

Therula turned deftly, so that her cloak was left on Cliodora's shoulders. The girl clutched it to her, still shivering.

"Don't worry, apple blossom," Therula assured her. "I'll be there, too. But first, can you do something for me?"

"Of course!" Cliodora straightened slightly.

"The queen wasn't here, I noticed," Therula said. She could understand why Alustra would stay away, but she wished she hadn't. Alustra's failure to bid her own son farewell was sure to raise questions—and not the right ones. "When you get inside, you must tell my mother what the king said. Give her his exact words."

"I can do that." Cliodora seemed relieved to have a job to do.

"I know you can. Hurry now." Therula gave her little sister a gentle push. Cliodora hurried inside.

Therula turned back to the courtyard. She stared after the departing soldiers, with the banner of Crutham floating so bravely above their heads. She thought again about Oskar's speech.

"I leave them in your hands," he had said, meaning the royal women—Alustra, Therula, and all the others. In Therula's experience that phrase, "I leave it in your hands," was a kind of code. The lords in council used it when they wished to be absolved of blame afterward. Oskar might as well have said, "If anything happens to them, it will be your fault, not mine."

Which implied that something was going to happen. Maybe the false king counted on Garican being too inexperienced to lead an effective defense, or maybe it was something else, but Therula knew in her gut he had some kind of surprise planned. After putting up with these intuitions for the past few weeks, she found she was coming to trust them.

Under the circumstances, then, Therula thought she had better undertake a precaution of her own. She just hoped Captain Garican would be as easy to browbeat as he looked.

CHAPTER TWENTY-FOUR
RACING TO DISASTER

HE lay, unable to move, for what seemed a very long time. Awareness came and went. Lottres felt hard floor boards. His temples throbbed against them. Then he felt he was falling through the floor. He wanted to struggle, to fight for his life, but he had no energy, no will.

A consciousness intruded into his dazed mind. Lottres shied from it, fearing Ysislaw's return, and fell into darkness. The being pursued him, steadied him. With relief, Lottres recognized Shaelen.

"Come back to me, heart-brother," Shaelen said. *"You must return to your body."*

"How?" Lottres managed.

"Let me guide you," Shaelen said. *"I spoke of a spell to banish fatigue. Do you remember? This will also clear the poison from your lungs. I will show you how."*

"All right." Lottres was too disoriented to argue.

Shaelen's presence enfolded Lottres with the security of a mother's embrace. He felt they were floating like thistle puffs, down and up and in and out, all at the same time. Yet his thoughts were coming clearer.

They had been in Eben's tower. Brastigan had triggered a trap. Lottres remembered Ysislaw's boasting, and the horror of realizing the only person who knew where they were had left them to die. Smoke had overcome him. Shaelen, too. He remembered her lying terribly still. How could she be helping him now?

"That was a ruse." Lottres sensed gentle laughter as Shaelen answered him. *"Remember, I was already meditating. I used that to protect myself. I heard Ysislaw say we were to share your king's fate, and I knew he was merely immobilized, not dead. I guessed that we wouldn't be killed, either."*

"You're right." Lottres had known it himself, that Oskar was still alive. He felt foolish for assuming the worst.

"I'm sorry for your fear," Shaelen said. *"Tormenting you is what kept Ysislaw from sensing that I wasn't as unconscious as I pretended to be. I waited and listened. Ysislaw has left the keep again. The battle will soon begin. I don't think he has any* eppagadrocca *here. We can try once more to escape."*

"This time, we'd better succeed," Lottres said.

* * *

Therula leaned on the stone archway, watching the soldiers depart. She waited, considering how best to handle Garican. Trampling on Garican might be the most efficient approach, but it was exactly what the false king would have done. She didn't want to be like him. Besides, Garican still needed the little credibility he had.

The soldiers were gone. The keep's outer gate closed with a thunderous clang. Therula missed her cloak's warmth as she moved toward where Garican was speaking with his squad leaders. The group broke up just as she reached them. Therula nodded in response to bows from soldiers hurrying away.

"Captain Garican," she called.

"What—Oh, your highness!" Garican sounded rattled. Maybe he had understood more of what Oskar said than she thought. "Princess, you must get to the inner keep. That would be the safest place for you."

"Of course, Captain, but I need a favor," Therula smiled winningly. "I know that Sergeant Pikarus's squad has returned from their journey. I would like to borrow them."

"Borrow?" Garican hesitated. "Your highness, we need every man on the walls."

"But Mother is concerned," Therula said. It was only a little lie, she told herself. Alustra would never know how Therula had used her name.

"Two squads have already been assigned to the keep, your highness," Garican said. She supposed he meant that to sound reassuring. It came off a stuttering parody.

"But we don't know them, and the king," Therula couldn't bring herself to call him brother, "said you were to take the greatest care with our safety. Mother trusts Sergeant Pikarus more than most."

Garican paused again. Therula let her lower lip roll out, and fixed him with an earnest pout. She watched a dull redness creep up Garican's neck and into his cheeks. Therula took a step toward him, laid a hand on his arm.

"Please, Captain," she begged in a low, dramatic tone.

Garican jumped as if her touch burned him. In an instant, his resolve crumbled. "If... I... Of course. Very well, your highness. Sergeant Pikarus and his men will report to you right away."

"Oh, thank you so much!" Therula beamed with breathless gratitude. "I'll go tell him."

"I can send someone, " Garican faltered.

"Oh, you're much too busy," Therula insisted. In truth, she didn't want Garican to start searching for Pikarus, and realize he wasn't in the barracks with his squad.

"Thank you again, Captain," she fluttered. "You've saved us."

* * *

Peace flowed from Shaelen, washing through Lottres like a river. He was on the floor again, feeling faintly ill. As his senses returned he instinctively copied Shaelen, summoning that same cool cleanliness from within himself. The swirling current carried away poison and fatigue. He was left calm and rested.

Lottres opened his eyes in darkness. The thick smoke was still there, but it didn't seem to matter. Lottres rolled to his feet. He sensed the furnishings and faint warmth from three unconscious men. The lightless surroundings were no more important than the drugged haze in the air. Others, however, didn't have such an advantage.

"I'll look for a candle." Lottres spoke softly, knowing Ysislaw might hear no matter how far off he was.

"And I'll get this door open," Shaelen said. Lottres could feel her stand by the stirring of the air. "The others will need to breathe when we wake them."

Pikarus had had the candle when they entered the room, so Lottres walked toward the bed. Once again, he noticed that it was harder to extend his senses as he drew nearer. Whatever the source of Ysislaw's blocking spell, it must be nearby. He could barely sense Shaelen at the door, to say nothing of the sluggish pulse of Brastigan's unconscious mind. Frustrated, Lottres resigned himself to relying on his normal sense of touch.

Fumbling fingers located Eben's headboard. He found the stand of twisted iron and a hollow shell of wax where one of the poisoned candles had been. No trace of heat lingered there. Lottres didn't trust himself not to trip over someone, so he circled behind the bed. A basin and pitcher rested on the flat top of the chest of drawers. At last, there was the candle.

Lottres sat on the edge of the cold mattress. His fingers traced the shape of the tarnished metal holder. The candle was a short stub, slightly greasy, with a brittle curve of wick on top. Lottres touched that gently, lest it crumble beneath his touch.

He held the candle before him and pictured it in his mind with the shapes his fingers reported. Then he imagined the flame, a yellow flower opening. Lottres focused his power and willed the fire to life. A little hiss, a brief crackle. A tiny round spark appeared like a golden pearl amid the false night. As it grew steadily, Eben's room emerged from nothingness.

Shaelen swung the door wide. She knelt and placed the wooden bar to block it open. Then her power gently stirred the air, trying to clear the fumes. It did little good.

"There's a trap door at the top of the tower," Lottres said. "If you open that, it should set up a draft."

Shaelen paused in the doorway, looking up the dark stairwell. "I don't sense any more guards," she said. "This won't take long."

Lottres nodded, and she slipped up the stairs. He carried his light around the bed again, and looked down on his fallen comrades. Two of them were right at the bedside. Pikarus lay half across Oskar, as if he had been trying to rouse the comatose king when the smoke overcame him. Brastigan was a little farther off, pointing toward the door. He must have been crawling toward Lottres when he collapsed.

"Like you could have done anything to help me," Lottres murmured. Nevertheless, he felt touched that Brastigan had put his safety first.

A distant thump echoed down the stairwell. Shaelen had the trap door open. Almost at once, Lottres could feel air moving. Slowly, it carried the smoke from the room.

He looked down at the three of them a moment longer, trying to decide who to wake first. Oskar looked worst of the three. His face was a sickly color. But, Lottres thought, Oskar might not be able to walk right away. He might need the other two to help him along. Brastigan wasn't likely to be enthusiastic about such a chore—not that Lottres blamed him.

All in all, Pikarus seemed a sensible first choice. Lottres knelt so he could place both hands on Pikarus's back. As he set the candle down, a flicker of movement under the bed caught his eye.

Curiously, Lottres moved the candle up and down. Nothing. He waved it from side to side. Now he saw clearly: something under the bed was casting a shadow. He probed with his mind and felt nothing. Yet there it was, a regular black shape against the glow of candlelight.

Lottres put the candle aside. He groped under the bed and emerged with what looked like a brick. It was dark gray, roughly hewn, with a coarse, abrasive texture, yet it was strangely light. Even with his hands, Lottres hardly felt the weight.

He felt his pulse quicken. Could this brick be hollow? And did it hold inside it the spell Ysislaw used to block their senses? A crucial element of his plan, and Ysislaw had hidden it under the bed. Lottres let go a whisper of laughter. Why, any child in Crutham could have devised a better hiding place than that!

"Can't you wake them?" Shaelen asked.

Lottres started. He hadn't realized she had returned. Shaelen knelt beside Brastigan, feeling under his chin for a pulse.

"Can you feel this?" Lottres asked.

"Feel what?" Shaelen frowned.

"This was under the bed." Lottres held up the brick. From her quick catch of breath, Lottres could tell she was thinking exactly what he was.

"May I see it?" Shaelen asked.

There was no closure on the outside. Lottres shook it, hoping to feel or hear something inside. Nothing. He held the brick up for Shaelen.

"It could be a type of puzzle," she said, frowning thoughtfully. "*Maess* has one like it. In fact, I may be able to open this."

"If you try that," Lottres offered, "I'll start rousing them."

Shaelen nodded, all her attention focused on the mysterious brick. Lottres turned back to Pikarus. Placing his hands on the soldier's back, he summoned peace and healing within himself.

* * *

The barracks were eerily silent as Therula entered. She was accustomed to a buzz of men and activity, but now found only beds and foot lockers along the walls. Untidy bedclothes and a scattered handful of darts hinted at a sudden departure.

"Javes!" Therula called. Her voice rang like a bell in the emptiness.

"Your highness?" Javes's voice floated down a flight of stairs to her left. She heard rapid footsteps above her.

Therula hurried up the stairs. She met Javes at the top landing. The rest of the squad stood in a loose cluster, watching them.

"He's not back yet," Javes reported in a low voice. "I guess we'll be assigned to the walls, but I'm not sure how to explain—"

"No, you're not," Therula interrupted. "I've persuaded Garican to send you to the inner keep instead." Javes opened his mouth to respond, but Therula raised her hand to silence him. "Do you know where Pikarus and Lottres went?"

Javes nodded.

"Go look for them," Therula said. "I'll let Mother know what's happening, in case Garican asks her about it. We need to know if they've found Oskar."

"At once, your highness." Javes turned to beckon. The soldiers gathered their weapons and began to come over.

Javes sounded calm, but Therula saw in his face the depth of his loyalty to Pikarus. He understood what she wasn't saying, the intense need to know her beloved was safe. Therula swallowed against a hard knot in her throat.

"Please find him," she whispered.

* * *

It was a surprise to wake up feeling refreshed and alert. Then again, he was surprised to wake up at all. After passing out in the choking darkness, Brastigan hadn't expected it. He blinked up at Lottres. His brother smiled at an unspoken jest.

"Yes, this is real," Lottres assured him. "Another useful spell Shaelen taught me."

"Thanks, then," Brastigan said, and he meant it.

He sat up slowly and raked the dark hair out of his eyes. Brastigan looked around warily. They were still in Eben's chamber. Pikarus stood at the door, sword drawn, listening for trouble outside. Shaelen sat cross-legged nearby. For once, she ignored Brastigan as she turned some kind of rock over in her hands with an air of complete concentration. Oskar lay on the floor beside the bed, as sickly and still as he had been when he was on it. As Brastigan watched, Lottres scooted over the floor to sit beside Oskar.

"Is he alive?" Brastigan asked.

Lottres nodded. He laid his hands on Oskar's chest.

"He lives," Lottres said, "but..."

"Dung," Brastigan put in.

Lottres smiled at that. "He's been imprisoned for a long time. You and Pikarus woke right up, but you'd only been asleep a few hours. Oskar may take some time to rouse."

Time, Brastigan thought. Time—and Ysislaw could be anywhere, doing anything, all the while.

"How long have we been in here?" he asked.

"I'm not sure."

Lottres's voice had taken on a vague, dreaming tone. If he was busy with his magic, Brastigan decided, he'd better just let him work. Shaelen looked preoccupied, too. Brastigan stood up, marveling again that he felt neither weakness nor nausea. He went to join Pikarus at the door.

"What time is it?" Brastigan asked.

"Well into daylight," Pikarus answered. "I don't know for certain, but Lady Shaelen said the battle has already begun at the city gates." His eyes turned to the two wizards, each rapt in their own magical problem. Pikarus murmured, "We need to go."

"I'm with you." Brastigan watched Lottres sitting beside Oskar. Nothing seemed to be happening, but Brastigan was learning that appearances were deceptive. Nothing happening could be everything happening.

Oskar showed no sign of rousing. Brastigan leaned against the door jamb and sighed. Then his eyes fell on the chest of drawers, with the ewer and basin on it. He stalked over and lifted the container. Something sloshed inside it.

Brastigan continued around the bed to kneel on the other side of Oskar from Lottres. "Mind if I try this the old fashioned way?" he asked.

Lottres's eyes focused briefly on the pitcher. "Fine," he murmured. "Just don't drown him."

"You take all the fun out of it," Brastigan smirked. He dipped his hand into the ewer and splashed a handful of stale water into Oskar's face.

Oskar caught his breath. His eyebrows and hands twitched. With a perverse joy, Brastigan continued flicking water into Oskar's face.

"Rise and shine, you worthless —."

"That's enough," Lottres cautioned.

Oskar's head jerked. His eyes flickered open. In the wan candle light, their color seemed as muddled as day-old soup.

"Wuz goin' on?" Oskar raised a feeble hand to rub his wet face.

"We're trying to save your backside," Brastigan snapped. "Wake up, or do you want more help?"

"Bras, stop," Lottres lectured sternly. "Oskar, you've been under a spell."

"I remember that." Oskar sounded confused, like a frightened boy. "I was awake sometimes, but I couldn't... Why couldn't I move?"

"Because you were under a spell?" Brastigan suggested acidly.

"If you're going to act like this, I'll send you to wait with Pikarus," Lottres warned.

"Good luck making me," Brastigan retorted, but he did stand up and take the ewer back to its place.

Lottres gently told Oskar, "I've just released you from the spell. Can you sit up?"

Oskar clasped Lottres's hand. He groaned as he pulled himself up, shuddered, and leaned back against the bed. Oskar's skin had a bloodless, pearlescent quality in the dim light. He swallowed heavily and asked, "How did this happen?"

Brastigan felt a pulse of rage in his chest. It was all Oskar's fault, everything that had happened, and he had the nerve to play the pitiful invalid!

"Your partner played a little trick on you," Brastigan bit out.

"Brastigan, go away." Lottres pointed at the door.

"No, let him speak." Oskar's voice was a little stronger, with some of its accustomed, lofty tone. "I must know the truth."

Brastigan didn't wait for Lottres's permission. He dropped to his knees, so his face was mere inches from Oskar's.

"While you've been getting your beauty sleep, Ysislaw took your place. He's wearing your crown, sitting on your throne. Crutham is right in the palm of his hand. And you gave it to him," Brastigan snarled.

He watched Oskar's face shift between arrogance and bewilderment, horror and shock. Oskar's eyes darted, assessing what this meant. Then he let them slide shut.

"He tricked me," Oskar groaned, too weak to generate the righteous fury Brastigan knew he must be searching for.

"I already said that," Brastigan replied without sympathy. "By the way, we know all about your plan to kill off our brothers."

Oskar's eyes snapped open. "That is ridiculous." He sounded sanctimonious, but his eyes were cat-cold.

Brastigan's heart seethed with fury, yet he felt perfectly calm as he aimed a punch at his brother's face. Lottres leaned forward to intercept his fist.

"You can't lie to me, Oskar," Lottres said. "I'm a wizard, too, and I hear the truth in your heart."

Brastigan jerked away. At least Lottres didn't bother to scold him this time.

"You?" Oskar gave a rusty laugh. Brastigan watched Lottres's face redden.

"Yes, me," Lottres retorted. "How did you think I revived you?"

"Your highness! Your majesty!" Pikarus called from the doorway. "Please, we should move away from here."

The three princes glared at each other. Then Oskar said, "I'll try."

He extended a hand, clearly expecting someone to help him stand. Brastigan sprang to his feet and stalked away. Oskar was a traitor, both to Crutham and his own kin. Lottres could help the fool if he wanted to, but Brastigan would have none of it.

Before Oskar could respond, Shaelen exclaimed softly, "Ha."

Brastigan pivoted toward her. Lottres's head turned, too. Shaelen had managed to push out a section of stone along one narrow side of her brick. She twisted the opposite end, and it slipped right off. As they watched, Shaelen shook the stone upside-down. A small, black object fell into her waiting hand.

"Is that it?" Lottres demanded. He turned completely away from Oskar, who let his hand drop with an annoyed expression. Brastigan prowled around the bed to where he could see what Shaelen held.

Shaelen nodded. "Yes, this is the center of the spell."

It was a small thing, a bundle of coarse black thread twisted into a complicated knot. No, Brastigan saw as he bent closer, it wasn't thread. It looked like dried grass.

"Are you sure?" Brastigan asked doubtfully.

"Yes," both Lottres and Shaelen answered together. Then Lottres asked, "Can you dispel it?"

"I don't know how," Shaelen said. She turned the knotted grass in her palm, barely touching it with her fingers.

"If you ask me, you should just burn it," Brastigan said.

"We could do that." Shaelen looked up at him. For once, she didn't flinch. She actually seemed to be considering his idea.

"We might be able to learn from it," Lottres protested.

"What Ysislaw has to teach, you don't want to learn," Brastigan said. Lottres glared up at him.

"The problem is," Shaelen said, "if we destroy this, the spell may become permanent. That is, no one would ever be able to see into Harburg with magic again."

"The queen wouldn't mind that," Pikarus remarked. Brastigan hadn't realized he had approached.

"I would," Lottres objected.

While they hesitated, Oskar sighed dramatically, drawing all eyes back to himself. Immediately, Pikarus knelt beside him.

"Your majesty," Pikarus said, "let me help you up."

Oskar nodded and extended his hand. Pikarus dipped his neck, allowing Oskar to rest an arm across his shoulders. They straightened slowly, Oskar balancing against the soldier. His face was still ashen, but he seemed in control of his legs. Pikarus, who was slightly taller, had to walk bent over.

Lottres and Shaelen scrambled to their feet, she with the twisted grass still balanced on her palm. "Maybe I should just bring this with us for now," Shaelen said.

Brastigan shrugged. He followed Oskar and Pikarus, making sure he didn't get too close so they couldn't demand his help. He was close enough to hear Oskar speak, though.

"Is it true?" Oskar asked, panting a little with the effort of walking. "Did Ysislaw take my place?"

As if Pikarus would tell him something else, Brastigan thought with disgust. Then he could ignore Brastigan and Lottres if he wanted to. But Pikarus gave Oskar no such satisfaction.

"I'm afraid it is true," Pikarus said.

"Did you know he killed Father, too?" Brastigan interrupted. Despite the danger, he wanted to hear Oskar admit his guilt. It might not change anything, but he wanted to hear it anyhow.

"He did not." Oskar dismissed the suggestion, but his voice held a tremor of uncertainty.

"Of course he did," Lottres said, striding up beside Brastigan. "And you knew — but it was all to your benefit, wasn't it? It put you on the throne.

That's why you didn't ask questions."

"He was only supposed to kill Eben," Oskar said.

Brastigan remembered all too well Ysislaw's bragging, how Oskar had begged for help when Eben revealed Oskar's conspiracy to Unferth.

"Oh, he did that," Brastigan said grimly. "He just didn't stop there. You see, Ysislaw agrees with you that the royal heirs should be eliminated. It's just that you're one of us, too. He only kept you alive so he could control Alustra if she got any notions."

Oskar didn't answer. Maybe he had to concentrate just on walking. Still, the less he said, the angrier Brastigan became.

"You know, I can understand why you'd take Rickard down," Brastigan went on. "He did plot against you with his uncle. And Mathas was always better looking, so maybe you were jealous of him. But why kill Luvan? He was just a boy."

"He was a threat to me," Oskar replied absently.

"He was a poet!" Brastigan choked, fists clenched at his sides.

Oskar stopped, swaying as he leaned on Pikarus.

"You're all threats to me." Oskar met Brastigan's eyes without flinching. In that moment, he looked very much like Alustra and nothing at all like Unferth. Oskar said, "I could never be secure in my position with a pack of mongrels lurking around. You attract intrigues like flies. There was always someone *looking* at you, wondering who was the strongest and scheming to bring me down."

Oskar spoke with outrage, as if he considered himself the victim.

"You are so full of it," Brastigan snarled.

"We're your brothers," Lottres added sternly. "We came when you needed us. If we hadn't..."

Oskar laughed at him. "I never knew you were such a dreamer." There was color in his face again, and his eyes blazed with years of concealed fury. It seemed his hatred gave him renewed strength, in spirit if not in body. "I did what I had to for the stability of the kingdom. I only regret that my man-of-work missed his mark."

Brastigan stopped short. It was impossible to miss his meaning, that Oskar had hired the assassin in the Dead Donkey. He supposed he should have known it from the beginning.

"Your majesty, please save your energy." Pikarus spoke with perfect courtesy. You had to know him as well as Brastigan did to sense his complete contempt.

Pikarus started walking, half pushing Oskar along with him. His action had kept Brastigan from swinging at Oskar, king or not. Maybe he knew it. Pikarus shot Brastigan a warning look over his shoulder. The two princes trailed after, walking stiff-legged with fury.

"Is it too late to put him back to sleep?" Brastigan muttered to Lottres without real hope.

"Don't tempt me," Lottres answered.

"Wait!" Shaelen cried just as they reached the door.

She spoke too late. Brastigan heard shuffling steps in the stairwell. A moment later, armed men burst in the door. Brastigan glimpsed black surcoats, and the gleam of metal from hauberks and helms. Pikarus gave a cry of alarm. Brastigan jumped forward, drawing Victory. He heard Lottres coming after. They were helping Pikarus, Brastigan told himself. Pikarus deserved it, even if Oskar didn't.

It turned out not to matter. The lead attacker stopped, flung out an arm to hold the others back.

"Sergeant!" A familiar voice exclaimed.

"Javes." Pikarus looked around from trying to steady Oskar and draw his own weapon at the same time.

Javes sheathed his sword and stepped forward. A group of Crutham soldiers filed in behind him. Javes nodded to Brastigan and Lottres. "I see you found them."

"Yeah." Brastigan let Victory slide back into her sheath. "Give Pikarus a hand, would you?"

Javes beckoned, and two of his men stepped forward to support Oskar. Pikarus straightened gratefully.

"Is that the king?" another soldier murmured.

"Yes," Lottres said. "This is the true king."

As the soldiers began to kneel, Oskar snapped crossly, "Don't do that! Form up, and let's get out of here."

"Oh, yes, your majesty," Brastigan sneered. "I would never have thought of escaping by myself."

Some of soldiers looked at Brastigan uncertainly, but they did as Oskar said. Soon they were moving down the stairs. Pikarus, Javes and Brastigan went first. Most of the soldiers came next, surrounding Oskar, and then Lottres and Shaelen.

"It's good to see you," Pikarus said to Javes, "but what are you doing here?"

"Princess Therula sent us," Javes replied. "She was worried when she hadn't heard from you and then everybody left."

"She was right to worry," Pikarus said. "We fell into a magical trap. Did you say everyone left?"

"Yes. The Silletsian army appeared during the night, pfft—" Javes made an upward gesture "— like mushrooms. They were hammering at the town gates before dawn. King Oskar led the princes and our armies down there. At least, we thought it was him." He glanced uncertainly over his shoulder.

They had reached the lower landing. The door stood open. Brastigan motioned to Pikarus, and they went through with swords drawn. No guards were in sight. An empty passage stretched before them. A short way down, another stairway opened to the left, leading down. Distant noises suggested the panicked evacuation of the keep.

"All right," Pikarus called. Javes and his men filed out slowly, with Oskar in their midst. Brastigan drew Pikarus to the side. Ymell had warned him, less than a day ago, to stay away from Ysislaw and let the dragons handle their own. With Ymell absent, it looked like Brastigan got the duty after all.

"If Ysislaw's gone to the gates," Brastigan said, "that's where I'll go, too. Someone has to warn Habrok. Pup," he called, "are you with me?"

"Yes." Lottres's reply came ringing down the stairway. He didn't even ask what they were talking about.

"Do you want my squad?" Pikarus asked.

Brastigan shook his head. "I'd love to have you, but you'd better stay here. Remember what I said? There are at least two Silletsians running around in Cruthan uniforms. Probably more than that. You'd better get Oskar to his chambers and block yourselves in."

"The princess wants us to guard Queen Alustra," Javes remarked from across the corridor.

"They're probably together," Pikarus said. "If we take his majesty to Alustra, we can defend all of them at once."

"Good," Brastigan said. The last of the soldiers emerged from the stairwell. Lottres and Shaelen came out last. He said, "Let's go, Pup."

"What should I do?" Shaelen asked.

Brastigan paused, staring at her. There was no more time for holding grudges, he knew, but he still felt a familiar ache inside.

"Bras," Lottres began to scold.

"If I may," Pikarus interposed, as usual. "I'd like to have a witch with us, too. Lady Shaelen, would you mind?"

She shrugged, trying to pretend the rebuff didn't bother her. Brastigan turned from her hurt-doe eyes to clout Pikarus on the shoulder.

"Thanks," he said. "Take care."

Brastigan strode past Oskar without a word and started down-stairs at a run. He immediately had to stop at the bottom of the flight. The level below was crowded as servants and nobles evacuated into the inner keep from the outer parts of the fortress. Brastigan paused, waiting impatiently, to let a pair of heavily laden serving men pass by. Lottres caught up with him.

"You know it's not her fault," Lottres began, aggrievedly.

"Don't start on me," Brastigan said. "I just can't deal with her right now. We have one big problem in front of us. I have to worry about him. Anything else will have to wait."

"How long?" Lottres persisted.

Brastigan didn't answer. He darted across the corridor when a clear spot offered itself, and started down the next flight of stairs. As they descended, they passed a half-dozen soldiers coming up the other way.

The one good thing about the situation was that Brastigan and Lottres should be able to move freely, just two more armored men among many. If someone was looking for them, they should be hard to spot.

"I hope you're right," Lottres said, following Brastigan's thought as usual. "We don't have time for any more delays."

CHAPTER TWENTY-FIVE
TANGLES AND TIES

LET go of me!"

Both Therula and her mother turned sharply as Oskar's strained voice cut through the babble in Alustra's chamber. The two women had been standing near Alustra's fireplace, trying to look calm and in control while surrounded by the tumult of evacuation.

"I tell you, I can walk!" Oskar insisted irritably. His voice came from the corridor just outside the queen's chambers.

Heads turned all over the room, now. Alustra abruptly strode away, leaving Therula flat-footed. Therula couldn't see her brother through the crowd of courtiers and servants. Still, her heart thudded in her chest. If Oskar was back, then...

"Your majesty, please let us help you," Pikarus said.

"I'm not an invalid," Oskar snapped.

Therula sank down on the warmth of the hearth, ignoring a serving maid who was trying to put wood on the fire. She had been standing stiff all day, as if that could really make her stronger. Now Pikarus was back. He sounded so like himself that she knew he wasn't injured. Relief left Therula weak. Her heart pounded with the force of panic she had been holding at bay.

"Sister, what's wrong?" Cliodora, who had been holding hands with her mother in a girlish gesture of dependence, rushed to Therula's side. Casiana was dragged behind, barely able to keep pace. Questions tumbled from Cliodora's lips: "Is that Oskar? Is he hurt? Are they already fighting outside?"

"Shush!" Casiana said. "It's too soon for that." Casiana was fair and delicate, pretty as a flower and about as sturdy. In this crisis she looked little older than her daughter, and nearly as fearful.

Therula opened her mouth, but then closed it, no word spoken. Faces all around her were pinched with worry. Princesses, concubines and servants, looked to her for reassurance, and she didn't know what to say. Alustra wouldn't want her to burst out with news of the imposter in Oskar's place, yet it would be hard to avoid questions. Oskar had just left to fight at the city walls. Now he was back again. How was Therula supposed to explain it?

Meanwhile, everyone interpreted her relief as a terrified swoon. That, at least, she couldn't allow. Therula stood up.

"I'll have to ask Mother," she announced. Truth to tell, she couldn't bear another moment without seeing Pikarus.

Therula made her way toward the door, though the crowd made swift movement impossible. Servants were bringing in furniture and baggage for the six princesses who had gathered in the queen's chambers. In addition to Casiana, Jenne and Tioma were there with their daughters. These were the last of Unferth's paramours who hadn't married and still lived in Harburg.

It had always been difficult for Alustra to accept her rivals, yet she tolerated their presence thus far. Perhaps Unferth's death made their rivalry meaningless. Whatever the reason, Therula was glad. She had no heart for her usual responsibility of pacifying jealous tempers.

Therula arrived in the doorway to see Alustra and Oskar in the hallway. Oskar stood between two soldiers, wobbling as he resisted their efforts to support him. Pikarus stood behind them. Shaelen was with him, but Therula hardly noticed. Her eyes were fixed on her beloved.

"Oskar." Alustra's voice, choked with emotion, drew Therula back to the drama before her. The queen had her hands on Oskar's shoulders. She stared into his face, as if she could see that he was who he seemed.

"Mother, please." Oskar's face was pale, almost grayish. His eyes burned a fevered blue. Only they seemed truly alive.

"My son." Alustra's hands trembled as she drew Oskar to her, kissed him briefly.

Just for a moment, Oskar leaned on her. The faintest tremor was in his voice. "I'm fine, Mother, but please, I've got to sit down."

"Of course. We have much to talk about." Alustra drew Oskar down the corridor, gesturing for someone to open the door ahead of them.

Therula stood aside, letting the soldiers pass, before she edged her way to Pikarus's side. She embraced her beloved, not caring any more who saw or what they thought.

"Javes found you?" she murmured.

"It's good you sent him," Pikarus said. "We ran into some problems. Once the king is comfortable, I will make good on your word and prepare to defend these chambers. Lady Shaelen has agreed to aid us."

He clasped Therula's hand briefly and stepped away. Reluctantly, she allowed him to go. For the moment, Therula was satisfied to know Pikarus was alive. Of future perils she would not think too deeply. Therula turned to Shaelen.

"We appreciate your help," she said. "We have gathered in my mother's chambers. Please join us."

"Very well." Shaelen's dark eyes darted, taking in her surroundings. Princesses and paramours crowded the doorway. Among them, Therula saw Margura.

"Was that... the king?" Margura asked. Ever the hopeful sycophant, Therula thought.

"Yes," Therula said. She spoke clearly, for all to hear. "So far as I could see, my brother isn't wounded. However, the queen is with him to give her counsel. I am sure she will advise us when the king can take visitors."

The anxious crowd pushed back slowly. Margura went with them, wearing a petulant expression. Since Oskar's chamber was adjacent to Alustra's, Therula had no doubt Margura would contrive to slip away.

Remembering Pikarus's suspicions, Therula resolved to find the queen's brazen attendant some pressing duty.

Unexpectedly, Shaelen leaned closer to murmur, "You cannot trust that one."

Therula nodded, trying to conceal her surprise. She gestured toward the doorway. "Will you please join us?"

There was a lot of worried chatter about Oskar's haggard appearance, but Shaelen's entrance created a further scandal. With so much happening, Therula had almost forgotten the Urulai woman's unkempt hair, her barbaric leathers and weapons. The courtiers gawked. Some curled their lips in disgust. Margura, who had the least reason for pride, edged away as if the brush of Shaelen's arm might soil her clothing.

Recalling her own first reaction, Therula didn't blame anyone for their shock. Nevertheless, it was wrong to scorn somebody who had come to help them.

"This is Lady Shaelen, from Hawkwing House," Therula announced. Her throat felt tight with loud speech and emotion. "She has come to aid us in our time of need."

A few of the bystanders made scanty curtseys toward Shaelen. Others looked ashamed of their staring, or merely returned to their fretful conversations. For her part, Shaelen's stiff shoulders showed her discomfort at being the center of attention. After a moment's hesitation, she crossed the room to sit on the hearth where Therula had been just moments ago.

More serving women entered the room, carrying trays of rolls, sliced fruits and cheeses. Therula stood aside to let them pass. This would be all the breakfast most of them had, until an emergency kitchen could be set up. Therula accepted a bit of cheese and nibbled without tasting it. She glanced behind her, making certain Margura was accounted for. Then she strolled slowly back toward the hearth.

Shaelen ignored the food offered by a passing servant. Her hands, cupped before her, held something small that Therula couldn't see. Whatever it was, Shaelen was concentrating hard on it. Nearby, Therula noticed Cliodora edging over toward the hearth. The youngest princess still held her mother's hand, but her face was alight with curiosity.

Therula moved to intercept her little sister, but Shaelen looked up. Her dark eyes warily examined the intruder.

"Excuse us," Casiana murmured. She tried without success to pull her daughter away. Rather than being abashed, Cliodora took Shaelen's notice as an invitation.

"Are you going to fight?" the girl asked, leaning still closer.

"If the battle comes here, I will," Shaelen answered.

"Why?" Casiana burst out, appalled. "Let the men do it. It's their job!"

"They will do it," Therula interrupted, aware of those who lingered nearby, listening. "Captain Garican will do his duty. Sergeant Pikarus is here, too. You need have no fear."

Shaelen glanced between Therula and Cliodora, who regarded her with great admiration. She seemed to weigh her words carefully.

"Cruthan ships once carried the exiles from Urland after its fall," Shaelen finally said. "Honor demands that we help you now."

"And we appreciate it," Therula reiterated, in case anyone was in doubt of Shaelen's welcome.

Casiana seemed little mollified, but Cliodora continued leaning forward as far as their linked hands would permit.

"What is that?" she asked, nodding to whatever Shaelen held in her two hands.

"There is magic in it," Shaelen replied. She pitched her voice lower, though Therula doubted she was hiding anything. The room was too small, too crowded. "If I can undo the knot and break the spell, that would be of great help."

Magic? Despite her intention to set a good example, Therula had to take a look herself. In the sorceress' calloused hands lay a twisted strand of some coarse, prickly-looking twine. It was dark, almost scorched. The strands curled in on themselves until you couldn't make out one end from the other.

Without thinking, Therula said, "If it's tangled, perhaps Jenne could help. She is a seamstress."

"That's right," Cliodora exclaimed. She turned to call out, "Auntie Jen, Auntie Jen!"

"Yes, I'm right here," Jenne said. She and Frella were standing just on the other side of Casiana. Jenne had her sewing basket over her arm, as always.

"Calm down," Casiana scolded. Cliodora, of course, didn't listen.

"Can you undo this?" she asked Jenne, gesturing toward Shaelen's knot.

"Let me see it."

Therula stepped back, allowing Jenne to come closer. Jenne leaned forward to see what Shaelen held, fishing absently in her sewing basket. Meanwhile, Therula had the sudden feeling she had been distracted by something trivial. She glanced around sharply, relaxing only when she caught sight of Margura assisting some of the servants in spreading sheets on the temporary beds.

Then she turned, eyeing the small door that connected Alustra's chamber to Unferth's—now Oskar's chamber. It was ironic to be keeping Margura away when she longed to slip through herself. Therula wanted to talk to Oskar, to find out what had happened to him and how it affected Crutham's defense, but she was trapped here along with the others. Trapped by her own words.

* * *

Brastigan worked furiously, throwing saddle and bridle onto his Urulai horse, while an agitated groom prepared a spare mount for Lottres. Except for the jingle of harness and slither of feet over straw, the stable was very quiet. Lottres rubbed his ears, though it did little good. Ysislaw's spell, which blocked his clairvoyance, was stronger than before. He felt as if he had a head cold, with congestion turning his head to a solid block of wood.

The groom had told them the false king went out in a group with the other princes. Those were the ones Lottres needed to find. Habrok or Calitar must be warned of the treachery to come. Lottres longed for the pressure to ease, for his second sight to return. Without his clairvoyance, he had no idea where in the warring city they might be.

Frustrated, he broke his silence. "Where should we look first?" Lottres asked.

"What?" Brastigan snapped, distracted.

"Where should we look for Habrok?" Lottres amended.

"You tell me," Brastigan shrugged. When Lottres gave an irritated sigh, he said, "No, I mean it. You can find them."

"I've been trying, but I can't," Lottres confessed. "It's driving me mad."

The groom led Lottres's horse over to him. It was a knob-kneed bay with a white splotch down its nose. Left behind for good reason, Lottres thought. He took the reins anyway. It wasn't like he had his choice of horses.

"Do what you can." Brastigan led his gray mare past, and Lottres followed. "We'll search the whole city if we have to. Let's hope your bag o'bones can keep up with Shadow."

Outside the stables, weak daylight filtered through a layer of low clouds. Brastigan swung into the saddle. Lottres was about to do the same when he suddenly stumbled. Merciless pressure crushed his skull, as if he had put on a helmet that was too heavy for him. Then it stopped. Ysislaw's spell was gone!

"What's wrong?" Brastigan demanded.

From the inner keep came Shaelen's exultant call: *"We got it! One of your sisters' maids untied the knot. The spell is broken."*

"I felt that," Lottres answered.

"Pup?" Brastigan leaned over to shake his shoulder, but Lottres moved aside.

"They broke the spell," Lottres told Brastigan. He climbed into the saddle and told Shaelen, *"We're just leaving the castle."*

"Good luck to you." Shaelen broke contact.

"So you can find Habrok?" Brastigan asked.

"I think so."

Truth to tell, the sudden return of his clairvoyance left Lottres a little dizzy. He had been trying so hard, straining against Ysislaw's power. Now it was too much, too fast. Lottres urged his bay after Brastigan's gray and tried to sort through the din.

There was a roar of voices, coming and going like waves of the sea. It was broken now and then by horn calls, or the shrill cry of steel, or a lone man's voice. The darkness wasn't just clouds, Lottres sensed with growing dismay. Sheets of smoke drifted over the walls. Harburg was in flames, and magic was all around him, foul spells assaulting the walls. It seemed to come from everywhere.

"Who goes there?" a man called from the wall above them. Lottres could hardly pick out his voice from the chaos.

"It's us," Brastigan yelled back. "Let us out!"

"The king has ordered these gates barred," the man answered. That was

Garican, Lottres realized. The newly made guard captain was trying to be a stickler for the rules, as if that could protect him from the approaching horror.

"I just woke up," Brastigan cried, making an effort at humor. "They left without me, and I don't want to miss any of the fun!"

For once, Brastigan's reputation worked in his favor. Lottres saw men grinning above the gate. He chimed in, "Besides, Oskar said to keep the invaders out, right? He didn't say no one could leave. We're going to go fight at his side."

Garican frowned. Lottres heard him thinking, *"Here they come again, all these royal brats telling me how to do my job."* He caught an image of Therula in Garican's mind.

"I'm the greatest swordsman in Crutham," Brastigan boasted, but his voice held an edge of desperation. "You can't keep me here at a time like this. My place is with my brothers!"

Remembering that Ymell had not compelled Johanz's cooperation, Lottres resisted the urge to force Garican's obedience. The captain relented on his own.

"On your own heads be it." Garican turned away, irritably gesturing for men to raise the portcullis. *"One less worry for me."*

Lottres tried not to hold that sour sentiment against Garican as they urged their horses forward. On the opposite side of the gate, Brastigan turned Shadow to face its towers.

"No, it will be on their heads!" he shouted back up at the walls. He gave a jaunty wave.

While Brastigan was strutting, Lottres looked out over beleaguered Harburg. Outside the keep, the overcast was even more oppressive. The very heavens seemed to press down like the lid over a boiling pot. Through veils of smoke, Lottres picked out the thick belt of walls. Beyond the battlements, the Silletsian army covered the fields like a dark, moving quilt. So many of them, Lottres thought with alarm. Even in the best of times, he didn't think Harburg's defenders equaled those numbers.

"What's burning?" Brastigan checked his horse beside Lottres.

"I think it's the harbor," Lottres replied, for the smoke over Harburg was moving on a brisk sea wind.

Indeed, there was movement on the sea walls. The battle had been joined. Black smoke billowed up where ships burned at the piers. Others had shoved off, trying for safety. Lottres could hear the frantic slap of their oars. But dozens of long, lean galleys cruised the choppy water of the great bay, like sharks waiting to feed. There would be no escape from Harburg by sea.

"Where do we go?" Brastigan asked.

"I'm trying to figure that out," Lottres answered.

Lottres didn't think Habrok would be at the harbor. He would have sent some of their brothers, perhaps Sebbelon and Eskelon. Habrok himself would be at the king's side, at one of the two gates—but which?

Then Lottres felt a surge of malevolent power. It was centered on the south gate. A queer glow lit the haze of battle. There was a rippling in the air. Then came a sucking gasp. One of the gate's towers sagged. At the gate, a commander was screaming orders. The voice might have been Axenar's.

"What's going on?" Brastigan demanded.

"They're turning it to sand," was Lottres's grim reply.

Brastigan cursed. Lottres's stomach churned. Then the whole gate collapsed. Men screamed as they were swallowed in a tide of debris. Lottres felt as if he were being dragged down, too, into the cacophony of war.

"We can't stay here," Brastigan growled.

Lottres clung to his brother's voice for stability. "I can't..." he gasped. "It's too much. I can't tell!"

"Steady up!" Brastigan shook Lottres's shoulder. "We'll have to make a guess."

Strangely, his words helped. If it came down to logic, Lottres was good at that.

"What do you bet," Lottres said, "Ysislaw has Habrok with him? He'll want to be sure what happens. Keep him in reach, just in case."

"I'd take that bet," Brastigan said. "Where's he, then?"

Lottres looked over the town again, feeling for the dull horror of his enemy's presence. Unlike Habrok, Ysislaw was easy to find.

"Bloody Square," Lottres said.

"Naturally." Brastigan urged Shadow forward. Lottres followed.

* * *

The peculiar cord Jenne had untied slowly burned to ash in the fireplace. Shaelen sat and watched it blaze for so long that even Cliodora got bored and drifted away. Suddenly, Shaelen stood up.

"They are coming," she announced.

Therula practically felt the chill in the room at the portent of Shaelen's words.

"That can't be," cried Agiatta from the window overlooking the inner courtyard. She babbled in her fear, "There's no one out there at the gate. We're safe, aren't we?"

Calm and purposeful, Shaelen strung her bow. Therula glanced at her, and then moved to lay a comforting arm over Agiatta's shoulder.

"It's best not to take chances," Therula said.

"But..." Agiatta began to argue.

"What's the point of having a sorceress, if we don't listen to her?" Diona snapped. Shaelen walked toward the door, and Diona called, "Let her through, there!"

"It's all right," Therula said. "Sergeant Pikarus and Lady Shaelen are here to protect us. We'll be quite safe."

Hoping to cut off the discussion, Therula turned to look out the window. The sky outside remained just as gloomy as the atmosphere of fear in the queen's chambers. In the uncertain light, Therula saw a group of soldiers emerge from the arched portal that led up toward Eben's tower.

"Here they come," Agiatta murmured fearfully.

With military precision, the soldiers jogged over to form ranks before the gate to the outer courtyard. Therula counted thirty men, including their officers. She tried to draw comfort from the familiar black surcoats with their tower device clearly visible. Thirty men wasn't a great number, but over a hundred more were positioned on the outer wall. Even if they took losses in combat, the remaining soldiers would retreat to the keep, bolstering the force within.

The soldiers' leader stood before them briefly. He must have been speaking, but Therula couldn't hear through the closed window. At his curt gesture, a handful of men trotted into the gate towers. The rest began to move toward the ground entrance to the keep. This brought them almost directly under the window where Therula and Agiatta stood.

"Those are our troops," Agiatta muttered irritably. "Some sorceress. Huh!"

Something about their grim faces and the way they hefted their shields made Therula anxious. Then she heard a faint, rhythmic clicking. The iron bars of the portcullis began to drop toward the ground.

Why was the gate closing? The men outside wouldn't be able to retreat. Therula's heartbeat quickened as a terrible idea sprang into her mind.

"Shaelen?" Therula turned, hoping the Urulai woman would refute her, but the door to the corridor was closed.

Trying to hide her fear, Therula pushed through the crowded room. She had trouble getting into the hallway because it was full of Pikarus's men. Barrels and spare furniture were stacked high in a barricade. The gleam of polished wood and fine fabric seemed out of place beside crates full of turnips and cabbages.

"Princess, stay inside," Javes began.

"Where's Pikarus?" Therula asked, but she did stop in the doorway.

"Here." The reply drifted to her through a wall of armored men.

"I saw them," Therula called. She tried to stay calm, not just blurt it out like Cliodora would. "They're wearing our uniforms!"

Javes's expression remained grim, but he didn't seem surprised.

"Ysislaw's brought in his own men," Pikarus answered. "We knew from what Brastigan told us."

"Did you see how many?" Javes asked.

"About thirty." Therula felt a little better that she could help at least this much. "Some of them stayed at the gate. And you should know, they've shut us in. Even if Garican figures out what's happening, he'll have to fight through them before he can help us."

The soldiers nearby exchanged grim glances. These odds weren't in their favor. They all heard the tramp of armored footsteps approaching.

"Get back inside," Pikarus said. "Keep everybody calm, but block the doors."

"I will." Therula shut the door with ominous footsteps thrumming in her ears.

Once again, all eyes were on Therula as she slipped back into the queen's chamber. She reflected on the grim reality as she bolted the door. This room held only women. There were no men at all. If Pikarus fell, they had only themselves to rely on. Therula wished her mother would come back, but

Alustra was still in Oskar's room.

"We will barricade this door," Therula announced. She gestured to the servants. "Bring those beds over here."

Moments of chaos followed as the servants hurried forward to obey. One of the older women, Giselle, took charge and started them all pushing Alustra's armoire toward the door. It was the largest piece of furniture, and heavy with the clothing inside. Claw feet moaned in protest as they moved it. The remaining courtiers and princesses stood back, murmuring among themselves.

Therula jumped as muffled shouts came from the hallway behind her. There was a great clatter, like hailstones against the window, but she knew it was the beat of steel on steel. Everyone froze for a moment. Then the servants redoubled their efforts, stacking temporary beds in the front of the armoire.

"What if they come in here?" Cliodora quavered, clinging to Casiana, who looked nearly as frightened. "What can we do?"

Therula didn't know how to answer. What *were* they supposed to do, if Pikarus and his men failed?

"Grab something heavy," Diona answered darkly.

Then, through the hurry and noise, she caught a furtive movement. The door to Oskar's chamber had just been open. It closed slowly, as if someone wished to avoid being seen. Therula felt her heart skip again. Her eyes darted, searching the throng. She didn't see her mother coming into the room with news. Margura wasn't there, either.

For moment, Therula felt foolish for her anxiety. Margura was Alustra's attendant. She might have gone in to tell the queen what was happening. Besides, her link with Oskar was clear enough.

Then Therula swallowed heavily. Margura's link was with the *other* Oskar — the pretender. That must be what Shaelen had meant.

"Sister?" Cliodora asked again.

"In a minute," Therula called over her shoulder. She ran to the connecting door. Resisting the urge to fling it wide, she opened it just enough to see through.

Except for the thunder of battle just outside, the room was very quiet. Oskar lay on the grand bed. Pillows propped him up. The glow of many candles gave his face the look of parchment, so pale and lined. Alustra stood on the opposite side of the bed, hands clenched at her sides. Margura was there, as Therula had suspected. She held a basket, and was just rising from a curtsey.

"I don't know, madam," Margura said demurely, apparently answering a question from Alustra.

It all seemed innocent, yet Therula found herself stiff-legged with rage as she stalked into the room.

"I do," Therula said. Her voice was brittle. "They are Silletsians, disguised as our own men. Pikarus and his squad are holding them off."

"Silletsians," Oskar said bitterly. He closed his eyes for a moment, as if the candlelight troubled him. Alustra looked as if she had something to say, but held her peace.

Meanwhile, Margura bent forward over her basket. She drew a dark green bottle from its depths and poured a flagon, which she offered to Oskar.

"Drink this, your majesty," she murmured soothingly. "You will feel better."

"What is that?" Therula demanded.

With gentle patience, Margura said, "I have merely brought a share of the food the staff provided. I thought his majesty might like some breakfast."

Therula stared at Margura, trying to find something sinister in her words.

"Close the door, daughter," Alustra murmured tightly.

Frustrated, Therula turned to obey. Looking toward the door, she realized this room was unprotected if the enemy broke through. Maybe that was something she could use, Therula thought. Bring in a bunch of servants to block the door, and Margura couldn't do whatever it was she had planned.

"Mother, we should —." Therula began. Then she saw Oskar listlessly accept Margura's cup. He raised it to his lips. "No!"

Startled, Alustra and Margura turned to Therula. She ran to the bedside.

"Don't drink it!" Therula cried. "You can't trust her!"

Oskar swallowed what was in his mouth. "Of course I can," he answered with a shadow of his former arrogance. "Margura works for me, dear sister."

Alustra began to scold, "Therula..."

"Oskar, listen to me." Therula trembled, controlling the impulse to slap the green bottle out of Margura's hand. "You cannot trust this woman. She serves the enemy!"

Margura ignored Therula. She offered Alustra a second flagon. "Your majesty?"

Alustra didn't take it. She stared at Margura, perhaps wondering if her loyal attendant could really be a traitor.

"Think, Mother," Therula urged. "As soon as Father was gone, she turned to Oskar. I'll bet they were very close." Therula glared at her brother. Oskar sat still. The flagon Margura had given him was poised at his lips.

"Then somehow Oskar was replaced," Therula went on, "and she started telling you how *old* you were, that nobody needed you. She kept you in your rooms, all to help the usurper push you out of public view."

"Your highness is overwrought," Margura reasoned. "You speak without thinking."

"I do not," Therula faltered, a weak rejoinder. She longed to shout that Margura had been with Brastigan as soon as he returned, and he had been in chains before the day was out. She swallowed those words, knowing it would be a mistake to mention any of their half-brothers.

"Your majesty," Margura turned, appealing to king and queen as one. "I beg you not to listen to this. Can you truly credit me with such sinister designs?"

"I don't know what to think," Oskar said. He sounded very tired as he put Margura's flagon down on a bedside table.

"In his hour of emergency, can you afford to take chances?" Alustra asked with cool pragmatism.

"No," Oskar agreed. His expression was set. "Leave us, Margura."

"Your majesty!" Margura gasped. Trembling, she clutched the flagon Alustra hadn't taken in one hand and the empty bottle in the other.

"Come, you heard the king." Therula spoke sharply in her relief. "Out with you!"

Therula reached for Margura's elbow, prepared to pull her away, but Margura whirled and dashed the contents of the flagon right in Therula's face.

"Oh!" Whatever was in the glass, it burned Therula's eyes like fire. She blotted her face with her sleeve and cleared her eyes just in time to see Margura swing the empty bottle at Alustra's head. There was a horrible thud. Alustra fell to her knees with a groan.

"Mother!" Oskar struggled to get out of the bed, but he was too weak to rise.

"Stop!" Therula cried. She lunged at Margura, trying to grab her arm.

Again, Margura was too fast. She whirled and struck at Therula. Therula yelped and tried to jump back, but she was too slow. The bottle caught her above the left eye. A dull thump and terrible pain filled her head. She felt as if her skull had split. Therula stumbled backward and fell over Oskar's bed. She lay still for a moment, clinging to consciousness. Faintly, she heard another thump nearby, and a cry that sounded like Oskar's voice.

Therula forced her eyes to open. She gathered her hands beneath her to push up off the bed. Alustra lay face down. Dark fluid pooled around her head. Her arms and legs were oddly twisted beneath her. Oskar lay against the pillows, semi-conscious. His eyes flickered, while crimson trickled from a livid weal across his forehead. Margura was bent over, reaching into her basket.

As Therula watched, the traitress pushed aside the rolls and cheese. She straightened with a knife in her hand.

SHADOW raced down the ramp, never faltering on the switchbacks. Brastigan could already pick out details in the open square below. Water washed over the cobblestones, displaced from the moat when the south wall collapsed. He could see a worse tide coming, though. Red tunics flooded into Harburg through the fallen gate, as if the city itself was bleeding.

Brastigan closed his eyes for a moment as they passed through a swirl of thick, rank smoke. Another section of wall was already tottering. He clenched his teeth with helpless rage. What could a man do, when the enemy turned his walls to sand?

"Bras, look!" Lottres kicked his gelding to make it catch up with Shadow.

Brastigan drew Shadow up and glanced where his brother pointed. Farther back in the gloom came the sullen glow of the Dragon's Candle. So it was still open, still vomiting out Ysislaw's troops. He could have sworn the light hadn't been there when they came out the castle gate.

"It wasn't," Lottres said, his voice high with excitement. "They're here, Bras!"

"Who?" Brastigan asked.

Then he saw them, huge and black against the leaden sky. Two dragons soared over the battlefield.

"Oh. Them," Brastigan said. "I thought they were still in Carthell."

Lottres shrugged. "*Maess* says they flew to Firice and opened the gateway for troops there."

"I won't complain," Brastigan assured him. He urged Shadow forward again.

Brastigan felt his heart rise. Maybe Crutham did have a chance, with those two in the fray. As the two princes approached the lower gate, the two dragons folded their wings and dove over the battlefield. Sheets of flame roared across the Silletsian lines in their wake.

Men cheered on the gate, though it was hardly likely the dragons could hear. Brastigan had to roar himself to get their attention.

"Hey!" he yelled. "Which way did the king go?"

The gate started to rise, and one of the soldiers made a broad gesture. "Bloody Square!"

As they passed beneath the pointed teeth of the portcullis, Brastigan thought about teasing Lottres. He held the jest in.

"Go ahead and say it," Lottres said.

Brastigan grinned. "Who needs magic?"

Hooves splattered in the shallow water as the two princes entered the central square. A stream of Cruthan fighters were retreating from the disaster at the South Gate. Brastigan and Lottres slipped into the traffic and let it carry them past the barricades and sentries.

Except for the soldiers, the city was completely empty. Every window and door had been barred. The citizens must be hiding, waiting for the battle to end. Brastigan hoped the precautions would do some good. One advantage to the bone men — if it was possible to find anything positive about such monstrosities — was their single-mindedness. They would follow orders and not break into looting parties.

The two dragons continued swooping over the battlefield. As Lottres and Brastigan approached the Bloody Gate, columns of black smoke rose to meet the dragons. Fires burned atop the great towers, where cauldrons of boiling oil were poured on the attackers. They also heard a repetitive, dull booming. A battering ram, most likely. Although Brastigan had to wonder why they bothered with war machines, if their magicians could make the ramparts fall apart.

"I think it's a diversion," Lottres said. "To keep everyone's eyes here while the south wall went down."

"Could be," Brastigan said.

All the barricades along the street were angled toward the Butcher's Gate, meant to repel invaders from that direction. They wouldn't be as good against attackers from the center of town. Word of the gate's collapse had reached the defenders, and men were frantically turning the defenses, though Brastigan could see it would take too long.

In the center of the barricades, just where the street met the square, he could see three things of great importance: the banner of Crutham, hanging dull and limp in the still air; Habrok's hulking figure; and a pair of dragon horns sticking up, much too close to Habrok. Brastigan drew Shadow aside for a moment, wondering if he dared approach Ysislaw so directly. But then, why not?

"Wait," Lottres whispered as Brastigan urged Shadow forward. "You can't just ride up to him!"

"He'll give himself away if he tries any magic," Brastigan said.

"But you —" Lottres faltered.

"Follow my lead," Brastigan said. "While everyone is staring at me, get Habrok to safety."

Brastigan didn't wait for Lottres's reply. He tightened his knees and Shadow crowded through the slow stream of moving men.

"Hail, Habrok!" Brastigan cried as he approached the Cruthan standard.

Habrok turned sharply. He bellowed, "Where were you this morning? We had servants scouring the keep."

"You didn't search Eben's tower, where I was lying in chains," Brastigan answered amiably.

As he spoke, Brastigan looked past Habrok, straight into the face of the pretender. Ysislaw's eyes were brilliant and cold under the shadow of his helmet.

"You are a fool to come here," he said in Brastigan's mind.

"I could say the same to you," Brastigan smiled through gritted teeth.

"We've no time for games," Habrok scolded. "I've been waiting to see you test your mettle, you braggart."

"You'll see that," Brastigan answered, "but Lottres would like a word with you, brother." Lottres, who rode close on his left, moved forward. Brastigan urged Shadow a bit to the right, bringing her between Habrok and the imposter. Shadow snorted, and Ysislaw stepped back slightly.

Brastigan could hear Lottres speaking quickly, in a low voice, and Habrok's startled exclamation, but Brastigan knew Lottres would need more time to convince Habrok. He leaned forward, resting his elbows on the Urulai saddle's high pommel, so he could look Ysislaw in the eye.

"You've lost," Brastigan said with relish.

"Why, brother, have you so little faith? The battle is barely begun," Ysislaw replied. There was tension in his voice, though. He must be realizing that since Brastigan was here, free, Oskar must be loose, too.

"No brother of yours," Brastigan replied, pitching his voice loud enough to be heard over the battering ram and the babble of voices around them. "For I know well you are no man, of Crutham or any other place. You —."

Ysislaw interrupted before Brastigan could say his name with too-hearty laughter. "Ever the prankster, Brastigan, but I find this jest ill timed."

His oratory was a fair copy of Oskar's broad style, but Brastigan knew bluster when he heard it. Ysislaw's eyes darted left and right, watching the bystanders for their reactions.

Indeed, men murmured around them, as if they had only just noticed how their king's helmet obscured his features and couldn't think what it meant. Ysislaw must have been using his magic to cloud their judgment, make them accept him without question.

"Do you call me a liar?" Brastigan demanded, even more loudly than before. In the corner of his left eye, he could see Lottres pulling Habrok back from the confrontation. "Well, I say that *you* are the liar. Aye, and traitor as well. You aren't my brother. You are a fraud!"

"Madness!" the pretender cried. "Fear has undone your mind!" Ysislaw edged backward, as if he feared for his safety. A line of men crowded near, dutifully protecting their nemesis. At that moment, Habrok broke away from Lottres.

"If what you say is true, I will not flee from my enemy," Brastigan heard him say. Habrok pushed his way forward.

"Psh. It's easy enough to see the truth. Take off your helmet." Brastigan grinned, daring Ysislaw to refuse. "Prove me wrong."

"Aye," Habrok cried. He strode around Shadow and stopped with fists planted on his hips. "Show your face, if you are the king!"

Whatever reply Ysislaw might have made was lost in a rush of hot, smoky wind. Everyone turned, looking up and up and up at the enormous black dragon that had just landed on the wall.

* * *

The knife was long and serrated, the kind a serving maid might use to cut bread. Margura held it as if she knew exactly how to use it.

"You should have just drunk the brandy." The traitress spoke with something like regret. "I wanted this to be easier."

Therula felt frozen, too terrified to move. Somehow, she forced herself to rise.

"Don't you dare," she croaked, though she held to the bed post for balance.

"Oh, I dare." Margura had the nerve to laugh, brittly and without joy. Her face was chalky white, as ashen as Oskar's was, but her eyes were wild and desperate. "I dare this and more to pay you all back for how you've treated me. But you don't need to worry, *Princess*." Margura sneered, mocking Therula's heritage. "You're wanted alive."

"I will never submit," Therula said.

On the floor, Alustra groaned again. Her hands twitched against the carpet. Margura swiftly turned from Therula. She knelt and grabbed a handful of the queen's hair. She drew back the knife.

"No!" Therula threw herself at Margura, trying to drag the woman away by her knife arm. "Mother, wake up!" Therula begged. "Run!"

Margura made a kind of shrug, fighting Therula's grip. "Get off," she snarled, "or you might get hurt after all."

"I won't let you touch her," Therula cried as they struggled for the knife. "Help me, someone! Help—Pikarus!"

Immediately, Therula heard the rattle of the door behind her. "Sister?" came Cliodora's trembling voice.

"Get help!" Therula shouted.

Margura cursed, trying to throw Therula off. The princess held on with all her strength, but Margura was stronger. She shoved and sent Therula staggering away. As she did, candlelight flashed off the blade on her hand.

Cliodora screamed at the sight of it, her shrill voice piercing even the rumble of combat in the hallway. Therula glanced around and saw her little sister doing a frantic dance in the doorway. Courtiers, concubines and servants crowded behind her, trying to see what was happening. Cliodora continued to shriek hysterical nonsense words.

"Move! Let someone in," Therula wailed, exasperated. Then, "Oh, no!"

Margura had stepped backward, assessing the situation. Her lovely face hardened into an ugly mask. She whirled and lunged at Oskar with the knife held high.

"The king!" Therula cried. She leapt after Margura, knowing she would be too slow, too late.

There was a sharp report, a blinding flash and wave of searing heat. Therula stumbled against the bed, clasping her hands to her ears. Through the haze in front of her eyes, she saw Margura slumped on the floor. The knife lay nearby, its blade blackened and wooden handle smoking. Oskar remained propped up in the bed, still unconscious, unaware how close death had come.

* * *

Silence fell over Bloody Square. Only the battering ram pounded on, monotonous in its destructive intent. For a long moment, everyone stared at the monster on the wall. Men who had never seen a real dragon before stood thunderstruck, speechless. Lottres sensed the mind of Ymell within the great beast. Ymell glared down at Ysislaw, who gave him back eye for eye. Lottres could feel their emotions like a hot mist in the air. No words were adequate to express the long centuries of their enmity. Ymell roared, and the very stones vibrated with the force of his hatred.

The result was predictable. Soldiers cursed and ran, or ducked behind their shields. Horses screamed in panic, including Lottres's mount. The bald-faced gelding reared and shook his head, fighting Lottres's hand on the reins. Only Brastigan's gray seemed immune to the screaming, bucking frenzy that gripped the beasts. Being of Yriatt's company, it must have been accustomed to a dragon's presence.

"There is your enemy." Ysislaw's voice rose over the chaos. "Archers, fire! Shoot the monster down!"

"No, he's on our side," Brastigan countered. "Habrok, stop them!"

"Hold, men of Crutham!" Habrok bellowed.

It did little good; Ysislaw's command fit too well with everyone's gut reaction. Arrows filled the air, a cloud as black as the smoke that rose from the gate. Ymell reared back, wings sweeping wide open. More cries of panic came, especially from the soldiers in the gate's towers, but none of the arrows touched the dragon.

"What was that for?" Ymell asked. He blew out a scornful breath, and arrows fell to the cobbles with a rattle like hail. Ysislaw did not reply answer, but continued exhorting the soldiers to shoot.

"There, there, there," Lottres crooned, trying to control his hysterical horse. Just as he had done in Altannath, he poured a feeling of calm into the animal's mind. "There, there, there."

When he finally quieted the beast, Lottres was facing away from Ysislaw and Brastigan. Thus he heard the shouts as the bone men reached the barricades. The battle had been creeping closer, street by bloody street. For a moment, Lottres felt as panicked as his horse.

"Brastigan! Habrok!" he cried with mind as well as voice. "They're here!"

Both men jerked around. Brastigan scowled at the interruption. Lottres could feel his brother's mind see-sawing between this new emergency and the ongoing confrontation with Ysislaw. Habrok reacted a little faster.

"We will speak more of this," Habrok told Ysislaw. He reached forward to seize the banner of Crutham from the startled bearer. Habrok bellowed, "Crutham, to me! Man the barricades! The black tower will never fall!"

With a massed shout, the Cruthan soldiers rushed to follow Habrok. Oskar might be king, but Habrok was a known and trusted leader. They followed him without hesitation.

Ysislaw showed no reaction to the defection. Perhaps he was even glad of it. Lottres sensed Ysislaw gathering his resources. His gaze was fixed on

Ymell, whose huge shadow plunged the courtyard into even deeper gloom.

Like Brastigan, Lottres didn't know what to do. Habrok needed them, yet he was afraid to turn his back on Ysislaw. He also feared Brastigan might attack the tyrant and get himself killed.

"Maen?" Lottres looked to the wall, hoping Ymell would give some guidance.

"Not now," Ymell answered curtly.

As Lottres watched, the dragon wizard kicked off the wall. He hovered a moment, falling in on himself like an empty sack. Wings shrank into robes, and great claws into feet. Ymell glided downward, shrinking as he came, until he set down lightly in his human guise.

"Give up," Ysislaw said. He spoke to Ymell, yet his words burned Lottres like hot embers. Lottres quickly threw up his mental shield.

"Never," Ymell answered with fierce resolve. *"I will no longer permit you to meddle with humans. Nor to harm my loved ones. The time has come to end this."*

Ysislaw gave an arrogant laugh. *"Let us see, then, who will have his end."*

"Let us see," Ymell agreed.

He raised his hands slightly. Lightning blazed, forming a shield around the horned man. Lottres sensed Ysislaw's power gathering in response. The very air around him shuddered with unseen fires.

Lottres felt Ysislaw's attack as a wave of pure force. The two wizards grappled, mind-to-mind, in an invisible combat. Even Lottres could hardly follow it. Still, he knew that Brastigan was sitting much too close to the action.

"Bras," Lottres hissed, hoping Ysislaw was too busy to notice.

The struggle at the barricades wasn't going well. Lottres heard the crash of steel and cries of the wounded. Swordsmen hacked at the oncoming foes with all their might. In the butcher shops along the street, their brother Miswald had his archers pouring streams of arrows into the advancing bone men. It made little difference. Lottres knew all too well how hard it was to keep those cursed creatures down.

"Bras, let's go." Lottres reached out to grab his brother's elbow. "There's nothing we can do here. Ymell will handle Ysislaw. Habrok needs us."

Brastigan seemed to shake himself. Lottres felt his brother's reluctance as he turned his horse toward Habrok's position. Brastigan drew his sword. Lottres concentrated, summoning his own power. In Altannath, Shaelen had taught him to make his arrows explode. He ought to be able to the same for Miswald's arrows, if he could get a clear view.

"I think not."

Lottres gave a choked cry as Ysislaw's presence shattered his barriers and flooded his mind.

"What is it?" Brastigan demanded. Lottres barely heard.

"Hold your hand, Ymell." Ysislaw's voice in Lottres's mind was rich with triumph. *"This is your* eppagadrocca, *is it not? Stand down, or I will crush his heart."*

Lottres gave a strangled cry. He couldn't move. His horse bolted, and he was jerked out of the saddle. Pressure squeezed Lottres's chest, so it was a struggle even to breathe.

"I do not hold slaves," Ymell replied. His guard didn't waver. *"Release him."*

"Leave him alone!" Brastigan yelled. He charged past Lottres with Victory held high.

"No!" Lottres croaked. "Stay back!"

Ysislaw made a bored, swatting gesture. Brastigan's horse shrieked and tumbled to the ground. Lottres watched in horror, fearing his brother would be crushed by the animal's weight.

"Do you care for these children?" Ysislaw gloated. *"Surrender, Ymell. Crutham is mine. Your grandson and your* eppagadrocca *are mine. You have no hope."*

Ymell stood silent, struggling with feelings Lottres could only guess at.

The gray mare lurched to her feet. She limped a few steps and stood with ears flattened, one rear hoof raised in the threat of a kick. Brastigan rolled on the pavement, groping for Victory, but Lottres felt Ysislaw's power reach out with brutal force. His will pinned Brastigan to the pavement.

"What shall be their fate?" Ysislaw taunted. *"I hold their lives in my hands. Choose, Ymell."*

Lottres, suspended in the air, felt his chest constrict ever tighter. Darkness closed in on his vision. Yet no matter what happened, Ymell had to protect Crutham.

"Maen, don't listen!" Lottres cried.

"Oh, be quiet," Ysislaw said with casual malice.

Lottres reached out frantically for the only one who could help them.

"Maess!" he cried. Yriatt must be here. He had seen her flying.

Lottres was surprised to hear an answering roar from very nearby. He looked up through another gust of smoky wind. Yriatt glided behind the towers of the gate. Flames leaped from the opposite side of the wall, putting Yriatt and the gate into silhouette. The ram's drumming suddenly stopped.

Yriatt landed on the wall, exactly where Ymell had been. Fire billowing from her mouth.

"Die," she said.

Ysislaw turned toward her, raising a protective shield. As he did, he let the two princes go. With a startled cry, Lottres dropped toward the pavement. He fell hard, struck his head, and knew no more.

* * *

Brastigan fought the irresistible force that pressed him down against the cobblestones. He felt like an insect beneath a man's boot. It seemed impossible to free himself. Then, suddenly, he could move again. Brastigan rolled over, snatching Victory from the pavement. He stayed low and looked around.

Ysislaw stood black against the dragon's flames, which stopped against an unseen barrier. Incredibly, he was laughing. Yriatt's fires died away, and Ymell's lightning crashed against the barrier. It didn't penetrate, either.

Lottres lay on the pavement, face up, eyes closed. A trickle of blood ran into his beard. Brastigan felt his throat constrict. Lottres was all he had left.

Dragon's fire exploded in his blood. Brastigan didn't plan. He lunged without thinking. Victory slashed in a high arc. Ysislaw started to turn, but too late. Brastigan felt the impact, heard a dull snap. The tip of Ysislaw's left horn flew off, spinning in the air.

"You..." Ysislaw grated. One gauntlet groped at the broken stub of his horn. "Do you know what you've done?"

"Yes, I do," Brastigan grinned, giddy with success, mad with rage that Ysislaw had hurt Lottres. "Your horns are your power, and I've broken yours. You're nothing but a man, just like me."

"I will kill you," Ysislaw said, a harsh whisper.

"You've told me that before." Brastigan laughed. "Come on and try it!"

He raised Victory in defiance, but Ymell struck first. Lightning snarled in the air. Ysislaw's barrier shattered with a shriek like broken glass. The evil wizard staggered beneath the onslaught. For the first time in millennia, maybe, Ysislaw the conqueror screamed in pain and fear.

"Well struck, Brastigan," Yriatt's voice said in Brastigan's mind. She projected warmth and pride, which abruptly turned to ice. *"Now get out of our way."*

Prudence overcame pride. Brastigan retreated to Lottres's side. He bent over his brother, and was enormously relieved to hear a moan of pain. Lottres's eyelids fluttered—he lived!

Yriatt landed, somehow making her dragon form fit into the courtyard. Ysislaw staggered as if trying to flee, but Yriatt sprang like a cat. Her talons slashed Ysislaw's steel hauberk like cotton cloth. She flipped him into the air, just as a cat tosses a mouse. He flew, spinning and screaming and shattered. Lightning roared upward from Ymell's outstretched hands. Then Yriatt's black head snaked up. She snatched Ysislaw from the air with a snap and a crunch. Then she shook her head and flung the limp body over the wall and out of sight. Ymell looked ready to follow and savage the corpse some more.

"Hey!" Brastigan called to them. "I don't want to seem ungrateful, but this doesn't solve all our problems."

He gestured toward the barricades, where Habrok's fighters were being overwhelmed. The banner still stood, but you couldn't guess how long. The walking skeletons had gotten in with the archers, too. Even with Ysislaw dead, the Cruthans could still lose the war.

"You are correct." Ymell inclined his head to Brastigan. "Come, daughter. There is much to do."

Yriatt folded her wings, which became her robe. Black scales blanched into fair skin. She and Ymell strode toward the barricades. Lottres sat up, wiping blood from his chin.

"I bit my tongue," came his mumbled complaint.

"What a crybaby," Brastigan jeered, but he was quick to offer his hand. If Lottres had died, Brastigan might as well be dead, too. "Heal it and come on. This day isn't over, Pup."

* * *

"Out of the way, girl!" Diona pushed Cliodora out of the connecting doorway, admitting a rush of servants and courtiers.

"Stay back," another voice commanded. Shaelen strode in from the corridor through the main door, which they never had managed to block off. "She is only stunned."

"Thank you," Therula said. Her heart hammered in her throat, now that the emergency was past. "I didn't know what I would have... Mother!"

Alustra pushed up on her elbow. Half her face was coated with blood. With a trembling hand, the queen wiped her eyes. She stared at her smeared fingers with horror. Therula's arms and legs felt shaky, too, but she managed to reach her mother's side.

"It's all right," Therula said. "Shaelen saved us. But come, let's move away."

"She struck me," Alustra murmured. Her voice sounded strange and thick. "I remember that. The bottle..."

"Come," Therula urged. She took Alustra's arm and helped her stand.

"How could she?" Alustra's voice was plaintive as a child's.

"You can ask her later," Therula said. "Help us, someone."

"Yes, Princess." Servants stepped forward, led by Giselle, who took Therula's place.

"This way," Casiana fluttered anxiously. "Oh, Cliodora, do stop your screeching!"

Cliodora did her best to obey, covering her mouth as she watched the servants lead Alustra toward the door. Therula let them go, looking anxiously toward Shaelen.

"Is it safe?" Therula asked in a low voice. She glanced anxiously toward the outer corridor, for battle cries and the clash of steel came much louder through the half open door. "Do they need you?"

"In a moment," Shaelen said. Her eyes were fixed on Margura with strange intensity. "I want a word with this one."

"Why?" Therula asked. "Oskar isn't your king."

Before Shaelen could reply, Cliodora gave a yip of fear. Margura came to her feet, wild-eyed, her fingers crooked into claws. She looked ready to rush at Shaelen with her bare hands.

"You witch! You've ruined everything," Margura screamed.

Margura sprang toward the knife, and staggered back as another blazing arc of lightning leaped from Shaelen's hands. Therula quickly put herself between Margura and Oskar.

"This is on your own head," Therula cried. How dare the faithless servant put blame on someone else?

Margura ignored her. She glared at Shaelen. The Urulai woman's dark eyes gleamed with some emotion Therula couldn't name. Sorrow, perhaps, or bitter humor.

"I spare you," Shaelen said quietly, "for the sake of the life within you, but

I warn you now to leave Brastigan alone."

"Him." Shame and fury twisted Margura's face. "You would defend him? After he abandoned me? That miserable excuse for a man —."

"Do not call him a traitor," Shaelen replied. "After all he had endured, you met him with betrayal. You put him in the hands of his mortal enemy."

"He betrayed me first," Margura shrieked back at her. "He gave his heart to someone else, after I told him not to forget me. So what if the wench is dead? I'm glad — she deserved it!"

Shaelen took a step backward, her face reflecting incredulous shock. Her lips parted, but no words came. Therula stood wondering why Shaelen was so angry on Brastigan's behalf. Then Therula heard voices behind her. Some of the courtiers still watched from the doorway.

"What, she's pregnant? Is that what this is all about?" Diona demanded.

Therula remembered how sick Margura had looked the night before. Just now, she had complained of being maltreated and abandoned. Therula wondered if her mother knew of Margura's condition. Alustra hadn't acted like she knew.

"Is this true?" Therula asked. "Margura, are you pregnant?"

Margura's crimson cheeks gave the answer even before she hissed, "Yes."

"Well, if Brastigan got her with child..." Jenne began.

"No," Shaelen interrupted. "The father is someone named Alemin."

"Alemin?" Cliodora squeaked.

"Isn't he married?" Diona laughed coarsely.

"Diona!" Casiana rebuked. "The girls are here."

"So what?" Diona cackled. "It's nothing they don't know already." Then she turned on Margura with fury. "So you've got a brat in your belly, and that means the kingdom must fall?"

"Diona, stop," Casiana pleaded. She tried in vain to push Cliodora out the door after Alustra. Now it was Lioda, Orlyse and Agiatta who stood gawking, blocking the exit.

"Dear child, look around you." Jenne stepped toward Margura, speaking gently. "There are four of us here who know exactly how you feel, and more down in the town. You could have come to any one of us."

"For what?" Margura straightened, sneering at them. "To be paid for and kept as a pet, while my children are pushed into the shadows? Maybe that was enough for you..."

"We would have helped," Jenne said, though she flushed at Margura's ungrateful words. "You had but to ask."

"She did ask," Shaelen put in. "She asked the help of Ysislaw of Sillets, who offered a position of power when he had conquered Crutham."

"Shut up, you witch!" Margura screamed.

She did leap at Shaelen then, but she met a wall of light before she touched her foe. Margura hung in the air for a moment, arms and legs jerking. Then she fell again, and this time she lay still.

"Fool," Shaelen said quietly.

Diona stalked past the bed to rummage in Oskar's armoire. She emerged with a belt, and quickly began to bind Margura's hands. Meanwhile, Casiana and Jenne were murmuring together. Casiana seemed to gather her resolve. Then she stepped forward.

"Let us care for her," Casiana said to Therula. "With all respect, you don't understand how it is. Leave this to us."

"Perhaps I don't understand," Therula acknowledged. "Keep her in her quarters for now. She must pay for what she's done, but since she was my mother's attendant I will let Mother decide what to do."

"Thank you," Jenne said quietly. She and Casiana stood back while Diona directed the servants in carrying Margura from the room. As Therula watched them go, she almost felt sorry for Margura. The woman must have come to Harburg with high ambitions, willing to do anything to get what she wanted, but she had chosen the wrong path to advancement and now it was all ashes.

Then Therula heard Oskar's breath catch as awareness began to return. She remembered her mother's bloody face. Therula felt no pity at all. She hoped Margura would have another of Diona's tongue-lashings before it all ended. Maybe more than one.

Oskar voiced a painful moan. Therula turned to Shaelen again.

"Can you help him?" Therula asked.

The Urulai woman had been watching after Margura. Her expression didn't show vindictive triumph, as Therula might have expected, but rather a kind of startled joy. Shaelen started when Therula spoke. She made as if to join Therula at the bedside, but then stopped.

"No," Shaelen said, her face grave. "I will not help him."

"But..." Therula began to argue.

"He is in no danger of dying," Shaelen said.

"We need him," Therula insisted. "He is our king."

"Perhaps, but this man is as much a traitor as Margura," Shaelen said. Her voice was calm, without malice, and her gaze was steady. "He conspired to kill his own brothers. Even the very men who saved him."

"No," Therula murmured.

"He said so in my hearing."

Something made Therula turn toward the bed. Oskar was awake, watching her. Instantly, Therula knew Shaelen was correct. Oskar showed neither guilt nor regret, only the defiant belief in his own righteousness.

"He lied to your mother," Shaelen went on, while Therula struggled for words. "He will try to lie again. You must not permit it. Accept nothing less than the truth."

Therula felt her heart drop, but she forced herself to stand straight. "I won't."

"I must go," Shaelen said, and she returned to the battle in the corridor.

Therula stared at Oskar with a strange sense of disconnection. He was her brother, fully blooded, and yet she felt she had never known him at all.

"Why?" she asked.

"Their presence is an insult to our mother, and to me," Oskar said, as if that made it all right. He extended his hand imperiously. "Help me sit up."

Suddenly Therula was too tired even to summon the proper feeling of indignation.

"You really are a liar," she said.

Therula turned away to find Cliodora still lingering in the doorway. Her eyes were round as marbles. Cliodora moved to answer Oskar's demand, but Therula caught her arm and guided her out the door.

"Therula!" Oskar cried, greatly wounded.

Therula closed the door and left him there, alone, as he deserved to be.

CHAPTER TWENTY-SEVEN
FACING THE FUTURE

SHADOW munched her grain and swished her tail, but her ears twitched restlessly as Brastigan gave her a rub down. Outside the stables, all was noise and hurry. Inside, it was quieter. The soothing ritual of water and curry comb helped to calm them both after the confusion of recent days.

The past week had been tense, as Brastigan sat on Shadow's back and kept watch over the captured Silletsians. The bone men had fought mindlessly until destroyed, but there were other soldiers, humans from various Silletsian territories. Few of them had offered any resistance once Ysislaw was gone. They had been rounded up into hastily built stockades in the nearby fields. It was a greater task to keep back the vengeful townsfolk than it was to watch over those cowed and defeated men. The prisoners hunkered down, refusing to look at each other or their captors. Only those from the provinces had asked when they could go home. None who came from Sillets itself wanted to return there.

None of the *eppagadrocca* had been captured, however. That could be because Yriatt, following her usual tactic, had made sure to burn them before going to aid Ymell against Ysislaw. Still, there were sure to be others left behind in Sillets. Without Ysislaw's control, who knew what they might do? The problem would have to be dealt with one day, Brastigan was sure. Personally, he thought it would be a boon to the world if the lot of them saw to each other. Crutham had already paid too dearly for her safety.

For Ymell's prophecy had nearly come true. A year ago, Unferth had had twenty-two sons. Only eight now survived—if the younger lads hadn't been picked off by assassins. Alemin's ship was overdue in Forix and presumed lost. Miswald had lost his sword arm, Leolin an eye. Calitar and Axenar's bodies had never been found in the muddy soup of the south wall. Eskelon lay as one dead, never knowing Sebbelon had gone before him. Even Ymell couldn't say when Eskelon might open his eyes again. Albrett remained in Carthell, and they were welcome to have him.

Oskar survived, though he would never walk without a cane. To Brastigan, that was the cruelest blow. Oskar, who had opened the door to this whole disaster, got to keep his throne and honors when so many others lost all. He complained of being tricked and held captive, but none of Unferth's other sons believed Oskar had suffered enough for his sins.

Shadow tossed her head and stepped on Brastigan's foot, just hard enough to get his attention. Only then did he realize how harshly he had been brushing her.

"Sorry, sorry." Brastigan eased his toes out from under the mare's hoof.

He finished his work quickly and gently. Shadow's ears and tail worked impatiently the whole time.

"You're bored with Harburg," Brastigan murmured. He patted her neck. "I know how you feel. I wish I could say we ride out tomorrow. We won't, but it will be soon. I promise."

"Bras?" Lottres's voice came into his mind, a sensation that no longer startled him. *"Remember, you promised Therula you'd be on time."*

"I will be," Brastigan answered. He spoke out loud, and it felt funny, like he was talking to himself. Lottres's presence withdrew.

Shadow whickered mournfully as Brastigan left the stables. It was late afternoon. The lowering sun slanted amber rays across the courtyard, where soldiers and servants went about their duties. Brastigan headed for the downstairs bath, to clean himself up now that his horse was cared for.

Used to be, he would show up smelly just to bother Alustra. He didn't have the heart for it any more. Besides, this was Pikarus's and Therula's day. He owed those two his best behavior.

* * *

"I'm so excited," Cliodora whispered, for what seemed like the hundredth time that day.

Therula smiled patiently. "I know."

Golden sunlight streamed into Alustra's chambers, where the bridal party had gathered. Therula was aware of her younger sisters cooing over each other's finery, while a flock of servants dressed them and put up their hair. The eldest princess eyed herself in the mirror, taking in the details of her own appearance. Her hair was still bright gold, her eyes blue as the sea. You couldn't say she had changed, and yet she felt very different.

Therula wore a simple gown for her wedding, creamy pink with an overdress of lavender velvet. An embroidered pattern of blackberries and doves ran along the sleeves and skirts as a unifying theme. Therula had deliberately chosen these gowns for the simple lines of the Cruthan style. No more foreign influences for her! As a last touch, Therula tucked her embroidered glove through her belt. At last she could wear it as the symbol of fidelity she had meant it to be, before Ysislaw's odious bet.

"Aren't you happy?" Cliodora asked, picking up Therula's somber mood. "You should be!"

"Of course I'm happy," Therula said. "After everything that's happened, I can't believe it's finally real."

Therula admitted to herself what she couldn't say aloud, that she feared Oskar might still change his mind. What if he refused to let her marry Pikarus? Until the ceremony was complete, she could not relax.

"All right, young ladies," Alustra called. "Line up and let me see you."

Cliodora gave Therula a quick hug, and ran to her place. The six princesses, Orlyse, Leoda, Alista, Agiatta, Frella and Cliodora, formed a line from oldest to youngest. They tried to stand quiet and demure while the queen inspected them, but the young women couldn't help exchanging excited glances and giggles of anticipation.

Even Alustra, Therula thought, couldn't find anything to criticize in the girls' attire or their presentation. With a war just over, no one was wearing anything really extravagant. They had all adapted existing garments, even Therula, who had been working on her gown with Jenne before Pikarus and Brastigan even left on their journey.

It was all quite proper. Still, Alustra's expression was clouded as she reached her own daughter. They stood uneasily for a moment, neither speaking. Alustra's eyes searched Therula's face. The queen's expression showed regret, imminent sorrow—everything Oskar ought to show, but never deigned to. Since he didn't compromise, neither would Therula.

Slowly, Alustra lifted the veil attached to the coronet in Therula's hair. She let the filmy black fabric fall over her daughter's face. Along the line, the girls began to whisper excitedly as the servants did likewise for them.

Alustra and Therula turned together, no word spoken. They left together, followed by the procession of princesses. The corridor had been scrubbed clean of blood stains. Its floor and walls practically glowed. However, the servants hadn't yet been able to remove the scorch marks that snaked along the ceiling, showing how Shaelen's lightning had decided the battle.

Now that she and Alustra weren't looking at each other, Therula felt a surge of her own regret. Matters hadn't been easy between them since the war's conclusion. Alustra had returned to full alertness, devoting all her resources to aiding Oskar during the reconstruction. After defending her son's interests for so many years, Alustra seemed all too willing to overlook certain uncomfortable truths—such as Oskar's lying to her, painting himself as the victim of Margura's machinations and minimizing his own misdeeds.

The surviving princes had convened a series of tense councils, which Therula and Alustra had both attended, where Brastigan and Lottres laid out the painful facts. For her part, Therula had abandoned her life long habit of placating everyone to support the effort to hold Oskar accountable. Her mother couldn't accept this.

It was Alustra who had said, after the last of these sessions, "If you are such a trouble to Oskar, why should he permit you to marry a man of your own choosing?"

This had raised every fear in Therula's own heart, for she knew a royal princess seldom had such a luxury, but she wouldn't show weakness, not even before her own mother. Therula had snapped right back, "If he doesn't permit it, then he will see how troublesome I can be!"

The two women had scarcely spoken since then. Still, Therula and Pikarus would be leaving for Gerfalkan within a few days. They would take up residence with his parents, at least for a while. It was Therula's first real separation from her mother. She didn't want it to have this sense of grim finality.

Impulsively, Therula reached over, putting an arm around her mother's waist. Alustra gave a kind of sigh. At once, she raised her arm to circle her daughter's shoulders. Something relaxed inside Therula. She blinked away tears as they descended the stairs and passed beneath the arch leading into the courtyard.

Soldiers saluted as the royal procession passed beneath the fortified gate. Above, the banner of Crutham fluttered quietly in the breeze. Below was the beautifully carved entrance to the great hall. At the doorway, Alustra paused. Therula could hear the susurrus of voices within. The two women gazed at each other through their veils, sharing a kind of farewell.

"I hope it will be all you wish for." Alustra spoke softly so Orlyse, behind them, wouldn't hear.

Therula hesitated a moment. A jumble of thoughts passed through her mind at once, especially the memory of how difficult her parents' marriage had been. Unferth had visited so many disappointments upon Alustra. Even though Therula had loved him, she knew it wasn't fair.

Quickly, before embarrassment overcame her, Therula whispered, "I hope you find someone else, too, Mother. Someone who treats you as you deserve."

Alustra blinked in surprise, then shook her head and gave a faltering laugh. "Oh, I long ago gave up on men to make me happy."

Therula wondered if that meant Oskar, too, but Orlyse was crowding closer, her face alight with curiosity. Alustra faced the doorway. Her shoulders straightened and her chin came up. Every inch a queen, Alustra signaled the herald to announce them.

Trumpets sounded, and Alustra stepped forward. The younger women followed. After the brightness of daylight, Therula felt she had entered a cave, dim and gloomy. As her eyes adjusted, the ranks of courtiers took shape. Some faces were smiling, some speculative, and all were watching her.

The next moment they were nothing but a backdrop, blurred and meaningless. Ahead of her, in a circle of candlelight, Pikarus stood with his family. All of Therula's fears dropped away. She smiled with confidence and anticipation.

Would this marriage be all she hoped for? Therula knew it would be. Soon Pikarus would be hers, as she would be his. No one could ever threaten to separate them again.

* * *

The four wizards stood together, yet isolated, among the crowd in the great hall. Yriatt and Shaelen had both borrowed gowns for the occasion, while Ymell and Lottres wore plain, dark blue robes. The dragons' horns set them apart all the same.

Brastigan had been quick to tease Lottres about his attire—"Have you been getting into Eben's things?"—and Lottres was aware of other whispered comments around them. Nevertheless, he felt more comfortable in the simple sorcerer's robe that he ever had in court garb. All those years, Lottres had been disguising himself, trying to be someone he wasn't. It was a relief to give up the pretense at last.

Looking around the hall, it hardly seemed they were waiting for a wedding to take place. Men had once outnumbered women in this hall. Now that was reversed. The throng was almost all women draped with black mourning veils. The few men present wore the black surcoats of military service. So many had died, so recently, the survivors were hard put to celebrate anything. So many of the dead were Lottres's brothers. Their absences made the crowd seem strangely thin, the room almost empty.

In a marked departure, Therula had declined to invite her two older sisters, who might have objected to her union with a lesser nobleman. The haughty Bessara and the abrasive Praxia had never spared a kind word for Lottres, yet he found that he missed them. Too many others were absent.

At the rear of the chamber, Lottres sensed Therula waiting with her mother and younger sisters. Pikarus, his parents and siblings formed a separate cluster nearby. Trumpets sang out again, raising echoes in the half empty chamber. Usually, the groom's father entered first, but since Alustra held the higher rank she claimed the right. The queen stepped forward, walking down the center aisle with dignified aplomb. Therula followed, and her sisters trailed after in a line.

Even as they drew left, forming a semi-circle to face the dais, Pikarus's father and mother came down the aisle together. Pikarus followed, and then his two younger sisters.

Before them all, Oskar's throne stood above the room. The king sat alone beneath a magnificent cloth-of-gold banner which fairly lit the room with reflected glory. Habrok and Brastigan and the others stood nearby, but none joined Oskar on the platform. They all maintained an uneasy distance these days. Oskar still depended on Habrok to lead his armies. Privately, Lottres had to wonder how long a king's reign could last when it had been so profoundly compromised by deceit.

Then Pikarus's clan had assumed its place, and Oskar leaned forward to address them.

"Welcome, Mother." He projected warmth and affection, but Lottres could feel his distaste. "What is your business this day?"

Alustra bowed, and her dark veils swayed with the movement. "I bring a petition to your majesty. My daughter, your sister, Therula of Crutham, desires to wed."

"With whom?" Oskar asked, as if the whole Gerfalkan family wasn't standing before him.

"With the son of your loyal subject, Perhalon of Gerfalkan." Alustra made a sweeping gesture. Pikarus's father stepped forward and bowed.

"I am Perhalon of Gerfalkan," he intoned, "come before you to join her majesty, Queen Alustra, in requesting the privilege of a marriage between Princess Therula and my eldest son, Pikarus of Gerfalkan. Our line is connected to the Dukes of Gerfalkan, although distantly."

"Does the Duke acknowledge the relationship?" Oskar interrupted.

"He does." Perhalon bowed again, and continued, "My son must already be known to your majesty, as he has served seven years or more among the guards of Crutham Keep."

"Both the couple are well known to me," Oskar said. "I do not question their fitness to marry. Mother," and perhaps he gritted his teeth just a bit, "what is the dowry?"

Perhalon retreated, and Alustra again stepped to the fore. She began to recite a long list of dower items, including silver coins, gold and pearl jewelry, horses, weapons, armor and even, to Lottres's surprise, a small estate between Gerfalkan and Begatt. Therula had grumbled to Lottres and Brastigan, that the dowry was mostly things she already owned. Due to the wartime emergency, she wouldn't receive the lavish gifts her older sisters had enjoyed.

Alustra's list went on, but it seemed Yriatt was bored with the ceremony. Silently, mind to mind, she inquired, *"Father, have you considered when you will move against Sillets?"*

"Yes, I have considered it," Ymell replied.

He said no more. Glancing aside, Lottres saw Ymell apparently giving all his attention to the wedding. Yriatt's head turned toward him. A trace of a frown betrayed her impatience. On the other side of Yriatt, Shaelen stood pensive, not listening to her mentors' debate. Her thoughts were shielded, but Lottres thought he knew well enough what she must be feeling.

"Don't tease me, Father," Yriatt said sternly.

"The time is not right to invade Sillets," Ymell answered. From his smugness, Lottres could tell Ymell had indeed been teasing Yriatt. And enjoying it, too. You could tell he was related to Brastigan—but Lottres made sure that thought stayed behind his own shields.

Ymell went on, *"They still have their ranks, their supply lines, and familiar means of communication. We must wait for the empire to collapse upon itself. The smaller kingdoms will be easier to manage."*

"There is one province isolated from the others," Yriatt countered, as if she had had a goal in mind all along. *"Our first assault could be against Urland."*

"Urland?" That got Shaelen's attention.

"True," Ymell said. *"The Urulai warriors have already gathered. Because they helped raise the siege of Glawern, they have the support of popular sentiment."*

"There are also the galleys we captured," Yriatt said. *"With them, we need not beg for transportation."*

Lottres turned his eyes toward Brastigan for a moment. He was sure this news would please his brother. Brastigan would want to help free Urland. If Yriatt took part in that, Lottres would go, too. They could travel together a while longer.

What Lottres sensed in Brastigan's mind made his attention snap back to the dais. Lottres had missed a good bit of the ceremony. Therula and Pikarus now stood facing each other. Their parents had joined their hands, and they were reciting the traditional wedding vow.

"...As our hands are joined, so our hearts are joined. Though distance may divide us, we shall remain united in body and spirit."

As they spoke, Lottres saw Oskar's face, pinched and bored. Lottres couldn't see Alustra, but Pikarus's parents stood nearby gazing into each other's eyes with undisguised love and pride. That reassured Lottres more than any mere words.

Hands clasped between them, Pikarus and Therula turned to face the audience. Cheers and applause began slowly, but soon filled the great hall. Therula was embraced by her mother-in-law, while Alustra gave Pikarus a more restrained kiss on the cheek. The newlyweds moved back down the aisle, greeting well-wishers who pressed in from both sides.

Through the din, Lottres felt the hollow ache in Brastigan's heart. Shaelen was a blank spot nearby, determined to conceal her emotions. It struck Lottres as sad, even a little silly, that those two stood alone. He slipped behind Yriatt and Ymell, who clapped politely, to touch Shaelen's elbow. The tall woman glanced around, then bent her head slightly toward him.

"You should tell Brastigan the news," Lottres suggested. "Tell him we're going to Urland."

Shaelen jerked away. She almost turned toward Brastigan, but then shook her head.

"He won't want to hear it from me," she answered bitterly.

"Is there another Urulai here to tell him?" Lottres challenged.

Shaelen gazed down at Lottres with an expression of betrayal. "You know what he thinks of me," she said.

"No, I don't," Lottres answered. "We haven't talked about you." He spoke softly, only for Shaelen, though he was aware when Yriatt turned slightly, listening.

"Don't assume you know what Brastigan will do," Lottres told her. If he had learned one thing, it was this. "People think all kinds of things, but they don't say it all. They keep some things to themselves for all kinds of reasons—like when they don't want to hurt someone's feelings. What they say out loud is what matters."

"I've never known Brastigan to hold anything back," Shaelen said with a curt laugh.

"Believe it or not, he does," Lottres said, though he smiled wryly. "Remember, he's not one of us. He can't guard his thoughts. Out of common respect, I try not to pick things out of Brastigan's mind. Or anyone's. We have to let them choose their own words. It's not fair, otherwise."

"I know, but..." Shaelen stopped and sighed. "You just don't understand."

All at once she looked tired, bewildered. Lottres felt a welling of sympathy. Being separated into two parts and then rejoined had affected her in ways nobody could understand, maybe not even Yriatt, who had performed the changes.

Lottres laid a gentle hand on her sleeve. "It's true, I don't know how you feel, but I know Brastigan doesn't like standing alone while Pikarus and Therula are overflowing with happiness. Just tell him. You might have more of a chance than you think."

"I thought you weren't reading minds," Shaelen accused, though she would have sensed it instantly if he tried to penetrate her shields.

"That was an educated guess," Lottres retorted, smiling. "You have to talk to him sometime, you know, if we're all going to Urland together."

Lottres felt Shaelen's flash of panic. He quickly lifted his hand from her arm, breaking the contact. Then he turned away, looking for a chance to congratulate Therula and giving Shaelen time to make up her mind. Lottres found himself under the level gaze of two dragons.

"You're quite the manipulator," Ymell said, but he clearly meant it as a compliment.

"Nobody ever listens to me," Lottres demurred.

"You've already learned not to abuse your powers by spying on your loved ones," Yriatt said with a hint of fondness. "You will have a good future with us."

Lottres nodded, feeling his chest swell with pride. He felt more confident with magic than he ever had with sword and shield. Magic was right for him. He knew it in his heart. So, whatever the future held, he was ready to face it.

* * *

"This isn't about me," Brastigan told himself. *"It's their day, Therula's and Pikarus's. I'm happy for them."*

Maybe he even managed to look happy. Brastigan pounded Pikarus on the back, glad to welcome the man who was no longer a mere brother-at-arms but a brother-in-law. Brastigan shared a bawdy joke with Habrok and did an impromptu dance with Cliodora, who was too elated to stand still. All the while, a big grin stretched his face in unnatural ways. It did nothing to ease the sick emptiness inside him.

He didn't even realize, at first, that he was working his way toward the door. Yet there was no denying his relief as long strides carried him up the stairs to the outer wall. The din of celebration had left him with a throbbing headache. He needed fresh air and room to move.

Out of habit, Brastigan headed for Eben's tower with its expansive view. Then he remembered that the dragons had taken over the tower, at least temporarily. It wouldn't feel right to go there now. Brastigan reluctantly changed directions, following the long wall toward the west, where the setting sun turned the sea to fire. He nodded to a sentry walking the other way. At the southwest tower, Brastigan stopped. He leaned his elbows in the recess of a crenel and gazed out over the capital city.

From here, you could see how badly Harburg had been hit, how close they had come to losing all. The harbor wall was intact, though its gates were too badly burned to shut, and the Butcher's Gate still stood to the east, but the south wall was a mere line of rubble. The moat was completely filled with muddy debris, which hardened daily into a kind of crude cement. No one was sure yet if they would have to clear the moat. Oskar might opt to expand his capital by moving the wall farther out and having a new moat dug.

Meanwhile the town stood blackened, riddled with holes like a fine old cheese. The dragons had used lightning to drive the invaders back, and that had set the buildings ablaze. The troops Yriatt brought from Firice had ended up fighting fires as much as they fought enemy troops.

Brastigan sighed in exasperated memory. There was so much to do in Harburg, so much to repair, yet he knew he couldn't stay here. Oskar's ascension was too offensive. Anyway, he was no closer to ruling than he ever had been. Oskar might not have any sons, but Habrok and Calitar did. For that matter, so did the traitors Rickard and Albrett.

The only things keeping Brastigan in Crutham to begin with had been Unferth and Lottres. Now Unferth was gone. Lottres wasn't likely to stay. Finally and completely, Brastigan had no reason to remain in Crutham.

It was funny, really. Coming from such a large family, Brastigan had never been alone, not ever. Maybe that was what spooked him so much when he was far from home and Lottres began to pull away. Brastigan, who feared no man or beast — or bone man, either — had been terrified. As he was now, because he could see it all happening again.

Brastigan restlessly paced along the edge of the tower, pausing when he faced true west. His gaze went past the harbor, seeking that smudge on the horizon where Urland lay. Then he shook his head irritably. Even if he looked Urulai, he wasn't. Anyway, he couldn't expect them to take him on as a leader. There had never been a king in Urland.

More than ever, Brastigan envied Therula and Pikarus for being so sure of what they wanted. Of course, Brastigan was sure, too. It was just that what he wanted could never be. He thought of the girl now with a strange disconnection. As if the whole experience had happened to someone else, long ago. However real it had been, past was past. Brastigan had lost too much to keep looking back.

Dusk was falling. Evening shadows swallowed the war-wracked harbor, and the empty air held no answers. Brastigan turned to leave and saw someone coming up the steps from the courtyard. Shaelen. There was no mistaking the dark fire of her hair, though she had exchanged her leather armor for one of Therula's dresses. The cloth was a blue satin, turned almost black by the orange glow of sunset. Pearls shimmered on the sleeves and bodice. Brastigan could see the dark disc of her *jeup* in the scoop of the neckline.

Brastigan watched her come, feeling the familiar clash of emotions. It was hard to resent Shaelen when she had helped rescue him, and then saved Therula and Cliodora as well. At some point, he might even owe her an apology. Yet neither could he forget the shadow girl whose life she had stolen.

Shaelen paused, as if she expected Brastigan to say something. When he didn't, she ventured, "Lottres wanted me to tell you, Ymell has decided. We go to Urland." Her voice sounded strange, faltering and rough.

Brastigan shrugged at the news, but he felt a stirring of excitement. He looked out across the water, where the last golden light touched the waves. Shaelen came to stand beside him, far enough away to respect his silence. She twisted a braid around her finger, and Brastigan saw the beads in her hair, red orbs turned to blood in the last daylight. Those were the beads he had given the girl, a day before she died.

The quiet stretched between them, taut with things unsaid. Shaelen said in a rush: "I have never been to Urland. I would like to see it. Will you go?"

Brastigan eyed her, analyzing her awkwardness. Shaelen had always been confident and competent. There was no reason for such nervousness, unless she was feeling guilty about something. Like what happened with the girl, maybe.

"It wasn't your fault," he said, ignoring the question about Urland. "Don't dwell on it. I'm trying not to."

Brastigan thought he was being generous, but Shaelen looked at him like a child about to cry. The red beads twisted over and under her fingers.

"It's not that easy, not for me." Shaelen's voice was strained. "If it is for you, then I have to wonder how well you knew her. What did you really think of her?"

"Thinking. That was the problem, wasn't it," Brastigan shot back.

He ought to walk away, he thought. Shaelen was the last person he would choose for an intimate discussion. Yet she was also the first person to ask how he felt about any of it—the girl, his father, the war.

"You met Margura, I hear," Brastigan spat with distaste. "Well, the court women are all like her. I'd never known anyone like the girl. Someone so... perfect. She was gentle and trusting, like a child. Not greedy, not wanting any favors, and she never judged me because I look different..."

Brastigan trailed off. Shaelen stared at him, her cheeks flushed, her eyes wide and dark. Then she gave a sad laugh.

"Perfect?" she asked. "She was a blank slate, Brastigan. You could imagine her to be whatever you wanted, and she would never tell you differently. Weak as she was, you could mold her however you chose."

It was Brastigan's turn to stare, seething with rage at the unjust accusation. After he'd been honest with her, too!

"It wasn't like that," he grated out. "She needed me when no one else did, and I needed someone to take care of. I was not molding her!"

"I know." Shaelen's smile was luminous, just as the girl's would have been, if she had ever been fully alive. "That's why I admire you. Everyone else saw her as a thing, even *Maess*, who should have known better. Only you saw that she could be more."

Brastigan scowled, trying to take in this reversal. He saw again how Shaelen looked so much like the girl. It just wasn't fair.

"How much do you remember from her?" Brastigan asked.

"Everything," Shaelen answered quietly. "Her feelings, her love for you... I received all of that when we rejoined."

Love? Brastigan took an involuntary step backward. He had known it, of course, that the girl loved him. It still hurt to hear the words and know she was gone. Abruptly he turned his back, pacing along the edge of the tower.

"Go away," Brastigan said.

He was sorry he had let Shaelen bring all this up. He regretted showing her any part of himself that was real. It only made him feel worse. Shaelen let go a harsh breath. She followed Brastigan, easily keeping pace with his long-legged strides.

"Do you think it's easy, having two sets of memories?" Shaelen demanded. "I remember going to *Maen* in Altannath, but I also remember staying with *Maess* and traveling with you—things that never happened to me. I don't even know who I am any more!"

Her yammering made Brastigan angry. "So you have her memories." He whirled and caught Shaelen in his arms. "Do you remember this?"

Shaelen stared up at him. He could feel her trembling.

"I remember," she whispered. She wasn't trying to escape, he noticed. "But you never touched her."

"That's right," Brastigan said, "because she didn't understand what she wanted, what it meant." He tightened his arms around Shaelen's waist until he could feel her heart, and his own, beating together with rage or frustration or something he was afraid to name. Brastigan bent his head toward her. "Do you?"

"Yes," Shaelen sighed, and leaned toward him.

Brastigan only kissed her because he was angry, but he felt Shaelen's ardent response and then he couldn't stop himself. Incredibly, he was kissing the girl at last, the way he had longed to. He didn't have to abandon her memory at all. Shaelen contained the girl's spirit, and yet had a mind of her own. Shaelen could be wooed like any woman. Brastigan called on all his skills as a seducer. Shaelen clung to him and demanded more. A long time later, Brastigan breathed, "Just tell me you don't already have a man."

Without his realizing, it had gotten very dark. Only embers were left of the burning sunset. Shuffling steps nearby hinted that sentries were trying to walk their rounds without intruding. Shaelen gave a low laugh and let her head rest on Brastigan's shoulder. The herbal fragrance from Hawkwing House clung to the curls of her hair.

"It would serve you right if I did," she said. "No, I've never been sought after. As a child of the conquerors, I must be despised. Yet there are so few Urulai women, even I have had suitors."

Brastigan growled playfully, pulling her closer. Shaelen laughed again.

"None of them stayed," she said. "I think *Maess* put them off."

"She'd better stay out of it," Brastigan said.

He bent to kiss Shaelen again, before she could argue with him. He let his hands wander, and Shaelen moaned softly. Just as Brastigan was wondering how he could get her back to his chambers, she pulled away again.

"Well," Shaelen teased, "have I convinced you to come with us to Urland?"

"Try to stop me." Then, more seriously, "Though I don't know if they'll want me. I'm a half-breed, too, even if I am the greatest swordsman in Crutham."

"You are the son of a beloved martyr," Shaelen answered fiercely. "You struck the blow that destroyed Ysislaw! No one would dare deny your right to go home."

"I was hoping you'd say that," Brastigan said, lightly, to disguise his relief. "The last time I saw my father, he told me my destiny lies in Urland. I think he was right."

"But," Shaelen said with a smile in her voice, "I must tell you the name of our country is not Urland. It is Urutchat."

"I can't say a word like that," Brastigan protested. "I was raised here in Crutham."

"I'll teach you," Shaelen reassured him. "Say it slowly, after me. U-rut-chat."

Brastigan did, and made a fumble of it. While Shaelen snickered, he whispered in her ear, "What's the word for..." And he made the picture very clear in his mind, so she could not mistake it.

She answered him with kisses.

www.ingramcontent.com/pod-product-compliance
Lightning Source LLC
Chambersburg PA
CBHW071841020726
47502CB00003B/567